PRAISE FOR THE GUILD HUNTER
NOVELS OF NALINI SINGH

"Paranormal romance doesn't get better than this."
—Love Vampires

"Intense, vivid, and sexually charged."
—*Publishers Weekly* (starred review)

"[A] remarkable urban fantasy series."
—*RT Book Reviews* (Top Pick)

"World-building that blew my socks off."
—Meljean Brook, *New York Times* bestselling author

"[A] heart-pounding, action-packed story line of love and loss; death and destruction; family and friends; intrigue and suspense."
—The Reading Cafe

"It's dark and edgy, and so atmospheric."
—Book Chick City

"Mesmerizing . . . Fascinating world-building."
—Bitten by Books

"The Guild Hunter series is not set in a peaceful world and Singh doesn't pull any punches."
—The Book Pushers

"Completely awe-inspiring."
—Fallen Angel Reviews

"Stunning, original, beautiful, intriguing, and mesmerizing."
—Errant Dreams Reviews

continued . . .

"[Ms. Singh] has a knack for writing characters that are truly believable, and admirably strong and resilient."

—Dark Faerie Tales

"One of the most immersive and consistently creative works in urban fantasy."

—Grave Tells

"[A] fabulous addition to the paranormal world."

—Fresh Fiction

"[A] powerful, riveting novel. I found myself wholly absorbed."

—Dear Author

"Dark, lush urban fantasy, steeped in violence and power."

—HeroesandHeartbreakers.com

Archangel's Viper

Nalini Singh

JOVE
New York

A JOVE BOOK
Published by Berkley
An imprint of Penguin Random House LLC
375 Hudson Street, New York, New York 10014

Copyright © 2017 by Nalini Singh
Penguin Random House supports copyright. Copyright fuels creativity, encourages
diverse voices, promotes free speech, and creates a vibrant culture. Thank you for buying
an authorized edition of this book and for complying with copyright laws by not
reproducing, scanning, or distributing any part of it in any form without permission.
You are supporting writers and allowing Penguin Random House to continue to
publish books for every reader.

A JOVE BOOK and BERKLEY are registered trademarks and the B colophon
is a trademark of Penguin Random House LLC.

ISBN: 9780451488244

First Edition: October 2017

Printed in the United States of America
1   3   5   7   9   10   8   6   4   2

Cover art by Tony Mauro

This is a work of fiction. Names, characters, places, and incidents either are the product
of the author's imagination or are used fictitiously, and any resemblance to actual persons,
living or dead, business establishments, events, or locales is entirely coincidental.

If you purchased this book without a cover, you should be aware that this book is stolen
property. It was reported as "unsold and destroyed" to the publisher, and neither the author
nor the publisher has received any payment for this "stripped book."

Birth

She pushed with a silent scream and it was born, the child that shouldn't exist and that she would love with all her being. But when she opened her arms for that longed-for child, she saw that the healer hadn't picked up the babe from the bed, was instead backing off toward the door.

Fury a savage storm through her, she sat up to rescue her helpless child . . . and saw.

1

Holly hugged her sister good-bye one final time, her heart aching. "Shoo," she said when Mia hesitated at the entrance to the security line. "You'll be late for your flight if you don't get going."

Mia sank her teeth into the fullness of her lower lip, her chin-length bob gleaming obsidian under the white fluorescent lighting inside the terminal building. "I miss home already."

"You'll be fine." Though Holly was going to miss her elder sister—and best friend— desperately, she took Mia's face in her hands, met eyes as brown as hers had once been, and said, "You're the smartest person I've ever known. You'll knock this out of the park." Her newly minted doctor sister had been offered a prestigious residency at Massachusetts General in Boston.

"I'll be so far from everyone."

Holly didn't point out that her sister's new base of operation was only a few hours' drive from New York, less at the speeds Holly liked driving. She knew what it was to be homesick. She'd felt that way in the vibrant city her family called home when she'd isolated herself from them for several long months in the aftermath of the attack that had changed her into a being who wasn't human, but who wasn't vampire, either.

Thankfully, she'd gotten over that stupidity—and her family loved her enough to forgive her. Of course, her mother reminded her of it every chance she got, but that was par for the course. Daphne Chang also reminded Holly of the time she'd snuck out of the house at seventeen, only to have to call home for help after her asshole date abandoned her on a dark street in Queens.

Holly still had to keep some secrets from her parents, her younger brothers, and Mia, but those secrets were for their protection: mortals didn't need to know about a blood-born archangel. As far as Holly's parents and siblings were concerned, it was a deranged mortal who'd abducted her friends and her, and who'd infected her with a dangerous virus. An angel had saved her by attempting to turn her into a vampire, but the transition hadn't gone smoothly because of the virus in her blood.

They had no reason not to believe the story.

"I'll drive up and see you anytime you feel alone," she said to Mia, this sister of hers who'd loved her with unflinching stubbornness even when Holly didn't—*couldn't*— love herself. "Just call."

"I love you, Hollster." Another crushing hug, Mia's body a sweep of soft, womanly curves.

Holly, in contrast, was still hoping her breasts would grow a little bigger if she wished hard enough. In the silver-lining department, at least she didn't have to waste money on bras. "Love you more, Mimi," she said through a throat that had gone thick. Not because Mia was heading off on a new adventure, but because Holly was horrifyingly aware of how life could change without warning, how a person could be laughing and living one instant and, in the next, be a bloodsoaked corpse.

She had a serious psychological problem letting those she loved out of her sight. Which was why she forced herself to release Mia; she wasn't about to steal Mia's dreams because of her own nightmares. *"Go."* Putting her hands on the soft gray of Mia's cardigan, she gave her sister a little push.

"I'm gonna hold you to your promise!" Mia called over her shoulder as she finally tugged her little roll-onboard case in between the ropes that led to the screening area.

That area was visible through the glass, so Holly stood and watched until Mia made it through—all the while fighting her impulse to jump the barriers and wrench her sister back to where Holly could watch over her, protect her. Smiling a little nervously, Holly's eldest sibling waved one last time from the other side, and then she was gone, lost in the stream of travelers heading out of a city Holly loved and hated in equal measure.

Jingle bells, jingle bells, jingle all the way!

"Ashwini, I swear to God . . ." Holly muttered as she scrambled for her phone.

That was *not* the ringtone she'd programmed.

Managing to cut off the annoyingly cheerful chipmunk singing at last, she put the phone to her ear as she headed out of the terminal. "Tell your wife I'm going to murder her the next time I see her."

Janvier laughed, as if threats against his beloved Ashwini weren't the least unusual. "You are still at the airport, Hollyberry?" he drawled in that lazy Cajun accent of his that fooled the unwary into thinking he wasn't paying attention to the world.

"Cut that out." It came out a snarled order. "And add Viper Face to the list of my future murder victims." Venom had given her that ridiculous nickname after she insisted on being addressed as Sorrow. The latter name had fit her at the time, but looking back, she could see she'd been acting a little dramatic.

So sue her. She'd been kidnapped and brutalized by a violently powerful and deeply insane archangel, her life suddenly a miasma of terror and blinding grief. She'd been only twenty-three at the time—and she'd had soul-shredding nightmares night after night. Waking to find herself curled up in a silent, fear-drenched ball on the floor of her closet had become a daily occurrence. As if her subconscious believed that the red-eyed monster wouldn't find her there.

He did, of course.

Always.

Because he lived in Holly's tainted blood.

She was allowed a few dramatics.

And it wasn't as if *Venom* could talk. "Yes," she muttered. "I'm at the airport. Just about to head back to Manhattan."

"I need you to do a pickup at the private airfield."

Holly froze midstep. "Oh, *hell no*." She knew exactly who was flying back into New York today. "That's your job."

"Alas, I am stuck in traffic," Janvier said. "A truck spilled chickens all over the road in front of me."

"Ha ha. I'm hanging up now."

"But this is no laughing matter, *'tite* Hollyberry," was the aggravating response, followed by the sound of a window being lowered. Indignant chicken squawks filled the line seconds later. "See? Janvier does not lie. I am surrounded by frustrated drivers on every side, with no way out, but you are only ten minutes away. Do the pickup."

"Is that an order?" Janvier and Ashwini were Holly's official bosses as of seven months ago, when the entire team in charge of her training—and sanity—had pronounced that she'd gained sufficient and stable control over the twisted, poisonous power that marked her as the Archangel Uram's creation.

Pride curled her toes at the memory of that day—Holly tried to focus on the trust the team was showing in her, not on how she remained on a leash nonetheless. Thanks to Ash's and Janvier's willingness to utilize her ability to make friends with those who lived in the shadows, she was now part of the small but efficient team that kept an eye on the murky gray underground of New York, a place far from the power-drenched environs of Archangel Tower.

Before her life broke apart in a spray of blood and fear and anguish, Holly hadn't known there was a hierarchy in the immortal world. She'd seen the angels who soared high above the skyscrapers and the vampires who stalked the streets as all the same: dangerously strong and hauntingly beautiful. These days, she knew two-hundred-year-old vamps who were homeless addicts with less to their name than Holly, and understood that when a being lived too long, he or she could forget any concept of humanity or empathy.

For many, torture and sex alone, often entwined, held any pleasure.

"*Oui*," Janvier said in reply to her edgy question. "It is an order. See, I am acting bosslike."

Holly's lips twitched despite herself. "Fine, I'll go pick up Poison."

"Play nice—no putting a *cunja* on him."

Holly stuck out her tongue at her phone before she hung up. A little boy wearing a tiny blue and yellow backpack saw her, stuck out his own tongue with a giggle. Holly winked. Looking over his shoulder, he waved at her.

She waved back.

That sweet kid, he didn't know that she was the creation of a murderous psychopath, that she had horrific urges inside her that caused her to break out in a cold sweat. He saw only a small-boned Chinese American woman in skinny black jeans decorated with appliquéd black roses on the left calf and thigh, her top a floaty orange silk, and her ankle boots a shining black with small gold buckles.

That ordinary woman's rainbow-streaked black hair was pulled back in a sleek ponytail, her face framed by blunt black bangs, and her nails painted in a wild mix of colors.

The only thing that made her stand out in a city overrun with the stylistically adventurous was the acid green that had taken over the light brown of her irises. The shade had been darker before, nearer to the vivid green of the archangel who'd used her as a human toy, but the acidic lightness had come in firmly over the past year and settled.

When strangers spotted Holly's eyes, they automatically assumed she was wearing contacts. It fit their impression of a woman who looked as if she'd been dropped in a vat of color.

Maybe a touch quirky or peculiar, but human. *Normal.*

Holly ached to be that normal human woman every single day. But in the four years since she'd been stripped naked and forced to watch her friends be dismembered alive, her throat torn and raw from her screams, she'd gotten over the first four stages of grief: denial, anger, bargaining, and depression.

Acceptance . . . well, that was going to take a hell of a lot more time, she thought as she slid into the Tower vehicle she'd been assigned. When Janvier had first told her she'd get a vehicle as part of her job as his and Ash's apprentice, she'd glumly expected a sedate sedan, but she should've remembered the kind of people who worked for the Archangel Raphael.

None were the sedan type.

Holly's car was a sleek black thing that looked like an arrow in flight. It wasn't new by any stretch of the imagination and had more than a few dents and scratches—all the better to fit the environs she prowled in the shadowy corners of the city. The tires were good, but not so good anyone would bother to steal them, and the radio only got about five stations.

Holly loved her ride with the passion of a thousand suns.

Inside this car, she could be free, could *fly*.

No leash. No blood that craved the monstrous. No flash-fire memories of a rust red hand stroking her hair as he told her to "Drink, girl," in a gentle voice that belied the carnage in which she knelt broken and beaten.

Today, she raced in and out of traffic with bare inches to spare as she made her way to the airfield that handled the Tower's private fleet. It wasn't the safest way to drive, but Holly was very careful not to put anyone else in danger. Only herself.

Yes, she needed therapy.

But Holly wasn't suicidal. Not any longer. Her head was plenty messed up, but never would she hurt her family by making that irrevocable choice. Her mom and dad, Mia, her younger brothers, had suffered more than enough in the immediate days and weeks after the slaughter, and in her months of confused, angry, scared silence.

It was Janvier who'd made her understand what she was throwing away.

"I will miss my sisters my entire vampiric existence," he'd said to her as they sat on the grass after a sparring session that had left Holly's body a screaming ache. "I have a big family that loves me so, but to grow up with another, ah, *'tite* Holly, that is a different bond." A sheen in eyes the shade of bayou moss that her deadly boss made no effort to hide. "Amelie and Jöelle . . . they live here." His fist on his heart. "Always they will stay safe within."

His gaze had gone to his wife, who was practicing a martial arts kata with cool hunter dedication. "And my dangerous *cher*, my Ashblade, she yet grieves for her brother and sister." As he'd risen to go tease Ash into a kiss, the Guild Hunter's fingers sinking into the chestnut brown of his hair, the copper strands within it glinting in the sunlight, Holly had felt understanding kick her. Hard.

Mia would be gone forever one day.

Alvin and Wesley would be gone.

Her parents would be gone.

She would *never* get back that time.

Holly had caught the subway home an hour later—to be greeted with tears and hugs and her favorite meal—followed by a grilling so intense it had threatened to set her hair on fire.

It was a memory she hoarded against the unknown future.

Zipping into a parking spot outside the airfield building located at the end of a long and deserted private road, she got out and showed her Tower ID to the guard. He gave her the hard eye regardless and pressed his finger to the receiver in his ear after muttering her name into the microphone on his collar.

Whatever he heard back had him nodding. "You're cleared." A faint curve to his lips. "Nice outfit. I didn't know the Tower let five-year-olds drive."

Eyes narrowed, Holly pulled out her best sincere tone. "Did you get your suit at Slick Vampires Are Us? Asking for a friend."

Smile wiped off, the vampire just looked at her, unblinking. Holly stared back, not about to be intimidated, even if he was at least five hundred years old according to the internal chronometer she'd developed over the past year.

A tingle ran behind her eyes.

Shit.

Though backing down was against her personal religion, Holly lowered her eyelids and took a deep breath. When she lifted them back up, the vampire was smirking. Gritting her teeth and refraining from pointing out that she'd been a second away from mesmerizing him into clucking like a chicken, she carried on inside. It was a relatively small area with a glass wall that looked out onto the airfield.

Air traffic control was high above in their own little aerie.

That had always struck Holly as funny: angels flew wherever they wished, but if they traveled in an airplane, they needed to obey the rules of airspace. Not that the man she was here to pick up had wings. Venom was a vampire. One of the Seven, Raphael's private guard. That, unfortunately, also meant he was far, *far* stronger than he should've been for his three hundred and fifty or so years of age.

All of the Seven were violent powers.

"Tower Airways Flight Three on final approach."

Holly looked up at the speaker system with a startled grin. "Very funny, Trace," she said, having recognized the voice at once.

Male laughter came through those same speakers. "I thought, my fellow adventurer into the wonders of worlds unseen, you might need a little entertainment," the vampire said in his warm tenor. "Would you like to come up?"

She caught sight of the plane heading in to land. Her heart began to beat faster. In preparation. Because with her and Venom, it was always a war. "No, but thanks. And since when are you an air traffic controller?"

"I'm keeping Andreja company."

Trace signed off with a line of poetry that made her heart soar.

Her and Trace's friendship was based in words, in the poetry in which they found wonder and comfort.

Then there was the man about to get out of the plane that had come to a smooth stop on the tarmac. He'd been part of her life almost since the hellish day when she'd watched helplessly, her body paralyzed by poisoned blood, as an insane archangel tore a screaming Shelley's arms from her body as if he was pulling the wings off a butterfly, then paused to kiss Holly with his red-rimmed mouth.

"Shh."

Hands curling at her sides as the hairs on her nape rose, she shoved away the past to focus on the man she was here to pick up, a man who'd irritated and angered her from their first meeting.

When the Tower had reassigned him away from New York just over two years earlier, she'd said good riddance. Only to realize that with Venom gone, no one in the city truly *saw* the part of her that was cold and deadly and eerily inhuman. The immortals who surrounded her were powerful and deadly, but no one else was so strangely *other*.

Venom was both immune to her capacity to mesmerize prey and the only person who could teach her how to deal with the ability. Which meant she'd had to have his annoying voice in her ear once a week over the time that he'd been away—in a place no one would mention by name to her. He'd been meant to return to work physically with her, but a strange, taut tension had gripped the immortal world in the interim, and Venom had made no visits to New York.

He stepped out of the private jet.

Of course he was wearing a flawlessly tailored suit in black, paired with a black shirt and no tie. Wraparound mirrored sunglasses obscured his eyes. Holly still hadn't figured out if he wore the sunglasses because his eyes were sensitive to light, so people wouldn't freak out, or simply because he was an asshole who liked to look impenetrable.

She'd bet on the last.

After striding down the steps of the plane with a battered brown—in an elegant way, of course—leather hold-all slung over his shoulder, he turned to look back at the plane, raising a hand toward the cockpit. The early-afternoon sunlight caught on the clean line of his jaw, the burnished brown of his skin glowing in the light. His slightly overlong chocolate-dark hair was brushed neatly, not a strand out of place.

The damn man looked like he'd stepped out of an ad for fine whiskey or luxury watches.

She was scowling when he met her eyes through the glass. She knew he was looking at her despite the mirrored sunglasses. Arms folded and feet set apart, she stared back.

He smiled and slid off the sunglasses.

Eyes slitted like a viper's met hers, the color a bright astonishing green. *I see you missed me, kitty*, he mouthed.

Holly gave him a sickly sweet smile . . . followed by the finger.

2

Sliding the sunglasses back on, Venom laughed. He was inside the waiting area moments later. The raw power of him crashed into her. Violently. Despite her earlier thoughts, she'd forgotten just how incredibly *strong* he was—she knew this was no power play; he wasn't trying to overwhelm her on purpose.

This was simply who he was: a vampire a hundred times more deadly than the guard outside.

"Damn," she said with a downturned face. "I was hoping you'd fallen into a crevasse." He'd mentioned in their last call that he was about to go out on a climb. "Too bad, I guess."

"I see those little kitten fangs of yours are still just as cute."

She wanted to hiss at him, controlled the urge only because it would amuse him—and because in the time that he'd been gone, she'd achieved iron control over the most obviously inhuman aspects of her nature.

As for the ugly voice that kept whispering inside her

when she was distracted, she'd strangle that, too. "Where's the rest of your luggage?"

"This is it."

Rolling her eyes, Holly put her hands on her hips. "Yeah, right. What did you wear for the past two years?" Venom had a suit for every day of the month.

"You don't know everything you think you know, kitty."

The world became tinged in acid green.

His smile was slow and satisfied. "There you are." He took off his sunglasses again to reveal those eyes even more eerie than her own. "Boo."

Getting her temper in check through sheer teeth-clenched grit, Holly looked up toward the speaker mounted on the wall. "Bye, Trace. Hope you and Andreja have a good day. Oh, I may be arrested for homicide soon. Please come visit me in prison."

"Adieu, my beautiful girl," Trace said with cheerful gallantness. "And, old friend, while you may provoke sweet Holly to homicidal rage, it is a pleasure to have you home."

"It's good to be back." Sliding his sunglasses back on, Venom looked at Holly. "You my chauffeur?"

"I'm the woman you don't want to piss off unless you plan to walk all the way to the Tower," Holly said before striding out to the car.

Venom paused to shake hands with the guard, then dropped his hold-all in the trunk. Coming around to take the passenger seat, he pushed it all the way back to accommodate his legs. He was whipcord lean, but he had wide shoulders, long legs, a lot of muscle. He could also move as fast as a cobra strike.

"They let you drive now?" he said in a wondering tone of voice calibrated to get under her skin. "I leave for a couple of years and miss kitty's first steps. Did anyone take photos for the baby album I sent you?"

"It's full of pretty pictures." Holly bared her teeth at him in a caricature of a smile. "Honor *is* a little concerned about how I keep drawing you with your head cut off," she said in a deliberately thoughtful tone, "but an artist must follow her instincts."

"Oh, Hollyberry, I'm deeply touched that you couldn't get me out of your head."

Holly deliberately skidded out of the parking spot before racing out so fast that Venom's head should've slammed back against his seat. Instead, he laughed, lazily bracing one arm against the frame of the open window as the lethal wildness of his scent blew across her skin. "Got that temper under control, I see."

"Oh, b—" Holly cut herself off before she said, *bite me.* She knew exactly what his response would be.

"I *am* looking forward to fresh blood." It was a liquid sound, his body languid in a way that simply wasn't human. "Blood hot from the vein is so much better than the cold, preserved stuff. Don't you think?"

Holly squeezed the steering wheel and tried to think of the calming exercise Honor had taught her in an effort to foster mental and emotional discipline at a time when Holly had been tearing herself apart. She hadn't needed that exercise for a while. Venom hadn't been in the city for a while.

Breathe in, breathe out, breathe in—

Blood pulsing in her victim's veins, drawn to the surface by quivering fear.

—breathe out. In, out, in, damn it, out.

The taste of hot iron on her tongue. Her mouth watering.

Staring at the road with grim focus, Holly refused to give in to the potent—and abnormal—hunger Venom's words had aroused. She didn't need that much blood to survive. And she definitely did *not* want to tear open a helpless mortal's jugular and bathe in a dark, hot gush of red.

Her stomach clenched, her gorge rising at the images

that filled her brain. Horrific, nightmarish images straight out of a fucking asylum for the murderously insane.

"Still fighting the reality that you're a vampire?"

"I'm not," she said, her voice holding no indication of her utter terror—because Holly was used to hiding the madness submerged deep within. "I have vampiric tendencies, but I don't need as much blood as you." What she craved was a more violent and deadly thing. "I also have other aspects to me that aren't vampiric."

"You mean the ability to mesmerize prey? Hate to break it to you, kitty, but I can do that, too, and I'm a vampire. Unlike you, my ability is no longer limited to mortals and very young vampires."

Holly was well aware he was taunting her. He knew very well what else she could do. "I need food," she still said, because at least trading barbs with Venom was her version of normal. "That hasn't changed in the time since the Tower decided Manhattan would be better off without your delightful presence."

"Stop, stop. I can't take the effusive welcome." Unruffled amusement in every syllable, he stretched out his legs. "You still craving samosas?"

"No." She'd gone to her favorite Indian restaurant three times last week and stuffed her face full of the fried *Wait a minute*. "What possible reason could you have to remember that?" she asked suspiciously, the admission about her craving having slipped out during a long-distance training session.

"Because it's another strange little Hollyberry fact to add to my growing collection."

"You're an asshole." The exchange described their entire relationship, she thought as she continued down the otherwise empty private road that led to and away from the airfield. Thankfully, they merged into a much busier multi-lane road not long afterward. It gave her an excuse to ignore

Venom and the prickling over her skin that wouldn't go away when he was in the vicinity.

. "So, what do kitties do on their days off?"

"Be quiet. I'm driving."

"Is that what you call it? I was thinking more lunatic roller coaster."

"I don't see you putting on your walking sho—" She wrenched the wheel all the way to the right as a huge black SUV shoved into her lane. "Jesus!" It hadn't been a mistake on her part—the driver of the fucking tank was still pushing with unhidden aggression, as if he didn't have three other lanes to choose from.

And now the bastard was beeping his horn at her.

"Stop the car," Venom said, his voice ice cold. "I'll deal with this."

Holly made it a point to disagree with everything he said on principle, but the idiot in the other vehicle was taking hazardous behavior to a whole new level. He could cause a crash—and most of the other drivers around her probably weren't vampires who could take far more damage than humans.

She pulled over onto the verge. The SUV screeched to a stop *beside* her, rather than behind her. "Great, looks like the idiot has road rage issues." Holly shoved open her door without regard for any marks it'd leave on the SUV's gleaming finish. The space was narrow, but workable for a woman of her size.

Venom was already on her side of the car, his speed vicious. But she got out in time to see the doors of the other vehicle slam open and a harsh male voice call out, "Grab the girl!"

Grab the girl?

Not. Fucking. Happening.

Holly kicked the gun right out of the first goon's hand. The second was flying back against his car before she saw

Venom move. The third took one look at Venom and went sheet white. "You're not supposed to be here!"

Barely hearing the fearful cry, Holly snapped a kick at the first goon's jaw, slamming his head sideways. But he was strong, a vampire of at least three hundred. He kept coming at her. Holly couldn't use any of her new abilities when things were moving so fast, had to fight using only the skills she'd learned from Honor and Ashwini and Elena.

All three Guild Hunters, all three used to fighting against stronger, faster opponents.

Holly was smaller than all of her trainers. *'tite* Holly-berry. That was what Janvier called her. The kids at school had just said "short." Holly didn't care right now. She cared only that the hunters and Janvier—and Venom—had taught her to fight in a way that *used* her size. She ducked under the goon's meaty fist and brought up a two-fisted punch of her own into his gut, right in the sweet spot.

His agonized groan was music to her ears . . . right before he was thrown back so hard against his vehicle that he left a person-sized dent in the metal. It matched the dent left by goon number two.

"I had that." Her chest heaved, her blood hot.

After straightening his unrumpled suit jacket, Venom said, "You're welcome." He nudged at one of the crumpled goons with his designer-shoe-clad foot. "This one looks the most alive. Let's see what he has to say."

It turned out to not be much.

"There's a bounty to grab her." The goon was all but quivering in front of Venom, his pallid white skin flushed and blotchy.

"How much? And who's behind it?"

"I don't know. Mike had the details but I think you bashed his brains in."

"He'll wake up. Eventually." A cold smile. "Then he'll discover the true meaning of pain."

The goon's teeth began to chatter. "I swear we weren't going to hurt her," he sobbed. "Just take her for the bounty."

Holly rolled her eyes. "I'm right here, moron."

Said moron was still frozen in front of Venom—and she knew Venom wasn't using his ability to mesmerize. "That's all I know," the guy blubbered out of a mouth that was swelling up from the gash on his lip. "We stalked her, realized that she was dropping off her sister today and would be driving back alone."

"Didn't you get a clue when I detoured to the private airfield?" Everyone knew it belonged to the Tower.

The goon's eyes didn't even flick to her as he said, "She drives like a maniac."

Venom laughed. "In that we agree." His laugh had the thick-necked goon flinching. "Now, the rest."

The man spoke so fast his words rolled into one another. "We lost her right after the main airport and, after fifteen minutes of searching, decided to pull over at a gas station, get some coffee, make a new plan. We'd just got back in the SUV when we saw her car fly past."

And the goons had figured it was their lucky day, too hyped up on the hunt to think about *why* Holly wasn't already in Manhattan when she'd taken off so fast that they'd lost her. Not bothering to shake her head at their incompetence, she said, "How were you supposed to contact the person who put out the bounty?"

"I think Mike has an address to e-mail a photo to." He swallowed, licked his lips. "You know, for proof."

Going to the goon whose head was crushed in on one side badly enough that she could see brain matter leaking out— gross, but far from the worst she'd seen—Holly searched his pockets until she found his phone. She unlocked it using his thumbprint, then scanned his text messages.

Nothing.

A reminder popped up onto the home screen before she

could check his e-mails: *Kidnap Holly Chang. E-mail photo.* An e-mail address followed.

Taken aback at the idea that this vampire had needed a reminder of his intention to kidnap a woman—I mean, it didn't seem like the kind of thing you'd forget—she showed Venom the note.

He met her eyes. "Can you pretend to look beaten and defeated?"

No. She was *never* going to look that way again.

"No," he said softly, "I didn't think so."

Shoulders unknotting when he let it go, she thought quickly. "I can look unconscious." She pulled a few random hunks of hair out of her ponytail, then climbed into the backseat of the SUV and slumped her head to the side—one of the goons had torn her brand-new top, so with that and the messy hair, she looked appropriately bedraggled.

Venom took the shot using Mike-the-forgetful-goon's phone, e-mailed it through. They still didn't have a response by the time a Tower team arrived to take the bounty hunters into custody. A tow truck followed, to haul away the SUV—Venom had damaged the engine when he'd thrown one of the goons on top of the hood.

"Whoever put out the bounty might have people watching the ones most likely to succeed," he said once they were back in the car and on their way to the Tower, the silent phone in the cup holder. "If so, the lookout would've seen us take down the bounty hunters."

Holly snorted. "If those three were judged the most likely to succeed, it's a seriously low bar."

"Not a surprise, kitty. Only the stupid or the desperate would go after a woman who belongs to the Tower."

Holly tapped a finger on the steering wheel. "Goons might not know that," she murmured. "I've only had a room in the Tower for seven months, and I try to keep my connection low-key." The weakest immortals, the ones who haunted the shadows, were aware she knew powerful vampires and angels and could get their concerns heard, but Holly wasn't considered a threat in her own right.

What a con I'm running.

She wanted to tear the steering wheel off its housing, wanted to scream out her rage. Too bad that super strength wasn't one of the abilities bestowed on her courtesy of her tainted blood . . . or that she couldn't forget the nightmare of her creation. She *hated* the emotions that had hit her during the kidnapping attempt, emotions that yet pulsed in her body.

Uram had taken her while she'd been heading out to the movies with her friends, the six of them laughing and talking about grabbing mint chocolate frappuccinos. She'd been wearing a flirty little yellow dress, and strappy high heels in an effort to make herself taller, and her makeup had been immaculate—it had taken an hour to apply.

Mia had helped her with her eyeliner.

Then had come the horror.

That feeling of utter helplessness, it was a stone in her gut, a memory she couldn't wipe after it had surged its way to the surface some two and a half years after the abduction, as if her mind had decided she hadn't faced horror enough.

More than eighteen months on from that searing instant of recall, and the nightmare echoes refused to fade. She'd screamed until she was hoarse, had fought to save her friends, but Uram had gutted them one by one in front of her, as if displaying his art to an appreciative audience. Holly had been the only one left, a bloody, naked, half-mad mess when Elena found her.

Often in the days afterward, she'd wished that she, too, had died in that charnel house. It was so much harder to be alive and to know Shelley would never again laugh her breathless and giggly laugh, that Cara and Maxie would never again dither over a shade of lipstick, and Rania and Ping never again gossip about the men in their lives.

There had been two other victims in that Brooklyn warehouse, women already dead and drained of blood by the time Uram took Holly and her friends to his house of horrors. It was much later that Holly had discovered their names: Kimiya and Nataja.

She'd been in no state to go to any of their funerals . . . and she couldn't bear to visit their graves. It *hurt so much* to think of her friends and those two strangers she'd never known—and never would know—lying cold in the earth.

"What I don't understand is why anyone would want to kidnap a kitty with tiny baby vampire teeth."

3

Venom's musing statement snapped her out of the loop of grief and loss and horror and rage. "Come closer and I'll show you exactly how helpless those baby teeth are." Her fangs dispensed an acidic green substance the Tower scientists had tested and declared a deadly poison.

"Sorry, kitty. Biting me will do you no good . . . though I have been told my blood is the best women have ever tasted."

Holly made gagging motions with the hand not on the steering wheel, incredibly glad right then for his aggravating and distracting presence—though she'd cut off her own head before she admitted it. "Some women will do anything to get into the Tower."

"You play mean, Hollyberry. Like poison."

Coming from anyone else, the latter words would've been an ugly insult. From Venom . . . "Did you just compliment me?" she asked, her mouth falling open. "Take it back!" She couldn't deal with Venom being nice to her in any way, shape, or form.

"Of course," he said, "your poison is nowhere near as venomous as mine."

She went to snap back a retort about men always thinking their package was bigger, when the import of his words penetrated. "Did the Tower compare the two?"

"We're the only two venomous members of the Tower. The sire needs to know our exact strengths."

"How much stronger are you?" she asked through gritted teeth, though his potency wasn't a surprise. Venom might look like he was maybe twenty-seven, but he'd lived a lot more life than she could imagine.

And he'd look that way forever, a sexual creature no one would ever dare call a "boy." Holly, in contrast, was stuck with the face of a twenty-three-year-old who'd still had a youthful softness to her when Uram altered the shape of her existence. The softness would've disappeared in another year; she knew because she'd watched Mia's transformation.

But Holly never got that extra year to grow into her skin and her womanhood.

Vampirism—or whatever it was that ran in her blood— would probably refine her features to something more adultlike in the future, but she'd never look anything but young. Not even if she lived to be five hundred years old. Of course, a long, near-immortal life was the best-case scenario.

"I've grown strong enough to take down a large number of the angels in the city," Venom said lazily. "It's a secret the Tower will execute you for speaking, so never share it—but I can shock the youngest ones into an intense involuntary sleep that the healers believe could lead to death, incapacitate the older with severe pain."

Holly scowled and said, "Bull," wincing inwardly at using language for which her mother would threaten to wash out her mouth with soap. Daphne Chang didn't care *what* Holly was; she did care that her daughter comport herself like the lady she'd been raised to be. Holly tried, she really did. But only when her mother was in the vicinity to bear witness.

Never again would Holly willingly cause pain to the mom who'd *never*, not once, looked at her as anything but her child. Her dad was less demonstrative, but he was the one who kept aside certain pieces of clothing for her in his dress shop, pieces that were always colorful and quirky and Holly.

Love came in many different forms.

"It's all true." Venom's hair lifted up in the wind coming through his open window, his profile so astonishingly perfect that her breath caught for a second. "I'm deadlier than the deadliest snake in the world, with the ability to impact strong immortals. But you're not too far behind."

"Try being used as a chew toy by an insane archangel," Holly said with a grim smile. "It does wonders for your poison, I hear."

No one knew exactly what Uram had done to her beyond making her drink his blood—that sickening memory, she'd finally recovered. But much of the time he'd spent with her after murdering her friends remained a blank. Either she'd been unconscious or he'd made sure she *wouldn't* remember, and it was just great to know that a bloodborn archangel might have been digging around in her mind.

Who knew what he'd left behind.

What Holly did have was a lot more information about angelic biology than even the majority of older vampires—she'd needed that information to understand what was happening to her.

"But," Venom continued, "as I was saying. I'm immune to your poisonous bite."

Holly scowled. She'd bitten him once or twice, back during her psycho-PTSD phase, and he'd shrugged it off, but those bites had been mere scratches—and her toxic kiss hadn't yet settled into its final form. "The scientists tested our venom against each other?"

Reaching over, Venom played with strands of her hair, which she'd scraped neatly back the instant after he'd taken the photograph. "You look like that pony toy with a unicorn tail."

She slammed up an arm to knock him off. "Answer the question. And unicorn hair was the point, Mr. Designer Cut and Dry." Every so often, Holly had to fight the urge to jump on Venom and mess him up.

"Complete neutralization." Venom turned slightly in his seat to face her profile—and the prickling over her skin turned into a swarm of stinging bees. "My venom cancels out yours and vice versa."

Holly stared straight ahead. "Is my venom the same as yours?" It was a question she didn't want to ask. "Like a viper's or a cobra's or another snake's?"

"No." His answer made her heart slam into her rib cage. "Mine tracks that way—though it's a unique mixture, but yours is unlike anything on the planet and it's growing in virulence."

Holly felt her muscles lock. The *thing* inside her, the psychic tumor she couldn't outrace, was getting stronger. She knew it, had felt it. Where would it end? In death? In psychotic madness like the archangel who'd been her blood sire? Worse?

"We could test it," Venom said in that languidly sensuous tone she'd heard him use on the women who panted after him. "Share our venom."

Holly found her feet again. "Oh, gosh, let me think about it," she said with a flutter of her eyelashes. "The answer is . . . A Big. Fat. *No*." She knew he was jerking her chain. He thought she was a spitting baby. She thought he was a conceited ass. That was the extent of their relationship.

"Why does someone want you enough to put a bounty on your head?" His tone was serious this time. "It was very definitely *you* they were after. Holly Chang, also known as Sorrow. That was the brief and it included a photo of you."

Holly nodded. "I saw." The photo had been stored on the chief goon's phone. It had been of her striding out of a café where she'd taken her mother for a cup of tea and cake. Daphne Chang had a weakness for cake that Holly fully exploited as she weaseled her way back into her mother's good graces.

"The instigator must know how you were Made," Venom continued, his power a sinuous wave that wrapped around her before sliding away. "Or they suspect."

Holly fought to keep her breathing even. Venom hadn't been messing with her just then—he played games, but not like that. Not in ways where they weren't on equal ground. She was sensing his power so vividly either because her own sensitivity had increased as a result of the ongoing changes in her body—or because Venom had grown stronger in the two years since she'd last seen him in person.

Or both.

"Your blood is valuable currency," he added.

"Unfortunately." Holly didn't carry the deadly toxin that had resulted in Uram's murderous insanity, but she carried *something* that wasn't standard issue in either the mortal or immortal world.

No one had quite figured out what yet. They just knew Holly was a "strangeness unseen in nature"—words spoken by a healer working on her case.

"There's another possibility," Venom said. "You're unique and such things rarely come along in an immortal life. As Zhou Lijuan collects the most extraordinary wings in angel-kind, so another collector may seek to acquire you."

Holly shivered inwardly at the mention of the seriously creepy Archangel of China. "How can she collect angelic wings? Does she cut them off?" she asked, horrified.

Venom's answer was chilling. "No, she prefers the whole body. Like pinning a dead butterfly to a wall."

"Fuck, immortals are twisted." And theirs was her world

now. "Did they react to you that way? Like a curiosity or a collector's item?"

"I wasn't as much of a shock. Not given the identity of my Maker."

The Archangel Neha, the Queen of Snakes, of Poisons.

"But," he continued, his voice a little distant, as if he was looking hundreds of years back, "I'm the only vampire she has ever Made who inherited so much of what makes her who she is. There were many who tried to lure me from her court at the conclusion of my Contract."

Holly was intrigued despite herself. "Was Raphael one of those people?"

His laughter was incongruously warm for a man with the eyes of a viper. "The sire has never had to lure anyone, kitty."

Hissing at him before she could stop herself, she braked to a hard stop in front of the gleaming spike that was the cloud-piercing form of Manhattan's Archangel Tower. "You can slither away now," she said when he didn't move.

"You'll be coming with me." His tone was unbending. "Dmitri will want to know about the kidnapping attempt."

Holly's gut tensed. She'd been afraid of that. And while she cheerfully defied Venom for no reason except that he was aggravating, defying Dmitri was a whole another matter. It wasn't that she was scared of him—though Dmitri could be terrifying. It was that she didn't want to disappoint him.

Spinning the car left and down into the underground Tower garage, she parked in silence and got out. Venom grabbed his hold-all from the trunk, then prowled beside her with a liquid smoothness she'd thought an affectation until she'd seen him fight and realized his eyes didn't lie—Venom had been changed down to his very cells during his conversion to vampirism.

She wondered why he'd made the choice and if it had

been worth it to lose not just his freedom for a hundred years in payment, but also his humanity in ways even most vampires didn't have to consider.

Stepping into the elevator, she kept her curiosity under wraps and her eyes resolutely trained frontward even as the sinuous slide of his power filled the small space. But she was conscious of him taking off his sunglasses and hooking them into the neck of his shirt. He rarely did that except with Raphael and others of the Seven.

The elevator doors opened smoothly on the floor of the Tower that held Dmitri's office. Holly hadn't been up there for a while, though Honor had told her about the renovation. The walls were a smooth gray, the carpet a richer shade of the same elegant color.

It had all been black beforehand, pure Dmitri.

Now, it reflected both the most powerful vampire in the city—and his hunter wife.

"What are those dents?" Honor had to be dismayed at the damage to her newly painted walls. At least the pretty artwork she'd picked out appeared to have survived unscathed.

"Looks like knives punching into the walls," Venom said after a quick glance, his lips curved in what looked like genuine amusement. "My guess is Elena and Dmitri."

Then there was no more time to prepare for what was to come; they'd reached Dmitri's office. Raphael's deadly second wasn't standing behind his desk—Holly had never seen him actually sitting in his office chair—but was out on the railingless balcony beyond. He didn't look a thousand years old, maybe in his early thirties at most. A dangerous man with black hair and dark brown eyes and sun-bronzed skin who "exuded sex," according to the media.

Dropping his hold-all in a corner, Venom strode straight out.

Holly followed with more care—she'd been warned over and over that while she was like a vampire, she wasn't quite one. And even a vampire would die if he fell from this height and his head separated from his body. That Dmitri and Venom were so cavalier about it spoke to the amount of power that ran in their veins.

Dmitri had been on the phone but hung up the instant he spotted Venom.

A smile breaking out over his face, he hugged the other man in a way that said they were friends rather than simply compatriots or brother warriors. More than six hundred and fifty years separated Dmitri and Venom, the oldest and the youngest in the Seven, but there was no distance in that moment.

As she watched, Dmitri slapped Venom on the back before the two men stepped apart.

"Holly."

Holly walked to meet Dmitri halfway and, when he drew her into the warm strength of his arms, she didn't resist. Where other women looked at him and saw a hard-bodied vampire who oozed sex appeal, Holly saw the man who'd found her at her lowest, full of self-loathing and guilt that she'd survived when her friends were all dead. He'd been so angry that awful night, had told her brutal truths about what would happen to her if she continued on her self-destructive path, but he hadn't abandoned her when she admitted her fear of what she was becoming.

He'd stroked her hair as they sat on a cliff with a glittering view of Manhattan, and he'd let her cry until she had no more tears left in her. Until she was ready to claw out some kind of a life for herself from the ashes of who she'd once been. In the time since, he'd watched over her development and made sure she didn't drown under the black waves of her nightmares.

Running his palm over her ponytail before he released her, he shifted so that he had his back to the precipitous drop behind him, while she and Venom stood in front of him. The wind whipped at his black T-shirt, the color the same as his jeans and his boots.

"Can we go inside?" Holly blurted out. She was loath to betray any weakness in front of Venom, but she hated seeing Dmitri so close to the edge.

To her surprise, Venom didn't comment at all as they slipped inside Dmitri's office. At which point he told Dmitri what had happened. Dmitri's dark eyes sharpened, the lethal predator in him suddenly evident—this was the man spoken of as being merciless, Raphael's "Blade" who made bloody mincemeat of his enemies.

"The bounty hunters specifically wanted Holly?"

"No doubts." Venom pulled out the phone they'd confiscated. "I'll have Vivek see what he can do with the e-mail address."

Dmitri nodded before turning to Holly, the violence of his power making her teeth ache. "Were you hurt?"

"No." She pointed at the torn shoulder of her top. "My father gave me this top just last week. The stupid goons ripped it."

Dmitri's smile was lethal. "If there's a significant enough bounty, this will only be the first attempt." He folded his arms. "The bigger threats will be the old ones so bored with life that risking death by attacking one of the Tower's people will be a dangerous thrill. They won't be as incompetent as this trio."

Holly got a prickling at the back of her neck. "I can take care of myself," she reminded him. "You made sure of that." He was the one who'd thrown her into training designed to increase her control over her abilities.

Pinning her to the spot with the darkness of his gaze, Dmitri raised an eyebrow. "Could you have taken all three vampires today?"

Holly opened her mouth . . . and couldn't lie. Not to Dmitri. "No," she finally grated out. Mike and his fellow idiot goons had been big bastards, and while Holly could fight, she wasn't an experienced hunter or warrior.

"You don't go anywhere alone until we figure out who it

is that wants you and why." The words were an order. "I'll speak to Janvier and Ashwini, see who best to assign you."

"I can babysit," said the aggravating vampire beside her, the one whose power kept sliding around her, the feel of it warm, living snakeskin across her body.

4

"Thank you for your generosity," Holly said in her politest "nice young lady" voice, her smile wide enough to cut into her cheeks, "but I'd rather shack up with a flea-infested rabid dog."

Venom's eyes did that fascinating thing they did sometimes—they nictitated. The flash of the membrane coming horizontally across his irises was so fast that no one else believed her when she told them what she'd seen. It was like they couldn't see it, the speed was so rapid. Instead of being creeped out by the act, she wanted to lean in close, see if she could track the movement.

She also wanted him to do it slower so she could fully appreciate the beauty of it: the membrane that came across his eye wasn't totally transparent or milky white like she'd seen in images of birds when she'd looked up the topic online. The translucent membrane was cracked through with white, creating a fine net through which the green of his eyes could shine. The effect was incredible.

And only visible for a millisecond at most.

"You're not exactly my first choice, kitty." A leisurely scan down her body. "I prefer to spend my off time with women."

Holly didn't rise to the bait. "I'm sure Ashwini won't mind if I hang with her." If she had to have a bodyguard, either Ash or Honor or Janvier would be her choice. Since Honor was teaching a class at Guild Academy this semester, and Janvier had extra duties while Raphael and Elena were away, that left Ashwini.

"Ashwini is in advanced combat training, as is Janvier," Dmitri told her. "They also have a heavy schedule of duties." He looked over at Venom. "I was planning to ask you to take over some of their tasks while Illium teaches them what they need to know."

"Isn't Galen involved?"

"What do you think?" Dmitri's smile was sharper now. "I think they're both already ruing the day they agreed to be in Elena's Guard." A glance at Holly, his amusement fading before he shifted his attention back to Venom. "This situation needs to be brought quickly to heel. It's your priority—keep an eye on Holly and find out who's after her. I'll split the other duties between the stronger vampires like Trace until you're done."

Holly folded her arms. "Sorry to break into your cozy little chat," she said, struggling past her desire to obey Dmitri, "but I'm a grown adult. Don't make decisions for me like I'm not here."

"You sure you're full grown?"

"Venom." Dmitri's cool voice cut Venom off before he could needle her any further. "Talk to Vivek, then get some rest. Holly can shadow me for the rest of the day."

She managed to keep her mouth shut until after Venom had left. "Dmitri, I won't fight a bodyguard"—no matter how much the extra leash chafed—"but don't stick me with him."

"No one will dare touch you with Venom nearby. He's

one of the Tower's strongest—and he's light-years ahead of you in utilizing his abilities."

"He's also an asshole."

"So, according to many people, am I," Dmitri said, clearly not bothered by that. "It's either Venom, or I confine you to the Tower."

Her hands fisted, her heartbeat accelerating. The world began to gain a hard clarity washed in acid green. In front of her, Dmitri watched her with no indication of fear or worry. "Holly, shut it down." The words were mild.

She screamed instead, the frustration inside her snapping out into a loud sound. "I've earned my freedom, Dmitri! I've done everything the Tower has asked, *everything*!"

Walking around his desk, he leaned back against it, his arms folded across his wide chest. "And you'll keep doing it," he said in a tone that demanded obedience. "Four years is nothing in an immortal existence, less than a heartbeat, less than a child's first breaths. You have no idea how dangerous you might be."

"So you plan to watch me forever?" He'd put her officially under Contract, but unlike normal vampires, she wouldn't automatically walk free after a hundred years of service in return for the "gift" of vampirism—the Tower would decide if she was ever safe enough to be freed.

"If that's what it takes." His words were pitiless. "But I have a feeling that once you have total control of your abilities and over your urges, you'll take the choice out of my hands."

The acid green continued to pulse in her vision. "Are you immune to my poison?" she asked, so angry it was a hum in her blood.

"No, but it won't kill me. I'm also fast enough to snap your neck before your fangs ever get close."

Holly blinked. The green faded.

Suddenly, her body wanted to sag. She was so tired of

this. Of fighting a world that viewed her as an unknown threat. Of fighting the cancer inside her that wouldn't let her be normal. Of fighting to stay alive, stay sane. "Venom and I think they might've wanted my blood," she said, forcing her tired brain to think. "Or maybe just to collect me."

"Possible. It's also possible they want to re-create the effect that Made you." Cupping her face in his hands, Dmitri spoke in a voice midnight with age. "Hate me if you want, Holly, but remember this: you're one of the Tower's now. You're one of *mine* now. That might mean chains, but it also means you have hundreds of vampires and angels at your back."

Emotion was a hot burn at the back of her eyelids. "All for a weird Chinese girl who had the bad luck to survive a massacre?"

A deep smile that reached the hard intensity of his eyes. "Let's go, my little weirdling. I'm Ash and Janvier's teacher for the next hour. You can watch."

Her sudden tiredness faded. Dmitri was lethal in combat, and neither of her two bosses was exactly a slouch. However, as she watched the session that hour, she realized she'd never before seen Dmitri at full speed. "That's insane," she muttered to herself where she sat at the very top of the bleachers that ringed the internal sparring area.

"Even many older immortals have trouble tracking him with the eye."

"Drat. I was hoping if I ignored the crawling sensation up my arms, you'd poof back to the hole you slithered out of."

Venom sat down on the top bleacher beside her, the freshness of his just-showered scent washing over her. He'd changed into black pants and a long-sleeved black shirt with the sleeves rolled up. For him that was casual attire. "Kitty's in a bad mood. Missing me again?"

Her skin felt his heat across the bare inches between them, absorbed it. "Like I miss the giant blister I had on my foot in tenth grade." Again, she didn't manage to spot what Dmitri had done that left Janvier groaning on the floor.

The chestnut-haired vampire called out something in Cajun French that made his wife laugh and Dmitri grin. Then he accepted Dmitri's help to haul him upright and swapped positions with Ashwini. Oddly, the hunter proved to be better at sparring with Dmitri than her older and more experienced husband. Ash was a vampire, too, but she hadn't even crossed the three-year mark since being Made.

"She's predicting his moves," Holly whispered, leaning forward, her eyes wide. "I didn't know she could do that." Ashwini had precognitive abilities; anyone who was around her long enough figured that out. But this . . .

"No," Venom murmured, "neither did I—it looks like she's glimpsing his move half a second before he makes it. In combat, that can change everything."

For the next ten minutes, they sat in complete harmony, watching Ashwini and Dmitri dance like demons. It was incredible how long-legged and lithe Ash was keeping up with a vampire who was over a thousand years old and who'd spent nearly all of that time as a warrior in one way or another. The hunter compensated for not being as fast or as strong by making idiosyncratic moves that had Dmitri grinning.

Her large hoop earrings swung with each move, light sparking off the gold.

Dmitri still got her pinned, but he was sweating by then. And when he hauled her back up, he said, "You just volunteered to be my sparring partner while Raphael is away."

Sauntering over to lean one bent arm on her husband's shoulder, Janvier's glowing pride unhidden, Ashwini said, "I'll think about it."

Holly felt her eyes widen even further.

"Still in awe of Dmitri, I see."

"I don't see you arguing with him." She turned to face

the vampire whose presence was a prickling across her senses. *"Venom,"* she said, mimicking how Dmitri had said his name in the office. "And off you ran like a good little vampire."

"Oh, how you have wounded me, kitty." Cool amusement in every word.

Probably because, unlike her, he was totally confident of his place in the Tower and in his skin. He wasn't some weird hybrid creation no one knew quite what to do with.

"To be wounded," she said, "you'd have to have a semblance of humanity." She shook her head, her face pitying. "Too bad you sold your soul to the devil centuries ago."

A nictitating moment, his expression icing over in a way that had her going motionless. Holly wasn't afraid—she had a predator inside her, too, and it was poised to strike. But then Venom smiled and it was the charming smile he kept for women he was trying to get into bed. Not that he had to try very hard: viper eyes or not, once he focused his attention and languorous charm on a woman, she tended to melt.

Holly felt like kicking those women's backsides and telling them to have a little respect for themselves, and to stop giving him further encouragement to be an asshole who thought he was God's gift to women. "Not even if the Hudson freezes over and turns into a candy-colored snow cone."

"Alas, kitty," Venom said from his lounging position, "you're too bite-sized for me. But I thought you might be starved for male attention, being that your prickles scare them away."

"Oh, you're so kind, so generous." She clasped her hands in front of her chest and beamed before dropping the act with a roll of her eyes that made him throw back his head and laugh.

It erased the lingering edges of ice, and of that charm she saw as a mask.

Refusing to let the warm sound wrap around her—or to

consider how handsome he was with smile lines cutting into his cheeks—she returned her attention to the sparring circle. Dmitri was leading Ash and Janvier through a series of moves that appeared easy enough—except that both were sweating. "What am I not seeing?"

"It's the muscle tension," Venom said with deceptive laziness. "It's the lack of speed that's the killer. Try to do this." He showed her a single arm move. "And hold."

Holly copied him because, his aggravating tendencies aside, Venom was highly trained. At first, it was fine. And then . . . Teeth gritted, she rode past the pain, past the haze of red that started to flicker in her brain.

Venom snapped out an arm toward her, so fast that she had to move or take a punch in the face. "Into beating up women now?" she snarled, careful to keep her voice low so Dmitri wouldn't hear.

Eyes glittering, the slitted black center onyx against the brilliant green, Venom leaned in close. "I thought you had your masochistic tendencies under control?"

Holly flushed. "I don't enjoy pain."

"No?" Venom's power slid over and around her, slow and sensuous and deadly. "Then why were you trying to snap a tendon by holding a pose that's not meant to be held beyond the pain threshold—at least not until you're an expert?"

Massaging her abused arm, Holly looked away. Venom was the last person to whom she'd admit that she'd rather feel pain than the viciously inhuman urges that had begun to rise up inside her more and more often. *I'm not insane*, she told herself even as fear gnawed at her insides. *I'm not a monster.*

"Some of us," she said aloud through a forcefully relaxed jaw, "like to push ourselves."

Venom didn't reply, but she could feel him staring at her with those astonishing eyes that had fascinated her from the first. It didn't matter. Venom had no right to her secrets.

Mia alone suspected something was wrong beyond Holly's continued fight to create a new life for herself, but Holly's sister was a mortal who had no knowledge of immortal horrors. She'd never guess that it wasn't just a terrible echo of trauma.

"Venom, *mon ami*!" Janvier called up at one point. "Come over tonight for dinner."

"I'll be there."

"You, too, Holly," Ashwini said before Holly could sidle away. "Let's dress up."

Caught, she nodded. It wasn't that she didn't love spending time with the couple—they'd become two of her favorite people—but being forced to make nice with Poison was not her idea of a good time. "Don't you have to go rest?" she said to him. "It must've been a long trip from . . . Where were you again?"

"Nice try, kitty, but knowledge of certain places in this world is earned." Rising to his feet with a muscular grace she grudgingly admired, he said, "I do need to check on a few matters. I'll pick you up at six for the drive to Janvier and Ash's."

Holly didn't say anything—but neither did she agree to meet him for the drive. Walking down the bleachers to the training area once the session was over, she shadowed Dmitri as he'd ordered. He went up to his and Honor's apartment to grab a shower first, leaving her to work on her laptop in a spare office on the same floor as his own office.

Holly had stopped her studies for two and a half years after the attack. When she'd picked them back up, her former major of fashion studies had seemed like the daydream of a silly girl. A girl who'd been offered an exciting position at a fashion house and who'd planned to finish up her degree part time.

Holly missed that girl sometimes.

After her return to school, she'd wandered through the curriculum aimlessly for two months before she'd found herself sneaking into psychology lectures—and staying for hours. Not hard to figure out why she was drawn to the study of the mind. Jeez, she was a textbook case of "physician, heal thyself," but that awareness of her own messed-up psyche hadn't stopped her from switching majors and starting from scratch since cross-credits weren't about to happen.

No one at the Tower monitored her schoolwork—that was her parents' job.

Daphne and Allan Chang insisted on paying as they had before: "This is our responsibility!" they'd said when she'd talked about taking out a loan. "Do you think we saved for your education so you could get a loan?"

Of course, that meant the two kept an eagle eye on her grades. They were also pushing her to go all the way and get a doctorate. Apparently, one doctor in the family wasn't enough. The old Holly would've been frustrated by their desire to be so involved in her life, but the Holly who'd died and lived again just smiled and sent her mom and dad copies of her exam results and graded essays.

Because her future . . . it was a total unknown. While the healers thought she'd have a vampiric life span, it was also possible she'd drop dead in ten years without warning—or go frothing-at-the-mouth mad and have to be put down.

Uram's bloodborn taint was a gift that never stopped giving.

Was it any wonder she was half crazy?

5

Venom wasn't the least surprised when Holly wasn't waiting for him at the front of the Tower for the six P.M. pickup. Since he knew she wasn't in any way stupid, he was very sure she hadn't headed out to Ash and Janvier's on her own. So he tracked her.

And found her at the very top of the Tower, her eyes on the glowing red golds of the Hudson under a startling sunset. Venom had called this land home for nearly two hundred years, but he still appreciated the magnificence of it. As he appreciated the wild nature and unbreakable spirit of the fine-boned woman who stood staring at the setting sun.

After what she'd undergone, Holly Chang should've been a candidate for what mortals had once called insane asylums. She'd teetered on that edge for a while, but she'd never fallen. Today, she stood dressed in a sleek black cheongsam that celebrated her femininity. Hitting her mid-calf, it was printed with tiny flowers in indigo blue. She'd pulled that silky hair full of color up into a high and equally sleek ponytail.

In her hands, she held a clutch.

And on her feet were four-inch black stilettos that brought her closer to his height.

When he reached her position and she deigned to glance at him, he saw that her makeup was both subtle and masterful. She'd loved fashion once, he remembered. As he'd once loved working with the textures and flavors of food.

"I see you did grow up a little in my absence, kitty." He'd witnessed her increased control over her abilities from a distance—but seeing her like this, so totally a woman who had now lived twenty-seven years on this earth, he realized she'd changed in deeper ways than he'd understood.

"Why do you think I care about your opinion?" she asked in a politely reasonable tone that held *just* the right amount of perplexed bemusement.

Venom laughed, delighted with her—though he'd never allow her to guess that. Holly had always challenged him in a way that ignited his instincts, and she did it with a cutting intelligence that spoke to his own. It appeared her increased control over her temper had only honed the razor edge of her wit. "Let's go have dinner."

She didn't take his offered arm, instead giving his hand-tailored suit of darkest brown and crisp white shirt a slow and critical once-over. On his way up to the roof, he'd been subtly invited to bed sport by four vampires and two angels, one of whom had run her hand down the lapel of his impeccably fitted jacket and murmured that he looked "good enough to eat."

Holly sighed. "I see the shares in Cheap Suits Co. are paying off."

"It did seem a wise investment."

Her eyes sparked laughing green fire at him before she spun on her heel and strode to the elevator, the back of her dress hugging the tight curves of her body. "Keep up, old man."

Venom felt the urge to bite her. Of course, she'd probably bite back harder. Walking into the elevator by her side, he rode down with her in silence. It was prickly, of course. It always was—as if the strangeness that lived in them both was irritated by the proximity. Just to see if contact would further the prickles, he touched the curve of her lower back as they stepped out of the elevator.

"Do you want me to break your wrist?" she asked with acerbic politeness.

"You're being very reasonable today." He did drop his hand, but only because he had to slide on his sunglasses. After three hundred and fifty years, Venom was well accustomed to using his looks to distract or to cause fear or to charm.

It turned out women liked the eyes if he gave them a certain look.

However, he didn't particularly enjoy dealing with horrified gapes. It reminded him too much of the most painful day of his existence, when he'd seen the same expression on the faces of those who meant more to him than his own life. Oddly, Holly had never given him that gape. Instead, she'd told him that if he left his fancy contacts in too long, his eyes would rot and fall out. Venom had known from that instant that the girl everyone thought broken would survive.

"I'm hoping it'll rub off," she said after they exited the Tower. "That you'll learn a few manners."

Venom had come from Neha's court, had been one of her favorites because of his smooth manners and charm. With Holly, however, he reacted from a more primal place. "Here," he said, opening the passenger door of his low-slung car. "A lady should go first."

"Oh, sir, how gallant of you." With that breathy statement worthy of an ingénue, Holly got in and crossed her legs, her purse in her lap.

Lips curved, Venom shut the door and got into the driver's seat. "Put on your seat belt." Vampires were near-immortal, but losing the head would finish them both off. And Holly wasn't *quite* a vampire. Like another one of the Seven, Naasir, Holly was unique. Neither one thing or the other. But while Naasir was at peace with his dual nature, Holly either ignored it or fought it.

"Of course," she said. "Safety first." She put on her seat belt with exaggerated care. "So nice of you to care."

"I always care for the kitties I babysit."

A rumbling sound from the passenger seat before Holly strangled the feral emanation.

Venom shot her a glance. "What was that?" he asked in genuine curiosity. "You sounded more like Naasir than anything else."

"It was human irritation," she muttered.

No, it hadn't been.

Venom thought back to what he knew of Uram's archangelic abilities and what the insane immortal might've passed on to Holly. Most vampires didn't receive anything but near-immortality as a result of the Making process, but there were rare exceptions: Venom was the way he was because Neha was the Queen of Poisons, of Snakes.

Uram had had no such reputation or inclination. And, since he'd died at the dawn of the Cascade that had awakened new abilities in all the living archangels, there was no way to know the inheritance he'd left to Holly when he'd forced her to ingest his blood.

Venom frowned. Was it possible Holly was directly feeling the power-birthing or boosting effects of the Cascade? It was meant to affect only archangels and a limited number of the most powerful angels, but Holly's Making had been unusual in every possible way. Maybe Uram had left such a strong imprint on her cells that she was catching the edge of the Cascade.

Normally, he'd ask Raphael these questions, but the archangel he chose to call sire was in Morocco for a meeting of the Cadre, the archangels who ruled the world.

Even had Raphael been here, he might not have had the answer. Because while Uram and Raphael had been friends once, they hadn't been close in all the years Venom had chosen to serve Raphael. The person who'd been most intimate with Uram during that time, and the one who'd know of any nascent abilities Uram might've developed, was the Archangel Michaela.

Who was also in Morocco—and who'd lie to Venom's face just for amusement.

Then there was the fact that Uram's blood had gone toxic. A toxin powerful enough to drive an archangel insane would've undoubtedly mutated whatever power it was that would've been Uram's in the Cascade . . . echoes of which now lived in Holly.

"Have you taken a vow of silence?" Holly's voice was sugar sweet. "Were you in a monastery while you were gone?"

"Yes, a monastery that permitted external calls to kitties in need of training." He took the George Washington Bridge across to the cliffs of the Enclave, where Janvier and Ashwini made their home. The exclusive area full of angelic residences boasted such stratospheric price tags—and such limited availability that usually only old or extremely powerful angels could afford it, but Janvier had been given a small property a hundred years earlier by an angel for whom he'd retrieved an object of great value.

"If I'm a kitty," Holly said in that same honeyed tone, "what does that make you? Hmm." A snap of her fingers. "Oh, I have it! Woof, woof! All slobbery tongue and drool."

"That tongue is quite in demand," Venom said mildly because he knew that would annoy her and annoying Holly was high on his favorite-things-to-do list. "Not that little Hollyberries know about such things," he added in a lazy purr of sound.

"Ah, such innocence you have." Holly crossed her legs the other way.

The long slit of her dress opened to expose a creamy

swath of skin that made his fingers curl tight on the steering wheel.

Venom glanced away with an inward scowl. Holly might have grown up, but she was still only twenty-seven years of age and marked by horrific trauma. Unlike Venom, she hadn't chosen to embrace the immortal world with all its beauty and its darkness. It had been forced on her.

She was the last woman he'd ever see as a partner for bed sport.

"There's the turn," she said at that instant, her voice back to polite and reasonable.

It made him want to irritate her just to get a rise. He knew full well this wasn't the real Holly Chang. The real Holly Chang was a complex and intense creature, sometimes bitter, sometimes sweet, and always dangerous. "Does it hurt to bite your tongue so hard?" he asked with faux concern.

Holly didn't miss a beat. "I'm in a car with you—I clearly have a high pain threshold," she said as he brought the viper green Bugatti Chiron to a stop in Ashwini and Janvier's drive.

She was outside by the time he moved around the car to open her door—and he'd moved with the striking speed of a cobra. "Well done, kitty."

Giving him a patently false smile, she brushed nonexistent lint off her arm before heading up toward the wrap-around verandah of Ash and Janvier's home, the railing decorated with tiny lights that sparkled in the quickly falling night. The couple came out just then, smiles of welcome on their faces.

When their chocolate-colored mutt of a dog, its paws as huge as saucers, bounded out to sniff at Holly, she smiled and, bending, petted him with the ease of a woman who'd done the same many a time. The dog's eyes closed in ecstasy at her scratch behind its ears, but it only allowed itself a moment before bounding over to sniff at Venom.

"Hello, Charlie," Venom said, going down on his haunches. Janvier had sent him photos of the abandoned puppy he and Ashwini had adopted, a puppy who'd grown into a rambunctious dog who never tired of play, but this was the first time they'd met.

He held out his hand for Charlie to sniff.

The dog took its time doing so . . . before laving Venom's face with a long lick, his tail wagging like a metronome.

Laughing, Venom played with the friendly beast for a minute before rising—to see Holly watching him with a small frown between her eyebrows. When he met her gaze, however, she looked away and returned to her conversation with Ashwini, while Janvier came over to take charge of the dog and welcome Venom.

Dinner was an unexpectedly relaxed affair—even Holly unwound and laughed with an open delight that made her eyes light up from within. Not with Venom, of course, never with him. However, she seemed at home with Janvier and his tall hunter mate. Out alone on the porch with Janvier at one point while Ashwini was showing Holly something inside the house, Venom took a sip of the wineglass of blood Janvier had handed him.

He shuddered and, pulling the glass away from his lips, stared at the swirling red liquid that gave an excellent appearance of being blood. "What *is* this?"

"Flavored blood." Janvier grinned and took a sip of his own abomination. "We're taste-testing this batch. What do you think?"

"Why does blood need to be flavored?" Good blood was a jolt to the system, a burst of pure life pouring through vampiric veins. "Blood—good blood—is beautifully pristine and perfectly balanced."

"It's this new generation of vampires," Janvier said sagely. "They're all about pushing boundaries and turning the old into the new."

. Snorting, Venom took a second sip—and shuddered again. "Reminds me of . . ." He frowned and made himself take another sip. "Actual red wine?" Amusement wove through his veins. "Someone has a sense of humor."

"Elena and her business partner have hired a 'renowned vampire nose' who comes up with the flavors. Monsieur LaFerge is, *mon ami*, a pretentious ass I wish to throw into the Hudson, but as my Ashblade loves the dark-chocolate-infused blood he is responsible for creating, I'm forced to leave him be."

"Not keeping your wife satisfied with your own blood, tut, tut."

"Talk to me when you have a woman for longer than a night," Janvier responded with the easy insult of a friend who'd known him for untold years. "Bringing home a bottle of chocolate-infused blood for my wife has certain advantages." A very satisfied smile on Janvier's face. "I am a most content husband."

Venom had been betrothed once—an eon ago. He hadn't thought of Aneera in as many years, having long ago left his past behind in a knot of grief and sorrow.

Janvier stirred. "Dmitri told us about the bounty on Holly."

"I'll keep her with me—they won't get to her."

"You're planning to look into who it might be?" At his nod, Janvier said, "Use Holly. She knows the shadowy corners of this city far better than you do."

Venom curled his lip. "She is an infant." It was a reminder to himself as much as it was a statement.

"She's been working with me and Ashwini for seven months," Janvier said, his Cajun accent making music of the unexpectedly serious words. "Not the part that involves hunting certain immortals who fall outside the purview of the Guild—but in talking to those too scared or otherwise afraid of directly contacting the Tower." A pointed look at Venom, the eyes that hinted at Janvier's marshy homeland darkened to near-black by the night. "You're too powerful. She isn't. She's one of them."

Venom wondered that Holly had managed to sell that piece of fiction: he knew full well that she was utterly unlike the broken, weak creatures in the gray underground. Holly was a predator, albeit one who hadn't yet woken to her full strength. When she did . . .

6

Holly bit her tongue all the way back to the city . . . until she couldn't stand it anymore. "Are you going to bed?"

A sharp look. "Why are my bed habits any of your business, Hollyberry?"

She fought the urge to tear off his stupid sunglasses. "I know you're old and probably need more rest," she said with mock solicitousness, "but we should head to the darker end of the city, talk to a few people who usually only come out at night." It frustrated her to have a leash, to have to ask his *permission* to go into her own world, but Uram hadn't damaged her brain when he'd Made her. Holly understood that if she slipped that leash, the consequences could well be deadly.

And not just for her.

In truth, these days she was far more terrified of what she might do than what might be done to her. Even now, she wanted to claw and bite and cause Venom pain, wanted to make him bleed until she'd created a shimmering ruby pool around his body. Hand fisting at her side, she gritted her teeth and silenced the horrific whispers that came from the madness inside her. But no matter what she did, one thing she couldn't afford to forget: that *she* was the nightmare in the shadows.

"Where would you suggest?" Venom's calm tone had the hairs rising on her arms.

But Holly wasn't afraid of the viper that lived in him. The darkness in her, the part that wasn't *other*, but simply part of who she'd become, stretched out toward him. "A lot of information passes through the lower-end clubs," she said. "I have friends who patronize those clubs."

One hand lying easily on the steering wheel, Venom turned his head toward her. "Wouldn't your friends call you if they'd heard something useful?"

"They're not that kind of friends," Holly said shortly. "If you can't be bothered—"

The tires squealed as he made a hard turn in the direction of the beauty and death of the Vampire Quarter. She knew the clubs with which he'd be familiar—Venom walked the dark side, but he was a *very* powerful vampire, one of the most powerful in the city. And power called to power. He'd be known at places that were elegant and drenched in money and strength.

Today, she intended to take him to the far seedier side of town. "You have to let me lead," she said, ready to fight him on this. "The people on the streets will talk to you out of sheer fear, but they won't tell you anything."

"How do you plan to explain my presence?" was his silken response.

"I'll tell them we're dating," Holly said flippantly.

Venom tapped a finger on the steering wheel. "Do they know about your abilities?"

"The jagged speed, yes," Holly said, suspicious of his suddenly serious tone. "I wasn't able to hide it well at the start."

"Then the two of us make sense." A slow, taunting smile. "They will assume you are my current pleasure toy."

Scowling because he was right, Holly didn't speak again until he was pulling into a dark parking lot protected only by an aged chain-link fence. "I didn't know you hated your car." This area wasn't exactly the safest.

He got out and shut the door, not coming around to her side this time. "No one will be touching this car."

She realized why when she saw the number plate: *VENOM*. "Vain much?"

"I'll get you a matching one that says *KITTY*."

She knew he was baiting her but had to fight not to react nonetheless. Thankfully, keeping her heels from catching on the gravel of the parking lot provided a good distraction. They were on the cracked sidewalk within half a minute. She strode confidently down the street, Venom prowling beside her. "How can you see out of those glasses?"

"Good night vision."

As she watched, he took off his sunglasses and folded them away into the top pocket of his suit jacket. And his eyes, they reflected the paltry light on this street in a way that was probably eerie, but that riveted Holly.

It irritated her to admit it, but Venom was as handsome as sin; the eyes were just the icing on the cake. "Do Neha's eyes nictitate?" On the surface, the Archangel of India had normal brown eyes, but since she'd Made Venom, there had to be more beneath the surface.

"Yes," Venom said, surprising her with the straight answer. "It's difficult to catch and it happens very rarely, but yes."

"Why aren't her eyes like yours?"

A slow smile. "They are—but only for milliseconds at a time. Most people have never caught the transition."

Holly tried to imagine Venom's eyes in Neha's regal face, couldn't. "What about other vampires in her court? Are many like you?"

"None. Though she has been trying to Make another me for centuries." Especially after he'd left her court at the end of his Contract: to serve the angels for a hundred years in return for the gift of near-immortality.

Neha had been more generous with her post-Contract settlement than mandated by their unusual agreement, and he'd had the money to travel, decide who he wanted to be. For the first time in a hundred years, he'd been free to live where he chose, serve who he chose, though he hadn't been certain he wanted to be part of *any* court.

Then had come Raphael.

Venom had slotted into the sire's tightly knit team as if he were a missing puzzle piece. Jason had even said as much at the time. "Finally, we are complete. We are the Seven."

Neha and Raphael had been friendly back then, so Neha hadn't fought his defection. She'd seen it as him being drawn to Raphael's youth. "Wild to wild," she'd said with an indulgent smile when Venom returned to her court to tell her of his plans. "Well, Venom, if I had to lose you to anyone, it would be Raphael."

Venom hadn't needed her permission. He'd served his hundred years with utmost fidelity, had earned his freedom. But archangels and queens like Neha weren't always rational—and this archangel had kept her promises to him. His visit had been a gesture of respect and honor.

"Has Neha ever tried to lure you back?"

Venom sent Holly another slow smile, wondering exactly how much she'd picked up of the current state of archangelic politics. It was probable that she had no idea Neha now considered Raphael an enemy, though Venom had the feeling Neha's hostility was intermingled with a deep sense of loss. When beings lived that long, their emotions tended to be complex, layered things where contrary feelings could exist side by side.

Venom wasn't that old. His emotions were less knotty—and his pleasures simpler. Annoying Holly ranked at the top. "Everyone wants me."

She snorted. "Doesn't being that delusional make it hard to function?"

He felt his lips tug up . . . right as Holly stumbled on a crack in the sidewalk. He'd snapped out an arm and curved it around her waist before she did more than sway a little. She'd reacted quickly, too—just not as quickly as him. The side of her body slammed into the front of his, his hand fitting into the curve of her waist.

She was gone as fast, jerking out of his hold with the inhuman speed that made her so much fun as a sparring partner. "If I wanted to be pawed," she said, brushing her arm as if brushing off his germs, "I'd go to a furry convention."

"If you thought that was pawing, kitty," he said with deliberate sophistication in his tone, "your education has been sadly lacking."

She forgot her coolly elegant persona and made a face at him. He'd reached out a finger and flicked her nose before he thought about what he was doing. Eyes narrowing, she hissed at him, flashing those tiny fangs he still couldn't believe were functional. "Next time you touch me, I'm going for blood."

"It's been said that once you go Venom, you never go back."

"Argh!" Holly fought the urge to take off one of her high heels and throw it at his smug head. But she'd spent good money on those heels, she reminded herself. Money she'd *earned* in the work she did with Ashwini and Janvier— work that meant she had far better contacts in this part of town than Smugface Venomous.

Taking a deep breath in an effort to control her racing heart as the otherness that lived in her stretched inside her skin, she turned her attention to the club that had appeared out of the darkness. The neon was pink and blazing and the outside walls matte black covered in creative white graffiti.

Used needles lying carelessly against one wall glinted in the neon glow.

"They like pretty boys here," she said to the deadly vampire who was very much a man. "You shouldn't have anything to worry about."

His hand was suddenly against her lower back.

Holly went to kick back her heel when he said, "Don't."

It wasn't the word that got her to pause, it was the tone. It was the same calm, dangerous tone he'd used just before they'd fought off the goons who'd tried to kidnap her. Scanning the area in the way Ash had taught her, she caught the furtive movement on the left, deep in the shadows to one side of the club.

Her chest eased. "I know them." She stepped away from Venom's coiled body. "Don't follow me."

He just *looked* at her.

Rolling her eyes, she patted the taut muscle of his biceps. "It's okay, Sir Venomous, Knight of the Tower. You can move fast enough to rescue the damsel in distress if she squeals for help." She turned and walked away before he could respond.

She could feel his eyes on her, but he stayed in position. *Thank God.* If he hadn't, the two skinny vampires loitering in the shadows would've been ghosts in one second flat. "Zeph, Arabella."

"Hol, hey." The pockmarked male vampire smiled at her, his face so badly damaged that she'd believed for the longest time that he'd been Made while in that state and that vampirism hadn't healed him though it healed most imperfections.

Then one night, she'd spent ten minutes with him; he'd only lasted three before starting to pick at his face with his ragged and dirty nails. His vampirism couldn't keep up with the constant wounds, especially since Zeph didn't exactly subsist on the best blood. Holly had tried to pay him for his information in good bottles of blood, but he preferred money—which he spent on honey feeds, where human junkies got high, then allowed vampires to drink from them.

As far as Holly knew, it was the only reliable way a vampire could get high.

Arabella, the equally skinny blonde vampire who was Zeph's shadow, was no junkie, but she couldn't deny Zeph, so it ended up the same. "Hi, Holly," the female vampire said with a natural sweetness that always struck Holly, her fingers twisting her limp dreads in her hands. "You sure look nice."

"So do you," Holly replied in a gentle tone, seeing in Arabella what could've happened to her if the Tower had abandoned her—or if she'd abandoned herself. Which, frankly, she'd been inches away from doing. She'd never judge Arabella for the choices she'd made or for her strange loyalty to Zeph. "Were you guys looking for me?"

Arabella darted a quick glance behind Holly. "What's *he* doing down here?" Her lush Southern vowels contracted, her fear a living being between them.

"He's with me," Holly said simply.

Arabella's eyes widened, the harsh edge of fear transmuting into an openly female admiration. "Wow, Holly. That's *Venom*. You did *good*."

Holly bit her tongue rather than crush Arabella's illusions. "Did you two want to tell me anything?" Every so often, the pair found her when they didn't have any information to trade but were really hungry. Then she gave them blood vouchers that couldn't be exchanged for money and were personalized to Zeph and Arabella so Zeph couldn't try to barter them.

Just because a person was broken didn't mean they had no value, no right to live.

"Um, yeah." Zeph went to pick at a scab, stopped himself. He was like that, tried to be "normal" as long as he could. "We heard some guys were going after you."

"They already tried," Holly began.

"No." Arabella tugged at Holly's arm before snatching

away her hand so quickly it was as if she was afraid
someone would hurt her for daring.

Holly glanced over her shoulder and gave Venom the
hard eye. He'd gotten closer, those irises of his penetrating
the shadows as if she, Zeph, and Arabella were bathed in
bright sunlight. *Go. Away*, she mouthed.

He slipped on his sunglasses instead.

Shifting her attention back to Arabella, she took the trembling woman's hand. "He won't hurt you." She'd kick his ass
if he tried. "What did you want to tell me?"

"There's more guys," Arabella whispered. "Someone
put a big . . . Zeph, what's the word?"

"Bounty." Zeph scratched furtively at a scab. "Like if
we kidnap you and give you to this person, we get a lot of
money."

Even though Holly already had that information, she let
the two think it was new. Pride was as important as food
when it came to survival. "How much?" she asked, not expecting a firm answer.

Arabella frowned. "I think we heard five million?"

Shoving his hands into the pockets of his dirty jeans,
bony shoulders poking out through his holey black sweater,
Zeph nodded. "Yeah, it was five mil. I thought I was zoned
out and hearing things, but I never had a honey feed last
night. For sure, it was five mil."

Five million?

Even in her wildest dreams, Holly wouldn't value herself at that extravagant amount. "Thank you for telling me
instead of attempting to kidnap me."

"Aw, Hol, you're our friend." Zeph pulled off his ubiqui-
tous knit cap to reveal hair of an astonishingly beautiful
auburn that surprised Holly each time she saw it. "We don't
got nothing else," he added. "Just the rumor. Some of the
other vamps were talking about maybe trying to get you, so
we heard."

"But most won't try," Arabella said with a reassuring pat of Holly's arm. "Folks know you're with the Tower and it'd just be stupid to get on the Tower's wrong side."

Unfortunately, if people were strung out or otherwise desperate, that wouldn't matter. "Here." She slipped them personalized blood vouchers as well as money; she'd put both in her evening clutch just in case. "Go get the good blood first, okay? I don't want anything to happen to you." It took a lot to kill a vampire, but if Zeph or Arabella got any weaker, another vampire might rip out their hearts or tear off their heads to get at their meager belongings.

"Thanks, Holly." Arabella touched her arm again and Holly noticed that the other woman's ragged military-surplus jacket had become even more so.

"Arabella, you need a new coat." It got cold at night, especially for a woman with no roof over her head.

"Not yet," Arabella said before Holly could offer to replace it. "If I have anything new, the others will take it. Maybe after it's a little colder?" A hopeful smile that was shaky at the edges. "I know a charity shop that has stuff."

"Just find me when you're ready." Waiting until they'd melted safely back into the shadows, Holly turned to walk back to Venom.

And nearly slammed into his chest.

7

Managing to maintain her balance, she scowled up at him. "You can't even follow simple instructions?"

"I waited until the vampires left," he said without a smile. "What did they say?"

"Take off those ridiculous sunglasses first." Holly hated not being able to see his eyes.

Slipping them off, he smiled at her and it held no mockery or amusement. "Happy?"

Her stomach did a strange flip. "I just want to see your snakeyness in the unlikely event that I begin to think of you as human."

His smile didn't fade. "The information, Hollyberry."

Holly wanted to refuse to share it. As soon as she told him, she'd put herself in an even tighter cage of supervision. Protective it might be, but it also suffocated.

Venom slid his hands into the pockets of his suit pants, as dangerous and urbane as Zeph had been shaky and broken. "Or would you rather I get the information from your friends?"

"You keep your hands off them." Neither Zeph nor Arabella had the physical or mental strength to deal with Venom.

He just waited with the predatory stillness she'd never mastered.

Fingers tightening on her clutch, she said, "The bounty—they heard about the rumored payoff."

"How much?"

"Five million dollars."

Venom didn't so much as blink. "That's a big enough number for certain immortals to risk Raphael's fury." His power slid sinuously around her. "It's also a big enough number that it'll draw reckless but nonetheless experienced bounty hunters from outside the territory."

"The goons in the SUV," Holly said, standing her ground against the intensity of his strength. "Has Vivek confirmed their identities?"

"It wasn't difficult." He turned to walk beside her when she swiveled on her heel to head toward the club, a silkily prowling presence. "We'll deal with them."

The hairs rose on the back of her neck. "What will you do to them?"

"Dmitri is in charge," was the simple answer.

And Dmitri did not take any attack against the Tower lightly—because at present, Holly was Tower property. "Didn't it frustrate you?" she found herself asking. "Spending a hundred years under someone else's control?" All vampires signed a Contract to serve the angels for the privilege of being Made near-immortal.

Venom's face gave nothing away. "I made a choice as an adult in full control of my faculties," he said in a cool tone. "Only the stupid regret choices. The smart learn to adapt."

"You didn't answer my question."

Venom looked over at her, his lips curving. "'Frustration' isn't the word I'd use, kitty."

They'd reached the door to the club. The big and muscle-bound vampire bouncer had become increasingly more pale the closer Venom got. Now he opened the door with a trembling hand. "Welcome," he croaked out.

Venom didn't respond, his hand once more on Holly's lower back as he ushered her in. She scowled up at him once they were inside the thundering noise of the club. "What? You couldn't be polite to a lowly bouncer?"

Leaning down to her ear, he said, "That lowly bouncer is maybe two decades into his Contract." His breath was warm against her ear, his body a tensile wall. "A vampire that young needs to be scared of me. Fear will keep him from running, and that means the Guild Hunters won't have to track him and haul him back. At which point, his punishment would be a violently painful affair."

His fingers moved in a slow circle on her lower back, his eyes shimmering in the pulsating darkness. "Fear," he said, "also fosters control. That's why the hundred years of service is necessary—so that the world isn't overrun by blood-maddened vampires, feeding and feeding and feeding."

Holly shivered.

Running his hand up then down her back, Venom held her gaze. "That's also why you need to be kept under watch. No one knows what lies inside you, what deadly urges you must be taught to throttle."

Holly wanted to refute his words, but damn it, he was right. There was a horrible something inside her, a monstrous creature that *hungered*. "Let's go," she said, jerking forward into the chaotic darkness of a club lit only by moody dark blue bulbs and glowing jewelry hung around necks or worn around wrists.

Booths circled the dance floor. Though every single one had a ragged curtain, only a few were pulled closed. In the nearest open one, Holly glimpsed a group of young vampires crowded together, drinking blood and laughing. A simple night out.

A knife twisted inside her.

She'd done that once upon a time. Gone out for a drink

with her friends. Poor Rania could never hold her drink, but she was such an adorable drunk that none of them minded. The last night they'd gone out before the torture and death, Rania had slung an arm around Holly and nuzzled into her neck, saying, "I love you lots and lots and even more than marshmallows."

Holly's throat threatened to close up.

Ripping away her gaze before Venom could catch her being maudlin, she looked at the next booth. This one held a sight more expected and more perverse. A bare-breasted female vampire was doing a lap dance for a heavy-lidded angel who sat with his wings draped behind him and his arms spread on the torn red leather of the booth bench.

The angel was clearly slumming. Angelkind was too powerful to be reduced to bars like this one. As for the vampires who ended up in this life, it was a combination of bad choices and fate. After serving their hundred years, all vamps were meant to be released with enough resources to start a new, independent life.

Some angels were more generous than others.

Zeph's angel had been—but he'd also treated the sensitive vampire so viciously during his Contract that Zeph was incapable of living life without the sweet oblivion of drugs.

"Your eyes are beginning to glow." Venom's voice against her ear, his hand curving over her hip.

Fighting the impulse to pull away because that would betray far too much, she said, "I'll get it under control."

"It's part of you. Why control it all the time?"

His response had her staring at him. "Didn't you just rave on about control?"

"Control and asphyxia leading to weakness are two different things." He slipped his sunglasses back on. "I am always in control—and I always have access to the full depth of my abilities." He glanced around. "You have friends here?"

"A few." Off-center, Holly moved forward through the crush of dancing bodies to the bar, Venom's hand sliding off her hip in the process. Space opened up around her, in front of her, without effort. She knew better than to think she'd caused the effect. Usually, she had to push and shove—and occasionally hiss—to get through.

More than one fuckwit was of the opinion that he could get in an ass-grab just because Holly was small and female.

"Holly!" The ebony-skinned bartender leaned forward and kissed her on the cheek. "You're looking far too fine for this pit of sin, love."

Holly laughed and patted his bearded jaw. Heavily tattooed and as heavily muscled, Magnus had been one of the first friends she'd made in this shadowy part of the city. "Looks like a busy night."

His light brown eyes gleamed. "It also looks like you brought in a wolf with you, then." He extended a hand across the bar. "Magnus."

To her surprise, Venom shook the bartender's hand with polite courtesy. "Venom."

Holly wanted to ask him, not for the first time, if he'd had another name once, if he still remembered that name.

"That, I know," Magnus said with a grin. "Don't usually get one of the Seven in my humble establishment." He pushed across a shot glass he'd just poured full of a rich amber liquid, the dragon tattoo on his forearm rippling with the movement. "On the house. After the rumor gets around that you're visiting, my business will go through the roof."

Venom smiled and threw back the shot before slamming the shot glass neatly back on the polished wood of the bar. "Goes down smooth."

Magnus went to say something else when there was a sudden rush of orders. As he moved away with a hand sign that meant he'd be back, Holly hopped up on a bar stool and put her back to the bar. Venom leaned his arm on the bar behind her, his body so close that her shoulder brushed his chest. She didn't say anything, instead crossing her legs with care and staring out into the heaving mass of bodies.

She could be staring right at people who wanted to truss her up and deliver her to a buyer. "Five million dollars is a lot to pay for a collectible."

Venom's answer was a single word spoken against her ear, his lips brushing the sensitive curve of it. "Uram."

Holly's hands clenched so hard that her nails cut into the palms of her hands. Her mind hazed. Her blood boiled. And she wanted to *scream*! As she'd screamed in that Brooklyn warehouse where Uram had butchered her friends and made her watch. As she'd screamed when he'd torn off her clothes and gripped her throat to force her to drink the blood pouring from his wrist.

"Do it." Venom's cold purr. "Scream."

Holly tried to breathe but the scream was choking her up. Then Venom was suddenly in front of her, cupping the back of her head and pressing her face to his chest. *"Scream."*

Holly opened her mouth. What came out was a sound of purest rage that went on and on and on. Venom's chest absorbed most of the sound, the rest lost in the loud pulse of the music. Her heart pounding in the aftermath, she immediately pulled away and turned around to get the assistant bartender's attention. She couldn't get drunk anymore, not with the metabolism she had, but there were other uses for alcohol. "Whiskey," she said. "Neat."

When it came, she threw it back.

The burn was acid and it was exactly what she needed to shock her system back into the correct rhythm. "I'm the last remaining piece of him," she said under her breath, since, obviously, Venom had very good hearing.

"You've always known that."

Yes, but she tried not to think about it. It was self-delusion, she knew that full well, hadn't needed a shrink to tell her. That shrink was a vampire who was part of the Tower medical team. A nice man, patient and kind.

Holly hated him.

Hated even more that he wanted her to face things she'd much rather bury as deep as possible.

"What's got you drinking whiskey neat?" Magnus leaned forward on the bar after making his way back to them.

Not waiting for an answer, he lowered his voice and said, "You're looking for info on the bounty, aren't you, then?"

Holly had known Magnus would be aware of what was going on—he knew everything that went on in the gray shadows of the city. He didn't always share that information, his loyalties myriad and complex, but he'd never put Holly in a position of danger. "Yes," she said past the rawness in her throat.

"Five million," he said, his eyes going from her to Venom and back. "You, my darling, are to be taken alive. Evidence—a photo—to be e-mailed to a throwaway e-mail address. Payment to be transferred into the kidnapper's choice of account once the kidnapping is verified: half pre delivery, half post."

Venom spoke even as Holly battled her renewed rage at being thought of as a commodity, a thing to be traded. "Why are people taking the bounty seriously? Anyone can put out the word like that, especially with the only contact an e-mail address."

"I'll be there in a minute, you arses!" Magnus yelled down the bar to an impatient group before lowering his voice to speak to them again. "Rumor is the initial word came from a man who's known to be a fixer in this kind of thing, someone the big mercenary fish all trust when it comes to their work."

"Who?" Holly asked.

Magnus shook his head, his tightly kinked black hair sporting a razored pattern on one side that paid homage to the striking emblem that now marked Raphael's right temple. "No idea, love. *Way* above my pay grade." A touch to her hand. "Be careful. I like you, and I'm not fool enough to defy the Tower, but even I was tempted by five million." He left to deal with the impatient group.

Swinging off the stool, Holly began to stride out. She didn't bother to wait for Venom, but she knew he was behind her. The damn rivers parted in front of her, people scrambling out of *his* way. She knew her eyes were glowing a hot green by the time they hit the cracked sidewalk. Not stopping, she strode onward to the parking lot.

They got into the car in silence. Then Venom drove. Hard and fast and edgy.

He took them through city streets where prostitutes lingered and junkies slept, past high-class establishments that were all about pain and blood, along a respectable row of clubs where suburban moms and dads came to party and pretend they were walking on the wild side. They took in a closed stadium, drove through streets with gracious mansions so ornate and covered with ivy that it was as if they'd been frozen in time.

Those houses screamed immortal money.

Behind them rose skyscrapers that glittered with light. But the tallest building of all was the Tower, a soaring spear of light that pierced the starlit night sky and made her breath catch. Angels flew in and out, their wings silhouetted against the night, their beauty extraordinary. "Have you ever fantasized about plucking off an angel's feathers?" It was the first time she'd spoken in the past sixty minutes as Venom drove them in and around and through their city.

"Illium's sometimes, when he gets too maddening," Venom said lightly. "Do you have anti-angel fantasies?"

"Just anti-Uram." Even saying his name made the scream build in her throat. "I fantasize about bringing him back to life in a way that means he's paralyzed, able to feel what I'm doing but unable to stop me." The latter was *very* important.

Even in her fantasies, Holly knew she was no match for an archangel. "Then I want to sit there and pluck off each and every one of his feathers." Gray with flecks of amber, those feathers had been far too beautiful for the ugliness they hid. "After which I want to stab and stab and stab at him until he's nothing but a piece of meat."

She exhaled loudly. "Go ahead, call me a psycho."

Venom shrugged. "I have high standards for the psycho call. You barely brush the surface." A glance out of mirrored sunglasses.

"Take those *off*!" Moving with that strange speed that lived in her, Holly tore off the sunglasses and threw them behind their seats.

Venom hadn't jerked the steering wheel despite her unexpected act. "Those are expensive," he said calmly. "You can't afford to replace them, kitty."

"Fuck you."

"Sorry, the line's too long for you to get to the top."

Her fangs dripped, poison filling her mouth.

And it was too much. The kidnapping attempt. Losing what little freedom she'd earned after *years* of teeth-gritted hard work. Having her genesis shoved into her face. Venom's provocation. She hissed and dove for his throat, not thinking about the danger of attacking him while he was driving, not thinking at all.

8

Venom slammed out a hand to grip Holly's jaw, keeping it away from his neck while he controlled the car with his free hand. She clawed at him, but he could take a few scratches. He could take her bite, too, but it'd affect him for a split second that could cause a crash. Gripping her jaw hard, he pulled the car over to the side of the street.

They were in a dark part of town, an area filled with business workers in the day and homeless people at night. None of those people would dare come near the well-known viper green of his car.

So he released Holly and sucked in a breath as her fangs penetrated his skin. Her poison burned for that split second before it was neutralized, but she didn't let go. Her nails dug into the other side of his neck, her fangs impaling him.

But she wasn't feeding, wasn't doing anything but holding him in place.

He lifted his hand, put it on the back of her head and pushed slightly. "Drink," he ordered in a voice that not many people would dare disobey. *"Drink."*

Holly dug her nails in deeper but refused to do as he'd asked. So he squeezed the back of her neck. Hard. "Or would you prefer that I drink from you, kitty?" he said in his coldest, silkiest tone. "I wonder what Uram's blood—" That did it.

She drank.

And fire raced through his bloodstream. *That*, he hadn't expected. Feeding could be erotic, but this was Holly, not a woman he planned to fuck. Gritting his teeth against the unexpected reaction that went straight to his cock, he pulled her off when her body began to go lax. "Enough. You're gorging now."

Eyes glowing acid green, she wiped the back of her hand across her mouth, smearing a droplet of blood across her cheek, and just stared at his neck.

Venom smiled. "Drop the act, Hollyberry. I know you're back in control." Angling his body, he gripped her jaw again before she could move. "You've also been a *very* bad girl."

Baring her teeth, she licked her tongue over her fangs. And his goddamn cock grew even more rigid, though he knew she was trying to get a rise out of him. "You haven't been drinking your quota of blood." Holly had been placed on a strict blood regime because she disliked the vampirish side of herself so much that she often "forgot" to feed. "What have you been doing to the bottles of blood that are delivered to you?"

Holly jerked her chin, but he wasn't about to let go. Reaching out, he used his thumb to wipe away that smear of blood she'd created deliberately as a distraction. With another woman, he might've sucked his thumb into his mouth, turned the act sensual. But this wasn't another woman. "Answer the question or we'll be here all night."

Smiling that sweet fake smile, she said, "Why drink bottled blood when I can have it fresh from the vein?"

"You haven't fed in at least three months." Most vampires couldn't go that long—but Holly wasn't *quite* a vampire. "And you just went into bloodlust."

She blinked, frown lines forming on her forehead. "No, I didn't. That was . . . the other thing."

Uram's taint. "Trust me, Holly. I know bloodlust when I see it." His voice turned cold, like the blood of the vipers who'd been part of his Making. "If I wasn't here to stop the bloodlust before it took full hold, you could've ripped out multiple throats today. And humans don't come back from the dead."

Her skin went pale. "I'm going to be sick."

Releasing her, he reached over and pushed open the passenger door. "Do it outside."

But though she hung out the side and retched in harsh pulses, nothing came out. Her body had been too parched for the blood to reject it. Finally slumping back in her seat with the passenger door open to the cool night air, Holly said, "I hate the taste of blood."

"You liked mine just fine." If he'd let her, she'd have gorged herself into a purring stupor—and fuck, that image of her lushly sated looked too good in his mind.

Her shoulders grew tight. "Like you said, I'd starved myself. I didn't taste it."

That might even be true. "Why would you risk going into bloodlust?" he asked in the viper's tone that was as much a part of him as his eyes. "You want to become your Maker?"

"Fuck you," she said again, but her hands were fisted and her voice trembled.

Reaching across to pull the passenger door shut, Venom began to drive. He went straight to the Tower garage. Once there, he got out and went around to pull open her door. Uncharacteristically, she'd stayed inside. "Let's go."

A grim-eyed look. "Are you going to turn me in to Dmitri?"

"I don't tattle, kitty." Holly had always been his to train—but he'd been reassigned to the Refuge because his duties to the Tower came first. He'd only had a single session with Holly per week—and that had been long-distance, making it difficult for him to gauge her development. That was no longer an issue. And it was becoming clear to him that, regardless of their skill and affection for Holly, the people who'd trained her on a day-to-day basis hadn't understood *what* it was they were training.

She got out, her heels making click-clack sounds on the floor as they walked to the elevator. He pressed the button for his floor. When Holly went to press the button for the much lower floor where she had a room, he stopped her. "We're not done yet."

Her small hand fisted again, her body all but vibrating next to his.

He knew the only reason she wasn't defying him was that she understood how bad things could've gone tonight: Holly was terrified of herself. That had always been part of the problem. She wasn't like that bouncer at the club. For him, fear would save his life. For Holly, fear could either cripple her—or turn her into a deadly threat who had to be executed.

They rode up in silence, exited in silence. He got lucky that no one else was up on the floor right then. Venom took Holly straight into his apartment—a massive sprawl with floor-to-ceiling windows and a large empty space in the center of his sitting area. There was no carpet there, only a square of highly polished stone that appeared to be a design feature that echoed the electric fire set into the opposing wall.

Shutting the door behind him, he locked it, then took off his suit jacket. Holly had gone motionless on entering, seemed to be taking in the apartment. He could tell it wasn't what she'd expected. But she could have the tour later. "Take off your shoes." He pulled away her clutch and threw it on a nearby chair.

Holly bared her fangs at him, but she was still shaky.

She actually obeyed an order, kicking off her heels. "Now what, master?"

Having folded up the sleeves of his shirt and kicked off his own shoes and socks, Venom waved her forward to the stone section; it was just big enough to act as a sparring ring. "Now," he said, "I want you to release the otherness inside you." He knew it lived in her because the vipers and cobras who'd been part of his Making lived in him.

Holly didn't move. "Why? So you can tell me I have no control?"

"Control isn't the same for us as it is for other people, kitty." That was what no one else understood, what Holly herself didn't understand. "I'm not strong because I leash my impulses. I'm strong because I use those impulses. So *use it*." Still, she didn't take action. "Fine." He *moved*, aiming to sink his fangs into her throat.

As he'd expected, she reacted out of pure self-preservation. And then the fight was on—but it was a normal fight. She wasn't releasing the thing that lived in her. Venom scraped his fangs over her throat. She hissed and swayed for a moment before shrugging off the touch of venom.

"Bastard." Eyes glowing, she jumped on him without warning.

The movement wasn't human, not anywhere near. But it was her.

Grinning as she clawed his chest, half ripping off his shirt, he pulled her off and threw her aside. She gave an "oof" as she hit the wall, but she was up and running toward him a second later when she should've had multiple broken bones. Venom knew her exact tolerances, knew that her delicate-appearing bones were *far* stronger than normal vampire bones, even the bones of vampires hundreds of years older.

Holly's bones were closer to angelic bones.

He slashed his nails tauntingly across her stomach as she tried to get to his throat again. It made her move with a speed even he couldn't avoid. He was facing her, and then suddenly, her fangs were sinking into his shoulder from behind and her nails were clawing at his chest. He reached back and ripped her off.

Blood dripped down his back. "No more blood for you, kitty." Holly might have been starving, but he was dangerously potent. She could drink herself into a coma. Oh, she'd wake up, but it'd take days or weeks.

Hissing, she jumped on him again.

He laughed in pure joy.

Because the way they fought now was nothing human, nothing vampire, utterly *other*. Their bodies were liquid, sinuous, bending in ways that shouldn't have been feasible and striking so fast that had anyone been watching, the movements would've seemed impossible. Exhilaration filled his bloodstream. He loved sparring with the Seven and Raphael, Janvier, even Elena, but this . . . No one else fought this way. *Like he did.*

She was young and untried and more instinct than thought—but the latter was the point.

Gripping her throat at one point, he pressed a kiss to her cheek that was more taunt than anything sexual. She twisted out of his grip in a liquid movement and shredded his back, hissing poison at him at the same time. He laughed and twisted around her to grab her thigh—visible through the torn skirt of her dress—holding on hard enough to bruise.

She smiled and kicked up in a way that had her bones going inhumanly fluid.

He avoided the hit, but not the nails across his face. Licking at his own blood, he grinned, and they were at it again.

Holly lay on her back on the stone in the middle of Venom's living area, her brain at absolute and blinding peace for the first time in years. She had no idea what had just

happened. The damn viper had goaded her until she'd decided to let him have it. But rather than yelling at her to shut
it down, he'd just grinned . . . and the rest was a haze of
acidic green across her vision, a sense of exhilaration, and
the thumping beat of her heart.

She raised her leg at the knee, felt a brush of air where
there should be no air. "My dress is ripped." That particular
fact didn't seem important, even though this was one of her
favorite dresses, a piece she'd saved hard to be able to afford.

"So's my shirt," said the man who lay on the floor beside
her, his breathing far more even than her own. "You're fun
to play with when you let yourself off the leash."

Holly inhaled, exhaled. It felt good to have the air ex-
panding her lungs, even better to release the slight tension.
Everything felt good, her entire body liquid. "Weren't you
the one who gave me a lecture about possible bloodlust?"

"Two different things." His voice was different . . . lethargic. Satiated. "You don't drink enough blood to remain
stable, you turn into a murderous monster. You let yourself
off the leash while stable, you fight with a speed and a natural fluidity that's extremely difficult to counter."

Holly tried to think that through, found it too much work.
"I'm drunk."

"No, you're just lazy after a good workout." He flowed
up into a seated position, moving in a way that was so boneless, she wondered if he even had a skeleton.

Letting the frivolous thought float away, she sighed. "I
don't remember most of what we did."

"You will," Venom said, flowing to his feet with that
same liquid grace. "This was the first high. The more you
do it, the more you'll begin to maintain rational thinking
even while surrendering to your *prana*."

Holly couldn't make herself get up, even though she knew
it was ridiculous to keep lying on the floor when Venom was
walking around doing things. "I don't know that word," she
said after several minutes. "It sounds like a yoga word."

A low chuckle. "It's Sanskrit. It has a complex depth of meaning, like all Sanskrit, but the easiest way to describe it in this context is the primal life force that lives in us." He knelt beside her. "I made you a cookies-and-cream shake."

Holly turned her head; it felt deliciously heavy. "Can I drink it lying down?"

"No. Up."

Exhaling again—and really wanting that shake—she managed to get herself up into a seated position. It was only after she'd taken two long draws of the shake through the wide straw that she realized one thing. "How do you know this is my favorite?" She shot him a suspicious look.

"Starting to come out of the haze, I see." He sat down on the floor, his hands braced behind him. "I know everything, kitty."

Holly thought about hissing at him, but the shake was delicious and he looked strangely delicious, too, with his shirt half-ripped to reveal smooth skin and rippling muscle overlaid with skin of honeyed brown. She was obviously more dopey than she realized, but right now, she felt too good to care. "Tell me about *prana*."

A shrug. "Many use the word to describe the energy that is life, but I've always chosen it to describe the part of me that came into being during my Making." His eyes nictitated.

Setting aside the shake, Holly went to crouch beside him on her hands and knees. She stared at his eyes. "Do it slowly."

A smile. "I can't." There it went again, that membrane that turned his eyes into a shattered stained-glass artwork.

"Pretty," she murmured, raising her fingers to his cheek.

He nudged her gently back. "Drink your shake."

Realizing that she was still acting drunk, Holly did as ordered. "So," she said after several more gulps, "what was this about?"

"Teaching you that you'll have better control if you stop fighting yourself."

Holly frowned and sucked up even more of the shake

that was a rush of sugar and fat and all those yummy things her body was craving. She was so glad she wasn't a full-on vampire. "The only good thing about Uram attacking me is that over the past four months, I've developed the metabolism of an Olympic athlete."

Venom yawned, his eyes slits of green behind lids gone heavy.

Rolling his shoulders, he lay down on the part of the floor that was stone. That seemed perfectly normal to her right then. Finishing off the shake, she put the glass carefully aside, then lay back down in the same stony area herself. And realized it was sumptuously warm. "Do you have a heated floor?"

"Just this part."

Yawning, she curled onto her side. "It's nice."

A pillow softly hit her face just as she was about to drop off. Squeezing it to her chest, she snuggled in.

Venom woke first. He'd known he would—Holly wasn't used to what they'd done last night, would take time to recover. She was curled up like the kitten he so often called her. In sleep, she'd made her way closer to him, so that his heat blazed on her back, while the floor's heat blazed into a large part of the rest of her body.

She slept with her head half on the pillow, was hugging the rest of the pillow to her front. Her right leg was pulled up to lie partially on the pillow. The torn sides of her dress fell on either side of her leg, revealing a sweep of creamy skin marked by a few small bruises and scratches from their tussle. He'd been very careful not to badly hurt her, but some wounds were inevitable.

She'd heal relatively quickly.

His eyes skimmed her leg again—"Rein it back," he ordered himself. "She really is a kitten." Small and new and finding her feet. He wasn't about to take a bite out of her.

Finding a soft, silky blanket, he threw it over her. She immediately tugged it right up under her chin and snuggled in for a longer sleep. He felt his lips kick up. When she wasn't awake and snapping at him, she was pretty cute. Though he had to admit he liked the snappy, snarky side of her.

A softer woman would've been crushed that first day of horror.

Leaving her asleep, he went and stripped off his torn clothes before stepping into the shower. He turned up the heat, let it sink into his bones. He tried not to act too "snakey" as Holly would put it, but he couldn't give up these burning hot showers. And why deny himself this one pleasure when there was so much he could never have?

He didn't step out of the shower until a long twenty minutes had passed. Drying off, he hitched the towel around his hips and went to check on his houseguest.

9

She was moving a little but was still on the floor. Her eyes half opened at sensing him. A big yawn before she snuggled back down, her body soon going motionless in a way that told him she'd fallen back into deepest sleep.

He went and got dressed in a dark gray suit paired with a white shirt, then spent a couple of hours on the sofa in the living area going through security reports and other Tower data that Dmitri had forwarded him to bring him up to speed with current events. Regardless of any other calls on his time and attention, he was one of the Seven and he'd taken a blood vow to protect Raphael and his territory.

That vow was a thing of honor, not compulsion. Venom could walk away at any time. He chose not to do so, chose to lend his strength to the reign of an archangel he respected with every fiber of his being. As he respected Dmitri and the others in the Seven. He'd already updated himself on most of this data on the flight from the Refuge, but he wanted to ensure he'd absorbed every detail.

He also didn't want to continue the search for those who

were hunting Holly while she was asleep and unable to assist. Venom understood what it was to fight your demons—he wouldn't steal her chance to conquer hers. His position on the sofa allowed him to keep an eye on her as she slept on.

He'd woken at nine in the morning. She was still fast asleep when he rose at noon to head back into his bedroom to grab his sunglasses. As he hooked them into the front vee of the shirt, he thought of how Holly had snatched them off his face. Most people were either fascinated by his eyes or repelled. Holly . . . the fascination was there, but there was also a sharp annoyance when he covered his eyes.

He was still thinking about that when he went back to the living area to see Holly sitting up with the blanket pooled around her. She looked a little confused in that soft "just woken" kind of way. Going to the bar to one side, he poured himself a glass of blood from the bottle in the underbar fridge. It wasn't his favorite way to intake it—fresh from the vein was always better, but this was convenient.

He didn't offer Holly any; she'd had more than enough to last her through today. Especially since she'd drunk from Venom. Sipping at the glass, he walked over toward her. She frowned and scrambled up onto her feet. Her hair fell around her, Holly having taken off her hair tie at some point. The strands were a slick waterfall of color-streaked black that reached past her waist.

Shoving them back, she glared at him. "What did you drug me with?"

"Your own spirit," he said with an amused smile.

"Yeah, right." She seemed to realize she was still holding on to the blanket, dropped it like it was a burning hot brand. "I slept on the floor. A *stone* floor."

"A heated stone floor," Venom supplied. "You're the only other person who's enjoyed it." Curious about his tendency to sleep on the stone, the others of the Seven had all tried it at one point or another. None had lasted more than a few minutes. Not even Naasir. The most feral of the Seven had enjoyed the heat, but couldn't understand Venom's liking for the hard surface.

Scowling, Holly stepped forward and past him. "I'm going to my apartment."

He didn't stop her. Finishing off his lunch, he made his way to Dmitri's office, the landscape beyond the Tower windows rain-washed dark gray. The other man wasn't there, so Venom left him a note stating what he and Holly had discovered the previous night. His next stop was the technical core of the Tower. The man who was now the heartbeat of that core was someone Venom had only met in person yesterday, but he was very aware of Vivek Kapur's skills.

All of the Seven had been briefed on the Guild Hunter turned Tower vampire.

It was relatively quiet when he walked in after a retinal scan to verify his identity, but the computers were humming and data scrolled through various screens. Strolling through the climate-controlled space, his sunglasses back on, Venom made his way to the very center—and the large circular control station that was Vivek Kapur's personal subdomain. It had been custom-built to his specifications, and gave him access to multiple screens, several of which hung down from the ceiling on electronically controlled arms.

"Vivek."

The other man swiveled around in a wheelchair that, Venom had been told, was as much a part of him as any of his limbs. Thin, with brown skin close to Venom's shade, the hunter-born male had lost all feeling below the shoulders as a result of catastrophic damage to his spine while he'd still only been a child.

But today, he lifted a hand. "Venom." A grin that was brilliant with life, his features handsome despite the lack of enough flesh on his bones. "Nice to meet you again."

"Likewise." Venom didn't offer to shake the other man's hand—vampirism had begun to have an impact on Vivek's injuries far faster than anyone had expected, but the changes were unpredictable; the hunter had gained movement in both arms and his torso soon after his transition, but there'd been no further change in the months following.

That wasn't why Venom didn't touch the other man.

After a lifetime of not being able to feel anything below the shoulders, Vivek had become excruciatingly sensitive in the same newly awake region. Literally. His skin was a carpet of pain that could be triggered by the merest touch. The healers were of the opinion that it was simply an outcome of his nerves being shocked awake after years of somnolence—he'd just have to grit his teeth and bear it.

The only mercy was that it was solely touch from another living being that triggered the pain; Vivek could sit and sleep comfortably, work his instruments without problem. Venom wasn't sure that was such a mercy, however: what must it be like to be deprived of the sensation of another's hand on your body for most of your life, only for that touch to become a punishment?

"Quite an empire you've got." He nodded at the work area, he and Vivek not having had much of a chance to talk yesterday when he dropped off the confiscated cell phone.

"I still miss my Guild station," Vivek admitted. "I pretty much built that from the ground up, ordered every single piece myself, customized the software."

"I built a house once," Venom found himself saying. "I'm a bad carpenter, but I built that house. And I still miss it." Mostly because of the people who'd lived in it, laughed in it, shared their bounty of rice and wild greens, lentils and handmade sweets.

Vivek nodded, the movement jerky, as if his body wasn't quite used to its new range of motion. "Things we build ourselves, they matter." He touched a screen, at the same time clicking the sensor that protruded beside his cheek, his wheelchair also designed to his specifications. "Sorry," he said afterward. "I spotted a piece of information Jason might be interested in."

Venom noted the glow in the other man's eyes, had to hide a chuckle. According to Dmitri, Vivek Kapur had a crush on Raphael's spymaster. Not a sexual crush. The crush of a man who loved having his fingers in every possible information pie—and Jason was the best at that there was. "Did you have a chance to dig into the e-mail address associated with the bounty?"

"Only for the past half hour—healers forced me offline for the rest of yesterday afternoon, and this morning, and I didn't want to delegate since you asked me to take care of it personally." A sour face as he began to work again. "They call it physical therapy and muscle recovery. I call it sadism."

Venom could imagine the pain Vivek had to bear every session. "Does it make a difference if the therapists wear gloves?" He assumed there'd need to be physical contact during the sessions.

"We tried," the other man responded with a scowl, "but then they can't feel the movement of my muscles as they need to. So instead I swear like a hunter, and the therapists wear earplugs." The last words were absent, Vivek's focus on his work.

Venom prepared to leave. "Send me a message as soon as you have anything."

"No. Wait." The hunter's eyes moved with rapid speed and Venom realized the other man was using software that read his eye movements, at the same time that he typed. "I've hacked the e-mail account. It's received four e-mails in total, not counting the one you sent using the confiscated phone. One is from Mike, whose skull you rearranged. He e-mailed to say he and his guys were taking the job."

"Professional of him."

"He's a regular CEO." Vivek's tone was bone-dry. "The

other three e-mails are from different parties who purport to have successfully snatched Holly."

He pulled up those three e-mails on the large screen in front of him. "Photos are doctored."

Two were bad, but the third . . . "That one would fool me if I didn't know her," Venom said, pointing to the picture of a terrified woman hog-tied on a concrete floor. Holly's eyes stared out of the screen.

Something dark and angry uncurled inside him.

"It's a very clever piece of photo manipulation." Vivek continued to work. "That's all there is right now. No money transfers to follow because, I assume, the buyer either knows these are forgeries—*or* doesn't know which e-mail to believe."

He used a second screen to bring up the photo Venom had taken, of Holly slumped in the backseat of the SUV. "That might be why you didn't get a response to your message, though I'm more inclined to believe your surveillance theory. Mike and his men aren't the sharpest tools in the shed, but they've got a better track record than any of these others—reason enough for the buyer to keep a hopeful eye on them."

Venom saw that the last forged photo, the one that looked genuine, had only been sent fifteen hours earlier. *After* Mike and his crew struck out—and after Venom's message. "You're monitoring the bank accounts associated with the bounty hunter who sent that final e-mail?"

Nodding, Vivek said, "No movement at all." A single account appeared on the screen that had originally held Venom's photograph of Holly. "I'll keep digging, in case he's smart enough to have hidden accounts."

"If this is what you can dig up in a half hour," Venom said dryly, "I'm guessing you'll have his entire life in sixty minutes."

A sharp grin from the other man. "It's a busy day, so maybe sixty-five would be a better estimate."

"Forward me the details of everyone who e-mailed." It'd give him and Holly a place to start interrogations as they attempted to track down the origin of the bounty. "And continue to monitor the e-mail address."

"Done."

Holly showered with a frown on her face. What the hell had happened to her last night? And why wasn't she more mad about it? Probably because her body felt *good*. It was like she'd slept in the lushest, most comfortable bed on the planet rather than on a stone floor. And it wasn't as if she was living in a hovel. This was the *Tower.* She only had a small room, not a sprawling suite like Venom, but most of the space she did have was taken up by a freaking huge bed.

That bed, an ornate extravaganza the size of a small continent, was courtesy of her parents. They'd wanted to give her a "moving in" present and what could she do but say yes? Mia had laughed her ass off over it until Holly had pointed out that a similar bed probably lay in her future, too.

The memory of her sister's aghast expression made her grin.

Leaving the shower after a long, hot time, she dried off, then stepped out and stared at the bed that had put that look on her sister's face. It was a white four-poster with a thick mattress and curtains tied to the posts. The posts were carved with love hearts, the headboard with a plump cherub pulling back his bow as he prepared to shoot an arrow at a whole bunch of hearts across from him.

"I have a giant princess bed drowning in hearts," Holly said to herself, not for the first time.

Then she smiled, because her parents had been delighted when Holly accepted the gift. Daphne and Allan Chang had even bought Holly a set of ridiculously expensive Egyptian cotton sheets and an equally expensive goose down comforter. The bed was cozy and soft and warm . . . and the stupid stone floor had still been nicer.

"Argh!"

Making her way around the bed, she opened the walk-in closet and stepped inside to dress. She really liked that she could do that; it meant she didn't have to pull down the blinds on the floor-to-ceiling window on one side of her room. There wasn't much of a view, not this low down in the Tower, but on a sunny day, the light was beautiful.

Today, it was a moody, water-washed gray.

Dressed, Holly sat on her bed, shadows streaking across her skin as she pulled on her boots. The rain wasn't heavy, more a constant mist, so she could still see beyond her window. In her direct line of sight was the building occupied by the Legion, the strange beings who'd descended on the city during Raphael's battle with Lijuan.

Pale-eyed and pale-skinned, with wings like a bat's, the Legion were the definition of eerie. Of course, who was she to judge? She wasn't exactly Ms. Normal. And she loved what they'd done with their building, turning it into a living creation swathed in lush green.

Holly had thought more than once about walking over and asking if she could look inside. She'd never done so because the Legion were so *other*, and so clearly powerful as to be beyond her reach, but today, boots on and hair scraped into a ponytail, she felt the devil take her. Or maybe it was that she wasn't quite ready to face what Venom had brought out of her the previous night.

Since the area between the Tower and the Legion building was archangelic territory no stranger could infiltrate, she didn't bother to alert Venom as she exited the Tower.

She did however send him a message: *Don't go hunting without me.* Fear of herself or not, she wasn't about to be sidelined. She just needed a few extra minutes to find her balance.

Despite the constant misty rain that felt like a cool kiss on her skin, New York carried on unabated. Steam escaped from a grate, suited office workers heading out to lunch flowed toward the subway entrance in the distance, and the warm, yeasty scent emanating from a nearby pretzel cart drifted over to tantalize Holly's taste buds.

The recently emancipated vampire with quick dark eyes and dark hair had been cheeky in setting up shop so near Raphael's stronghold, but he'd quickly created a number of high-powered fans. She'd seen angels swooping down to grab a pretzel before flying back up.

Today, she diverted from her course to grab one for herself. No bounty hunter was going to try to kidnap her with an entire angelic squadron within earshot of a scream; hair damp and expressions committed, they were seated on railingless balconies relatively low down on the Tower. A bluewinged angel with eyes of extraordinary gold and black hair tipped in blue—Illium—hovered in front of them.

Post-combat-training discussion, Holly thought, having seen the same sight multiple times since she'd moved into the Tower. The latter fact made her parents so proud they dropped it "casually" into any conversation with even a faint bearing on the matter.

Oh, our Mia? She's a doctor now. And our Holly works for the Tower. She took her brothers to visit her apartment—she has an apartment right in the Tower, did I forget to mention that?—and well, the two couldn't stop talking about it.

"My first customer of the day!" The pretzel seller beamed at Holly when she stopped in front of his cart. "Had to start late today—trouble with my cart, wouldn't you know it, but here you are before I even finish my setup." His hands moved quickly to half wrap the pretzel in greaseproof paper. "You get a free pretzel for being a good omen."

Holly accepted the gift with a grin, reminded of her dad. Allan Chang had been known to give his first customer of the day a fifty percent discount. "Ready for the post-training rush?" That entire angelic squadron would soon descend on him.

"It never ends, cutie." A wink. "It never ends."

Holly bit into the soft, chewy pretzel as she waved good-bye and continued on toward the Legion building. Stopping halfway, she gave her dad a call to touch base, exchanged comments with her gorgeous little brothers—who, at five foot eight and five foot nine, weren't actually so little anymore—over their favorite social media platforms, then messaged her mom. Daphne Chang *loved* the text app on her phone.

Is your hair still a rainbow? was the reply.

Yes, Mom.

You have such lovely black hair, Holly. I just don't understand you girls.

I love you, too.

Her mom sent back five rows of heart emojis.

Laughing, Holly pocketed her phone. She'd talk to Mia later in the day, as her sister had done a night shift for her first day on the job and was probably asleep right now.

She made it to the Legion building without being stopped, though she had no doubts the Legion were watching. They sat like gargoyles on buildings a lot of the time, silent and unmoving. People often forgot they were there until they opened their batlike wings and flew off.

"Hmm." She stared at the bottom of the building. If it had once had doors, those doors had long ago been sealed up. The bottom three floors had no exits or entrances that she could see, and were covered in green from the plants crawling up and down and growing outward from the wall itself, as if the walls had somehow been turned into vertical patches of soil.

She took another bite of the pretzel as she considered her options. Before she could put her plan into action, however, her skin prickled. But when she looked around, no one was there.

So she looked up.

10

Venom was standing high up on a railingless Tower balcony, so high up that she couldn't see anything of his features, especially with the misty rain blurring her vision—but she knew it was him. The way he stood, the way his suit so impeccably fit his body, it was pure Venom. And she knew he had his eyes on her; the rainbow hair was pretty and it made her happy, but it wasn't exactly good for blending in.

Holly thought about waking up on his stone floor, of the honey in her veins after their insane sparring session, and knew that way led trouble. Dangerous, deadly trouble washed in sin. She made herself look away, forced her mind back to the problem of how to get into the Legion building.

Her free hand tingled at that instant.

She looked down . . . and saw her skin fading in and out. "No," she whispered, curling her fingers into her palm to hide what was happening as she deliberately continued to eat her pretzel.

Nothing strange here, people, just a woman staring at

the Legion building while stuffing her face as tiny droplets of rain dotted her hair and skin. Perfectly normal. Lots of people stared at the Legion building. The tourist buses didn't dare cross the Tower's territorial boundaries, but the non-Tower buildings lucky enough to have a direct view of part of the Legion building made good money renting out their roofs so the tourists could gawp at the beauty of a building bursting with greenery in the center of one of the most cosmopolitan cities on the planet.

Pretzel eaten and her misbehaving hand fully visible again, she put the scrunched-up wrapper in her pocket, then walked over to the thickest-looking vine and, taking a strong grip on greenery turned slick by the rain, began to climb. Her bones went liquid, her instincts sharpened, and her breath changed. She climbed like this was what she'd been born to do—and it wasn't the human part of her that was in charge.

Exhilarated by how easy it was to scale the building, she didn't care.

I'm not strong because I leash my impulses. I'm strong because I use those impulses.

Maybe Venom was right when it came to certain aspects of who she'd become . . . but Holly knew there were also things inside her that should never be set free.

When she reached the balcony in front of the opening on the fourth floor that functioned as both an exit and an entrance—a large section with transparent hanging flaps of thick, heavy plastic that she figured must help maintain the temperature within—she straightened up and said, "Hello? Can I come in?" It wasn't polite to just invite yourself into someone's house.

If no one answered, she'd climb back down and try again another day.

But one of the Legion landed beside her in deathly silence. Her heart thumped. "Good afternoon."

Rising up from his crouch, he looked at her with eyes

translucent but for an outer ring of blue, his hair the same
midnight as Raphael's, and his face *too* flawless. He
appeared . . . unfinished in some strange way. As if life hadn't
yet put a mark on him. And yet, paradoxically, the sense of
age that clung to him made her bones ache.

Angling his head slightly to the left in a way that simply
wasn't human, he said, "What are you?"

Holly fought the urge to touch his face, discover if he
was warm or cold. "That's the million-dollar question."
Suddenly remembering that the Legion were meant to be
thousands upon thousands of years old, she said, "Do you
know the answer?"

A slow shake of his head, his utter calm unnerving. "We
are losing memories as we exist in this time and this place,
but it isn't only memory that makes us. We have knowledge
woven into our bones."

"And what does that knowledge tell you?"

"That you are new." He cocked his head deeper to the
side—she was almost afraid he was going to do that thing
owls did and turn his head upside down. "But you are old,
too, though not yet fully awake."

Holly swallowed hard. "The otherness inside me, what
is it?"

"You and not you." With that cryptic statement that
made her want to shake him, the Legion being turned away,
folding his wings neatly to his back. "You are new. You can
come inside. My brethren will wish to see you."

Though she suddenly felt like a science exhibit, Holly's
curiosity nonetheless compelled her to move forward. A
wash of humid air hit her face the instant she walked
through the flaps behind him. That made sense, if— "Holy
crap." She felt her mouth drop open, her eyes widen.

The entire building had been hollowed out except for
levels that jutted out here and there. Thick vines twisted up
the sides, ferns grew from impossible angles, flowers bloomed
in giant clumps, and below her feet was the thickest moss

she'd ever felt. When she looked down to the ground floor, she saw trees heavy with pink and orange fruit. There was no sense of rot, of fallen leaves or fruit ever left forgotten. The scent in the air was a fresh amalgam of green and light and growth.

Holly stared and stared, wonder filling her heart to overflowing.

"This is so *beautiful*." So much a thing of pure, unadulterated life.

Whispers surrounded her, coming from so many throats that she couldn't separate one from the other. It was creepy, but this was the Legion after all. Creepy was their normal modus operandi. But then they started landing around her on wings of silence and she thought, *Oh shit.*

"You are new," said the Legion being who'd brought her inside. "They have never seen you."

It was a strange way to put it. Not *something like you*, but *you*. "You've seen Venom," she said. "He's like me."

"He is a one being, too," her guide said, as the others continued to whisper . . . *without moving their mouths.* "Like you but not you. Different."

Since the Legion was staring full out at her, Holly decided to stare back. She'd heard it said that when they'd arrived during the climactic battle of the fight between Raphael and Lijuan, they'd all looked *exactly* the same. Dusty gray hair without color, eyes utterly translucent, no sense of sunlight to their skin, wings as devoid of pigment as their hair.

These beings, however, while as similar as brothers, weren't identical. Hair colors varied in subtle shades, skin tones were beginning to diverge in minute increments, and their otherwise still-translucent eyes bore rings of pale blue and pale green and pale brown and pale hazel. Only the one she'd first met had a more vivid ring, the color closer to Raphael's intense blue.

"Why are your eyes so freaky pale?"

"We are becoming, too," said a hundred voices, maybe more. "You are an echo who is not an echo. You are new."

Holly was starting to understand why Elena looked as if she wanted to pull out her hair after she'd been talking to the Legion. "What does that even mean?"

But the Legion had gone quiet. A motionless, silent second later, they flew off on their batlike wings to settle all over the inside of the building—or to fly straight up to the roof exit that sat open to the misty rain and portentous clouds of darkest gray.

Only one was left, and it was the one who'd led her inside.

"Tell me what that means?" Holly asked softly. "Please?"

"That you are an echo who is not an echo. You are new." He flared out his wings and was gone before she could reply.

"You guys are like the worst possible version of some inscrutable guru!" Holly shouted up.

They kept looking at her with that strange and oddly innocent curiosity. "Come back," a hundred voices said. "We will be new together. After you are not an echo."

Throwing up her hands, Holly stomped out—to slam into Venom's chest. He caught her by the upper arms. She broke the hold and scowled, her face reflected back by the lenses of his sunglasses. "Do you know how to speak Legion?"

A slow smile. "Did our friends turn cryptic on you?"

"I asked a question." She just barely stopped herself from tearing off the sunglasses and stomping on them.

"No one speaks Legion except the Legion," Venom said, his dark hair glittering with tiny jewel-like drops of rain. "The sire and Elena are still attempting to work out the meaning of something the Legion said to them when the Legion first landed in New York."

Holly looked over her shoulder, where the plastic flaps disturbed by her passage had already gone still. "Do you think they get off on messing with people's heads?"

"No." A pause. "The Legion aren't anything human or understandable. Try to imagine having an eon of knowledge inside you, of knowing so much that explanations are redundant. I think, in their own minds, they're being perfectly clear."

You are an echo who is not an echo.

Holly didn't want to think about that word: *echo.* She was scared she knew exactly what it meant. "Are you stalking me?"

"No need. I just followed the blinding glare of your hair."

"A man who wears the same outfit over and over has no room to criticize my fashion choices." Never would she tell him that he looked beautifully dangerous in the gray suit and white shirt that had survived the rain unscathed but for the odd droplet here and there.

Protected by the partial overhang above this railingless landing area, he'd soon dry off. Holly had done so inside the warmth of the Legion building.

"Look at this," Venom said now that the exchange of insults was over. "It's a faked photo of you."

She frowned, took his phone. It was a shock to see herself looking so beaten. "I'd never look like that," she said, ice crackling her words. "Even if they beat me to a pulp."

"The individuals behind it clearly didn't research their target." Venom took the phone back. "This one's the best manipulated image but there were two others. Vivek was able to track down physical addresses for all the fraudsters— I thought we should pay them a visit, see if any of them got a bite back via a channel we can't monitor."

"Let's go." Holly felt like kicking some ass.

Not waiting for Venom, she began to make her way down the vine. She heard him laugh, and then he was moving beside her. They landed at the same time, tiny droplets of rain glittering on their skin and clothing. "You don't climb like me," she said, curious despite herself. He was fluid like her, but his bones didn't move in the same way.

"We can compare techniques later." Striding across to where he'd parked his distinctive Bugatti, he got in, waited for her to take her seat. "I've sent you the files on the ones who said they'd caught you. See if you recognize any names. All are vampires."

Holly took out her phone, brought up the list he'd sent her. She didn't really expect to see any names she knew, but— "Son of a bitch. That asshole."

"Which one?" He turned away from the Tower, the world beyond washed in gray.

"Marlin Tucker. Low-level scumbag who deals in information when he can't deal in honey feeds. Vampire. Hundred and seventy years old."

"Perhaps your relationship will make him cooperative."

"We don't have a relationship. He's one of Ash's contacts— she thinks he's an asshole, too, but he's an asshole who belongs in the gray and people talk to him." She went through the other names. "I don't know anyone else and these addresses aren't likely to be real if they're the official ones on their driver's licenses or whatever."

"Vivek dug deeper." A sideways glance out of eyes she couldn't see. "Nice outfit. Taking fashion advice from Dmitri?"

Holly narrowed her eyes at him. She'd chosen skinny black jeans today, paired them with a three-quarter-sleeved and fitted black shirt that she'd tucked into the jeans; the outfit was completed by boots that laced up to midcalf. Not spike boots. Work boots. "I haven't seen Dmitri wear daisies anytime lately." Those daisies decorated her boots.

Venom's grin was a wicked, wild thing. *Real.* "Definitely not Sorrow anymore."

Holly wasn't so sure. She'd changed her name back to Holly because of the sadness on her family's faces each time they called her Sorrow, but the girl she'd once been was gone forever . . . and deep in the night, when she was alone and the world was distant and no one could see her vulnerability, Holly mourned for her. For that hopeful, color-drenched girl who'd loved fashion and who'd had a crush on one of her lecturers.

With his sandy blond hair, a smile that creased his cheeks, light blue eyes, and a habit of wearing cardigans over his shirts, he'd made her heart flutter. Shelley and Maxie had dared Holly to make a move on him after they graduated and she'd laughingly taken the bet. Because back then, her life had been like that. A bubble of joy and possibility. A weight-less, gossamer thing.

"Do you ever miss who you were?" The words were out of her mouth before she could think about what they might betray.

Venom didn't ask her what she was talking about. "It was a long time ago," he said. "Another few decades and it will be four centuries since I was Made."

"Janvier isn't that much younger than you and he still talks about his sisters, still goes to see their descendants." He and Ashwini had ridden to New Orleans a month ear-lier for a *fais do-do*, which Holly had worked out meant a party; the two had come back with joy written on their skin and colorful beads hanging off the handlebars of Janvier's motorcycle.

"People make different choices." Venom's voice was cold in a way she'd never heard from him—he might have the eyes of a viper, but for the most part, Venom was mock-ingly amused at the world. "What do you plan to do? Stay in touch with the next generation and the next, or fade away?"

Holly frowned and looked out at the gathering darkness, the clouds so heavy at this point that the world looked closer to six P.M. than just after one. This wasn't about her. But an inherent sense of fairness made her answer his ques-tion because she'd pushed him to answer hers. "I lost my

family once," she said. "I'm never going to do it again."
Turning back to face him, she saw the tightness in his jaw.

Venom never acted like this. This mattered. It wasn't to
be taken lightly.

"I want to be like Janvier," she said. "I want to have those
ties, have that sense of being rooted in humanity. He's the
most . . . human vampire I know aside from Honor and
Ash—and they just got Made, so it doesn't count. I think it's
because he's maintained strong ties to his family through
the centuries." A year ago, his great-great-multiplied-by-who-
knows-how-many-greats-grandnephew had stayed with him
and Ashwini for six months while the boy attended a theater
workshop in Manhattan.

Venom shot her a look made unreadable by the mirrored
lenses of his sunglasses. "Fighting the inevitable, kitty?" It
was a murmur, the last word almost affectionate.

Her eyes burned, her throat suddenly thick. Turning to
stare out the window again, she watched the passing traffic.
Streetlights began to flicker on, their systems triggered by
the lack of light. "I know I'm not human," she said when she
could speak again, her voice caustic because otherwise, she
might cry. "Bit hard to miss with the glowing green eyes and
the ability to break people's bones without touching them."

"What?" Venom's tone was hard.

"It's a new development," Holly said, her voice as color-
less as the landscape around them. "I was sparring with
Janvier and he was showing me how to move and I was
thinking that if I could get the angle exactly right, I'd probably break his forearm."

Bile burned her throat. "I wasn't planning to do that—I
was just thinking of how it might be helpful in a real fight
if I could take my attacker out of commission." She swallowed, the sickening sound of the bone cracking loud in her
head. "And then his arm was broken."

"He'd have healed quickly," Venom said. "He's old and
strong enough."

That didn't change that Holly had harmed someone who'd only ever been good to her. Janvier had even invited her along on the most recent visit to his family. She'd said no only because she'd wanted to spend the time with Mia before her sister's move to Boston.

Venom's power slid around her, a sinuously graceful thing. "Did he ask you to do it again?"

11

"How did you guess?" An edge of surprise in Holly's question.

"Because that's his job." Venom turned down a dingy street with several broken-out streetlights just as the rain thundered down in truth, but though he saw everything despite the acutely low visibility, the alertness part of his nature, his mind was on Holly's revelation. "That ability isn't vampiric."

"No. It's closer to angelic."

"No, kitty. You know as well as I do that it's closer to archangelic." The idea of that much power in her fragile body . . . "How are you still alive?" It was a serious question. Archangels were built to handle the violence of the power that lived in them. Even Illium, the strongest angel among the Seven, had nearly died when the Cascade forced extraordinary power into his flesh.

Holly continued to stare out the window. "It's only a droplet of power," she said in an eerily toneless voice. "It builds, then releases in sudden violence or . . ."

"Or?" Venom should've already had a briefing about her, but other events had overtaken the normal order of things when one of the Seven returned to the city after a long absence.

"Want to see a cool trick?"

Venom glanced over to see Holly holding out a hand . . . before it faded out of view only to flicker back in. He sucked in a breath as he turned his attention forward again. Glamour, the ability to walk unseen among the populace, was a *strictly* archangelic ability. "How long can you be unseen?"

Holly laughed as the rain transitioned from downpour to steady drizzle. "You mean how long can my *hand* be unseen? Because that's the only body part with which I can do my parlor trick."

A droplet of power.

Suddenly her words made more sense. "But you can summon the power on cue?"

"Depends on the day of the week. It comes and goes." She shifted slightly forward, pointing to their left. "That's the address of the idiots who think I'd cower. That three-story building with the graffiti of a flying dinosaur. Creative."

Venom double-parked his vehicle knowing no one would touch it. If they did—well, they might just get stung by a viper's bite. Getting out into the damp dark, he looked up at skies of heavy gray. "Have you been told of the Cascade?" Rain kissed his cheekbones.

"No. What is it?" Holly asked, trying not to watch the rain whisper across Venom's skin. "I won't share the information. I know not to talk out of turn about Tower business." That way lay certain death—after hideous torture.

She'd already had her fill of both.

Venom didn't answer until they'd crossed the street, his

body moving with liquid grace. Holly couldn't help it; she watched him. There was something deadly about Venom. Not just power, but *him*. She wondered if he'd been like this as a human, too, dangerous and beautiful.

She blinked, shook her head. Obviously, if she was starting to think Venom beautiful, it was time to break her self-imposed celibacy and go get laid. She had the primal rage inside her under control now, wouldn't terrify the poor men she picked up in the bars.

Her mind flashed to that . . . thing with Venom last night, when she'd gone full weirdo crazy on him—and he'd laughed. Because he was nuts, too.

"The Cascade," he said, once they stood in the rain-protected shadow of the building next to their target location, "is a once-in-an-eon event that causes massive power fluctuations and other changes among those who are Cadre."

Holly's fingers rose to her right temple. "Raphael's mark?"

"Yes, that's part of it. As are your new friends in the Legion." Venom scanned the otherwise empty street with lethal focus. "The Cascade also has unknown effects on the weather. Today's rain darkness could be a natural phenomenon, or it could be Cascade-linked."

Holly had the sense of glimpsing a vast world of earth-shattering power far beyond her understanding—and perhaps that was as it should be. For an immortal, she was still only an infant. She wasn't meant to consort with archangels . . . or with vampires as deadly as Venom. "Why are you telling me this?"

Taking off his sunglasses, he gripped her chin, held her gaze. "Because the Cascade most strongly impacts those with archangelic blood."

And Holly had been force-fed so much archangelic blood that it had changed her on a cellular level. "My parlor trick with the hand, breaking Janvier's arm," she said without severing the eye contact, "they might be connected to this Cascade?"

A nod. "No way to know for certain, but it would explain why you're developing abilities no one outside the Cadre should possess." He ran his thumb over her chin, slow and deliberate. "Be careful who you trust, kitty. Many would pay far more than five million for a woman who possesses even a single droplet of archangelic power."

Closing her hand over his wrist, his skin warm under her touch and his power curling around her so tightly that she felt it as a stroke across her skin, she tugged off his grip. "I appreciate the information—and the warning." He'd given her a tool to understand a little of the craziness around her, and she was grateful, but she couldn't have him touching her.

Not when her entire body seemed primed to respond.

His lips curved in a smile she couldn't read. Then, sliding the sunglasses back on, he slipped out of the shadows and up the steps of their target building. Holly followed, the two of them pausing by the front door.

Venom's body went inhumanly motionless. "It's too quiet."

Looking around, Holly saw no obvious signs of trouble. "They might just be crashed out after drugging themselves with honey feeds."

"You sound very sure."

"When you're in a situation like this"—she indicated the dirty, graffitied environment, a blunt illustration that these vamps weren't exactly living the dream—"escape, even illusionary escape, has a powerful draw."

Venom pushed his sunglasses to the top of his head, the slitted green of his eyes smashing into hers. "Have you fed from a drug addict?"

"No," Holly said flatly, not adding that, in the darkest depths of pain and despair, she'd thought about it, about the sweet oblivion of just letting go. It was the idea of the state she'd be in afterward—weak and vulnerable and unable to protect herself—that had stopped her.

Then there was the whole sucking-blood-from-a-living-being thing, which continued to turn her stomach.

So yeah, no thanks—but not for the best reasons.

"We going in or what?" she said when Venom continued to look at her with disturbing intensity, as if he saw her most terrible secrets.

Slipping his sunglasses back down over his eyes, he put his hand on the doorknob and turned. It offered no resistance and they slipped inside, shutting the door behind themselves.

The air that hung heavy inside the hallway leading to the chipped paint of the internal staircase was foul with the smell of unwashed bodies, urine . . . and more. "Old blood," Holly whispered in a harsh undertone, her gut twisting and lurching as images of mutilated and decapitated bodies piled in a red-streaked pyramid, while a mad archangel drank from a wineglass filled with the blood he'd drained from a living victim, shoved into her brain.

Fingers touching her neck, gripping painfully tight when she would've slashed out in a panic. "Focus, kitty."

The two words acted like a bucket of cold water thrown into her face. She froze, found her center as Honor had taught her, then breathed shallowly through her mouth. "Sorry." Heat flooded her cheeks.

Releasing her, Venom said, "The smell would turn anyone's stomach, much less that of a woman who was found coated in her own dried blood."

Holly scowled, though his matter-of-fact judgment made her feel a little less like a child confronted by a nightmare come to life. But, because she *had* reacted like that child, she moved on ahead of him.

Do not act stupid because you're scared and want to hide it. Do that and I'll kick your ass black and blue for a week running.

Ashwini's voice in her head.

And if you ever act like a horror movie dumb chick, I'll personally lobotomize you.

Holly's lips tugged up a fraction, her hunched shoulders straightening. She made sure she was cautious and alert, and not in any way driven by fear as she moved on down the hallway. Reaching the bottom of the steps that led up to the second floor, she stopped and glanced back at Venom, fighting an inexplicable urge from within that told her to *climb*, go higher.

"Up or down?" His sense of smell was more acute than hers; it made sense to ask rather than relying on her own strange compulsion.

He looked up along the line of the stairs, the damp, dark strands of his hair sliding back. "The old-blood smell is strongest up there." Scanning the lower floor and taking in the multiple doors on either side of the hallway, he said, "We clear these together."

Holly didn't argue. Ash and Janvier had taught her that you never left your partner alone in an unknown situation. "We should lock the front door." It'd make it harder for anyone to sneak in behind them and launch a stealth attack.

Removing the old-fashioned key from the lock afterward, she put it in her jeans pocket just as the bare lightbulb dangling from a wire in the ceiling flickered for a second. It had been on when they entered, and while its light was anemic, it was better than the storm gray gloom.

As it settled again, throwing shadows into the corners, she watched Venom's back while he opened the first door. No sign of life, the room beyond empty of anything but a broken-down sofa with cigarette burns on the arms, the foam stuffing visible where the dirty fabric was torn.

Holly took the next door; she was half expecting Venom to attempt to hijack the search, but he remained at her back, an alert, watchful presence while she looked inside and pronounced the room free of threats. He took the door after that, Holly the next, until they'd completed the entire first floor.

All the internal walls were painted a teal blue shade that had been discolored by time and cigarette smoke to have a sickly yellowish edge. Several boasted holes probably caused by punches, while one had a large black stain. As if someone had thrown a jar full of ink at the wall.

The majority of the rooms were furnished with either a ragged foldout couch or a dirty mattress. Clothes were scattered about on both couches and mattresses. Bedrooms of a sort, she realized. The last room proved to be a living area set up with three large couches that all sagged in the middle and faced a curved television screen that took up most of one wall.

Unlike every other item in the place, the TV was clean and cutting-edge.

A second later, she spotted the box that had held the TV. The lack of stains or cobwebs on it seemed to indicate the television was a recent purchase.

Holly gripped Venom's arm when he would've stepped inside to examine the items on the glass-topped coffee table that sat between the sofas and the TV. "Needles," she said, pointing down.

His lip curled. Taking off his sunglasses, he hooked them in the front of his shirt. "Someone's mother didn't teach them to keep a clean house."

Holly blinked. Though she'd asked him about his family, she'd never really thought of Venom as a man who'd had a mother. And definitely not one who'd taught him how to maintain the cleanliness of a home.

"Just be careful." Vampires weren't vulnerable to disease, but being stuck was still disgusting—and ever since the Falling, no one could be certain a needle hadn't been adulterated with some kind of virus or infection that could affect immortals.

Holly probably shouldn't know that it was the Archangel Charisemnon who'd created the disease that had struck vampires and dropped angels from the sky, but it was hard to work in the Tower with high-level vamps and not pick up information. After what Venom had told her outside, she figured Charisemnon had gained a disease-causing gene in the Cascade.

Not a gift she'd want, but she wasn't an archangel bent on power.

"I'm guessing there're a lot of syringes lying around," she said. "The vamps shoot up the junkies right before a honey feed, so that the high is stronger, lasts longer. No one's in a state to care about the syringes afterward."

Nodding, Venom walked to his original destination. He picked up something rectangular with squared edges, opened his hand to let it fall.

"Whoa." Holly stared at the hundred-dollar bills floating from his hand, then took in the new TV again. "Vampires who live in this area don't have access to that kind of cash." Most were out of Contract and had used up the money they'd been given when that Contract was complete—but not found well-paying jobs in the aftermath.

Venom rubbed a white powder between his fingers, brought it to his lips for a small taste. "Cocaine. From the amount of dust on this table, it's likely the source of the cash." Dusting off his hands, he said, "Let's go up. There's no threat here."

Holly headed up the steps in front of him, his presence a coldly silken danger at her back. She knew he could kill her as fast as a cobra strike—Venom might wear three-piece suits and look like he'd stepped out of a high-fashion magazine shoot, but he was a predator under the skin.

Rotting blood. Old urine. Other, more noxious body fluids.

Holly pressed a hand against her stomach as she tried

not to breathe in the increasingly fetid odor. "They're up here . . . and they're probably dead, right?" The idea made her stomach lurch, the response primal.

"Not necessarily. Our targets aren't human."

Exhaling, Holly nodded. Vampires could survive significantly more blood loss than humans. They could even survive multiple-limb amputation in traumatic circumstances. She'd heard the limbs *would* eventually grow back—but for most vampires, that would take a long, long, long time. It wasn't as if they were angels, after all.

For vampires like Dmitri and Venom, however, she had a feeling the timeline was shorter—a *lot* shorter. "Have you ever lost a limb?" she asked in an effort to distract herself from the smell.

"Once," Venom answered easily as they took in the layout of this floor. "It was in battle—my left arm."

"How long for it to regenerate?"

"Three quarters of a year. I was a lot younger then."

Three quarters of a year was still nothing in comparison to the vast majority of vampires. Holly knew a century-old vamp who'd lost his pinky in a bar fight when another brawler bit it off. A month after the incident and it was still a ragged stump.

"I'll go first into these rooms," Venom said, his eyes glinting at her.

Holly straightened her spine. "I don't need to be protected."

"I'm stronger. If these vampires are drug maddened, I'd rather put them down quickly than watch you flail about."

Holly gave him the finger. *Asshole.*

Smile becoming deep, taking him from handsome to fucking handsome, the beautiful asshole turned and walked to the first doorway. Holly watched his back instead of giving in to her bizarre compulsion to enter that room. He didn't say anything about the room, though he spent thirty seconds standing in the doorway.

He then quickly checked the other rooms.

"Let's clear the third level," he said after he was done. "Then we can deal with the mess in the first room." He turned on a light in the hallway, as if there was no longer any reason for stealth.

The hairs rose on the back of Holly's neck.

12

Holly had to consciously will herself away from the room on the second floor.

The third floor was heavily graffitied and littered with spent bottles of liquor and more syringes, as well as—randomly—several bottles of milk that had gone off. But it was devoid of life—or bodies. "They lived like pigs," Holly said, walking around a pair of underpants crumpled on the floor. "Even my homeless friends live more tidily than this."

"Some vampires find life outside a Contract challenging," Venom said. "They're indoctrinated to follow orders by their angels—having to make their own decisions leaves them floundering."

Holly was startled. "You feel sorry for them?"

"No," he said flatly. "I have no sympathy for those who'd rather be in gilded cages than scrabbling to make a living in freedom."

"There are some who can't," Holly said softly, thinking of Zeph and his pockmarked face. "They're too broken by what was done to them."

Venom's eyes remained unforgiving. "Unless it was a forced Making, those vampires chose to enter into a Contract in exchange for near-immortality. Choices have consequences."

Much as Holly pitied the broken vampire, she couldn't argue with the truth of Venom's words. That truth was the same reason Guild Hunters could, without guilt, do their jobs in retrieving vamps fleeing their Contracts. Because every mortal in the world had witnessed over and over how cruel immortals could be. Any choice made to enter into that world as an adult with full use of your faculties was made with eyes wide open.

"At least with a proper Contract," she muttered, "there's an end date. My sentence is open-ended."

"Life is what you make it, kitty." Venom ran his fingers through and over the long tail of her hair. "Prove yourself to Dmitri and Raphael and you'll never have to worry about your freedom."

Holly twisted her lips as she moved away from his touch. "You really think Raphael will allow a threat to live and thrive in his territory?"

Fangs flashing as he smiled. "Do you really believe Dmitri isn't a threat?"

"He wasn't tainted by Uram."

"I was Made by Neha."

When Holly just looked at him blankly, he said, "I forget, you aren't aware of the political currents in the archangelic world. Let's just say that Neha and Raphael are no longer friends as they once were. If she could, Neha would separate Raphael's head from his body and laugh while doing it."

Yet Venom, who bore Neha's imprint in a way no one could miss, walked by Raphael's side.

"Come," Venom said before she could respond, "we have business to attend to."

Holly had to enter that room that reeked of old blood and

other ugly things, had to see what lay within, but she had one more question to ask. "I know Raphael's too powerful to worry about you being a threat to him personally, but Dmitri and the others . . . Don't they worry that you might have a lingering loyalty to Neha?"

"You call me a viper. Some believe I am one, a snake in the nest." Venom's voice became flat, his eyes cold. "But Dmitri and the others in the Seven? Janvier? Trace? No. The bonds between us—and with Raphael—were forged long ago and made unbreakable by countless acts of trust and fidelity."

"I call you a viper because of your eyes and your general snakeyness, not because I think you're some kind of a great betrayer," Holly said with a scowl. "Stop calling me kitty and Hollyberry and I'll stop calling you Viper Face and Poison."

His chuckle sent ripples down her spine, made her breath catch in a way that shocked. "But, kitty," he said, the ice no longer in evidence, "I don't think that's a bargain I want to make."

Fascinated by how his eyes sparkled when he laughed, Holly had to grit her teeth to control her inexplicable reaction. A purely sexual response, she would've understood: Venom was darkly handsome and had a body even she couldn't deny was the stuff of female fantasies. But wanting to see him laugh, feeling that laugh wrap around her like a full-body kiss? It was just weird.

With a stern reminder to herself that he'd kill her should she show the least indication of being a danger to the Tower, she headed down the stairs to the second floor, and, shoulders squared, turned to the room of old blood that drew her so strongly. Venom didn't stop her, but his prowling presence was suddenly very close. And she thought—*He'll catch me if I fall.*

God, she really was losing it.

Then there she was, in the doorway. At first, she had

trouble figuring out what she was seeing in the darkness created by the drawn curtains, the only illumination coming from the hallway light at her back . . . and the small light over the pool table.

The horror burned into her brain in Polaroid flashes.

An arm, attached to nothing, bloody tendons trailing from it.

Three heads lined up neatly on the pool table.

A being without a head or legs propped up on its bloody torso by the fireplace, as if just waiting to lean forward and welcome them.

Two left hands lying side by side on the dirty carpet.

"Where are the rest of the pieces?" she said through the buzzing in her skull that wiped out all else.

"Look right."

She did, saw the pile in the shadows. Torsos. Arms. Legs. All piled up neatly, as if someone hadn't wanted to make a mess.

Venom spoke, his voice soft. "This is your nightmare, isn't it, Hollyberry?"

"Yes."

Which was why she stepped inside the room of horrors and, swallowing her gorge, walked carefully to that pile. There were no hiding places in this room furnished only with old chairs and armchairs and that spotlit pool table turned into a macabre display, but she'd seen too much horror to lower her guard.

She knew some monsters could walk right up to you and you'd never see them. Uram had been in full glamour when he'd taken Holly and her friends.

They hadn't stood a chance.

The only reason she didn't watch her back was that Venom was there. He'd execute her should she lose her mind to the vicious thing that lived in her, but until then, he'd protect her the same as he would any other partner.

The closer she got to the pile of body parts, the more real it became and the more her mind wanted to scream.

Bones poked out, shattered and gleaming white.

A rope of intestines was looped neatly around a torso.

Two right hands lay palm to palm, their fingers interwoven.

"You sure Uram hasn't come back to life?" The question came out near soundless.

"One of these heads," Venom said from where he stood by the pool table, "matches the ID photo Vivek was able to locate of the bounty hunter who sent that very well-doctored image of you. The other two match photos of known members of his crew."

Deciding she'd faced her fear long enough, Holly stepped back from the pile of meat that had once been living beings and turned to Venom. "Cocaine, drug-dealer-type cash lying around, used syringes everywhere—it looks like the three weren't exactly upstanding citizens. All kinds of things could've come back to bite them on the ass." There was no way to know if this massacre was connected to the bounty on Holly's head. "A psychotic vamp, or even a hopped-up human junkie, could've done this if the three were blazed out of their minds on honey feeds."

"Possible. We'll have a better idea when we track down the others who sent in false reports." Venom slipped his hands into the pockets of his suit pants. "I suppose I'd better call in a cleanup crew."

"Tower rule is we have to call the cops unless it's an issue that requires Tower handling." Or one that dealt with angelic secrets. "I think general bad guys being chopped up is probably a cop call."

"I'll bow to your greater knowledge on the topic," Venom said with no sign of mockery.

It was as Holly was pulling out her phone to make the call that a faint gasp whispered into the air. Venom's eyes nictitated, his head jerking toward that pile of cold body parts.

Holly's hearing wasn't sharp enough to have pinpointed the origin of the sound, but there was literally nowhere else in the entire room where someone—or some*thing*—could hide.

"Jesus." Sliding away her phone, she moved to the pile with Venom.

She had a very dangerous knife hidden down the side of her boot, the weapon one in which she'd had extensive training. Working in the shadows required that she learn to handle weapons, but she had difficulties with guns; they just didn't feel right in her hands. And, given her speed, a knife worked as well—even better when it came to situations that required silence.

But today, she decided not to reach for the blade. "Keep watch," she said to Venom.

He was stronger, could react faster to the possible threat.

Then, though her stomach twisted and churned, bile burning the back of her throat, she forced herself to move the body parts to one side, trying to think of the pieces not as butchered people but as inanimate objects. It was hard when the skin was sickeningly pliable under her fingers and when the smell of putrefying blood and other, nastier—

"No, *no*." Horror chilling her skin, she knelt in front of the thin naked woman covered in blood who was cringing into the wall. Knees and arms tucked into her chest and her eyes stark, she breathed in short, shallow gasps.

It was a wonder she could breathe at all—her throat had been slit.

Vampire.

Holly slammed her hand over the woman's wound. "Venom. Feed her." She'd do it herself but her blood was tainted, could well do more harm than good.

"Tilt up her head and hold her mouth open," Venom ordered. "I don't want to have to tear her off if she starts to gorge. I could kill her."

Heart pounding like a racehorse's, Holly used her free

hand to squeeze the woman's jaw until her mouth fell open
to reveal fangs not much bigger than Holly's, managed to
tilt back her head. Blood dripped into the brown-haired
vampire's mouth, Venom having cut himself using a pocketknife she'd somehow never expected him to be carrying.

He'd tipped his wrist over the woman's mouth.

When—because the woman's fangs weren't buried in
his skin—the wound began to heal, he reopened it.

The skinny woman with pale white skin didn't react for
at least five seconds—a near-impossible period for a starving vampire being given an infusion of powerful blood, and
then she jerked so hard toward Venom that had Holly not
been holding her, she'd have clamped on to his wrist. Venom
pulled away his wrist at the same time, cutting off the flow
of blood and making the vampire whimper piteously.

"Venom."

"She can't handle any more. I'm not a baby vampire,
kitty—my blood's *old*. And if I were you, I'd watch my throat."

Holly jerked back just in time.

The woman had lurched up surprisingly fast to end up
on her hands and knees on the worn carpet. Limp and dirty
hair hanging around the sides of her face, her eyes rimmed
with red, she hissed at Holly. And Holly traveled back in
time. She'd been too scared to hiss at Elena when the hunter
had found her, but she'd been as broken. "We're here to help
you," she said gently.

The woman screeched and clawed out at Holly, moving
with scrabbling speed across the carpet on all fours. Holly
scrambled back, unwilling to hurt a traumatized victim.

The vampire crumpled onto the carpet like a doll with
her strings cut.

Holly glared up at Venom. "What did you do that for?"
He'd taken the brunette down with a simple hit to the back
of the neck.

"I really don't have time for you to play chase with a feral
vampire," he said lightly. "And this is no longer cop business."

"Why?" She went to check that the vampire was alive, found a jerky pulse. "She looks like a junkie. Probably freaked out after witnessing the massacre."

"Vampires don't hold drugs that long inside themselves," Venom reminded her. "She had to be under that pile of body parts long enough for the parts to go cold and the blood to coagulate on the floor. *And* I fed her my blood—that should've shocked her back to full consciousness. She was acting . . . Not like a vampire in bloodlust, but close."

Holly shook her head. "She was acting terrified and psychotic." Driven by the primal impulse to survive. "That's how you act when you've been abused, then nearly murdered."

Venom put away his phone after making a call to the Tower. "She is not you." It was an oddly gentle comment.

"Maybe she is." Holly brushed the woman's dirty brown hair back from her face after turning her onto her back. "She's really thin." Thinner than the haunting vampiric slenderness flaunted by the older vampires who'd been so refined by their vampirism that they were ethereal in their beauty.

"Why doesn't Dmitri look like the old vamps? The ones who are all preternatural slenderness and translucent skin?" she asked, the thought one she'd never before contemplated. "He's all hard edges even after a thousand years."

"He's a warrior and he's stayed a warrior through time," Venom said, coming to crouch by the woman. "Vampirism shapes us as we choose it to shape us. For Dmitri, that's meant his muscles are stronger, more difficult to injure."

The woman coughed, her eyelids beginning to flutter. *Venom's blood.*

She wouldn't have recovered this quickly otherwise. But she wasn't quite there yet, and since she might go feral again when she woke fully, Holly took this opportunity to scan the rest of her. "Bruises," she said, pointing out the ones visible even through the rust red of dried blood. "Probably from being thrown at the wall." There was a noticeable dent in the wall against which the vampire had been cringing.

"Whoever killed the other three likely slit her throat and threw her at the wall and thought the job was done," Venom murmured. "She's young enough that she should have died— but the throat slit must've been just careless enough to give her a shot at survival."

He angled the woman's head slightly to the side to look at the wound. "It appears the killer didn't cut through her spinal cord. And she would've had blood dripping onto her face from the body parts for a period. Some would've gone into her mouth."

Sometimes, the *worst* times, Holly wondered if she had blanks in her memory because Uram had made her feed on the blood of her dead friends. Remembering something like that could drive an already half-crazy survivor all the way insane, so maybe she'd chosen to forget.

"These bruises, however," Venom said before the horror could dig into her brain, "they were made by a hand gripping hard and the color makes it clear they're older." He was pointing to marks on the woman's thigh.

"She must be really young if she's healing this slowly."

"It isn't always a matter of age. Some vampires of ten thousand will always be weak. Others will be powers at two hundred."

Holly nodded. At around two and a half centuries of age, Janvier was a walking example of the latter. "It looks like her leg was broken recently, too." There was a jagged scar on her right shin, as if bone had poked through.

Rising, Venom circled the thin brunette. "The bottoms of her feet are burned. Scarred." His voice was cold. "That's torture."

The woman's watery blue eyes, eyes ringed in pulsing blood red, flicked open. And this time, they focused on Venom. Her fear was a vicious curling up of her body, a tiny creature cringing in dread. "Please." A rasped whisper. "No more."

Sliding on his sunglasses, Venom hunkered down beside

the fallen woman. Then, to Holly's surprise, the most well-dressed vampire she knew slipped his arm behind the filthy woman's back and helped her up into a seated position with gentle care. The woman shivered violently, her bones rattling. Taking off his jacket—which probably cost thousands—Venom put it around her shoulders.

The brunette clutched the lapels closed over her naked breasts, shooting Holly looks so hopeful that it was all she could do not to cry. Holly thought of what her mother would do if she found someone like this, and reached out to brush the woman's matted and dirty hair off her face.

Sobbing, the vampire fell into Holly's arms. And said, "I thought you were dead. I'm so sorry. I thought you were dead."

The words made no sense . . . and they sent a chill up Holly's spine.

"Holly."

She glanced at Venom, startled at his use of her actual name.

He spoke quietly. "Watch her fangs. There's something not normal about her."

13

Holly wanted to tell him to go fuck himself. This woman could've been her not so long ago. But the ring of red around this broken vampire's eyes was a warning she couldn't disregard. Holding her nonetheless, she made sure she was very aware of the woman's mouth and fangs.

The vampire cried until she went limp . . . then jerked back so hard that she tore herself out of Holly's arms. Scuttling backward like a spider crab until her back was to the mound of body parts, she took harsh, hard breaths, her eyes scrunched shut. As tightly clenched as her hands where she gripped the lapels of Venom's jacket.

Holly was almost expecting the blood red eyes that met hers when the woman flicked her eyelashes back up. "Help me." This time, her voice was as rough as coarse sandpaper.

Venom was there before Holly saw him move.

Seizing the vampire's wrists with a single hand, he used his other to hold her jaw with enough force that she couldn't turn her head and try to sink her fangs into him. "Fight it," he ordered. "You have my blood in your veins now. You have power."

The vampire's throat moved as she swallowed. "More," she pleaded in a whispery tone that was eerie in its lack of humanity. "Please."

Holly expected Venom to say a flat no, but he said, "Holly."

"What do you want me to do?"

"Hold her wrists."

"I have them." The woman's bones felt like a bird's, so thin and fragile—but Holly knew not to be fooled. The stranger was still a vampire.

Raising his own wrist to his mouth, Venom tore open a vein and, tipping up the woman's head using his grip on her jaw, dripped his blood into her mouth. The woman swallowed frantically, blood splattering her lips when she missed.

"Enough," he said after a few moments, when his vein began to knit naturally. "You'll die if you glut yourself on me."

Holly stared at him. He was right, of course he was right. He was too powerful for a weak vampire to take— but he'd let Holly drink her fill of him last night. Which said certain things about her that Holly didn't want to face just now.

The vampire licked her tongue around her mouth to get all the splattered drops and at that instant she wasn't human at all. But a heartbeat later, she smiled, and her eyes, they were devoid of red. "Thank you," she whispered, tears rolling down her cheeks again. "I haven't felt clean inside since . . . a long time."

"What's your name?" Holly asked.

"My name?" The woman looked at her blankly. "I . . . I had one, once. I d-don't remember."

Holly's fury was a cold rage in her heart. "How about Daisy? It can be your temporary name until you remember your real one." Everyone should have a name, should have the dignity of an identity. "Or you can choose another name you like."

A shaky smile. "I like Daisy, it's pretty."

"Look at me, Daisy." Venom hadn't raised his voice, but it demanded attention nonetheless.

Daisy turned her head, and, after examining her face, Venom released her jaw, though he shot Holly a look to ensure that she kept hold of Daisy's wrists. "What are you doing here?" he asked the vampire. "Were you with one of the dead men?"

A hard shake of Daisy's head, hate in the stare she shot toward the decapitated heads lined up on the pool table. "My master gave me to them for a week," she spit out. "To reward them for something."

Holly's stomach twisted. This was why she would've never voluntarily signed up for a normal Contract. Those under Contract had few rights. For a hundred years, they were the playthings of the angels. It wasn't always like that, of course. Dmitri had been with Raphael since the start, and he'd said things that made Holly think the two had been friends even before Dmitri was Made.

Janvier had come out of Neha's court far more educated, and experienced in travel and diplomacy than when he'd gone in; he'd also been trained in how to use the *kukri* blades with lethal skill. Ashwini was treated like an asset by the Tower. So not all those under Contract were destined for a hellish life—but there was no way to know, was there? You could end up with someone powerful but "human" like Illium, or you could end up with a bastard who lent you out to his friends for them to abuse.

"Who is your master?" Venom asked.

"He'll hurt me if I tell." It was a rasping whisper.

"You're not going back to him," Holly said before she could stop herself.

Venom's head lifted, turned toward her. But she refused to back down. "I'll talk to Elena," she said, speaking to both him and Daisy. "She'll help." The Guild Hunter turned angel was still human inside, didn't look at the world through the jaded eyes of an immortal.

"The name of your master," Venom said, returning his attention to Daisy.

This time, his voice demanded absolute obedience.

Daisy had no hope of standing against him. "Kenasha," she whispered. "My master is Kenasha."

Venom's expression didn't change. "When did you sign up to be his?"

It was an odd question. Vampires didn't get to choose under which angel they served out their Contract—the Tower was in charge of assigning new vampires to angels. And not all angels qualified; they had to be strong enough to control newborn vampires. Holly knew there had to be other prerequisites, but she'd never had reason to find out what.

"He's been my master for . . . a long time," Daisy said lifelessly. "I don't remember." Her eyes returned to Holly. "I thought I knew you. But I don't remember anymore. Why don't I remember?"

"It's all right," Holly soothed before Daisy could panic. "You're exhausted and weak. We'll talk when you're stronger."

There were noises lower down in the house, the sound of steady, unhidden movement echoing up the steps. Venom glanced back over his shoulder. "The Tower team has arrived."

Holly forced herself to release Daisy into that team's care. "She needs medical attention," she said to the powerful vampires who'd responded to Venom's call.

They ignored her.

Holly had learned to live with the reality of being the lowest non-mortal on the Tower totem pole, but it still made her grit her teeth . . . as something inside her whispered: *You can kill them all.* Strangling that mad voice she tried to pretend didn't exist, she anchored herself firmly to the here and now—where she was weird but didn't pulse with power like those around her.

The Tower vampires turned their cool, dangerous eyes toward Venom. "Take her to the infirmary," he said, indicating Daisy's hunched-up form. "Keep her away from anyone else—and under constant guard. I want her blood tested. It'll have mine mixed in with it."

"Yes, sir." Two of the vampires left with a terrified-looking Daisy, two remaining behind. Holly noticed with a corner of her mind that they were all wearing plastic covers on their shoes.

The last thing Holly saw before the three disappeared from sight were Daisy's panicked eyes as the woman twisted to look back at Holly, tears melting from her irises. Not about to leave the weak and abused vampire alone among strangers, Holly moved to go after her.

Venom closed his hand over her biceps, holding her in place. "You can't help her." An unforgiving statement.

"Fuck you." She tried to wrench out of his hold, failed. "What're they going to do to her?"

"Exactly what I said." Releasing her only when it was too late for her to catch up to the ones who had Daisy, he spoke to the other vampires who'd responded. "Clean up this mess and tell me about anything unusual you find."

"Yes, sir."

"There could be clues here," Holly muttered, rubbing at her arm.

Venom's sunglasses were still on, but she could tell he was looking at the place where he'd gripped her, and where she was now rubbing. She dropped her hand, not about to appear weak or soft in front of him.

"They're a fully trained forensic team," he told her, right as the others said they were going to retrieve their gear from the van. "Let's leave them to it."

Holly had to admit she was glad to be outside; it was still

dark gray and drizzling faintly, but the air she drew into her lungs was welcomingly fresh. The stench inside had begun to get to her. "Why did you ask Daisy that?" she asked after Venom hung up following a low-voiced call. "About when she'd signed up to serve this Kenasha bastard?"

When Venom glanced at her, she reached out and snatched off those stupid sunglasses. She was half-tempted to throw them in the gutter and stomp on them, but, cognizant that they were probably worth six months of her salary, she folded them neatly before closing her fingers around them.

He smiled at her, tiny water droplets catching on his eyelashes. "When are you going to give those back?"

Never. "Maybe if you answer my question."

She expected him to block her. If this was Tower business, she had no right to the information. She spoke to cut him off as they crossed the road to where he'd left his car. Of course it was still there, not a scratch on it. "I'm part of the team that works in this section of the city. I need to know if something is going on that shouldn't be."

She didn't know if it was her words, or if he'd decided to trust her—after all, she'd made it clear she wasn't about to incur Raphael's wrath by spilling secrets—but he said, "I know who Kenasha is, and, as I suspected, he currently has no vampires listed as being under his care."

The last word was hard.

Holly frowned, her eyes tracing a water droplet streaking down the gleaming viper green of the car's hood. "The Tower didn't assign him Daisy?"

"No. Kenasha is never assigned newborn vampires." Unlocking the car, he waited for Holly to get inside, then got in himself. "If the angel officially in charge of her wanted to transfer her, he or she should've contacted the Tower."

"Why?" Holly's empty hand fisted, Daisy's words about being "given" to the three dead vampires as a "reward"

ricocheting inside her head. "It's not like the Tower inter-
feres to stop the newly Made from being abused."

"They make their choice, Holly," Venom reminded her
without an ounce of sympathy in his voice.

Holly's other hand tightened at her side, over his sunglasses, something Elena had said to her over two years
earlier rising to the forefront of her consciousness. Holly
had been feeling sorry for a vampire the Guild Hunter had
recently retrieved when Ellie had pinned her to the spot
with the silver-rimmed gray of her gaze.

And then she'd asked a question.

*If you'd had a choice, would you have chosen to sign
over a century of your life for the promise of hundreds,
perhaps thousands of years of life?*

Holly had said, "No," with harsh finality. She'd grown
up in a city filled with vampires and angels, had seen what
it meant to be part of the immortal world. The dark, seduc-
tive beauty, the wealth . . . and the horrific terror.

Raphael had once left a vampire's shattered body in
Times Square for three terrible hours that had turned New
York silent, people's blood running ice cold in visceral fear.
The rumor was the vampire had betrayed him. By the time
Raphael got through with him, the vampire's body had
been held together by nothing but a few stringy tendons.

His jaw had hung wrong, his skin torn and flesh missing
in places.

Holly had thrown up after seeing the news reports.

No, she'd never have chosen to serve beings so remote
from humanity that they could do that to another living
being. She still didn't understand how Elena could love an
archangel who could deliver such a punishment—but then,
betrayal was betrayal. And immortals had such long lives
and such an intense ability to heal that punishment had to
be vicious for it to count.

"What does it mean that the Contract transfer wasn't run
by the Tower first?" she asked past the ice in her blood.

"Likely venal politics." The lights of the Bugatti cut through the storm gray heaviness, but the rain against the windshield made it feel as if they were cocooned in a world apart from the life and chaos of New York.

"The reason for the rule," he continued, "is so that utter incompetents like Kenasha don't ruin intelligent vampires who could become long-term assets." His hands guided the car with an ease that made it look effortless. "It also wouldn't do for a low-ranked angel to build himself a harem of young vampires—quite aside from issues of control, there is a hierarchy."

"Here I thought it was to protect the vulnerable."

"Daisy would've torn out your throat, then buried her face in the wound and fed on your blood until she was glutted."

Holly put his sunglasses on the seat beside her before she broke them. "She was obviously starved. You'd act insane, too, if you weren't fed for so long that you became emaciated." Daisy's ribs, her collar bones, had stuck out sharp as blades against her paper-thin skin.

"No. Her reactions were off." Venom's tone left no room for argument. "She's young enough that the amount of blood I fed her originally should've shocked her back into full sentience. It's possible there's a drug in the mix."

"A honey feed?" She frowned. "The effect usually wears off much faster. Maybe it hit her harder because she's so thin."

"It doesn't have to be a honey feed." Venom's words were a surprise. "There are always chemists trying out new formulations. Every so often, they roll the dice and play with vampiric lives." His voice turned grim. "Did Janvier and Ashwini tell you about the drug named Umber?"

Holly shook her head. "I probably don't have the clearance." It was weird, but when her bosses told her that, she accepted it, conscious she had to earn her way up the ladder. When Venom told her the same, she wanted to claw out his eyes. It was irrational, but then her reaction to him had never been a rational thing.

"You definitely don't," he said. "But you need to understand certain facts to protect yourself if you're working in the shadows."

Caught, Holly turned partially in her seat to listen.

14

"You reacted to Daisy as if she was simply another abused vampire—that could get you killed." Granite in his expression. "You need to watch the reactions of any vampires you come into contact with, weigh those reactions against what you know to be normal."

He swung the car to the left, heading in the direction of the bridge. "You have to be conscious a vampire might be high off a honey feed, or on some new designer drug. All of the latter eventually end in bloodshed. Umber caused a voracious blood hunger that led users to murder and brutalize the people closest to them."

Holly released a quiet breath, her hands flexing. "Okay, you're right," she said, and the world didn't end. "I'll be more careful. I just . . . I felt sorry for her." She wanted to kick herself as soon as the words were out—what the hell was she doing exposing her vulnerable underbelly to Venom of all people?

"I know." No judgment in his tone. "Why do you think

I gave her my jacket? My tailor will be appalled when I ask for a replacement and tell him why I need it."

Holly rolled her eyes, but her lips wanted to tug up. "Why do drugs have such a dangerous effect on vampires?"

Venom's shrug was liquid. "Vampire physiology is complex and it's delicately balanced. Honey feeds work because our bodies are designed to filter the blood we intake—it just so happens that some of the drug isn't filtered out and creates the high. But that high isn't enough to upset the balance of the vampiric system."

Holly thought of Zeph, of the emotional pain he tried to drown in blissed-out oblivion. "People try the designer stuff even knowing it could be deadly because they want a longer high."

Venom gave a curt nod as his car prowled smoothly along the bridge, the lights of the other cars passing by in a rain-smudged blur. She had no idea what speed he was going except that it was *fast*. She liked it. "Are we going to find the asshole, Kenasha?"

"Yes. Marlin Tucker and our other target can wait—call Janvier and ask if some of his and Ashwini's snitches can keep an eye on Tucker's apartment as well as that of the third fraudster in the interim."

Holly made the call, got Janvier's agreement.

That done, she settled back in her seat and watched the world speed by. There weren't many people she'd trust to drive this fast on rain-slick streets and keep the car under control, but Venom's reflexes were even quicker than her own—and she was inhumanly fast.

Her skin chilled as the thought whispered through her mind, the strange thing inside her, the thing that wasn't in any way human, feeling as if it was salivating and readying itself for a rampage. She fisted her hands, took a deep breath, exhaled. And still, the thing *spread* itself inside her. It was as if she had a pair of huge wings trapped inside that wanted to tear out of her flesh.

God, she was going batshit insane.

That was why she hadn't told anyone what was happening when the whispers began. She still remembered the first time—it had been as Raphael fought Lijuan in the skies above Manhattan. Holly had wanted to volunteer to help in some way, but her control had still been erratic at that time, too erratic for anyone to trust her in the field.

So she'd watched the battle from a distance and she'd heard a whisper from deep within: *I can kill them both.*

The sheer madness of believing she could kill two archangels had staggered Holly. But that had just been the first sign of crazy from her psycho mind. She'd gritted her teeth and ridden it out each time it happened, and hoped it was the last time. But the mad, whispering voice—and the accompanying sensations—were getting stronger, not weaker.

"Kitty, you're growling." It was a relaxed comment.

Holly swallowed the feral sound with jaw-clenched will. "Damn it. Sorry."

A shrug. "Doesn't bother me—I told you, use what lives in you instead of fighting it."

Holly parted her lips, almost told him that she wasn't sure what lived in her should ever be allowed out into the light of day. Snapping her mouth shut before the words could escape, she turned to look out the window again as they hit the Angel Enclave. She might've had a death wish once but she'd gotten over that. Her parents didn't deserve to have their hearts broken by having to bury Holly because the Tower had decided she was too dangerous to be permitted to live.

Unable to see clearly because of the rain-fogged glass, she rolled down her window to the cool air. Fine droplets of rain settled on the skin of her face in a welcome burst of freshness. The world was even darker outside, the Angel Enclave a place of tall gates amid taller trees and heavy foliage. The homes beyond were far distant, at the end of long drives. The most exclusive perched on the cliffs that looked out over the Hudson to the glittering spectacle of Manhattan.

The only Enclave home in which Holly had ever been was Ash and Janvier's.

Elena had invited her to drop by for a visit, but Holly preferred to stay out of Raphael's view. She had the uneasy feeling the Archangel of New York would see through her to the madness that whispered egotistical, horrific, and frankly insane thoughts at unpredictable moments.

"What's Raphael and Elena's house like?" she asked, her curiosity trumping even her horror at what she was becoming.

"A home," was Venom's simple answer.

Odd as it was, she understood. To her, Raphael might be the deadly Archangel of New York, a being whose notice she never wanted to attract, but to Elena, he was the man she loved, and to Venom, he was the archangel Venom chose to serve. An archangel who'd protected the city with his own life and who Elena said had honor stamped in his soul. "Could you get a place along here if you wanted?"

"The land is tightly held." Venom took a curve with smooth grace, though their speed was deadly. "I prefer the city in any case. It's too quiet in the Enclave. Who needs all this green and peace? I'd rather listen to cabdrivers yelling at one another while the smell of hot dogs and pretzels makes me wish I could turn human for fifteen minutes."

Holly found herself surprised into laughter. "That's what I think, too. About it being too quiet." The homes were undeniably beautiful, with stellar views, but she'd rather be in the chaotic busyness of the city.

Venom turned right, heading away from the exclusive cliff-front real estate and deeper into the Enclave.

"The incompetent Kenasha's not top tier?" As Venom had so bluntly stated, there was a hierarchy. At the top were the archangels, then angels like Illium and Aodhan, who were powers in their own right.

"The waste of angelic space is four thousand years old," Venom told her. "I could take him without breaking a sweat—give you a few more years and I'd put my money on you rather than him." A short pause. "Scratch that, kitty. You could take him right now."

Holly blinked at that harsh assessment. "He's that weak?"

"He *keeps* himself that weak. Even if he never developed an innate power, he could've built himself up physically over time to become a formidable warrior like many of those in the Tower squadrons."

Thinking of the squadron members she'd run into, Holly nodded. Many of them did pulse with inborn power that pushed against her senses, but not all. Some were simply strong and fast and dangerous.

"Angels," Venom added, "have an incredible physical advantage in how quickly they heal and how strong their musculature can become with far less effort than required by vampires or mortals who want to achieve the same aim. But Kenasha prefers to sit on his ass and live off the money his parents accumulated. Raphael once said he thinks they went into Sleep out of embarrassment."

"Huh." Holly chewed on that. "Somehow, I didn't think angels could have deadbeat sons." It defied logic that a being of that age could have wasted his entire life. "Shouldn't he have achieved something out of sheer boredom?"

"You would think so, but he is a parasite who sucks at his parents' teat." Venom's lip curled. "He's a disgrace. A son is meant to care for his family."

Holly usually forgot Venom's age, he was so urbane and *now*, and then he'd say something like that. But of course, it wasn't only a case of age but the deep impact of a culture where elders often lived with the younger generation. Like Rania, the girl who'd been Holly's friend since fourth grade, Venom had been born in India.

"Not just a son," she said, an ache of loss and memory

thickening her throat. "My siblings and I will be taking care of our parents when they're older and can't live alone anymore." The idea of caring for the elders in the family was as ingrained in her as it apparently was in Venom. "My paternal grandfather and grandmother used to live with us until they passed."

"You've made up with your family?"

Holly nodded. "My mother lays a guilt trip on me every so often, though." She folded her arms and imitated Daphne Chang's scowl. "'Do you know how we felt? Do you, Holly? We raised you to know you were loved, that you could come to us with anything. And what do you do the first time you have a small problem but turn your back on your family! For shame!'"

Venom's shoulders shook. "A small problem?"

"Oh, shut up." But she was laughing, too. "That's how she always puts it. As if waking up needing to drink blood to survive is the same as being fired from a job or having a car battery die." Laughter turned into a smile. "She's going to be mad at me forever, but she'll love me while she's mad at me."

Venom was quiet for a long time as they drove along the rain-dark streets of the Enclave, no other vehicles passing them. If angels flew overhead, she couldn't tell in this weather.

"You're lucky, kitty," he said at last. "Cherish the family you have for as long as you have them. Hold them tight as Janvier does his."

Surrounded by the quietly falling rain, a hushed privacy between them, Holly felt the barriers melting away. "What happened to your family?" she asked softly.

She didn't think he'd answer, as he hadn't answered before, but he said, "A vampire son is one thing, but one with the eyes of a viper?" A shake of his head.

Rage crashed through her in a violent wave. "You did it for them, didn't you?" she said. "Signed up for a Contract."

Already turning into the drive of an angelic home, Venom

didn't answer, but Holly didn't need one. She knew. A son who'd been brought up to look after his parents and other family members would do anything to give them a good life. Even barter his own.

That they'd abandoned and rejected him at such an incredibly vulnerable time because the cost of his sacrifice wasn't what they'd expected? Holly wanted to tear their disloyal forms limb from limb. Too bad they were all already long dead.

She was still furious when they rounded a corner of the drive, and . . .

Her mouth fell open, her eyes taking in the monstrosity ahead. The rain had helpfully paused, as if the heavens wanted her to get the full picture. "So . . . you think Kenasha likes turrets?" The place was an atrocity of turrets and curlicues and God knows what else. She just knew it looked like the eighteenth century had thrown up on the seventeenth. Or was it the sixteenth?

Architectural history wasn't her strong point. But one thing she knew—the building in front of them would stick out like a mutant sore thumb in any century in which you dropped it.

"The last time I saw this place," Venom said after bringing the car to a halt, "it only had nineteen turrets." He pointed to the right. "That one's new."

Holly squinted to see what made this turret such a must-have. It was skinny, with four round windows that didn't match any other part of the house. "He has a turret-at-sea fantasy?"

"Let's ask him." Venom held out his hand. "I'll need my sunglasses for this one. Kenasha fears what lies beyond them."

That, Holly understood and accepted. So she handed over the sunglasses—but not before saying, "They come back off the instant we're in the car again."

Viper green eyes, slitted and unearthly, held hers. "Agreed."

*   *   *

Even as he spoke, Venom was wondering once again why it mattered so much to Holly that he not wear his sunglasses around her. Most people preferred he keep his eyes covered up—the only exceptions were those who'd known him for centuries and who considered him a friend. None of the Seven, nor Raphael, seemed to care that his eyes were different than theirs. The same for friends such as Janvier and Trace.

In the Refuge, Jessamy had banned him from screening his gaze when the two of them were speaking. "I want to see your eyes," she'd said when he'd asked why. "Just like I like to see Galen's eyes, and the eyes of anyone else with whom I'm talking."

Venom didn't know why when his eyes weren't readable like human eyes. He'd even stared at his own eyes in the mirror and tried to see if they reflected his emotions. As far as he could tell, they were as unreadable as the eyes of the vipers who had a part in his Making. The odd thing was that Neha hadn't meant to torture him—she'd liked him, had actually asked him to consider being Made well before he'd ever thought of taking that road.

"I have a strong feeling I'm going to attack Kenasha." Meeting him in front of his car with those words, Holly scowled up at the turret house. "I'll fang him if you don't keep him away from me."

"You'll hurt him if you do." Venom slipped on his sunglasses. "Despite his age, he's weak enough that my venom would kill him."

Dmitri would probably rip him a new one for sharing so much information with Holly, but it was time people stopped babying her and gave her what she needed to survive in their world. She wasn't a normal vampire and they couldn't treat her like one. And should Holly betray them, Venom would hunt her down himself. He had a feeling he was the only one who could—she was moving far differently than she had when he left the city two years earlier, a predatory confidence to her that he didn't think she realized.

"Oh, that's *interesting*." Holly looked up on that considering statement . . . and smiled, showing off those tiny fangs that were ridiculous and that fascinated him. "That means my venom should make him writhe about in pain for a while." Her eyes glinted a glowing film of green. "Let's go."

His own predator nature uncurled deep in his gut, called to the surface by her deadly, beautiful otherness. "You don't act without my go-ahead," he said, regardless of the cold part of him that was in total agreement with her dark intent. "This is Tower business. If Kenasha has earned a punishment from Raphael, then Raphael is the only one who will deliver it."

"I'm not suicidal, Viper Face. I'm not going to step on an archangel's toes." A shiver. "But if Mr. Turret hasn't done anything that requires Raphael's attention, then can I bite him?"

Venom smiled despite himself. "We'll see, kitty."

Growling deep inside her chest, Holly stalked beside him as they headed to the front door. It was already open, being held that way by a tall and skinny vampire with ghost white skin and pitch-black hair. "Sir." He bowed so deeply he almost bent his skinny body in half.

Montgomery could teach this one a few things, Venom thought. Raphael's butler was in a class of his own. "We're here to see your master."

Still bent over, the vampiric butler said, "Master Kenasha regrets to inform you that he's not taking guests at present."

"How unfortunate for him." Venom turned his voice to the silken menace that always got a result.

Pulse thudding hard in his neck as he rose to his full height, the butler swallowed. "Perhaps you'd like to leave a card?"

"Perhaps you'd like to tell your master to meet us in two minutes or we'll be leaving here with his head and no other part of him."

Going paler, if that was even possible, the butler said, "Of course, sir. Please wait in the living area." He waved to their right.

15

Venom prowled into the room as the butler scuttled away. He was aware of Holly shooting him a sideways look, but there was no fear in her, only a slight glee. "You enjoyed that, didn't you?"

"The butler has a repugnant taste for young flesh."

"Ugh. How come old vampires are so creepy?"

"I'll ask Dmitri."

"I'll punch you if you so much as mention that question to him," Holly threatened. "I don't mean Dmitri or Trace or other sane vampires. I mean the creepy ones that just get off on pain and ugliness." She poked at an ornate gold cushion edged with thick black satin rope. "Money clearly doesn't buy style."

Venom watched her take a seat on the equally ornate sofa, a small and deadly woman with acid green eyes who crossed her legs and watched the doorway. Her intense focus would surely terrify Kenasha. Amused by the idea, Venom moved to the left, so that Holly was who Kenasha would see when he walked in.

That happened moments later, the short and thickly built angel blustering in. It really took a lot of work for an angel to make himself unattractive—the angelic race was extraordinarily beautiful. So beautiful that an angel could still sometimes stop Venom's breath. He didn't want to own an angel as some vampires coveted. He didn't even want to sleep with one—he'd been there, done that, but he could admire their sheer physical beauty the same way he could a stunning work of art.

Kenasha, however, bucked the trend. His body was flaccid and without shape—and fat on an angel took serious commitment, as flight burned so much energy. His hair was a blond pompadour that might've been in style a few centuries back, but even then wouldn't have suited his round face.

His wings were patchy. In the three hundred and fifty years or so since Venom became a vampire, he'd *never* seen such a sight. The only times he'd observed angels missing feathers had been after an accident when they'd lost part of their wing and the feathers were in the process of regenerating. Kenasha, by contrast, appeared as if he'd fallen victim to a disease that was causing his feathers to waste away and drop off.

"What's the meaning of this?" the angel said in an exaggeratedly angry voice before freezing as his eyes landed on Holly. "Who are you?" It came out slightly squeaky.

Holly smiled slowly and didn't move a muscle. "Holly. And I *really* want to claw out your eyes, then crush your glistening eyeballs under the heel of my boot." Her smile never faded.

Kenasha gulped and took a stumbling step backward.

It took effort for Venom not to laugh. Keeping his expression impassive only through centuries of experience, he stepped out of the shadows. Kenasha swayed on his feet at first sight of Venom, though his wraith of a butler had to have clued him in as to the identity of his visitor.

"We have something to discuss," Venom said mildly. "You should sit."

The angel didn't argue, instead sinking into a large arm-chair that was a catastrophe of dark red and yellow and green. Ugly. Really ugly. Just like the being who occupied it—and Venom wasn't talking about Kenasha's physical appearance. "We found a vampire today who belongs to you. A female. Brown hair, blue eyes, thin."

"Oh." Kenasha's tensed shoulders relaxed. "I lent her to some friends of mine. She isn't lost. Thanks for coming to check."

As if Venom was the lost and found. "Holly," he said, warning in his voice, when he saw her start to uncross her legs.

"Just one eye," she said in a pleading tone so unlike her that he almost lost control and laughed.

Kenasha, however, took her seriously. "Look here," he said in a pompous manner, "I have every right to lend out a vampire who belongs to me. I pay for her blood, her room and board. I *own* her."

Venom felt the viper within uncurl. "Why is her Contract not registered with the Tower? Who transferred ownership to you?" Because that angel was also in deep trouble.

Tongue flicking out, Kenasha wet his lips. "She is post-Contract. Signed to serve me of her own free will."

If that was true, the Tower would have no reason to chastise him. But Venom was very, very good at sensing the ages of fellow vampires and Daisy had read as young to him. Extremely young. "Ask your butler to retrieve her papers so I can confirm." He continued to stare at the other man, unable to imagine how this creature was part of the same race as the magnificent being whom Venom chose to serve.

Kenasha didn't argue, calling in the wraith and sending him off to his study. They waited in silence, Holly staring unblinking at Kenasha the entire time. The four-thousand-year-old angel flushed, couldn't stay still in the hideous armchair.

"What happened to your wings?" Venom asked, wondering if he had to alert Dmitri to some kind of new disease. Angels weren't usually vulnerable to disease, but Charisemnon had gained the ability to infect immortals with disease in the Cascade. His last attempt had caused the Falling, when many angels fell out of the sky to lie broken on the earth. Perhaps he'd gotten more subtle in the intervening time.

"My wings?" Kenasha unfolded one and stared at it, as if he hadn't noticed the patchiness. "Oh, that. I think perhaps I ate something that didn't agree with me."

Venom caught the shiftiness of the angel's eyes, knew he was lying. But he held his silence and when he glanced at Holly, he saw that though she remained hotly angry, she was in control.

The butler walked in at that instant, the papers in his hand. Venom took them before dismissing the wraith. "This contract is dated four years ago." To be exact, it was dated a month after Raphael executed Uram, following a battle in the sky that had half destroyed Manhattan.

"Has it been that long?" Kenasha gripped the arms of his chair.

Venom scanned the document. It appeared to be in order—a female vampire named—

Well, that was intriguing.

The woman had agreed to serve Kenasha for twenty-five years in return for the "usual care." Foolish girl. A smart vampire would've asked for very specific terms and conditions.

Her signature was shaky, however, and the sole witness the wraith. "This contract is invalid." He threw the papers on the floor. "Your butler is not an impartial witness." The Tower did not meddle in the affairs of vampires who'd served out their Contract—they were adults who'd lived a hundred years already and were considered capable of making their own decisions.

However, despite the Tower's hands-off policy, there were certain rules in place to protect all parties. One of which was an impartial witness to any such contract. "Explain yourself." He walked close enough that he was looming over Kenasha.

The angel went red. "This is an outrage," he squeaked out. "I'm an angel. Your better."

Venom could've displayed very easily why this man was a bug to him, but he didn't want to play games. "Would you rather talk to Dmitri?" The leader of the Seven terrified most people—it was useful on occasion.

Kenasha lost all color in his face before slumping in his seat. "I found her," he confessed in a whisper, his throat moving as he swallowed. "She was half dead and in the Hudson. I saw her one day while I was flying and got curious, pulled her out." He shrugged. "I don't know why. I just thought it might be interesting to see a corpse."

It was a repulsive thing to say, but Venom didn't expect much else from Kenasha. "But she wasn't dead?"

"No, she was alive. And she was pretty then." He twisted his hands together. "I brought her home without thinking much about it."

"Liar." Holly's silken voice came from behind the angel.

Kenasha jumped, having clearly taken his eyes off her when Venom came closer.

Leaning over, Holly whispered in the angel's ear. "You wanted to fuck her, didn't you?"

Kenasha had frozen at the realization that he was surrounded by predators, but now jerked his head up and down. "I thought she'd be grateful I'd rescued her, and do things for me. That's not bad," he added. "I saved her life."

True enough—vampires couldn't drown, but a lack of

blood would've eventually made her so weak that the water and its creatures would've separated her head from her body. "How did you end up owning her?"

The angel's eyes shifted right. "She asked."

"Liar, liar," Holly whispered in Kenasha's other ear while scraping her nails delicately over his jugular.

Kenasha began to hyperventilate. "I wanted her!" he almost screamed. "She had something inside her that I wanted! I drank her blood and it was delightful! So I kept her!"

Venom's eyes met Holly's over the top of the angel's head. She looked as confused as he felt. "You drank *her* blood?"

"Yes. I've always liked a little blood and her blood smelled so good that I took a sip while she was unconscious." He shuddered in gross ecstasy. "It tasted so good, made me feel so powerful that I couldn't let her go."

"So she didn't agree to be your slave?"

Kenasha gave him a sly look. "It's her word against mine."

Leaving that for now because the not-very-bright angel had already incriminated himself many times over, Venom focused on the more interesting fact. "You felt good after drinking her blood? Any other effect?"

Kenasha opened out his wing again. "This. I didn't realize it until later, but my body couldn't process all the blood I was taking. That's why I started lending her out. When she's here, I can't stop feeding from her."

Venom saw the rage on Holly's face and shook his head slightly. She hissed but turned away to stalk to the other end of the room.

"Do others feed from her?" Venom asked.

"I never gave them permission for that!" Kenasha's tone rose. "I just told them they could use her as a toy. Her blood is mine!"

Obviously, the Tower techs needed to test Kenasha's blood and feathers to see why a young vampire's blood had caused such a strong negative reaction. That could be arranged easily enough. "Can you fly?"

"I'm weak," the angel admitted. "But I can get across the Hudson."

"I want you to go to the Tower and present yourself for blood and other tests. If you don't, I'll come to take the samples myself. Understood?"

"I'll do it now." A long breath, a shaky exhale. "It was *so* good. If you'd tasted her blood, you'd want to keep her, too. And, after a few months, she stopped fighting."

Venom didn't stop Holly this time. She sank her small, venomous fangs into Kenasha's neck and when she tore them back out, spitting on the floor to rid herself of his blood, the angel's body began to convulse in his chair, his eyes bulging out and his face a rictus of pain.

Venom stayed only long enough to make sure the angel was in no danger of death, then told the butler to take care of his master. "He will be expected at the Tower before dawn. Make sure he's there or the consequences will be infinitely worse than what he's currently experiencing."

The wraith bobbed his head so hard that Montgomery would've been mortified for his lack of poise. "Yes, sir."

Venom deliberately took Holly's hand as they walked out of the room. He didn't trust her not to go back and have another go at Kenasha. She actually curled her fingers around his palm and held on tight, as if she didn't trust herself, either.

Going out to the car, the air currently clear of rain, Venom opened the passenger door and waited for her to get in, then shut the door and made his way to the driver's side. "Feel better?"

She wiped the back of her forearm across her mouth. "Yes, except for the taste of el creepo I have in my mouth."

"Open the dash. There should be a bottle of energy drink in there."

Holly found it, took a swallow, and swirled it around her mouth before opening the door of the not-yet-moving car and spitting the mouthful on the ground. After shutting the door, she nodded. "That's better."

Venom started up the car, turned it, and headed back down the drive.

The dangerous woman in the passenger seat looked at him. "Why did you let me do that?"

"I didn't want to get the taste of el creepo in my own mouth."

Holly's laughter filled the car, and the otherness in Venom sat up and took notice all over again of this broken girl who'd become a fascinating, strong woman while he hadn't been looking. "There's one thing, Holly," he said, telling himself once again that she was far too young for him to play with.

"What?"

"The vampire's true name? It's Daisy."

16

Holly's mouth dried up, her tongue feeling too big for it.

Gulping more of the energy drink in sheer desperation, she said, "You're not messing with me, are you?"

"No. She signed the contract as Daisy Scaldini." Having already removed his sunglasses as per their agreement, he glanced at her out of eyes unique and stunning. "Did you meet her at some stage?"

"Not that I remember," Holly said, "but what other explanation is—" Mouth bone-dry again, she saw what he undoubtedly already had. "Do you think she was in that warehouse with me and my friends? That Uram did to her what he did to me?" And some part of Holly had remembered her, enough to pluck her name out of thin air.

"It's possible. Her fangs are smaller than is usual, but she doesn't have eyes like yours and she can't have the speed, or she'd have torn Kenasha to pieces by now."

"Not if he made her weak from the start." Holly's nails cut into her palms as the rain thundered down again. "It sounds like he abused her from the get-go—she probably never had the chance to grow into her strength."

Venom pulled onto the bridge. "Yes, and then there's the fact her blood caused Kenasha's feathers to rot. That's in no way a normal reaction."

"Jesus." Holly shuddered in her seat. "That *could* have been me," she said, horrified. "If it was a deviant like Kenasha who found me and not Elena and Raphael."

"You gave me trouble from the first, kitty." Venom's power twined around her in a silken twist as he spoke. "Your relentless will is your greatest strength."

The sinuous kiss of his power sliding across her, around her, it didn't make her shiver. It felt normal; this was who Venom was, the increase in strength a part of his natural growth. As for the rest . . . "I just wish Daisy had had the same chance," she said, her gut full of lead. "I wish I hadn't forgotten her."

"No one can fight an archangel determined to erase their memories," Venom said with a cool pragmatism that was weirdly comforting. "If Daisy was there, he made you forget her for a reason."

Mind clearing, Holly frowned. "Yes, why wipe her from my mind?" After all, he hadn't touched the ugly memories of her friends' torture and deaths.

"Right now, we can't be certain she *is* connected to Uram. I'm going to tell the Tower to run her blood against yours, see what comes up." After making the call, he said, "There's no point in speculating until we get the results."

Holly rubbed her face with one hand, then, gripping the energy drink bottle between her thighs, reached back to tighten her ponytail. "Damn it, if I have to say 'you're right' again, the earth will crack open and spew forth banjo-playing three-headed demons."

Venom's laugh was open and startled and deeply masculine. The sound washed across her senses, sank into her skin, going deep, so deep. Breath a little shallow, she forced herself to take another gulp of the drink in an effort to find a distraction. "Marlin," she said on a burst of inspiration. "Let's go talk to Marlin and see if his attempt to hook a big fish got a response."

Alas, for pudgy and bald Marlin, it appeared the fish had taken the bait. And gotten hungry when Marlin couldn't produce the payoff. "Okay," Holly said, staring down at the bloody, hacked-apart pieces of the vampire con artist and all-around slimy individual, "whoever is after me isn't only serious, they're *deadly* serious."

Having crouched down to examine the butchered remains placed in a neat pile in the middle of Marlin's living area, atop an unexpectedly tasteful Persian rug, Venom nodded. When strands of his hair slid forward, he pushed them back with an absent hand, his forearms flexing with casual power. She could see those forearms because he'd folded up his shirtsleeves to reveal skin she'd seen more than once already.

Today, however, the sight of that skin was doing strange things to her stomach.

"There's little doubt now that the killings are connected." He got up. "There hardly seems a point in checking the address of the third individual who tried to fool the buyer, but we should be thorough."

He called a Tower cleanup and forensics team first, however, the two of them not leaving until the team had taken charge of the scene. As for Janvier and Ash's snitches, they knew to scatter quick smart when someone of Venom's lethal power came in the vicinity. Payment for their work would come directly from Ash or Janvier.

The third address was in a slightly nicer part of town—the graffiti was classier and there were even potted plants in a few windows, but the scene inside their target apartment was a repeat of Marlin's. The only difference was that this time, the killer had piled the butchered pieces on top of the coffee table, the wooden floor below a mess of rust red streaks alongside larger coagulated pools of darker red.

This scene was also the oldest, the smell so putrid that even Venom stepped outside into the shared hallway to wait for the Tower team. "This isn't anger—the cuts are too precise, the way the body parts are piled up too theatrical," he said. "This is a message."

"Try to swindle me and you'll pay the price." Folding her arms, Holly tried to stand a little closer to Venom so she could draw the scent of him into her nostrils—she needed it to wipe out the noxious stink from inside the apartment. "Someone doesn't like having their time wasted."

"And is strong enough to have killed the vampire inside—unlike Marlin Tucker, this vamp was big, muscled. I also saw no signs of drug use that would've slowed his responses."

Holly scuffed her shoe on the floor. "I know I should focus on this psycho who's put a bounty on me, but I can't stop thinking about Daisy." About what the other woman had suffered, the horror followed by abuse and cruelty. "Don't let me near Kenasha unless you want him dead."

Uram was out of her reach, but Kenasha was very much within it.

Venom ran her ponytail through his fingers. "For a woman with unicorn hair, you're very bloodthirsty. I approve."

Holly smiled grimly; she had the feeling he, too, was considering the value of Kenasha's continued existence.

Dmitri looked them both up and down, a dark glint in his eyes that matched the night that had draped the city in black while they discovered two dead bodies, examined the locations, then waited for the Tower teams to arrive. The lights of Manhattan sparkled beyond the glass wall at Dmitri's back, the city finally free of rain, though black clouds continued to obscure the stars.

It looked more like midnight than six in the evening.

Dmitri stood with his hands braced on top of his desk, his arm muscles bunched tight. "I put you in charge so you'd control her," the leader of the Seven said to Venom.

Words shoved at Holly's throat, but she bit her lip. Venom didn't need her to fight his battles. As he proved right then.

"So you'd have patted Kenasha on the head and walked away after the piece of shit admitted to enslaving a half-drowned woman who didn't have the strength to stop him?" A raised eyebrow.

Dmitri's jaw clenched as he rose to his full height and folded his arms. "Keep the bastard out of my sight." It was a dangerously quiet statement. "I'd be tempted to tear off his head and then Raphael will have to deal with angels who think I'm too powerful."

"You *are* too powerful." Venom smiled. "That's why they're all so scared of you."

Dmitri's responding smile was of a kind he never gave Holly—it was between friends, between equals. Yet she didn't feel left out. Because her relationship with Dmitri was different. When he held out an arm, she went around and tucked herself under it. "I want to be in charge of finding out more about Daisy and what happened to her."

Dmitri hugged her a little closer to the hard strength of his body. "You can't lead yet, Holly. You haven't earned the right."

Again, because it was Dmitri who'd said those words, Holly could accept their truth. "Then give it to Venom and me together," she said, her eyes connecting with those of viper green.

Dmitri looked at Venom. "You're fine with handling this alongside the ongoing bounty situation?"

"Yes. Do you need me on security?"

His question reminded Holly that with Raphael gone, New York was vulnerable to an assault by another archangel.

It's all about politics, Honor had told Holly. *Successfully sacking the city that Raphael calls home and taking his Tower, his center of command, will have far more impact than an invasion of another part of the territory.*

"Is there a risk that Charisemnon or another archangel will attack?" she asked, her mind overflowing with images of blood and death from the last battle, a battle that had forced a mass evacuation of Manhattan.

It was Dmitri who answered. "No. They're all at the same meeting."

"Wow." Holly couldn't imagine the entire Cadre in one place. "Even Lijuan? I read online that no one's seen her for two years."

"Zhou Lijuan is AWOL," Dmitri confirmed.

That, Holly realized, was why the city was on high alert, why all the warrior angels and vampires had an edginess about them that wasn't normal. If the Archangel of China wanted to take New York, now was the best possible time. Its citizens, mortal and immortal, would all fight to the very end, but Zhou Lijuan was one of the Cadre—and only an archangel could kill or defeat another archangel.

"Clear up this situation with Holly as fast as you can," Dmitri told Venom. "We don't need groups of bounty hunters thinking they can come after a woman under the Tower's protection."

He pressed a kiss to the top of Holly's hair before releasing her. "As for Kenasha—he's always been a lazy waste of space, but your report on the condition of his wings concerns me. We need to make sure the vampire you rescued isn't a carrier of disease."

"We'll get to the bottom of it," Venom promised. "Let's go, kitty."

"I'd be delighted, Viper Face."

Lips curving slightly, he slipped on his sunglasses as they left Dmitri's office. "Daisy's our first stop."

"Why are you wearing your sunglasses in the Tower?"

"Because we're going to the infirmary level and the junior healers there don't often come into contact with me." His fingers brushed her lower back. "I try not to scare baby healers."

Her hand still itched to rip them off his face. "Do you think the healers will have a result on Daisy's bloodwork by now?"

"They haven't messaged me to say so, but that might be because they know I'm in the Tower and are expecting me to drop by."

The two of them stepped into the elevator side by side, rode down in silence. Every hair on Holly's body prickled, her skin suddenly acutely sensitive to Venom's presence. His face was pristine in profile, his skin glowing with health even under the artificial light. She wanted to touch it, rub her cheek against his like the kitten he called her.

Viper Face, Viper Face, Viper Face, she repeated mentally to snap herself out of the startling desire. *Yes, he's pretty. But he's also lethal, and I might yet become his prey if he discovers the mad, whispering voice inside me.*

Thank God the elevator doors were opening. Because the cold reminder to her psyche wasn't exactly working to calm the electric response of her body. Stepping out in front of him, she began to stride her way to the end of the corridor.

"Hollyberry, where are you going?"

She threw him a frowning look over her shoulder. "Daisy's in the isolation ward at the end." The Tower had built that ward after the Falling.

"How do you know?" Venom angled his head to the side in a way that wasn't human.

Holly parted her lips to reply . . . and had no answer. "Where else would they put her?" she said through a suddenly parched throat, her heart pounding.

"But you're not guessing, are you? You *know*."

"I can feel her," Holly admitted, realizing it was point-less to try to hide her reaction if she wanted to get to the bottom of the connection between her and the emaciated vampire.

"Smell? Sound? How?"

Shaking her head, Holly lifted a hand to a point between her heart and her stomach. Fisting it, she bumped that spot. "Here. I feel her here—like she's calling to me."

"I go first." Venom's face was hard. "If there is some-thing wrong with her, you're the more vulnerable."

Holly didn't even think about what she was doing—it wasn't a conscious decision at all. It was driven by the thing inside her. She pivoted on her foot and she ran. She had to get to Daisy first. Had to—

A strong arm around her waist, lifting her off her feet. Then Venom threw her harder than Ashwini or Janvier or Dmitri ever would. Hard enough that she flew back down the corridor . . . and connected with a wall in a liquid slide. None of her bones broke, nothing bruised, her body ending up in a crouch on the carpet in a way that had her blinking as she snapped back into control.

"What just happened?" she whispered half to herself, half to the man who was watching her from the other end of the corridor.

His fangs flashed. "Don't try that again or I'll really throw you."

Holly rose to her feet, and it felt as if she was melting her bones back into place. "This is seriously weird. Why am I not in pieces?" She moved gingerly toward Venom, afraid she'd imagined the whole thing.

"You trusted your instincts." Turning his back to her, Venom began to stride toward the isolation chamber.

Deep as Holly's confusion was about what had just occurred—both her mad flight in Daisy's direction and her subsequent liquid fall—she ran to catch up. But this time, she stopped a footstep to Venom's left. She had no desire to be thrown again when she didn't know how she'd saved herself the first time.

Not sure the thing inside her would behave, however, she took Venom's hand.

He didn't question why she was reaching out to him voluntarily, just wrapped his fingers firmly around hers. Warm and strong, his hand held a power that told her she wouldn't be breaking free; for once, Holly was glad of a leash. Losing her mind and acting erratically because of the whispering otherness inside her wasn't exactly high on her to-do list. "How did you know I'd make it?"

A shrug. "I didn't. But you wouldn't have died."

Holly punched him on the arm. "Asshole." But she was more astonished than angry—because Venom, of all people, was the only individual who never treated her as broken. He expected her to take care of herself.

Showing no reaction to her hit, his body undoubtedly sleekly muscled, Venom squeezed her hand. And because he'd thrown her down the hallway, expecting her to survive it—because he believed she had the *capability* to do so— she didn't fight the connection. The palm-to-palm touch felt peculiarly intimate, the essence of him pulsing through his veins and speaking to a craving inside her.

It wasn't vampiric hunger. Deeper than that.

Then he was opening the door to the outer unit of the isolation chamber by punching in a code on the electronic keypad and they were walking through.

17

The door closed automatically behind them, leaving them in front of a large window that provided a view into the isolation area beyond: Daisy lay strapped down in a white hospital bed. She'd been given a bath, her hair appearing clean and dry, but she was clearly not doing well.

As Holly watched, the other woman wrenched up off the bed and twisted hard enough that she'd have broken bones if she hadn't been strapped down. Holly continued to feel a tearing sympathy for the abused vampire, but even she could tell that the twisting wasn't simply the scrabbling panic of a woman who'd been made helpless in a strange place.

Her teeth were bared to reveal small fangs just a little bigger than Holly's, inhuman growls and grunts erupting from her throat and filling the observation chamber when Venom pushed a button to the side of the window.

"It's like she's possessed." Nausea churning inside her, Holly stepped closer to the window. "She doesn't look like the scared but sane woman we saved." Daisy's face was viciously contorted, her eyes swirls of rampant madness.

Was this what lay in Holly's future?

A healer entered the observation chamber even as the chilling thought iced Holly's blood. "She has no indications of disease," he said in that gentle healer way, the wings that arced behind his shoulders to nearly touch the floor a rich cream interspersed with feathers of sparrow brown. "We're keeping her inside because it's the easiest way to control her—and keep her safe—if she finds the strength to break those straps. The entire floor can be locked down with the flick of a switch."

"Is that a possibility?" Venom asked as Holly pressed her hand to the glass in a vain effort to calm Daisy.

The healer sighed. "She's emaciated and even the blood you fed her shouldn't have done much more than ease her hunger. It shouldn't have given her any kind of strength. But as you can see . . ." A wave toward the wrenching, twisting woman on the bed. "Yet her madness doesn't feel like blood-lust to healer senses. We'll need to monitor her longer to have any hope of working out the demons that hold her captive."

Holly's fingers clenched around Venom's palm. "I need to go in there," she said, the healer's words just a background buzz by the end.

Venom didn't stop her when she released his hand and walked to open the inner door, but she was aware of his prowling presence at her back, ready to intercede should Daisy break her bonds. Her heart pounded, her skin hot, the mad whisper silent in her head. She turned the knob, stepped inside.

Daisy stopped twisting. Her head snapped toward Holly.

And the *thing* inside Holly, it spread its jagged wings with so much force that she slammed back into Venom, her hands reaching back to claw into his thighs. Panic gripped her throat in a brutal hold, cutting off her air as the otherness tried to shove out through her skin. In the hospital bed, Daisy fought her straps to strain toward Holly, her eyes pleading and red-rimmed with insanity at the same time.

Venom's arms came around Holly, bands of heated metal that shoved her back into herself, crushing the strange, serrated wings that scraped at her insides. One of his hands closed over her shoulder, his arm across her body, and then his lips were at her ear. *"Fight."* It was an order.

Holly wanted to tell him she wasn't exactly hula dancing right now, but she was trying too hard not to come apart at the seams. When her head dipped, when her fangs shoved against her lips, water lining her tongue, she didn't even think about it. She sank her teeth into Venom's upper forearm.

It wasn't a good place for blood, but the taste was enough.

Power punched through her, a power so deadly and arrogant that it immediately cleared her head.

Releasing him, she breathed harsh, deep breaths, her eyes locked with Daisy's. The other woman's cracked lips parted, the whites of her irises suddenly awash in crimson. "It's calling to you," she said in a guttural tone. "It wants to be together." Her back arched in a spinal curve so brutal that Holly reached out a hand, wanting to push her down before she broke her back.

And a . . . *what-the-fuck* exploded out of Daisy, moving so fast that not even Venom's speed could save Holly. It slammed straight into her chest and burrowed in.

Venom swore as Holly crumpled in his arms, her body suddenly dead weight. Scooping her up, he backed out while yelling for the healer. The wide-eyed angel was beside them in a heartbeat. The man put his fingers to Holly's throat, checked her pulse, listened to her breathing. "She's alive," he said definitively.

Venom went to tear open Holly's black shirt to expose

the wound . . . but there wasn't a mark on her clothing. No burn. No tear. No bloodstain. He unbuttoned her shirt regardless, but there wasn't a mark on the smooth cream of her skin, either. But he hadn't imagined it. A substance or an entity had come out of the vampire on the bed and punched itself into Holly.

Yet Holly's skin was warm and smooth under his fingers, her chest rising and falling in a shallow rhythm. "Explain this."

The healer shook his head, his thin woven braids falling around his face as he examined Holly. "I can't."

Laying Holly on the carpeted floor of the observation chamber with conscious gentleness, Venom walked back into the much more medically spartan isolation room and toward the motionless body of the vampire they'd rescued.

Daisy wasn't moving, wasn't breathing, her head having flopped to one side. Dark strands of hair obscured her face. When he got close enough to move that hair aside with care to ensure she didn't sink her fangs into his wrist, he spotted a trickle of blood coming out of her nose. More blood dripped out of the corner of her mouth.

The scarlet stain on the white sheet below her was already significant.

It was often difficult to tell if a vampire was dead. They were almost-immortals, after all. Usually, the only way to be sure was to cut off a vampire's head or take out the heart. Though Venom could easily survive heart loss, as could the other vampires in the Seven. He was also near-certain that Dmitri was strong enough now that separating his head from his body would take the strength of an archangel.

As Venom had told Holly, Dmitri had been a warrior through time—add his potent raw power to that, and the structural foundations of his body might as well be formed of iron at this point.

"Venom." A senior healer's voice. "Let me through."

Venom stepped aside for the diminutive angel with wings of dark gray spotted with white. "Check her heart."

The healer—Nisia—already had her small, narrow hands on Daisy's chest. "The heart's gone, exploded inside her chest cavity from what I can tell." She frowned, as if peering deep within the sickly thin vampire's body. "Her other organs are also liquid." She indicated the slight swelling of Daisy's belly as fluid built inside the body cavity. "The poor tormented child is dead."

"She won't heal?"

"No. She was too weak to ride out the damage—especially with the loss of her heart."

Venom glanced back to make sure Holly wasn't alone. Seeing that the other healer was still kneeling beside her, his hands gentle on her as he continued to check her for injuries, Venom focused his attention on Daisy. "Something came out of her and went into Holly."

"I cannot sense an answer," Nisia said. "But Illium suggested we monitor this room in new ways." She waved vaguely toward the corners of the room.

Venom looked up.

Cameras.

"Do an autopsy," he ordered, making an effort to keep his tone respectful. Nisia was a trusted member of the Tower team and one who'd earned Venom's respect in the brutal aftermath of the Falling. "Don't remove her from isolation. We'll destroy her body here if need be."

The healer's soft brown gaze went to Holly. "That child should be in isolation, too."

Venom thought of how Holly had known where Daisy was being kept, of how she'd felt the compulsion to go inside the isolation chamber, and shook his head. "It's done now. Holly's not going to infect anyone." *She'd* been the target.

And he'd allowed her to walk in, believing he could protect her from all possible threats. Cold fury in his blood, directed at his own arrogance.

"No," Nisia murmured, her eyes still on Holly. "Whatever this is, it is not, I think, about anything as simple as disease."

Stepping out into the observation chamber to find that the healer had buttoned Holly's shirt back up, Venom bent down to scoop her up into his arms. She was so small. Sometimes, he forgot that. He'd forgotten it when he threw her down the hall—when she was awake and aware, all he saw was the wild, inhuman energy of her. An energy that was the closest to his own that he'd ever glimpsed.

There is no one like me. But Andi sees inside me, and knows me, and we have secrets together. And one day, we'll have cubs who'll be half like me.

Naasir's joy at his mating had made absolute sense to Venom, though he wasn't sure his friend and fellow member of the Seven had understood how deeply the words resonated. To the world, Venom was a vampire. And there were millions of vampires. But he was the only one with the eyes of a viper and the deeper, less visible changes that shoved him far outside that well-defined box.

Like Naasir, he was and had always been alone among millions. Until Holly.

"Come on, kitty." He cradled her higher against his chest. "You've said 'fuck you' to fate before. Do it again."

But for once, Holly didn't give him lip. She was silent and unmoving in his arms as he took her upstairs to his apartment. Ignoring the comfortable bed in his bedroom, he went straight to the heated stone floor in front of the windows. Placing her on there, he went to find a blanket . . . and by the time he returned, she'd curled into a tight ball, one hand spread palm down against the stone.

His entire chest expanded as he finally took a real breath.

Shaking out the soft cashmere blanket over her, he made a note to thank Naasir. It was the most primal member of the Seven who'd suggested the stone floor.

I make my lair outside the Refuge, because I like it out there. But my aerie is hot because I don't like snow. A shiver, the metallic silver of his eyes wild in a way that was nothing human. *You like the city, but you need your sunstone. Make one.*

Venom had never thought of it that bluntly, but in his defense, he'd been very young and not used to the freedom to create his own home when Naasir had discovered him searching fruitlessly for the heated stone surface his body craved. His first sunstone had been just that—a large flat stone that he'd dragged over from a distant spot and kept in the wild gardens that had once surrounded the Tower.

As the Tower morphed into its current form and the gardens disappeared to be filled with the manic, beautiful life of New York, he'd worked with the architects to create this sunstone deep inside his home. Deciding Holly needed a little extra heat, he switched on the large lamp that covered the entire ceiling above the sunstone.

The square of ceiling blazed to glowing life.

She sighed in her sleep.

Crouching down, he undid her ponytail so she'd be comfortable, then removed her boots and put them aside. That done, he watched to make sure her chest was rising and falling, her pulse steady. Because Holly wasn't a vampire. Not quite. She was human enough that such things were an absolute necessity for her survival.

When his phone buzzed in his pocket, he realized he'd become mesmerized by the rhythm of her, as if it spoke to the cobras that had been part of his Making alongside the vipers. That hadn't happened to him for a long time. Venom was very aware of his weaknesses as well as his strengths. But this was his home and it was filled with people who'd protect him to their last breath.

They didn't—*couldn't*—truly understand the sinuous core of him, but they were his friends.

His family.

And so he'd lowered his guard enough to slip into a state that was deeply restorative.

Rising to his feet after running his knuckles over Holly's cheek, he stepped away from her and the sunstone before answering the call. "Dmitri," he said. "Nisia called you, didn't she?"

"Inexplicable as it is, our competent and strong Nisia is intimidated by you, when she has been known to pat me on the cheek and ruffle my hair," was the bone-dry response.

Venom took off his sunglasses and set them aside. His eyes reflected back at him from the sleek square mirror on the wall that had been a gift from Elena. The two of them weren't exactly best friends, but the mate of his sire had owed him a forfeit after he beat her in a sparring session where they'd both had to fight using unfamiliar weapons.

She'd paid the forfeit with this mirror. At first, he'd thought it a somewhat unimaginative, though acceptable, payment. Then he'd noticed the delicate motif carved into the left white edge of the frame—a viper hanging off a tree. It was beautifully done. *Aodhan's work*, he'd realized at once. Done specifically for him.

Sometimes Elena made it very difficult to be annoyed with her for the weakness she'd created in the archangel Venom chose to serve. She was the only chink in Raphael's armor, and his Seven had come to terms with it—but that didn't mean they were all okay with it.

"Holly isn't infectious," Venom said. "Whatever it was that came out of Daisy, it *only* wanted to go to Holly." He felt the truth of that in his gut. "I don't know of any disease that punches out of a person and into another."

"I'm going to look at the footage. You want to meet me in the tech room?"

Venom glanced over at where Holly slept so peacefully.

She'd been here before, wouldn't be disoriented if she woke alone. "Yes."

It was time to uncover the shape of the thing that had burrowed into Holly.

The same thing that had lived inside a vampire who'd gone utterly insane in the hours before her death.

18

Dmitri was already in the elevator when Venom stepped into it; from the other man's tumbled hair and the faint scent of cold night air that clung to him, Venom figured he'd been up on the roof.

The leader of the Seven shot him an assessing look. "Holly's getting under your skin."

"She always has," Venom admitted to a friend who'd never betray him. "But she needs a little seasoning." Needed to get tougher . . . else, she'd never survive the immortal world. "You've all been protecting her under the guise of keeping an eye on her."

Dmitri's expression was amused. "I'm not exactly known to be a soft touch."

"Let her go, Dmitri," Venom said quietly. "We need to find out what she's capable of—but she needs to learn the truth about herself most of all." He held the other vampire's dark eyes, only then realizing he'd forgotten his sunglasses upstairs. "Release the chains."

Dmitri didn't answer until they were outside the elevator

and in the lighted corridor that led to the circular room of the Tower's tech core. Windows lined the entire hallway, would've poured the colors of New York inside had it been morning. "That could be deadly," the other man said at last. "Not just for others, but for Holly."

"If you don't release her soon, she'll die anyway," Venom said flatly. "She's a wild thing. Not built for a cage." He ran his fingers through his hair. "Neha . . . she understood me even if she was no gentle mistress. She gave me the freedom to figure out what the fuck I'd become." For the first five years after his Making, he hadn't been "human" even in the vampiric sense.

"There's a critical difference between you and Holly," Dmitri reminded him.

"Uram."

"Uram." Dmitri began walking again, the two of them going to the tech center in silence.

Vivek was waiting for them. His breath caught when they entered, and Venom quickly realized it was the first time the other man had faced his eyes unshielded. "Do you have infrared vision?" Interest glittered on his face.

Venom smiled, the curious reaction a far preferable one to quivering fear or horror. "You'll have to court me with roses and diamonds before asking such intimate questions."

Vivek snorted. "It's just like working for the Guild—place is full of smartasses." He swiveled his wheelchair around. "I've already cued up the footage in the private viewing room." That room lay behind his gleaming control station, and it boasted three massive screens, each taking up most of a wall.

The video from the isolation room was cued up on the wall directly opposite the door.

Vivek waited for them to shut that door before he started to play the recording. "This is slowed down a hundred times," the Guild Hunter said. "That's how deep I had to go to see anything."

Venom could see movement at far faster speeds, so the recording progressed at a glacial pace for him, but it proved useful in picking up all the details. It was a glowing red spark that had erupted from Daisy. Not even fist sized. Nowhere close. Maybe the size of a quarter. But it had slammed into Holly with phenomenal force.

"I felt that," he said as the moment of impact played out on the screen. "It was like she'd taken a punch from a heavyweight boxer. The impact flowed through her body to mine."

"But nothing penetrated your body?"

Venom shook his head in response to Dmitri's question. "It was aimed only at Holly, wanted only Holly." He didn't know if he could explain it, but he tried. "It wasn't a random eruption—it waited until Holly was within reach, so close that she couldn't avoid the impact. And Daisy spoke to Holly beforehand, said something about being together."

"Audio caught that." Vivek rewound the tape.

"It's calling to you. It wants to be together."

The guttural words, Daisy's voice far deeper than it should be, were clearly directed at Holly.

"Run it forward again." Feet set apart and arms folded, Dmitri looked at the screen with grim attention. "Zoom in on whatever it was that jumped from the vampire to Holly."

Vivek did so in silence. The red spark was actually a very small ball with a spiked surface . . . and its heart pulsed an acidic green.

"Fuck." Venom knew that color—it was the same shade as Holly's eyes had become. "Uram definitely touched Daisy, changed her."

"Get Kenasha in here now," Dmitri said, his tone unbending.

"He'll be incapacitated for a little while longer."

"No, he won't." Ice in every word. "I'll choke him on my own blood if I have to, to fight the effect of Holly's venom, but he's going to speak to us *right now*."

"My blood will work better." It'd counteract the venom

faster. "Illium's in a pissy mood. I'll ask him to go out—he'll enjoy dragging in an asshole." The blue-winged angel usually had the most joie de vivre of the Seven, but when Venom had searched him out yesterday prior to heading to the sparring circle to watch Dmitri, Ash, and Janvier, he'd found the other man brooding on the roof.

Illium was powerful, violently so, and as darkly angry as he was at the moment, he'd scare the piss out of Kenasha. That worked well with Venom's sense of justice.

"Do it," Dmitri said.

Leaving without further words, Venom made his way to one of the railingless Tower balconies and scanned the sky. He could talk to the sire with his mind, the gift one fostered in him by Raphael. He didn't, however, have the ability to reach out to others in the Seven on his own—not yet. But he didn't need it.

He had a phone.

Not spotting Illium's distinctive silver-edged blue wings in the sky and well aware the angel loved all things technologically inclined, he made the call. Illium answered in an unusually curt tone. "Yes?"

"I need a favor. A pickup. He enslaved a woman when she was too weak to say no."

"You always give me the best gifts. Where?"

Venom gave him the location before adding, "Holly bit him, so he'll be a little out of it."

Laughter down the line, Illium sounding more like himself when he said, "I've always liked your little kitty."

Venom's hand clenched on the phone. He had to fight the urge to tell Bluebell not to call Holly that—that was a *private* game between him and Holly. "Thanks for the pickup."

"No problem." Illium hung up and, less than five seconds later, Venom saw his form arrow out of the sky to skim above the tops of the brightly lit skyscrapers. He was a bullet as he crossed the Hudson, going so low there that his passage agitated the water into crashing waves.

Yeah, the laughing angel known as Bluebell was *not* in a good mood.

Sliding his hands into the pockets of his pants, Venom decided to wait for Illium to return. That he wanted to go back to his suite and check on Holly was another reason he forced himself to stay in place. The last time he'd felt even a faint glimmer of this type of protectiveness about a woman, she'd been his betrothed, and look how fucking well that had turned out.

And while Holly had grown up, she remained a baby in comparison to him. He wasn't about to put his hands on her—well, he might throw her around to teach her to embrace the power inside her, but he wasn't about to fuck her. Not even if his body was starting to stir more and more that way each time he saw her.

"Jesus." He shook his head as he spotted Illium over the waters of the Hudson once again; even for Bluebell, the speed of the pickup was extraordinary. The angel was holding Kenasha carelessly with one hand on the back of the other angel's neck. Kenasha's wings drooped uselessly. The wasted-away appendages had to be creating massive drag, but Illium didn't look strained in the least.

There was a reason certain archangels had put out feelers to lure Illium to their side, to take up a position as their second. Many believed the increasingly strong angel must be starting to chafe at holding a lower position in the Tower hierarchy than Dmitri. But Illium's answer had always been a flat no.

He'd chosen his loyalty and it wasn't only to Raphael, but to the Seven.

"Dmitri's more experienced and he's known the sire since the sire was young enough that Raphael treats him as an equal," the angel had once said to Venom. "I, meanwhile, was once a baby angel Raphael rescued from a river after I took a dunking. The next time I fell in, it was Dmitri who plucked me out."

He'd laughed, golden eyes dancing. "I'm not meant to be Raphael's second, or to hold a position above Dmitri. Power isn't everything—the bonds that tie us to one another, forged by emotion and battle and friendship, that's what makes us strong." A silver-edged feather of wild blue had drifted down to the ground from his wings as he resettled them. "No, I'm meant to occupy exactly the place I hold among us."

That soul-deep bond would change one day in the distant future, Illium's destiny written in his power. But it would never break. The Seven would always have each other's—and Raphael's—back. As the Archangel Elijah would never move against the Archangel Caliane.

He'd once been her most trusted general, carried that loyalty in his heart to this day.

Less than half a minute later, Illium dropped Kenasha's quivering body on the balcony in front of Venom's feet. "That was quick," Venom commented.

Landing on the balcony, Illium folded back his wings. "I was racing myself," he said, his eyes turbulent with emotions that were starkly *human* in a way it was rare to see in an immortal of Bluebell's age and power.

"Who'd you fight with? Ellie?" Of all the Seven, it was Illium who was closest to Raphael's hunter consort. "No? Then it has to be Aodhan." The other angel—and fellow member of the Seven—was Illium's best friend. Two wholly different men in personality, Illium and Aodhan had known each other since childhood. Sometimes, when they sparred in the air, it was like watching two halves of a whole, their reactions were so in sync.

Illium didn't answer, his jaw grinding. "Why do your friend's wings look like those of a half-plucked chicken?" he asked just as Dmitri exited onto the balcony. "I do like the rhythmic twitching, though."

"That's Holly's work." It was obvious her venom was yet causing Kenasha considerable pain.

"This makes me sad," Dmitri said without an ounce of sympathy. "Sad for all the children who might've seen this creature and thought him an example of angelkind."

"Don't worry," Venom replied in as cold a tone. "He doesn't fly. Daisy's blood did something to him."

Dmitri knelt beside the angel whose eyes were bulging out of his head—whether in pain or fear, Venom couldn't tell. "Hold him still."

Lip curling at the idea of touching the other man, Venom nonetheless knelt down and did as asked so that Dmitri could use the syringes he held in his hand to take blood samples. He held out both capped syringes toward Illium. "Fly these down to the infirmary so they can start on the tests. Gentle hold. You don't want to accidentally crush one and get contaminated by the blood."

Gingerly taking the samples, Illium said, "I have no desire to look like a plucked chicken. Been there, have no wish to repeat the experience." A pause. "Though . . . to be clear, I looked more like a fluffy duck—cute, not as if I had a molting disease." Illium was gone in a wash of wind seconds later.

Venom had seen Illium's feathers regenerating after an accident, but he was also aware the angel had once been stripped of his feathers as punishment for the crime of speaking angelic secrets to a mortal woman he mourned to this day. The latter had been before Venom's time. "Were Illium's feathers different before he lost them the first time?" he asked Dmitri, realizing he'd just assumed they'd regenerated identical to the original.

Dmitri gripped Kenasha's mouth, forced it open with the vise of his grip.

Ready, Venom used his pocketknife to slice his own wrist open, then dripped the blood into the contemptible angel's mouth.

"No," Dmitri said as Kenasha's throat began to move spasmodically. "Our Bluebell didn't have the silver then."

A faint smile. "He was vain before. Imagine how much worse he got when glittering threads of silver began to appear in among the filaments."

"When you're this beautiful," Illium said, coming up to hover on the other side of the balcony, "you have no choice but to be vain." He buffed his nails on his arm, then blew on them, and at that instant, he was once more the angel Venom knew: intelligent and generous and with a warm playfulness to him.

Most immortals had lost that playfulness long ago. Even Venom.

Kenasha choked and spluttered but Dmitri was relentless. Venom could easily donate this much blood within a short period of time, but he'd have to feed soon to make up for it. He wouldn't be weak if he didn't, but he'd be weak*er*, and Venom preferred to be at full strength. When his wrist began to heal, he slit it open again.

It took a lot longer than he'd estimated for Kenasha's body to stop quivering.

"Holly's strong," he murmured, pleased deep within.

"Want a bite?" Illium held out his own wrist. "This is first-class blood, available only to a select few."

Venom felt his lips kick up. "Thanks." He had no problem taking blood from his fellow members of the Seven—as he had no problem donating blood in turn. And when it came to Illium, he only had to drink a small amount.

Bluebell packed a punch.

Not as strong as Raphael, but more than strong enough that one day, Venom knew he'd look up into the sky and see an archangel with wings of bluebell blue glittering with silver threads.

His heart ached when he thought of that distant moment in time.

How much worse must it be for Dmitri, who'd watched both Illium and Aodhan grow up? Because as the moon followed the sun, when Illium ascended to become an archangel, Aodhan would go with him as his second. The angel with wings of shattered light had been the hardest of the Seven for Venom to get to know . . . and yet he'd given Venom an extraordinary gift.

"You're strong," Aodhan had said quietly a century earlier. "Your eyes might be of a viper, but you have the heart of a lion. You demand the world bow to you. I wish I had your courage, Venom."

As Illium's blood hit his bloodstream, Venom felt his veins pulse and hoped Aodhan was finding his own lion's heart in Lumia, where the angel had accompanied Raphael and Elena for the meeting of the Cadre. That lion's heart had always been there; Aodhan was a warrior through and through. He'd lost his faith in himself after an act of horror that nearly ended his light—but that faith, it was coming back. And an Aodhan Venom had only ever glimpsed was emerging.

"Thanks," he said, lifting his head from Illium's wrist after about ten seconds. "Janvier told me Elena's company is doing flavored premium blood now." It always struck him as hysterical that the Guild Hunter had fallen into a business that catered to a strictly vampiric clientele.

"It's one of *the* hot new businesses in Manhattan, according to *Immortal Insider* magazine." Illium ran his fingers through his hair, the blue-tipped black strands falling back in place around his face afterward. "You should go visit one of their blood cafés," he said with a straight face belied by the amusement in his eyes. "It'll give the business a big publicity boost among the fashionable crowd."

Venom snorted, not about to become a poster boy for *flavored* blood. What the fuck?

"I think our guest is fully compos mentis." Dmitri rose to his feet.

So did Venom, while Illium continued to hover just off the edge in a casual display of brutal strength. They gave Kenasha the courtesy of allowing him to get to his feet, though it was a dubious courtesy at best, since the angel looked scared stiff of the precipitous drop mere feet away. And that was beyond pitiful. As an angel, the other man should've been far more comfortable here than either Venom or Dmitri.

Then again, his wings appeared even more useless now that he was standing. The muscles and tendons drooped, like those of a marionette with its strings cut. "Are you sure you're not sick?" Venom asked, concerned for Illium and the other Tower angels.

"If I am, it's because of Daisy's blood," Kenasha whined. "She did something to me."

"Are any of your angelic friends displaying similarly wasted wings?"

Kenasha paled under the midnight cold of Dmitri's voice, a trembling figure framed by the lights of a city that didn't know the meaning of sleep. "No. I didn't tell any of them about her blood. I'm the only one who drank from her." He ran shaky hands down his front in a futile effort to smooth the wrinkles in the bruise-colored velvet of his ornate topcoat. It was embellished with two strips of yellow brocade and frog closures.

Venom wondered what Holly would think of Kenasha's sartorial choice.

Dmitri made fleeting eye contact with Venom, passing the baton, since Venom knew more about the situation. The problem was that Kenasha couldn't meet Venom's eyes—his terror of Venom's gaze was worse than the general fear that clung to him and stunk up the air. No matter. It wasn't like the angel could lie his way out of this, not with Venom, Dmitri, and Illium all focused on his quivering face.

"Tell us *exactly* how you found Daisy."

19

Kenasha repeated the story of rescuing Daisy from the Hudson. "After I realized she wasn't a corpse, I thought I'd be a hero," he whispered. "Like the other people who helped during the Falling. I thought if she was important, I'd be able to tell everyone I'd rescued her."

Venom wanted to slap the self-obsessed prick. "What did she tell you about how she ended up in the river?"

Kenasha shifted his feet. And Dmitri spoke with silken menace. "It seems you'd prefer to have this conversation with the sire."

The angel looked so horrified at the idea that it was comical. Venom could actually feel Dmitri's grim amusement. There weren't many people who wanted to come face to face with the Archangel of New York. Venom had never understood that—he knew Raphael burned with power, but he wasn't capricious or cruel without reason.

Yes, he ruled with a steel hand. However, that hand didn't get involved in the petty business of people's lives.

"No, no." Kenasha tugged at the white ruffles poking out

of the top of his coat; it was a miracle he didn't choke in the
froth. "Daisy said she was attacked by an angel who picked
her up and flew her across the city to a warehouse. She escaped from him when he was glutted on blood, somehow
ending up in the river—she couldn't remember the details
of how. I think she was probably hallucinating and disoriented because of the drugs. We all know angels don't get
blood-glutted."

Illium, Dmitri, and Venom had all gone predator-still
halfway through Kenasha's monologue.

"When?" Venom asked softly.

Face stark white, the other man didn't try to prevaricate.
"Not long before Raphael fought Uram in the sky."

His ignorance of how the two events were connected
wasn't a surprise. The Tower had managed to keep the details of Uram's unprecedented descent into insanity and
murder limited to a tight group of people. The world did not
need to know that the vastly powerful beings who ruled
them could fall prey to ravening madness.

"What else did she say about the attack on her?" Venom
pressed.

Kenasha frowned, and Venom could almost hear the
gears in his brain grinding as he thought back. That, at
least, wasn't an affectation. The old immortals weren't always good at keeping track of their memories—or even
storing them in a linear fashion. They'd lived so long that
their memories were tangled skeins it took time to unravel.

"She said he plucked her up from the street while she was
walking to work." Kenasha's frown grew deeper. "I knew she
must've been on drugs when she told me that no one could
see her, even though she struggled to free herself."

Glamour.

Not every archangel possessed it, but the ones who did
could also disappear objects and people held close to their
body, the field of glamour not limited to their own flesh.

"Then she said the angel fed on her blood and put himself in her." Kenasha shrugged. "She was quite pretty before so I can understand why the angel wanted to use her in such a way."

Venom felt ice crawl through his veins. "Those were her exact words? That the angel 'put himself *in* her'?"

Kenasha nodded. "I remember because . . ." Going red, he clammed up.

Illium chose that second to buffet his wings, creating a churning eddy of wind that nearly sucked the other angel off the edge.

Squeals leaving his mouth, Kenasha scrabbled for purchase.

"Talk," Dmitri said without mercy.

Chest heaving where he'd collapsed on the floor, Kenasha blubbered. "I remember because I was thinking how delicious it would be to take a woman who'd already been claimed by a much more powerful angel—he had to be powerful, didn't he? I mean, he'd flown her all the way across Manhattan."

Illium just shook his head. Venom knew that carrying a single human or vampire didn't make most angels break a sweat—Elena was an exception, her immortal strength yet growing in her bones, and still, she could already carry children. When it came to the angel-born, even the youngest Tower angel, Izak, could pull off carrying an adult any day of the week with one arm tied behind his back.

Illium, in contrast, could stop helicopters and planes.

He'd infamously turned a chopper upside down in midair after the paparazzi began to pursue Elena as if she was a mortal they could hound at will. Needless to say, the consort had never again had to deal with such dangerous tactics from the press.

Kenasha, Venom thought, was—*what was the word Holly had used?*—yes, a deadbeat. The angelic equivalent of the work-shy mortal slob who sat on his parents' couch, sucked up all their energy and money, and came to eventually resemble a tub of lard.

No strength, no muscle. No backbone.

"What else?" Venom asked this particular tub of lard.

A blank look. "That was it. I never did take her. I tasted her blood, you see," he whispered on a disgusting shiver of pleasure, "and afterward, it was all I wanted from her."

Venom prowled closer, causing Kenasha to scramble back until he was a hairsbreadth from the edge and a fall that shouldn't be deadly to an angel of his age—except that Kenasha had made himself so weak that it was highly probable he'd turn to red paste intermingled with rivers of fat when he hit the ground.

It was an amusing visual Venom would have to share with Holly. "When you say it was before Raphael's fight with Uram," he said, "exactly how much time are we talking?"

Gulping, Kenasha tugged at his frothy collar again. "Um, the day before? Yes, I think so. The day before."

That meant there was a good chance Daisy had been taken around the same time as Holly and her friends. It was highly possible the two women had been in close proximity to one another, their fractured memories hiding the truth but not managing to erase it out of existence.

I thought you were dead. I'm so sorry. I thought you were dead.

Daisy's chilling words made all too much sense now. The other woman had escaped Uram but left Holly behind because she believed Holly was already dead. Venom couldn't judge her for that belief, not when he'd seen the carnage Uram had created—it would've been difficult to separate the living from the dead in that charnel house, especially if Holly had been unconscious at the time and Daisy mentally disoriented.

"Look at me," Venom said to the gutless creature who'd stolen any chance Daisy had to reclaim a life for herself. "That is not a request."

Kenasha lifted his face, his lips trembling. All it took was an instant of connection with a man this weak, and

Venom had him mesmerized. The angel was his puppet now. Venom took him through the whole sequence of questioning again, adding a few new ones along the way.

The answers were the same. "He didn't lie."

"You realize that is extremely creepy?" Illium had come to stand on the balcony a couple of minutes earlier, and now waved his hand up and down in front of Kenasha's face. "What would he do if you asked him to jump off the balcony?" he asked in an intrigued tone.

"Don't," Dmitri said before Venom could demonstrate. "I'd just have to waste a Tower team's time on scraping him up."

Venom lifted his hands, palms out, to Illium. "Sorry." Then he glanced at Dmitri. "What will you do with him?"

"He'll be losing those wings first of all." Dmitri's expression held no mercy. "I don't care what he says—we have to eliminate any risk to the other angels in the city. Then he'll be under house arrest until Raphael's return. Kenasha's a coward and a self-centered piece of shit, but he's old enough that his punishment should come directly from the sire."

After a short pause, the leader of the Seven added, "I wouldn't worry that he'll get off easy; Raphael has a dim view of enforced captivity." Dark, unsaid things in his tone. "Daisy didn't choose to take a Contract. Nor did she choose to become a blood donor. Kenasha has no defense for his actions."

"I can do the wing slice now," Illium volunteered, sliding out a heavy broadsword from his back that hadn't been visible until then and that Venom knew was currently Illium's third-favorite blade of choice.

Illium's ability to hide the sword wasn't quite glamour, but it was close to it, at least on a small scale. And unlike with Holly's "droplet of power," Bluebell could control his ability, could disappear his weapons at will.

"Too much blood and mess on the balcony," Dmitri said. "Take him to the healers so they can get a sample of his

wings—and any other samples they need—then fly him back
to his home. Do the excision there. Incinerate his wings
afterward."

Golden energy arced between Illium's fingertips. "Is he going to be zombie Kenasha the whole way?" he asked Venom.

Venom shook his head. "The connection will break once
he's a short distance from me. He should be like this while
in the Tower, though—it'll make it easier for the healers to
get samples without him throwing any dramatics."

Nodding, Illium took charge of the other angel and
dropped down to the infirmary level.

"Uram marked her," Venom said quietly. "Do we tell the
sire?"

"Only if it's something we can't handle ourselves," Dmitri
replied, his gaze on the glittering city that spread out around
them, dark water in the distance. "He's surrounded by
enemies right now. We can't afford to divide his attention."

Venom nodded. "I'll work on this."

Dmitri folded his arms as the cold night wind ruffled the
dark strands of his hair. "You have it. But Venom, this
changes things." He released a harsh breath. "You have to
treat Holly as an unknown threat. She could have things
hidden inside her far beyond what came from Daisy."

Venom had seen the way Dmitri hugged Holly to his
side, witnessed the affection of his kiss on top of her
rainbow-colored hair. This from a man who otherwise only
interacted that way with his wife—and with Naasir, whom
he'd all but raised. "What would you do if she does?" he
asked softly. "Would you execute her?"

Darkness, dangerous and old, swept across Dmitri's face.
"It's your job to make sure that doesn't become a possibility."
His eyes locked with Venom's. "Don't let me down."

Holly woke feeling as if she'd just spent ten hours on the
weight machine at the gym. Every freaking muscle in her

body ached. Even the ones in her toes. But at least she was someplace warm, where the heat seeped into her bones and made her want to stretch out and never leave.

She curled her fingers into the luxuriantly soft blanket that covered her, and smiled. *This stone floor is so nic—*

Her eyes snapped open. She wasn't the least surprised to see Venom sitting on the thick light gray carpet on the other side of the stone. Dressed in black pants and a steel gray shirt open at the throat, he wasn't looking at her. His back leaning against a sofa, and his hair not as flawlessly combed as usual, he was staring out at the lights of the night-cloaked city, one of his legs raised and bent at the knee.

There was something starkly distant about him at that moment.

She spotted her boots near the edge of the stone, managed to use her foot to get one under the blanket without alerting him. Reaching down to quietly bring it up without altering her curled-up position on the heated stone . . . she threw it so that it landed with a thump next to Venom.

His attention jerked to her, a smile curving his lips. And he wasn't distant and unknowable any longer. "So, the sleepy kitty is awake." He prowled to her on all fours. It should've looked wrong, but his body flowed like liquid and it was perfectly normal.

Coming to a stop on the stone floor about a foot from her, he went to his stomach and, folding his arms under his chin, propped his head on them. "Have a good sleep?"

She wanted to reply with a snarky comment just because it was Venom who was asking, but she was too warm and comfortable—aside from the aching muscles. Yawning, she snuggled the blanket back up to her chin. "Yes. What happened?" She had a vague memory of being punched by Daisy but that didn't make sense—Daisy had been strapped down and too far away to hit Holly.

"Something interesting," he said. "But you should eat first. You missed dinner."

"How long have I been out?"

"Approximately five and a half hours." A quick glance at his watch. "It's currently exactly one minute past midnight."

Holly's aching body contradicted the hours of rest. "I feel like I went twelve rounds with Dmitri in a bad mood," she admitted.

A tilt of his head. "Has he ever sparred with you?"

"A little. But he doesn't really let go—I think he's worried he'll break my neck without realizing it."

"You're not that easy to break."

Holly thought again of how he'd thrown her, and of how her body had just kind of . . . flowed. "How do I learn to do that consciously?" she asked. "The boneless glide down walls?"

"Instinct," was the unhelpful response. "Stop fighting yourself and you'll do it the same way you walk and breathe." His eyes were so pretty and wildly green.

And she was clearly faint from lack of food.

Her stomach rumbled right on cue. "Did you know they deliver takeout to the Tower?" The first time she'd placed an order, she'd gone out front to wait, worried the delivery guy would get scared off by the genuinely scary vampires on guard. Even Holly didn't dare mess with those grim-eyed men and women.

To her shock, the middle-aged delivery guy had rolled up to her with a grin and a small bag of free chocolate chip cookies still warm from the oven. "After that last order," he'd said, "the Tower is our best customer by a country mile."

It had taken Holly a while to discover that the last order had been placed by a squadron of angelic fighters who'd had a hankering for deep-dish pizza. They'd ordered fifty . . . then fifty more after a second training session.

On the same day.

"I cooked you something." Venom's eyes held hers, and this close, she glimpsed the golden striations in the extraordinary viper green. In contrast, the slits of black were such a pure shade of obsidian that she could almost see her own reflection in them.

Lifting her hand without her conscious volition, she brushed the very tip of her right index finger across his eyelashes.

20

His lashes were straight and dark and uncompromising . . . but they felt like the softest of feathers, a whisper of a touch. He didn't stop her, just watched her with that unblinking gaze he got sometimes; it tended to frighten people who didn't know him. Those people erroneously assumed it was a threat when it was simply another part of Venom's nature.

Holly just felt . . . at peace.

She couldn't hurt him if she lost control. She couldn't terrify him. She couldn't even shock him. She *could* annoy him, but they both enjoyed that—a dirty little secret neither one of them would ever speak aloud. "What did you cook?" she asked in that peaceful, lethargic, oddly content state.

"Fried rice with fresh crab and scallops."

Holly jerked upright into a seated position. "Really? Give it to me!" She loved seafood fried rice so much that she'd learned to cook it; of course, hers was never as good as her mom's. Daphne just threw in "this and that," mostly leftover bits and pieces, and it always turned out fantastic.

"You're competing with my mom's top-shelf cooking, just so you know."

"I am warned." Flowing upright in a way that made it seem as if he had no bones in his body, Venom walked barefoot across the huge living area and up three small steps to the kitchen area. The gray of his shirt sat flawlessly on his shoulders, the fabric of his pants hugging his butt. What? She couldn't look? She was human and Venom was built like a racehorse, sleek and muscled and fast.

When he turned to lift a lightweight and aerated cover off the wok that sat on the counter, she noticed all over again that his shirt was open at the collar, revealing a strip of golden brown skin. "It's still hot," he told her with a faint smile. "Perhaps the scent lured you out of sleep."

"You think you're joking but seafood fried rice—*good* seafood fried rice—is serious business."

Holly sat cross-legged on the stone and watched as he dished out the rice onto a glass plate, her mouth watering and stomach rumbling. She was ready to chew the plate itself by the time he returned to put it into her hands, along with a fork.

"Now," he said, "for the review from a connoisseur."

Holly took a deep breath and scented ginger, garlic, shallots, a hint of chili. Her first bite was heavenly, the moan that rose up out of her throat pure, unadulterated pleasure. She'd never, not in a million years, tell her mom, but Venom was at least equal with her in the cooking stakes. Then she didn't think, just ate, her starved body in ecstasy.

When Venom disappeared for a while to the kitchen and returned to place a glass beside her, she didn't pay attention except to glance at it and make sure it wasn't the dark red of blood. *Ugh.* She so didn't need a mug of blood.

It was only halfway through the plate of food that she felt the need for liquid with which to wash it down. Taking a sip from the blood-free glass without looking, she felt her eyes widen. "Mango lassi?" It was a whisper.

Venom tilted his own glass at her from where he was once more leaning up against the sofa—but this time he was facing her, very much in the present. With her. Not in the distant past where she could never go.

She took a sip and felt her toes curl at the tangy sweetness. "How can a vampire be this good a cook?" she muttered before diving back into the fried rice with its succulent chunks of crab meat and equally juicy scallops.

The next time she came up for air, it was to find he'd brought the wok over.

Smiling at her imperious demand for more, he dished her another full plate.

She ate it. And she drank three glasses of the cold yogurt drink he'd made fresh. Stuffed, sated, she fell back on the stone with her arms out on either side of her in what her yoga teacher had called the corpse pose. Holly hadn't lasted long in yoga. She'd felt as if she'd explode out of her skin at the slowness of it all.

"Is my belly sticking out?"

Venom chuckled. "No. Though I have to admit, I don't know where it all went."

"Me, either." She just knew she'd needed fuel and the fuel he'd provided had been delicious. "You're a vampire. You don't eat." Yes, he could have the odd small thing— like that glass of lassi, or a few bites of a food he particularly craved, but he couldn't digest entire meals.

"I wasn't always a vampire."

She turned her head to look at him. "Don't tell me: you were a cook in your human life."

"Yes."

Holly blinked. She'd been joking. The idea of Venom as a cook simply did not compute. "Really?"

An incline of his head, his hair falling farther across his forehead. "My family had an inn along a Silk Road corridor. We fed and housed hungry and thirsty merchants, couriers, travelers of all kinds."

Fascinated, Holly turned over fully onto her side. "What was it like?"

"A good life," he said simply. "I had the freedom to create and I created tastes so renowned that even angels stopped especially at our little inn." No pride in his tone, just the ache of memory. "Neha wanted my skills in her kitchen—I had a standing offer to come to Archangel Fort and apply to become a vampire. She told me I'd be accepted without delay and that I'd hold a distinguished position in her kitchens."

Which meant, Holly realized, that Neha had already managed to get hold of his blood to confirm he was compatible with the angelic toxin that turned a mortal into a vampire.

"Is that what you did for her as a young vampire? Cook?"

"No. I was too altered after my Making—she realized I'd be far more useful as a warrior. So I trained for that instead." A faint smile. "Though, every so often, I'd break into the kitchen at night and cook a feast for my friends. Neha discovered us one day and told me she'd chop off my head if I didn't invite her next time. She used to sit with us at the wooden slab of the kitchen table, her wings brushing the floor, and laugh, eat."

He shook his head, the movement slow and thoughtful. "She was different then. A dangerous queen, yes, one capable of cruelty as well as mercy, but also a warrior like Raphael. Present. *Real.*"

Holly couldn't wrap her mind around the scene Venom was describing. The Queen of Snakes and Poisons was stunning, deadly, and unmistakably regal. The idea of her joining an impromptu midnight feast was incongruous . . . and it made Holly piercingly aware of the divide of life and experience that separated her and Venom. "You weren't tempted to open your own inn after you'd completed your Contract?"

"Sometimes, kitty," Venom murmured, "you can't go back."

Holly thought of the fashion templates she'd thrown away, the exquisite fabrics she'd made her mother donate to a local charity shop, and felt a stabbing sense of loss. "Who says?" she said defiantly, suddenly furious at herself for giving away a piece of silk she'd adored and planned to make into a dress. "*We* are the ones who make the choices." And she was going to choose to find another piece of silk for her dress.

Venom's response was a smile that said a thousand unspoken things. "Do you intend to make the choice to get up anytime soon?"

"Nope." Holly snuggled into the stone—that sounded so weird, but she didn't care. "Is Daisy all right?"

Venom's smile faded. "No, kitty. Daisy is gone."

Holly was seated cross-legged by the time he finished telling her what had taken place after she entered the isolation room, her tears for Daisy dry tracks on her cheeks. Venom had loaded the recording from the room onto a large tablet and she watched and rewatched the slow-motion replay until it was burned into her brain.

"Uram touched her," she whispered, her mouth so dry it was dust.

"There is more." Venom told her of how Daisy had ended up in the Hudson.

Pressing her palm on the tablet, over the image of a woman who'd never stood a chance, Holly felt a renewed burning in her eyes. "Why not me?" she whispered. "Why did I get to survive and she had to die?"

"Because you're stronger." Venom's answer was so definitive that she stared at him. "It's the only answer that makes sense. Whatever Uram hid in Daisy, it needed a host and she was starting to fail because of Kenasha's abuse. It relocated."

Holly tore open her shirt, uncaring that she was exposing her body to Venom—right now, she was more concerned about the strip of skin down the center of her chest. That skin was smooth and unmarked. Heart thumping, she put her hand on the part of her chest where she'd seen the *thing* penetrate. "I don't feel any different. Just . . . *greater.*"

Oh God. Oh fuck.

Her breath punched out of her. "Like it's bigger." A whisper. "The otherness inside me. It's gotten bigger."

The serrated wings stretched wider, straining her skin, cutting her from the inside.

Curling the fingers of the hand on her chest into her palm, she gritted her teeth while fighting to hide the pain from Venom. He watched her, his eyes flicking to her tightly fisted hand. She flexed it through conscious effort of will. *He can't know that I am awake*, the madness inside her whispered. *He will kill us to protect Raphael.*

Holly didn't trust that insane voice but she also knew she was becoming something that shouldn't exist, an abomination of creation. But she didn't want to die. Not now. Not when she'd decided to live. And, she had the otherness under vicious control. She wasn't a threat. If the madness tried to escape, she'd confess her sins, bear the punishment.

The one thing Holly would not do was repeat Uram's murderous rampage.

"The tests on her and Kenasha's blood," Venom said at last, "are taking time to complete. The healers say they've never seen the like."

"You need my blood, too. It has to be a new, post-incident sample." Skin cold, Holly buttoned up her shirt, taking the opportunity to break the dangerous eye contact with a man who was as intelligent as he was lethal. "Or did you take it while I slept?"

"I don't need to violate women, kitty. They beg me to take their blood and their bodies."

Happy to be back on a familiar footing, Holly pretended to gag before she rose to her feet. "Let's go donate my blood, then." She watched him get up before a thought struck her. "Have you fed?"

"Yes."

Holly slammed her mouth shut before she could ask the name of his donor. She didn't care. She *shouldn't* care. Yet the question was shoving so hard at her throat that it threatened to bruise. "Did you try that bottle of premium blood at Janvier and Ash's? Ash said Ellie's company is about to extend their flavor range."

"To humor a good friend is one thing, but I will never voluntarily consume that mockery of blood," he said with such an offended scowl that she had to laugh.

This, this was the man who'd once run his own kitchen.

But he wasn't done. "Anyone who adulterates such a pure and perfectly balanced liquid should be banned from the business of blood."

"You're a blood snob," she said teasingly. "Ellie knows how much I hate drinking blood, so she brings me a bottle of the expensive dark chocolate one when she visits." Holly's budget didn't yet stretch to that. "I pretend it's syrup and pour it over my ice cream." Of course, she hadn't consumed any blood for months before that near-bloodlust incident with Venom; it was a mistake she had no intention of repeating. "Next time, I'm going to put it into a milkshake."

Venom shuddered. "Stop, before I throw up." He pointed to the next level. "I have some of your things in the bathroom if you want to shower."

"I'll be quick." She kept her word, though she did have a moment's pause when she picked up her panties to slide them on. The idea of Venom handling the delicate peach satin and white lace . . .

Going downstairs afterward, dressed in tight blue jeans and a simple white shirt with the sleeves rolled up partway, canvas trainers on her feet that she'd painstakingly hand-painted with pink and orange stars, she said, "Thanks for getting a change of clothing for me. I didn't expect the shoes." The boots she'd placed neatly by the door definitely wouldn't have suited this outfit.

"It wasn't me," he said absently, his attention on his phone. "Ashwini turned up with all of it."

Exhaling quietly, Holly headed out. Venom came with

her, and the two of them were soon in the testing area. The sweet-faced angel who drew her blood also took her blood pressure and did a couple of other tests, "since you're here anyway." The healers loved getting their gentle—but intensely curious—hands on her, the people she dealt with all senior Tower staff who knew her history.

"It's like you get a hard-on when I'm around, Lucius," she said to the angel with wings of softest yellow that children couldn't resist. Angels generally didn't like getting their wings touched by strangers, but many seemed to make an exception for the littlest mortals.

She'd once seen Lucius sitting quietly in a sun-drenched corner of Central Park, his wings spread out behind him, while a group of five tiny children patted his feathers with their baby-soft hands.

"We all have our vices, sweetheart." He threw her a wink over his shoulder. Built tall and strong, with blond hair and sparkling gray eyes, he was handsome and kind and funny—but she didn't want to jump his bones.

It wasn't the wings; she'd gotten over her phobia of those. Lucius was just too old, too much from another time.

Problematically, she *was* beginning to experience the bone-jumping urge when it came to a vampire who'd lived more than three centuries and counting. This attraction laughed in the face of her earlier justification about Lucius. But then, Venom had always been an outlier when it came to Holly—he'd made her react, made her fight, even when she'd been at her lowest.

"Timeline, Lucius?" Venom asked.

"It's going to take a while longer. All the samples you sent us are . . . odd." He ran his fingers through his hair. "That is not scientific and I strive to be so, but there it is. It's all as odd as Holly's blood, and our lovely Hollyberry has set a high bar for oddness."

Holly threw a forgotten lab glove at his head. "I'll see you in a month, you bloodsucker," she said when he laughingly caught the glove out of the air. She had to turn up for a regular monthly checkup until her blood stopped being so mutable.

Who knew how long that could take?

"Highlight of my calendar, sweet girl."

Venom spoke after they'd closed the door to Lucius's lab behind them. "I didn't realize you were close to Lucius."

"He's been my lab tech pretty much from the start." Though it seemed strange to call Lucius that—he was so much more. Like Kenasha, Lucius had only a little innate power in angelic terms. But unlike the deadbeat angel, Lucius had spent his three thousand years of life learning endless medical techniques.

This decade, he was content practicing his skills doing bloodwork and other tests.

"What's our next stop?" Even as she spoke, she fought the urge to rub the knuckles of her fisted hand against her chest, to quiet the pulsing that had begun within. It was very low, barely detectable, and it had the rhythm of a heartbeat.

Holly tried not to hear it, tried not to feel it . . . because that *wasn't* her pulse.

21

Choking down that chilling realization because there was literally nothing she could do about it unless she wanted to confess and end up with her head on the chopping block—or her body caged in an isolation room—Holly said, "I'm wide awake and it's only one thirty in the morning." In immortal terms, the night was just beginning.

A sudden thought hit her before he could speak. "What about you? Have you had enough sleep?"

"I don't need as much as small kitties." Unaffected by her scowl, he said, "We still have to track down the individual behind the bounty on your head."

Holly had nearly forgotten that with everything else that had happened. "What we know so far is that the buyer is deadly serious and doesn't appreciate his or her time being wasted with false reports." She bit down on the side of her lower lip, frowning at the idea of the hours she'd lost. "Anything else come to light while I was napping?"

Eyes on her mouth, Venom shook his head. "Your phone

did ring several times while you were out. No one spoke
when I answered." He handed it over. "Fully charged."

"Thanks." Holly pulled up her call log, saw several familiar numbers. "These are pay phones in Zeph and Arabella's patch." She called one.

No answer.

The second one was picked up by Big Irma, a human
who was an unlikely mother figure to a number of down-
and-out vampires. "Holly!" she said in her energetically
overloud voice. "Zeph was wanting to talk with you!"

It took a couple of minutes for Holly to narrow down
where she'd be most likely to find Zeph and Arabella tonight. "Thanks, Irma."

"Just remember who helped you next time you're down
here!"

"I never forget." And she knew Irma's poison of choice—
menthol cigarettes.

Venom's eyes glinted after she hung up. "You have a
scent?"

"Maybe. Let's go see."

And all the while, the quiet, stealthy pulse continued to
beat in her.

The streets felt eerie and treacherous tonight, the squathouse to which she tracked Zeph and Arabella using Irma's
information looming out of the night like an inanimate
monster. Senses jacked up and the long knife she'd signed
out of the Tower armory safe in the spine holster she'd hidden under a bright pink hoodie, Holly glanced at Venom
and sucked in a breath.

"Don't kill anyone," she said. "No one in the squat is
capable of being a threat to you." Certain serious powers
did hang out in the shadier parts of the city, but they had
better things to do than prowl the dirty, graffitied dens
claimed by squatters.

"I kill only those who need killing," was the non-comforting answer.

He parked the Bugatti right in front of a group of skinny vampires with black scarves tied around their heads who were smoking outside the ramshackle building—the tobacco didn't do anything to vampiric bloodstreams, but the taste and oral addiction seemed to work the same as in humans.

Prowling up to them, he said, "A single scratch and I'll be extremely disappointed."

The entire group had frozen at his appearance.

Now, one of the vampire gang found the courage to squeak, "Yes, sir."

Not bothering to wait around, her gut churning at the heaviness in the air, Holly went straight to the doorway of the squathouse. The door itself was lying on the asphalt of the footpath, but that didn't signify anything: Holly couldn't remember the last time she'd seen the door—tagged with multiple gang signs—in place.

Venom joined her just as she stepped into the humid semi-darkness inside the building, full of old air breathed out by countless people who had nowhere else to go . . . or who preferred to live in the shadows. The only light was provided by the miraculously whole streetlamp outside—its yellowish glow coming in through the uncurtained windows—and by a standing lamp someone had plugged in.

The entire first floor was open plan; the stairs that led up to the second level hugged the left wall.

Bodies stirred on the floor at her entrance . . . before going preternaturally motionless. Holly knew she wasn't the reason for their fear—most of these people had seen her around. Some were friendly, some not, but so far, she hadn't had any trouble with them. Glancing back at Venom, she told him with her eyes to let her take the lead.

He slipped his hands into the pockets of his pants, the suit jacket he'd put on over the top of his shirt so perfectly cut and fitted that she knew it was bespoke—and created to hide his weapons. Looking at him, no one would guess he was armed with two short swords worn in a crisscross harness on his back. Holly had seen him move with those blades; "deadly" wasn't a strong enough word.

"Don't brush up against anything," she muttered, "or that'll be the end of your fancy suit."

His sunglasses reflected back her own image.

Scowling at the barrier, she returned to her examination of the squathouse's first level. About half the people within were curled up asleep under ragged blankets or piles of newspapers, while the rest sat hunched up against the walls, trying not to meet her gaze. Holly soon spotted the telltale signs of a fight—bruised faces, clothing torn and damaged worse than usual, scrapes of what looked like fresh blood on the floor.

The bad feeling in her gut intensifying, she did a careful round of the area while Venom stood by the doorway, his mere presence ensuring that no one dared move. "They're not here," she said to him. "We have to go up."

She was about two footsteps away from the stairs when a hand closed over the top of her shoe. Heart jolting, she glanced down to see a dirty and round face bordered by curly brown hair. *Brynn.* Holly knew her, knew, too, that Arabella often used her meager store of money to buy food for this mortal who wasn't quite right. Even Zeph, junkie though he was, would Dumpster dive behind restaurants to make sure Brynn didn't starve.

Sensing Venom stir behind her, she shot him a quelling look, then crouched down. Brynn was nearly lying on the floor, only her head raised. "Where's Zeph, Brynn?" Holly asked gently.

"He got hurt," the distressed woman whispered. "Real bad. Arabella, too." She waved Holly to the darkness under the stairs and to two unmoving lumps it took Holly at least a minute to make out, the murk was so deep there. "I can't wake them up."

Sitting up, Brynn twisted her stubby fingers together, her eyes wet. "I tried to give them my blood even though Zeph says I never have to, but they won't drink, Holly."

Swallowing hard, Holly focused on the bloody drag marks on the floor below her feet. "Did you move them?"

Brynn's lower lip quivered. "To keep them safe until they woke up, but they aren't waking up."

Holly went to the deathly quiet bodies of her friends and peeled back the old brown blanket with which Brynn had covered them. "Oh, God." Fury was a tempest in her blood.

Coming down beside her, Venom took in the damage. "The woman is alive despite the meat pulp someone made of her face. Him . . ." Pulling down the blanket, he shoved up Zeph's dirty T-shirt. "Heart wasn't gouged out, so there's a chance."

Holly knew most vampires would regenerate from a beating this brutal, but most vampires weren't as weak as Zeph. "Can you give them your blood?" He wasn't cruel, had fed Daisy when necessary.

"I could, but they'd be better off getting an infusion direct to the bloodstream." He slid his arms under Zeph's body, uncaring of the dirt and blood that had to be soaking into his suit jacket. "Can you and the mortal carry the woman?"

"Yes." Arabella didn't weigh much.

Brynn followed her instructions without deviation, and soon the two of them were carrying Arabella's badly beaten body to the car—which had no backseat. But Venom had already managed to fit skinny Zeph in the spacious passenger side footwell, now placed Arabella atop him, part of her body on the seat itself. "It's a short ride," he said when Holly went to protest the manner of transport. "Once you're in, you can cradle her against your body."

Turning to Brynn, he gripped the woman's chin in his hand, but Holly could tell the grip wasn't hard. "What happened to your friends?"

Brynn's huge eyes held no fear of Venom; in her artless mind, that he was with Holly and had helped Zeph and Arabella meant he was safe. "Was a big fight," she said. "People screaming so loud." She pressed her hands over her ears. "I just hid until after, but Zeph and Arabella got stuck in the middle."

"Shit," Holly muttered. "We'll never find out who started it unless Zeph or Arabella know. Things just erupt sometimes."

The skinny vampire gang yet lingering in the same spot as earlier had no answers for them, either. "Heard there was a big fight here, came to see," the one with the squeaky voice said through a haze of cigarette smoke, his skin a pasty white and his nails sharpened to points. "But it was all over by then." A shrug. "Just the bottom feeders losing their shit."

Holly felt her hand curl into a fist, but she didn't plant it in the ass's smug face. "Brynn, will you be okay?" She didn't know how long Zeph and Arabella had been watching out for the other woman, or how well Brynn could survive on her own.

"I lost my things in the fight," the mortal woman whispered. "I only got my blanket." Brynn still had possession of the latter because they'd carried Arabella out in a sling formed of the blanket.

To Holly's surprise, Venom peeled off several large bills and held them out to the skinny gangbangers. Dressed in white wife-beater tanks and low-hanging cargo pants in camo green or black, those stupid kerchiefs on their heads, they looked like children playing at being grown-ups. Holly wouldn't trust them with her imaginary dog, much less a flesh-and-blood mortal like Brynn. But Venom wasn't done.

"Use this money to get Brynn the food and supplies she needs, and keep her safe until her friends return." His voice was mild as he added, "You really don't want to cheat her, attempt to feed from her, or otherwise harm her. She is now under my protection."

Irrespective of the wildly differing hues of their skin, the vampires paled as a group.

Their unintentionally choreographed response might have been funny in other circumstances, but tonight, all Holly cared about was knowing they were too fucking scared of Venom to defy him.

"No, sir," Mr. Squeaky said. "She can hang with us. We got cattle at home, don't need to feed from some other vamp's donor."

Brynn, her wrists and neck badly scarred from old bites, seemed happy enough with that solution. Wrapping herself up in her blanket, she joined the gang in their spot. Before Holly left with Venom, however, she made sure of the other woman's safety by tapping into her own insanity until it colored her voice. "I have lots of eyes on the street. You'll be watched."

The cold words had the gang giving her a distinctly wary look.

Satisfied, she got into the car.

Venom drove straight to a twenty-four-hour clinic that catered to both mortals and vampires. The harried vampire physician on duty took one look at Zeph and Arabella and immediately hooked them up to blood IVs. "Best blood we have," he said, his ebony skin dull with fatigue. "I sure hope you two are covering the bill or my ass will be on the line."

"Send the bill to the Tower and it'll be taken care of," Venom said before Holly could respond. "We need to speak to them. Is there any chance either will wake soon?"

The doctor, dark circles under his eyes, took in both patients again. "Him, no chance. Her . . . give it a quarter hour and then, if you're willing to donate half a glass of your own blood, you might be able to jolt her to consciousness." A faint smile. "No clinic has access to blood as strong as yours."

The wait was excruciating.

"Why did you help Brynn?" Holly asked as the two of them stood with their backs to the scratched and nicked wall outside Zeph and Arabella's room.

In truth, she wasn't expecting an answer, but Venom spoke. "The mortal reminded me of a girl in my village. Maina was as . . . innocent. Childlike while being a woman. Even though I was only ten to her sixteen, I already knew to treat her like I did my younger siblings, rather than like other girls her age. Her family married her off to an old man who beat her, until one day, she just didn't wake up."

So many memories in his head, so much dark history. "I'm sorry."

"So was her family, but they were the ones who chose to think of her as a burden they had to shed." Pausing after that harsh summation, he said, "The two within use Brynn as a donor?" The question was dangerously impassive.

"No," Holly said at once, wanting him to know the hearts of the people he'd helped save. "Zeph and Arabella just pretend she's their personal donor so that other vampires will leave her alone. It's considered bad form on the streets to poach a donor who's been claimed." The two had been near starvation more than once and still never touched Brynn. "All those scars she has, they're from before, when she was alone."

"Maina's family was high ranking in the village," Venom murmured, "but your friends have more honor than they ever did. I'll personally ensure they have no debts as a result of their medical treatment."

Holly didn't know why she did it; maybe it was the hopelessness she'd smelled in the squathouse, the hollow pain of a history that could not be changed, or because Venom had just ruined another suit jacket and pledged his own funds to help people he could've disregarded as not worth his time . . . but she closed her hand over his.

Neither one of them moved until the doctor returned to ask

for Venom's blood. He injected it straight into the IV, so it'd directly hit Arabella's bloodstream. "That's all I can do," the doctor said afterward. "If she's not awake in five minutes, she probably won't come to consciousness tonight."

A loud beep had the medium-height male rushing off to handle an emergency.

It was only thirty seconds later that Arabella's swollen eyelids fluttered. "Zeph." It was a croak.

"In the bed next to yours," Holly told her, sliding two ice chips between the other woman's bruised lips at the same time. "He'll live, but you're both going to be in the clinic for a few days."

A struggling flicker of panic in the hazy blue of Arabella's eyes. "I'll pay," she managed to whisper as the melting ice wet her throat. "Zeph . . . he can't."

It took Holly a second to understand. "The Tower's taking care of the bill in thanks for your information about the bounty on my head." Everyone had pride and this small lie would protect Arabella and Zeph's. "You won't have to sign up to serve an angel to pay it off."

Her relief unhidden, Arabella turned to take in the sight of Zeph's motionless form and of the IV running red down his arm. "Brynn?"

Yes, Holly thought, her outwardly powerless and broken friends had far more honor than many. "Safe." She touched her fingers to an unbruised part of Arabella's hand. "Do you know who did this?"

"Just a stupid fight. People acting crazy. Zeph said they smelled off, like bad stuff was coming out of their sweat."

"It might be a new drug," Venom said. "I'll alert Janvier and Ashwini, have them follow up."

Arabella had shivered at Venom's voice, but found the courage to continue speaking. "Yeah, Zeph heard rumors of a new high." A cough that shook her rib cage. "I made him promise a long time ago never to take any of the new stuff. Just honey feeds or I'd leave him."

That was probably the only reason Zeph was still alive. "Is that why you and Zeph were calling? To tell me about the bad drugs?"

"No." Arabella's eyes fluttered. "We were hanging out in Times Square—I like the lights." She smiled softly. "It got real crowded. I don't mind so much but Zeph's not good with it, so we found a place inside the closed doorway of a dress shop."

Holly nodded, conscious that Venom had shifted so he was no longer in Arabella's line of sight. "Did you see something?" People often didn't notice those like Zeph and Arabella, who were used to fading into the shadows.

"No. Heard it." Her eyelids fluttered again. "Two older vampires stopped near where we were hiding and we went real quiet because we know they're mean. They were talking and one said, 'Word came down straight from Walter Battersby. Score is solid.'"

As Holly frowned, Arabella took another shaky breath and added, "We couldn't hear all of the rest . . . but we're sure the second vampire said . . . Chang." Arabella's eyelashes shaded her cheeks, her badly hurt body pulling her into a deep, healing sleep.

"Who," Venom murmured in the ensuing silence, "is Walter Battersby?"

22

According to Janvier, Battersby was a broker who acquired coveted items for wealthy immortals. Janvier's distinctive Cajun accent dark honey down the telephone line, he said, "Neither my Ashblade nor I have ever met him, but we've heard his name in connection with stolen antiquities and gemstones."

Of course this mysterious broker didn't live in the tormented, dangerous darkness that Zeph and Arabella and Brynn called home. He lived high up in an exclusive skyscraper that was all glitter and gloss. When Venom stopped his beautiful and very expensive car out front, the valet looked like he was going to have a heart attack.

Venom threw him the keys. "Don't dent it."

The poor young male looked caught between ecstasy and terror. He still hadn't managed to utter a single word by the time they were out of earshot. "You enjoy doing that," Holly said, trying for a scowl when she wanted to grin. "Making people lose their shit."

Eyes hidden behind his sunglasses, Venom said, "It's an

amusing little hobby." He nodded politely to the composed mortal doorman, then waited for Holly to enter the grand marble lobby before entering behind her.

Holly shivered.

His hand brushed her back over the top of the hoodie he'd called "a monstrosity that may burn my irises to blindness." To be fair, she'd told him he looked like an Indian Ken doll in his gray shirt and black suit; he was still wearing the suit jacket, having managed to find a rag at the clinic to wipe off the worst of the dirt and blood that had gotten onto it.

Dark as the fabric was, the damage was no longer visible to the naked eye.

"You're cold?" A low murmur of sound that sank into her bones.

"No, not really." Holly told her hormones to cut it out . . . and heard that stealthy second pulse she'd thought had gone mercifully silent.

Her blood turned to ice. "It's all this marble," she somehow managed to say, "it's cold."

Walking over to the reception desk, Venom asked the receptionist to buzz Walter Battersby. The cool-eyed and black-haired vampire on duty, her cheekbones like razors, nodded and did as asked . . . before offering Venom a deep smile with lush lips painted a rich pink. As if to make sure he didn't miss the silent invitation, the slinky woman leaned forward, her impressive cleavage plumping up in the deep vee of her dark blue top.

"You could lose a chicken leg in there," Holly muttered under her breath.

She thought she'd said it quietly enough that Venom wouldn't hear, but he shot her an amused look before thanking the receptionist. "My pleasure," the woman said in a lightly accented voice—Welsh, maybe?—before sliding her hand forward to shake his.

Holly turned away and rolled her eyes.

Waiting until Venom joined her out of hearing distance, Holly said, "Did she slip you her number?"

He showed her the card in his hand. "Unfortunately, she didn't pair it with a chicken leg or you could've had a snack."

Holly snorted out a laugh, blocking it with the back of her hand before it could echo off the marble. Slipping the card into a pocket of his jacket, Venom nodded ahead. "That elevator—it's coming up from the basement garage and is programmed to stop for us. Mr. Battersby has invited us up."

"How nice." Holly folded her arms and stared at the doors without saying a word. She wasn't bothered he'd kept Chicken Leg Breasts' card. "I thought you had better taste than that."

"Really? She has big eyes, soft lips, and enough curves for a racecourse." A shrug. "Fits the bill for pleasurable sexual release."

Holly turned very slowly to stare at his insanely perfect profile. "You're laughing at me." She could *feel* it.

Leaning close, his lips curved, he slipped the receptionist's card into a pocket of her hoodie. "You make it so easy, kitty."

Holly hissed at him just as the elevator doors opened. The well-dressed matron on the other side, her skin near Venom's brown but her eyes like Holly's, looked taken aback. "I say, young lady. Didn't your mother teach you manners?" was the stern question, followed by an intense second look. "You're Daphne's second oldest."

Holly prayed desperately for a sinkhole to open up under her feet and swallow her whole. No such luck.

Groaning inwardly, she stepped into the elevator with a silent Venom.

How in the bejeezus did her mother know *everybody*? It wasn't as if she was rich and swanky like this matron with her necklace of gleaming black pearls and a handbag that probably cost five grand. She looked like she was getting back late from an upmarket party. Daphne Chang, in contrast, ran a little deli beside the dress shop run by Holly's dad. Yet that damn deli was like a pot of honey that drew every single nosy matron in the city.

The elevator doors closed, cutting off all avenues of escape.

"Yes," she said, putting on her sweetest manners. "I'm very pleased to meet you."

The matron gave her a considering look up and down and just shook her head, before turning her attention to Venom. That he was a vampire—a very dangerous vampire—seemed to escape her. Or maybe she didn't care. At a certain age, Daphne Chang's friends seemed to stop giving a flying fuck about anything. In a very ladylike way, of course.

"Lovely suit, young man," she said, her tone warm with approval. "So nice to see young people who care about their appearance. My Everett used to wear a suit very well."

Her eyes landed once more on Holly's jeans, painted canvas trainers, and hoodie. Not saying a word—*loudly*— the matron stepped out of the elevator two floors below their destination. "Hissing, my dear. Really."

The doors shut.

And Venom's shoulders began to shake. She punched him in the side but it had zero impact. "Shut up. I'm going to be getting a call from my mother at the crack of dawn."

"The hoodie is an insult to clothing, but I like your shoes."

"I swear I'll stab you if you keep going."

Laughter still lingering around his lips, Venom put his hand on her lower back as the elevator arrived on their floor. He glanced right. "There. That looks to be Mr. Battersby's apartment."

The door opened at that instant, the vampire who stood within the doorway a compact and dapper man of maybe fifty with short silver hair and a skin tone that fell between Holly's and Venom's. He was wearing an old-fashioned smoking jacket. Deep blue velvet, it boasted lapels of black satin. Below the jacket, Walter Battersby wore silk trousers in the same black, along with fancy slippers of dark gold that curled up at the tips.

Unlike Kenasha, he pulled off the flamboyant outfit with aplomb.

"I'm afraid you caught me just as I was retiring for the night," he said genially when they reached him, holding out a hand to Venom.

The men shook before Battersby turned his cordial face to Holly. "And who might you be, my dear?"

Holly smiled her "matron smile," dead certain he hadn't needed to ask that question. "Just Holly." She wasn't quite sure what to make of Walter Battersby. He didn't set off her creep radar, but he was dangerous, of that she had not a single doubt.

"Ah, Holly." No surprise in the pale hazel of his eyes, his features so even and unremarkable that Holly had the thought this man could blend in anywhere, *become* anyone.

"I'm being rude," he said right then. "Do come in." He led them into a spacious apartment decorated with furniture that was a little too dark and heavy for Holly but tasteful nonetheless. Three framed black-and-white prints lined one wall, all depicting people in clothing at least a hundred and sixty or seventy years out of date. Those people stood stiff and formal . . . and one of them was a young Walter Battersby.

"Were you born in the 1800s?"

Battersby smiled at her question. "1812," he said, before going to a decanter in the corner and pouring two glasses of blood. He offered one to Venom, the other to Holly.

When she demurred, he asked her if she'd like to try a "raspberry liqueur with bite" that he'd recently acquired from a collector in Bavaria. Still unable to pigeonhole this man into the category of "unscrupulous asshole," Holly nodded, and he poured the liquid into a beautifully cut liqueur glass with a short, faceted stem.

"You must tell me how you like it," he said after she accepted the drink. "I have a terrible addiction to all things fine and I couldn't resist when I saw this bottle on the market . . . But that's not why you're here. Please sit."

Venom took a chair that gave him a view of Walter in his leather armchair, while he'd catch any movement from the direction of the door with his peripheral vision. By contrast, Holly chose a chair that put her back to the wall but also placed her directly across from Battersby. She trusted Venom to kill any threat that came through the door, but this intelligent and cultured man, he was another kind of danger altogether.

"Five million?" she said softly, holding the clear hazel of Walter Battersby's gaze. "I'll get an inflated opinion of myself if you're not careful."

To the vampire's credit, he didn't attempt to pretend he didn't know what she was talking about. "The client's choice, I'm afraid." He took a sip from his glass. "I did try to advise said client to lower the bounty so as not to be inundated with false reports, but . . ." An apologetic shrug. "The client was insistent."

"Have you alerted this client that I'm currently in your apartment?" Holly asked, her eyes on him and only him. There was no view behind him, the windows blocked out by heavy blackout blinds. An interesting choice in a city where views fetched a premium. Maybe Walter Battersby didn't like looking out and seeing the twenty-first century looking back at him.

Everything in this room, from the handwoven silk rug on the floor, to the ornaments on the mantel, to the chair in which she sat, came from another time. There was even a candelabra on the writing desk to the left, and the melted wax on the candles as well as on the metal of the candelabra itself told her Battersby used it often.

"No, no my dear." Walter Battersby shook his head. "I would never dip my hand in the cookie jar." Setting his glass aside on a small occasional table that was probably a valuable antique, he steepled his hands under his chin. "My job is *only* to facilitate certain transactions. I get paid handsomely for that. I don't need to make enemies of mercenaries and bounty hunters by poaching their target."

"How about the Tower?"

Venom's silken question had Walter Battersby's face going stone-still for an instant. It was the first time the urbane male had shown any indication of fear—and he recovered quickly.

Spreading his hands, he said, "I wasn't aware that Holly was special at the time I accepted the commission. I knew she lived in the Tower, but word on the street was that she'd earned that room by dint of her work with the darker denizens of the city. No one high-end, so to speak." Another look of sincere apology. "No one the Tower would miss."

Holly knew the Tower kept track of all its people. *No one* was expendable. "How much did you get paid?" she asked as the unashamedly opulent scent of the liqueur rose to her nose. "How much was enough to risk going after even a small fish in the Tower pond?"

"Two million."

That meant someone had laid out seven million to get her. *Seven fucking million.* Her head spun. "How much is this apartment worth?"

Battersby smiled. "Fifteen million. No, I'm not hurting for money—but one must have intellectual challenges or one fades away into ennui and that's a waste of near-immortality, is it not?"

He leaned forward. "Now that I know of the Tower's interest, I'll be returning the payment to my client and pointing out the clause in our contract that says they have to warn me of any unexpected dangers. Hazard pay is extra, you see—and this hazard, I do not wish to chance. There is a difference between acceptable risk and foolish stupidity."

Holly stared at him. "There's a contract?"

"I'm a businessman." Battersby rose—after glancing at Venom—and went to a sideboard where he picked up a document. "This is it."

Holly examined it first. It *was* a contract and it laid out the responsibilities of both parties "in the matter of the live capture of one Holly 'Sorrow' Chang." It was signed in blood on Battersby's part—the gold-banded fountain pen she'd noticed on his writing desk suddenly took on a whole new meaning.

The client had accepted the contract via a short e-mail that was attached to the contract. "There's no name on the e-mail," Holly said, handing the contract to Venom.

"No, my dear." Once more ensconced in his armchair, Battersby picked up his glass. "This client isn't unintelligent. I don't dig too deep, but I try not to work with distasteful types—for example, I don't truck with those who wish to do adult things with little ones, or who want to Make a mortal unwillingly—but I couldn't find anything on this individual. As he or she wanted to capture an adult vampire, there was nothing overtly wrong with the request."

"Except for the fact it was a kidnapping," Holly pointed out, the entire well-mannered conversation so surreal that she felt as if she'd fallen down the rabbit hole.

Battersby smiled at her dry tone. "Facilitating such things is part of what I do, alas." Pausing, he said, "If I may be indelicate . . . your fangs are rather small. Was your Making unsuccessful?" He actually looked distressed. "If you're under Tower care for medical reasons, I do apologize. I don't work with clients who target the unfortunate."

The *unfortunate*?

Holly looked at Venom, unable to believe this guy was for real.

Putting away his phone, Venom tucked the folded contract into his coat. "The Tower has accessed your technical devices. We'll wait while they verify your story."

Battersby leaned back in his seat, his eyes wide. "My

protections are state of the art. I may have been born more than two hundred years ago and still prefer the mores of that time, but I've kept up with the changes in the world."

Venom didn't say anything, didn't explain. Taking off his sunglasses, he just waited in an unblinking silence that had Battersby's fingers going bone white around his glass. Holly, however, was deeply curious—and since they had the time . . . "How did you end up in this line of work?"

A touch of color returned to his cheeks. "It's what I did before I was Made—for mortals, you understand," the other vampire said. "After my Making, I realized immortals had a need of the same type of discreet service and began while I was yet under Contract. My angelic master at the time was intrigued by my ability to build connections and obtain information while facilitating transactions, and gave me carte blanche so long as I hid nothing from him. We are friends to this day."

"Why don't you live in the darker part of the city?"

"Fleshpots and pain citadels are not my drug of choice," he replied with a smile that didn't quite reach eyes tinged with fear so deep, it couldn't be hidden. "As I can afford to live near the art galleries and fine wine bars that *are* my drugs of choice, I do."

"But you retain your connections in the streets?"

"Yes. A man in my profession only needs a few trustworthy go-betweens to ensure the word gets out about certain matters. Such as the significant bounty on the head of a just-Holly."

Holly smiled at his gentle mimicry of her butterwouldn't-melt tone at the door. "Aren't you afraid of angering the wrong person and losing your life?"

"That, my dear, is the point." Battersby put aside his half-empty glass. "The thrill of risk." He turned to look at Venom. "If I may be so bold, why have you never displayed any signs of ennui?"

Venom's tone was impossible to read when he replied,

his eyes still trained on Battersby, "Why do you perceive I haven't?"

"You've never been spotted in any of the usual haunts of those pushing their senses to the edge in an effort to feel something—and when photographed by the magazines that seem to enjoy following you, you are alert and aware. There's no sense of boredom to you."

It was true, Holly thought. Venom could give an impression of languid carelessness when he wanted, but he was never *actually* careless. He was interested in the world, noticed everything. Tonight, he smiled. "You are an intelligent man, Walter," he said. "But unfortunately, if you've crossed the Tower, that intelligence won't save you."

A fine layer of perspiration broke out over Walter's upper lip, but he didn't beg or plead. "I accept that I let myself down by not digging below the surface—I should've realized Holly was the Tower's." Returning his attention to Holly, he said, "In an effort at redemption, I'd like to warn you that much of my information on you came from an individual you may trust."

23

Holly trusted few people. And could see none of them betraying her. "Who?"

"David Shen."

Holly curled her lip. "That weenie? I should've guessed." He'd been a mistake during a period when she'd been fighting brutally hard to cling to normality. Of course, David hadn't known the truth of her transition at Uram's blood-soaked hands. His life would've been forfeit had she told him; she'd given him the same story she'd given her family.

David had been suave and sophisticated and onboard with dating a vampire. It gave him a certain cachet in his friend circle—composed of fellow financial advisors and other smug bastards. He didn't, however, have the balls to handle waking up five times in a row with his girlfriend staring at his jugular.

It wasn't as if she'd bitten him.

"What did this 'weenie' tell you about Holly?" Venom's tone hadn't warmed up, his form that of a predator who was keeping an eye on his prey but wasn't yet ready to strike.

Even Holly had to admit he was doing a good job of being coldly terrifying.

"Mr. Shen informed me that Holly was a failed attempt at a Making, and that she was only under Tower supervision because of the need to make certain she wasn't at risk of falling into bloodlust." Walter took a careful sip of the blood once more in his hand. "You haven't tasted your liqueur, my dear."

Holly tilted up the glass, looked at the astonishingly dark pink color that swirled within the crystal. It was pretty, no doubt about it. As for the taste . . . the first sip made her sigh quietly. "Definitely a drink you could use to seduce your lady friends." Holly had grown up in a cosmopolitan city filled with mortals and immortals both; she'd seen that love had facets as complex as the crystal of her liqueur glass—it couldn't be assumed that a man would always prefer a woman, or that a stable and committed relationship could only feature two people.

However, one of the black-and-white images on the wall was of Walter with his arm around a woman, his hold openly proprietary. Given the way he chose to dress and furnish his home in the fashion of another place and time, the broker struck her as a man who was very firm in his inclinations and desires. It'd be women for Walter Battersby.

Now, his eyes filled with a joy that was at odds with the fear that cloaked him. "That is good to know." Another sip of his own drink of choice. "The perfidious David also led me to believe that the Tower wouldn't care too much if you simply disappeared—you took up 'a lot more bandwidth'—his words of choice—than justified."

"Ass," Holly muttered, unsurprised . . . but hurt all the same. She'd thought she'd loved David once, enough to excuse his overweening ego and obsession with wealth and status. It was only after their relationship went down in flames that she'd realized the entire thing had been built on her desperate desire to be "normal."

She hadn't loved David; she'd loved the idea of him: normal, mortal, *human*.

So no, theirs hadn't been a grand romance, but to talk of her as disposable? What kind of person did that?

"I thought the same," Walter murmured. "I'm afraid your abnormally small fangs did lend weight to his words."

"You, of course," Venom said, "didn't rely only on the words of a weak and faithless man."

"No, indeed," Walter said as Holly caught the sharp edge of disgust in Venom's frigid statement. "I spoke to those who haunt the shadows where Holly works, and all were of the opinion that she wasn't a vampire Made by choice." Anger lit his expression as he returned his attention to Holly. "People said the circumstances of your Making had caused you to be angry and difficult to control, especially as those circumstances put you outside the Contract structure. You were an annoyance to the Tower."

If only this man knew how much she'd give to be on a standard Contract.

Venom's phone vibrated at that instant. Walter Battersby went motionless.

Taking out the phone, Venom scanned the message, then slid it back into an inner pocket of his suit jacket.

"So." Walter put down his glass. "Are my years of life over?"

"It appears you are to have a stay of execution." Finishing off the glass of blood Walter had given him, Venom rose to his feet and held out a hand for Holly.

She took it because . . . because, after hearing what David had said about her, she needed not to feel like a monster, and Venom did that for her. Warm and strong, his fingers closed over her palm.

"However," he continued without glancing at her, "you now work for the Tower in the matter of the bounty on Holly."

"Of course." Walter got to his feet and bowed with old-world courtliness. "I will pass on any information that comes to me, though it's unlikely the client will contact me now that my part in this is over."

"It's a long game, Walter. Play it well." The warning was clear.

Venom didn't speak again until they were in the elevator. "You are unique, kitty. The Tower considers you many things, but the one thing you are not is disposable."

She squeezed his hand hard as her throat thickened. She couldn't speak, not until they were in the car. And then she didn't talk on the subject of David and his view of her worth. "You liked Walter Battersby, didn't you?"

"I've always had a soft spot for the hustlers of this world." He floored the pedal, zooming them out of the tony street and startling the drivers of the gleaming black town cars that prowled this part of the city.

Holly laughed, exhilaration in her blood.

Grinning, Venom threw his sunglasses into her lap . . . without slowing. His speed was deathly fast, his reflexes insane. As he displayed when he brought the car to a sudden halt in front of a crosswalk where a homeless man was pushing across his cart. Holly's seat belt had jerked her safely in place, but her heart thumped a bass beat. "How did you even *see* him?"

"Do you think I would drive this way if I couldn't?" He took off as soon as the man was safely past.

Holly screamed and it was a sound of sheer excitement. The roads were quieter at this time of night, but with New York a city loved by night-owl immortals and mortals both, they definitely weren't empty. Yet Venom made his car flow like liquid around all possible obstacles until she thought that if anyone was watching from above, his car would look like a lightning streak against the black of the tarmac.

They'd just hit a stretch of road that was miraculously empty when Venom came to a total stop. She went to ask him why . . . and glimpsed vivid flame red out of the corner of her eye. Dmitri's Ferrari, a low-slung crouching tiger of a car, sat on the other side of the passenger window. Dmitri's hair was windblown and he was laughing, a grinning Honor waving to Holly from the passenger seat. Holly waved back, astonished at this side of Dmitri.

He looked . . . young.

Without warning, Venom gunned the engine and they were off, Dmitri streaking along beside them. Holly whooped as the two vehicles built for speed powered down the straight at insane speed. The waters of the East River rushed up at them.

Venom swung left and onto the road that paralleled the water.

There was more traffic here, but that didn't stop either Venom or Dmitri. They wove through the traffic as if it didn't exist. She glimpsed a flash of hot red in her peripheral vision before Venom pulled ahead and the other vehicle disappeared. "You're winning!"

"Dmitri's fast, but he's not a viper." Grin wild, and his own hair flying back in the breeze after he lowered his window, he pointed up without losing control of the vehicle. "Look right and up."

That was when she saw there was a third player in the game. Wings of brilliant blue edged with silver raced over the water alongside them, Illium's speed in the air a thing of beauty. "How can he keep up?"

"He's the fastest angel in the city, probably one of the fastest in the world." Venom swung past a lumbering people mover, slid in front of a sedan, then moved back into the other lane so quickly that she wasn't sure the other drivers had even seen him.

Dmitri's red Ferrari appeared behind them a second later. The leader of the Seven went to overtake, but Venom blocked his every move. Illium, meanwhile, kept pace as the two vehicles screeched into another turn that threatened to spin the Bugatti.

But the torque forces didn't win against Venom's handling and they rocketed away. All the way back home, where he brought his vehicle to a stop in front of the Tower itself. Dmitri pulled up two heartbeats later, looking over through the open window of his car. His grin was as untamed as Venom's, and when Illium landed in between the two cars, he completed the trifecta of beautiful, dangerous men.

Venom's fingers touched the back of Holly's neck, his arm stretched out and braced on the back of her seat as he leaned across to speak to the others. A sudden, sharp sexual awareness rippled through her body, the tiny hairs on her arms rising. She thought she'd caught it in time, but Venom's hand curled around her nape.

He rubbed his fingers gently over her hypersensitive skin.

She couldn't look at him, her heart beating so hard in her chest that she could barely hear the conversation the others were having. She heard Illium laugh, saw Honor's hand on Dmitri's cheek as she turned his face toward hers for a kiss, watched Illium and Venom bump fists. And felt Venom's fingers brushing her skin in a slow, rhythmic motion that went straight to her core.

". . . tomorrow."

She caught the last word before Dmitri pulled away to drive his vehicle around and down into the Tower garage. Illium lifted off a second later in a wash of wind that blew her hair back from her face.

"Kitty." It was a liquid enticement. "It's the adrenaline. Your blood is pumping."

Forcing herself to look at him, Holly sucked in a breath. His eyes glittered with the same atavistic sexual heat that burned in her. "Why not?" she whispered. "Have you ever been with a woman even a little like you?"

"You are a kitten," he said, but he didn't take his hand from the back of her neck. "I don't fuck babies."

"And I don't fuck anyone anymore." She stared into those wild eyes without fear. "I'm too scared I'll kill mortals and I'm terrified I'll plunge vampires into horrific pain." All it would take was a single brush from her fangs.

"You're safe," she said, twisting in her seat and moving with instinctive speed to fist a hand in his hair. "You want me." He was doing nothing to hide his reaction.

"You'll regret it in the morning." He tugged her hand out of his hair, his grip on her nape tightening as he hauled her halfway across the center console. "I don't do relationships, either. You're a relationship type of kitten."

Holly wanted to spit back a sarcastic comeback, but he'd muzzled her with the truth. Despite the horrific madness growing bigger and bigger inside her, she still craved a normal life. She was the girl who'd grown up planning her wedding, the girl who'd played house with her dolls. Uram had altered the path of her life, but he hadn't changed the fundamental heart of her.

"That," she said, running her finger over his lips, "doesn't mean I want to build a relationship with you." Venom was too dangerous for her peace of mind; he saw too deep, understood her in ways she didn't understand herself. "I just want to scratch a bad physical itch."

"That, I can do." Dropping her back into her seat, he swung the vehicle around and raced away from the Tower. She didn't ask him where they were going—it was clearly not to a bed where she could satisfy the craving low in her body, tumescent and hot and ready.

He brought the car to a halt near Central Park just as she'd finished taking off her hoodie in a vain effort to cool down. Getting out, he removed his suit jacket and threw it inside, then unbuttoned his shirt sleeves and rolled them up. After which he removed his shoes and socks and put them in the car.

Then he leaned close to her and whispered, "Run, kitty."

Holly's blood rushed to the surface of her skin. She was moving before she'd consciously decided to do so, the most primal part of her taking over. He'd give her a head start, she knew that. It'd make the chase more interesting.

She ran into the park with all of her preternatural speed, and she did things she hadn't believed herself capable of until that instant—flowing up trees and down others to confuse her trail, moving through the darkness as if it was her world. When she saw the glittering windows of the buildings that overlooked the park, she bared her teeth and wondered if the people within had any idea of the lethal predators that prowled below.

At last she went motionless and quiet, curling up as immobile as the snake that lived in Venom's eyes.

He found her, but she'd expected that. Having positioned herself up in a tree, she jumped onto his back, taking him to the ground and pumping her venom into his shoulder through his shirt. She was gone before he could flip over, but she was close enough to hear him laugh. An inhuman response.

But neither one of them was exactly normal.

Surrendering to the otherness inside her, she ran as if the trees weren't there, moving around and through the trunks in ways that weren't possible with human anatomy. The serrated wings inside her, they shoved and shoved at her skin, the pain constant. She couldn't fly like the otherness wanted, but she could run, and running . . . racing, it pumped her body full of adrenaline once more.

The madness was sated. For now.

Going flat to the ground three minutes later, her body stretched out on the dark grass, she went motionless again . . . and Venom passed right by her. Her lips curved, a deep happiness in her gut that she couldn't explain. She waited unmoving for at least ten minutes, not the least uncomfortable, before flowing up and back in the opposite direction.

They played in the night-dark park as if it was a playground. Whenever Holly happened near groups of vampires who were also using the park—or the odd, brave human—she veered away. This was a private game. She'd been running full tilt for at least five minutes when Venom appeared out of nowhere in front of her.

She had no chance of stopping.

Arms coming around her, he took her to the ground in a single move.

24

Holly's breath rushed out of her.

Hair falling around his face and his eyes brilliant in the fading night, Venom pinned her wrists on either side of her body. His chest heaved, his shirt dirty and torn. And his smile, it was a thing of primal beauty.

Holly didn't think. She just snapped up her head and captured his lips with her own.

Venom pushed her back down, his body erotically heavy and his tongue lashing hers. Her fangs nicked him. He ignored it. Emboldened, she licked her tongue around his own fangs. He made a sound that she couldn't describe except to say it wasn't human. His erection a brand against her, he deliberately nicked her lip.

She hissed out a breath, and he was sipping from her.

Holly groaned, her spine arching. She hadn't known that being fed from could be erotic. Sliding his hands down her body after releasing her wrists, he grazed his thumbs over the sides of her breasts even as his mouth moved down her jaw and to her vulnerable throat. He nicked her there, too, just enough to release her blood but not enough to hurt.

He fed on her in little sips, like she was the appetizer to a main meal. He didn't rip her shirt off her. He undid the buttons one by one, using both hands to push the sides open to expose her breasts before he dipped his head and captured a taut, sensitive nipple in his mouth . . . and then he nicked her there, too.

Holly screamed, uncaring of who might hear.

Venom flicked his tongue against her flesh, his hand on her neglected breast. It was too small, she knew that, but he was doing things with the pad of his thumb that were making her legs twist and her body curve. She kicked off her shoes and socks, tried to find a foothold in the earth, but it kept disappearing under a haze of need.

Smiling at her when he raised his head, Venom said, "I like your scream."

He'd opened her jeans and his hand was between her legs before she could process the words. She screamed again, her tightly wound body coming apart on his fingers. When he tugged off her pants to expose the peach-colored lacy panties she wore underneath, she didn't feel the least bit exposed. Twisting up with the primal speed he'd shown her she possessed, she switched their positions.

He let her unbutton his shirt to expose the hard, toned plane of his chest. His skin was the same beautiful burnished brown as on his face. "You go shirtless?" Older vampires found it difficult to tan, but Venom's skin color was natural—it should still have been paler on the parts of his body that were most often covered.

"I spent a lot of time in an outdoor training ring while I was away," he said, lying there unworried that someone might come upon them. "Extended combat training."

Holly loved watching him move when he sparred— though she'd never tell him that. Leaning down, she played her hands over the ruthlessly toned plane of his chest before pressing her lips to his skin. The contact wasn't enough. She wanted to rub herself against him, wanted to be skin to skin far more intimately.

Sitting up on his body, she went to peel off her shirt when the wings inside her spread out in a violent burst.

Venom knew he was making a mistake, but it was the most erotic mistake of his life. He watched with barely leashed anticipation as Holly opened up her shirt, exposing the taut mounds of her breasts, the plump flesh making his fingers curl into the grass. She was smiling at him in a slightly predatory way that made him feel a little hunted.

Venom liked it. No woman had ever looked at him that way. Like he was *her* prey.

A heartbeat later, her back arched violently, her head dropping back as her chest began to burn with an acid green glow that formed into the shape of wings. Not angelic wings. Not bird wings. Strange, jagged wings with sharp edges that looked as if they might cut. The color was viper green and acid green and light, light green, rippling shades that seared bright enough to glow in the darkness.

He snapped up into a seated position, his hands on her waist. "Holly!"

Her fingers clutched at him, gripping so tight to his biceps that her nails cut into his skin. Pain, he realized, she was in pain. He made the only decision he could. Using his fangs to tear open a vein in his wrist, he held it over her mouth. He didn't know if his blood would help her fight this, or if it would just fuel the effect, but he had to try.

Her throat moved. Again and again, his blood sliding down her throat.

The wings flickered . . . and faded.

Holly's head came up into a normal position. Wiping the back of her arm across her mouth, the blood smearing the white of her shirt, she stared at him with eyes that were stark. "What happens now?"

Do I die? was the unasked question in those eyes stripped bare of all shields, all protections. *Will you execute me?*

Venom gripped the back of her neck and tugged her close. "Now," he said, "we find out some answers."

Holly's chest still ached at ten the next morning, when she got out of the shower and began to dress. She'd had about five hours of dark, dreamless rest, which was enough to not leave her feeling like a zombie.

Amazingly, she'd actually fallen asleep on the short drive back to the Tower after they left Central Park, so exhausted she'd felt wrung dry. She'd woken with a start when Venom opened the passenger-side door of his Bugatti in the Tower parking garage, her heart thundering at what was to come.

He'd brushed his fingers over her cheek, his gaze inscrutable. "You're in no state to have a discussion with Dmitri, kitty. Get some sleep. We'll talk in the morning."

Now it was morning, and she had to face the judgment she'd tried to avoid for so long. In a way, it was a relief to have it all out in the open. No more hiding the howling otherness within her, the *thing* that was becoming ever stronger. No more pretending that she was getting better.

Having pulled on a pair of sleek black jeans, Holly stared at her naked upper half in the mirror tucked into a corner of her room. It was a freestanding one with an ornate frame that she'd painted pink. What that mirror reflected at her was smooth, unblemished skin. She ran her fingers over the centerline of her chest. Her flesh ached, but there was no visible bruise. Just an internal one.

When her hand brushed the slight curve of her breast, she paused, looked at herself again, this time as a woman. Her body was slender but had gained a lithe layer of muscle in the years since the attack. Her breasts, however, were exactly the same size as back then—she'd always hoped they'd get bigger if she had children, but she was part vampire now. No matter what, her body would spring back to this same state relatively quickly.

Slitted green eyes glinting at her, a man who saw nothing amiss in the small and taut mounds.

Color flooded her cheeks, her behavior of the night before a little embarrassing in the bright light of day. What had she been thinking?

Exhilaration. Heat. A dangerous, beautiful man who wasn't afraid of her.

Her core tightening, she turned away to pick up a dark pink tank top and pulled it on. Over it, she pulled on another tank in blood orange, layering the two so that you could see both colors. It covered everything very neatly. Had her sister worn this, their mother would've called her an "advertisement"—Daphne Chang wasn't the most emancipated of women when it came to her ideas about appropriate clothing.

Mia's more generous assets tended to overflow tank tops. She always made faces when Holly dressed in tanks, jealous that she couldn't wear them without being at risk of a wardrobe malfunction. Holly, in turn, had lusted after the lusciously gorgeous bras in her sister's lingerie stash. One memorable night while Holly was in high school, Mia had helped her stuff a bra full of tissues so she could see what it'd be like once her boobs grew.

Grinning despite the knot in her gut, she picked up her phone and snapped a picture of herself after pulling on a long silver chain with a small bottle at the end. That bottle had sparkling "pixie dust" in it. Also on the chain was a tiny black high-heeled shoe, and an equally tiny pair of scissors forged in silver. Mia had given Holly the long necklace on Holly's eighteenth birthday.

She added a message to the picture, the kind of message

you could only send to a sister you'd played with, fought with, and grown up with: *Thinking of you, Boobs.*

Mia must've been awake despite having worked the night shift, because her reply came at once. *Stupid boobs hurt because I decided to go for a run and didn't wear the right support. Pull your hair back in a tail. Did you hear Wesley is trying out for the youth philharmonic?*

Alvin mentioned Wes was considering it when I went over to watch his baseball game last week. A talented violinist himself, fifteen-year-old Alvin was more interested in being in a heavy metal band and was currently rocking a sneakily pierced ear under his shaggy haircut—he was working on the theory of ask parental forgiveness, not permission.

Holly had bought him a small stud for his birthday. *When are the tryouts?*

A month I think.

Holly made a mental note so she could give her brother a good-luck call, then re-sent her picture after pulling her hair back in a tail as Mia had advised: *My sparkly painted boots or the ones with the sunflowers?* Holly had bought both pairs at a charity shop for twenty dollars, then gone to town decorating them.

Sparkles. The word was followed by a smiley face. *I'm glad you're back, mei mei.*

Me, too, jie jie.

Sliding away her phone after that affectionate exchange, big sister to little sister, she decided to message her two brothers, then call her parents, too—and that was when she realized what she was doing: saying her good-byes. Because Holly would fight to the death to live . . . but not if it meant freeing the monstrous and bloodthirsty thing inside her.

"I hear you're hissing at handsome young men," was her mother's opening statement. "I was going to call you but since you were out so late with that handsome young man, I thought I'd wait. Well?"

"He's not a young man. He's one of the most powerful vampires in the city."

"You should bring him to dinner."

Holly was momentarily diverted by the idea of Venom at her mother's dinner table; his wicked smile would surely charm Daphne. Shaking off the strangely compelling image, she managed to nudge the conversation along to other matters, then spoke to her father after her mother had to hang up to deal with a customer.

"Are you all right, Holly?" Allan Chang asked in his gentle way.

"Yes, Daddy." Holly hadn't called him that in years, but today, she felt like a little girl who needed her father's embrace.

One last time.

Ending the conversation a far too short time later, her appointment with Dmitri looming on the horizon, she pulled on the black boots she'd spent two weekends painting so that they sparkled in the light, but not too much. They also had enough of a heel that she didn't feel Lilliputian next to all the tall people who occupied the Tower. It was like there was a height requirement or something.

"Good things come in small packages," she reminded herself as she pulled on a thick black watch on her left wrist, then added a bunch of colorful bracelets she'd picked up from a shop in Jackson Heights.

The eyes that stared back at her remained too stark, too scared.

Bringing out the cosmetics her sister had taught her to use when they were teenagers, she focused on those eyes, coloring her eyelids in a pink and orange pattern of sweeps that was probably over the top, but who cared when she was going insane anyway. Her lashes she mascaraed in thick black, after using a glittering silver pencil to line her lower lid.

Ready as she'd ever be, she stepped out of her room and began the walk to the elevators. Her heart was a cold drumbeat, her skin icy. When the elevator doors opened to reveal Venom, however, she didn't hesitate, just walked straight in. Because from the day she'd first heard a psychotic whisper in a voice not her own, she'd known this was coming.

He punched the button for Dmitri's floor and her eyes caught on his hand, on the fingers that had caressed her body, clenched in her hair.

Not ready to think about how he'd made her feel viscerally alive, she said, "Did you tell Dmitri already?"

"No. You can tell him."

Holly folded her arms across her chest. "It's never been like that before. I was glowing, wasn't I?" She'd just barely caught the glare of it before agony arched her spine—a futile attempt at escape.

"Wings," Venom said with a glance at her she wasn't ready to meet. "Unnatural, serrated wings, glowing in your chest."

Holly nodded, as if she understood the insanity of it all. When Venom's hand came to her upper abdomen and he picked up the delicate set of pendants on her long silver chain, she didn't stop him.

"A gift from my sister," she said, refusing to acknowledge the curls of desire aroused by his mere proximity, his scent clean and fresh and undeniably masculine. "The scissors because I used to make clothes for her even in high school." Tops that flattered Mia's lush figure while not scandalizing their conservative parents. "The high heel because I love shoes." She pointed down to her boots. "And the pixie dust because . . ."

Venom didn't step out of the elevator when the doors opened, his unshielded eyes on her fading smile. "Because you're a dreamer."

"Once." Holly tugged away the necklace and stepped out to face what might be her final hour of life.

25

I'll fight it. I'll run.

The defiant thoughts were hers and they came from deep within.

Fuck the world if it thought it could crush her. She hadn't asked to be changed and made into this nightmare. She had a *right* to exist, a right not to be prejudged, a right to be given the chance to fight the monsters within. If she failed, that was a different matter. She'd put her own damn neck on the chopping block then. No one had the right to steal the battle from her, steal her chance at life.

Driven by fury, she strode into Dmitri's office . . . and came to a sudden halt. The leader of the Seven wasn't alone. Illium stood staring out through the wall of glass that faced the balcony, while Honor stood on this side of the desk, frowning, the deep green of her eyes on the blue-winged angel's back.

Dmitri's gaze was on his hunter wife.

"I'm sorry," Holly said, having the feeling she'd interrupted something.

Dmitri's dark eyes landed on her. "No, come in."

"I asked that Honor and Illium be here." Venom touched his hand to her lower back.

Holly looked up at him. What was he doing, aligning himself so openly with her? Didn't he know she was toxic? A creature who fit nowhere. But he didn't break contact. "The change in Holly," he said, "it's escalating."

Then, though he'd told her she'd be the one who'd have to explain, he laid out the bare facts to set the stage. It gave her enough time to find her balance so she could tell her side of the story. "There's been . . . an alien thing inside me since the attack." It took furious effort to keep her voice flat instead of giving in to the screaming terror of the memories that haunted her.

"I always thought you were having trouble accepting the changes inside you when you spoke of them as if they were *other*," Honor murmured, propping her hip against Dmitri's desk, her soft ebony hair woven in a braid and her body clad casually in a fitted T-shirt and well-worn jeans that hugged her perfectly. "But I was wrong, wasn't I?"

"Yes, and no." Anger simmered in her yet, but the pause earlier had given her room to breathe; she knew she'd achieve far more if she put her points forward in a rational manner.

And Honor . . . Holly couldn't yell at Honor. Ever. Her heart wouldn't permit it; she wanted never to cause the hunter any hurt. Honor had conquered her demons, but as far as Holly was concerned, the woman who'd taught her that she could trounce grown men if she used her body right had already suffered more than her quota of pain.

"Uram," she began, "changed me in a way that goes bone-deep." It was no use fighting that truth. "But there's a part that's foreign, and always will be."

The whispering madness had never integrated with her psyche.

Holly had worried it was a sign of severe mental illness,

a total breakdown of her sense of self, but mental illness didn't make serrated wings blaze on a woman's chest that *other people* could see. "It feels too big for this body, too powerful."

"Did the changes accelerate only after Daisy?" Dmitri asked, while Illium put his back to the glass wall and just listened, the extraordinary beauty of his wings shot through with the cutting sunlight of a New York that had shrugged off yesterday's rain with the nonchalance of a catwalk model switching outfits.

"No. The . . . intruder inside me has been increasing in strength for a while," she admitted, her feet set apart and her arms folded. "I didn't say anything because I didn't want to be put down like a rabid dog."

Dmitri's dark eyes glittered with anger. "I see."

But Holly wasn't backing down. Not this time. Tears threatened to burn her eyes, but she refused to be that broken girl anymore. "I have no place," she bit out. "I have no stability. My right to exist is conditional." She wanted to throw something, to scream and shout, but that was partly why no one took her seriously. Because she was young and scared and sometimes, she panicked.

No more. "Who are you to hold my life in your hands?" she said to this man who'd made her feel so safe—and who might yet order her execution. "What gives you that right?" Her voice trembled from the sheer force of her determination. "Just because I don't fit your perceptions of what life should be permitted to exist?"

A slow whistle. "Looks like the kitten has grown up, Dmitri." Illium's voice.

Dmitri didn't look away from Holly. "Come here." It was an order.

She almost glanced at Venom for backup. Strange as it was, she had the feeling she might even get it . . . but this was her fight. Joining Dmitri as he stepped out from behind his desk, she didn't hesitate to follow him when he walked out to the sunlit balcony beyond. The wind was lazy today, but it was by no means dead calm, the danger of the fall beyond the railingless edge as perilous as it was on any other day.

Holly promised herself that regardless of what he said, what decision he made, the one thing she would not do was reveal how much it hurt that he continued to view her as a threat, one he was ready to eliminate at any time. Dmitri had become important to her. Not a father. She had a father whom she loved. But someone as significant.

Because she loved Dmitri, too.

"Why are you standing there?" he asked in a grim tone when she stayed safely in the middle of the balcony, while he'd stalked to nearer the edge. "I thought you enjoyed flirting with danger."

"I'm trying to be more mature and sensible."

To her shock, he laughed, throwing back his head. The indolent wind took full advantage to riffle its fingers through his hair. When he held out a hand, though anger and hurt yet choked her throat, Holly stepped forward to take it. She'd never have accepted the silent command had it been Venom who'd given it.

Her and Venom . . . they were equals. Not in power, but in other, vitally more important ways. Their relationship had never been and never would be like the one she had with Dmitri, where the power dynamic was so skewed, the imbalance was permanent. "Do you feel this way with Raphael?" she asked when she stood face-to-face with the vampire who had seen her at her pitiful lowest and darkest. "Like he's your senior."

A shake of his head, his hand protective on hers. "Raphael and I were friends when he and I were both pups in our own ways. We've grown up together."

As I'm growing up with Venom.

How strange to think that, when Venom had lived an eon in comparison to her butterfly existence, but it felt right. He'd told her she hadn't accepted the changes that marked her, but Holly didn't think he was at peace with himself, either. "So," she said, her hurt spilling over. "Do you plan to throw me over the side and rid yourself of the pesky problem of Holly once and for all?"

His face brutally hard, Dmitri dropped her hand only to grip her jaw while New York glimmered a patchwork quilt of streets far below. His eyes were chips of granite, his hold unforgiving. "If I'd wanted to rid myself of the problem of Holly," he said very, very quietly and very, very dangerously, "I'd have snapped your neck years ago."

It was a callous statement, but Holly wasn't scared. Because this was Dmitri. Who'd been harsh, but who'd always kept her safe—even from herself.

That was when she understood.

Dropping her eyes, she released a shaky breath. "I'm sorry," she whispered. "I know you wouldn't put me down like a rabid dog."

"Would you want to live if you became that way? A mindless, mad creature who hungered only for blood and death?"

Holly didn't need to think of her answer. "No. I will never be Uram's legacy." Lifting her head again, she said, "You told me once that you'd end me if necessary, that I'd never see you coming. Promise me you'll do that if I become a monster."

Fingers dropping off her jaw, Dmitri turned to stare out at the water far in the distance. It glittered and sparkled, as if there was no darkness in the world. As if monsters didn't exist.

Holly turned the same way and, when vertigo threatened, she gripped the back of Dmitri's black T-shirt. "Why do I always feel like a child with you?" she muttered.

A rough chuckle before his arm came around her and he tucked her close. "Yet you're asking me to execute you. A father should never have to execute a child under his care."

Holly heard so much pain in those words, so much dark

history, knew she was asking a horrible thing . . . but she couldn't ask Venom. The why of her reluctance wasn't something she was ready to face. "When did I become safe?" she whispered. "When did I cross the line from being a possible threat to a person you'd protect?"

He didn't deny that she *had* begun as an unknown danger it was his task to watch and perhaps eliminate. "I don't know," he said, his body strong and warm against her. "Probably at some point between wanting to strangle you and feeling pride when you successfully fought your way out of hell."

"I don't think we'll ever be friends," she said, the words solemn.

Turning to face her, he smiled again at last. "I don't think so, either."

Holly's lips curved. Because that was okay. Dmitri was something else to her.

Venom felt a conflagration come to life deep inside him as he watched Dmitri and Holly through the floor-to-ceiling window at the back of Dmitri's office. The conflagration was paradoxically a cold thing—emanating from the part of him that hadn't existed before a viper's bite—and a violent, heated flow of magma that altered him on a fundamental level.

Jealousy.

He blinked back to his senses the instant he identified the emotion. Because that was fucked up. Dmitri loved Honor with a passionate devotion that was a thing of chaos and beauty and legend. The leader of the Seven would destroy empires for his wife, if that was what she asked. Honor *owned* Dmitri heart and soul.

And she was looking out at the two on the balcony with a soft smile on her face. "I hate it when they fight," she murmured. "Everything seems out of sync."

Venom looked again at the tableau outside and called himself a fool. The way Dmitri was holding Holly protectively against his side, the way she looked up to him with such a willingness to accept his word, that wasn't a stance between lovers. There was too much inequality there.

His mind flashed to an image of her riding him, her body arched in a sensual bow.

Holly would never look at him the way she was looking at Dmitri. Not even if he put a gun to her head. Not even if he pumped her full of poison. Not even if he promised her a billion dollars and her own personal empire of fashion.

Holly Chang would never ever, *ever* consider Venom her superior in any shape or form.

Venom smiled, the conflagration ebbing to a flickering anticipation, as Honor went to join Dmitri and Holly. Which left Venom alone with Illium for the first time since he'd tracked the angel down on the day of Venom's return to New York. "In a better mood now, lovely Bluebell?"

A scowl from the other man. "None of your business, fledgling."

Venom hadn't been called that since about three decades after he'd come into Raphael's orbit. "I'm not the one who had fluffy baby feathers not once but twice."

"Once, only once. I'll have you know there was no fluffiness the first time around." Illium shoved his hands through his hair on that muttered comment, the blue-tipped black strands falling this way and that when he dropped his hands back to his sides. "I let Aodhan leave without saying good-bye."

Venom had never had a friendship like Illium had with Aodhan. The two had known each other from the cradle. Illium was a little older, but only by a matter of maybe ten years, which meant nothing in angelic time. Angelic children grew so slowly that both would've been babies still.

All of Venom's childhood friends were long dead.

He'd had a vampire friend who'd been Made around the

same time, but they'd gone in different directions when their power diverged . . . because Venom couldn't bear having a friend who was weaker.

Weaker people died. They got broken.

He hadn't seen Sahil in a hundred and fifty years and still he thought about his friend, still he listened for news of him. So he understood what it meant for Illium to have sent Aodhan into dangerous territory without a good-bye. "What happened?"

Eyes of aged gold bearing a mix of pain, sadness, and anger, Illium spread out his wings, then snapped them back in with vicious force. "You weren't there after we found him. If you'd seen . . . And now he tells me he doesn't need my care?" His hands fisted.

Venom had already been accepted into the Seven when Aodhan was captured by a twisted angel who wanted to own Aodhan's beauty, but as the most junior member, he'd been stationed in the then-rugged wild of New York. The hunt for Aodhan had taken place far from there.

By the time Venom was fully trained and cleared for Refuge access, where Aodhan made his home, the angel was back but not whole. Fundamentally fractured. "I've never really known Aodhan as he was before," he said to Illium. "I've only known the angel who buried himself in the Refuge and who shut out nearly the entire world."

Illium looked up, frowning. "He came to New York when you first joined the Seven. We all did."

"Yes," Venom said. "But he could only stay a week. And that week was full of training sessions with all of you, with only scattered downtime." Most of which the Seven had spent together, bonding quickly into a cohesive unit.

Aodhan had been acting as Raphael's personal courier then, and, seven days after his arrival, the sire had needed him to deliver an important package; he and Venom had shaken good-bye with a smile, knowing they had centuries to forge a deeper personal friendship. "Then, he was gone."

For a length of time that was difficult to think about even now. "And so the man I truly know is the one from after. I have no substantial memories of him from before."

Illium stared uncomprehendingly at him. "Venom, he was dazzling. Strong, a lightning bolt in the sky, an angel who didn't speak as often as the rest of us, but who'd back down from no challenge—and who'd be our shield in any battle. He was the *best* of us."

"Then why are you afraid now that he's becoming himself again?" Venom had seen the changes from a distance, witnessed it in the art Aodhan had begun to produce. The angel had always been gifted, even in his darkness, but this new art, it carried a subtle inner light missing from the work he'd produced after his rescue.

Illium stared at him for so long that Venom almost expected an archangelic glow to limn the angel's wings. "I'm not afraid," he said at long last, a hitch in his voice. "I've waited so long for him to find his wings again."

"What if it means those wings will take him far from you?" Venom said softly. "What if it means Sparkle and Bluebell will no longer be spoken of in one breath?" He could see the problem because unlike Raphael or Dmitri, he hadn't watched Illium and Aodhan grow up, wasn't locked into the perception of the two as an unbreakable unit. He saw them as the best of friends—but friendships could break.

Illium physically staggered, bracing himself against the window right before Holly and the others walked back into the room. Venom didn't say anything further. This was a conversation he and Illium had needed to have in private, and now it was done—and Venom had other priorities.

He looked at Holly. She met his eyes, came to join him . . . after a pause long enough to make it clear the decision was her own. *Bright and wild and fragile.* Nothing like the others in the Seven. Nothing like the people with whom Venom had surrounded himself after the last of his brothers died of old age.

And yet he didn't move from her side.

"When you feel the alien power," Honor said from where she'd taken a seat in Dmitri's executive chair, her husband leaning his folded arms on the back of the chair, "is it purely a sensation of pain, or more?"

Holly rubbed at her forehead. "It's overwhelming," she said slowly. "Pain . . . but also a pull." The last words seemed to startle her. "I didn't consciously realize it until now, but it's an insistent low-level draw that's been present since what happened with Daisy." A jagged exhale. "It's getting stronger in front of me, harder to ignore."

Venom took in the delicate lines of her face and thought of those wings with feathers sharp as blades shoving at her. "Is the pull to a person or a place?"

"I don't know. A . . . direction." Placing her hand on her chest, fingers outspread, she took a couple of steps backward to give herself clear air, then began to turn in a slow circle. And a faint acid green glow speared through her fingers.

26

Venom heard Dmitri suck in a harsh breath, but the other man didn't ask Holly to stop. She did two full revolutions before coming to a standstill. "This way." Her voice was definitive. "And it's *far, far* from here."

Lifting her hand, she pointed.

"Europe," Illium said into the silence. "That way lies Europe."

Michaela.

The other archangel's name was a silent vibration in the room. "It makes sense," Dmitri said, as if they'd spoken the name aloud. "Michaela was also impacted by Uram. Holly could be drawn to her the same way she was to Daisy."

Holly nodded slowly. "When we entered the house where we eventually found Daisy, I *did* feel a compulsion toward the room where she was hiding, but it was like static. Cutting in and out. This is far stronger, must be linked back to whatever passed from Daisy to me." Her fist on her chest, knuckles massaging the impact spot.

"Except," Illium said, "there's a problem." He took out a slim black phone and brought up a program before asking Holly to point again and holding the phone out along the same line as her arm.

As the acidic glow reappeared, the blue-winged angel said, "If we draw a line from Holly's fingertip to Europe and keep going, we slice right through Budapest."

The heart of Michaela's territory.

"Then what's the—" Dmitri bit off his question. "Michaela's currently with the Cadre and away from home."

"Exactly," Illium murmured as Holly finally lowered her hand and, with a wince, breathed deep. The glow pulsed for another three seconds before disappearing.

Honor leaned forward on Dmitri's desk, deep green eyes tilted up at the corners troubled. "It could mean Michaela has Made someone else like Holly."

"A possibility." Venom knew too well that people were always driven to replicate the unusual and unexpected. "Holly, do you feel a draw toward Morocco?"

"Add the path to China to the mix," Dmitri said. "I planned to call you and Illium in for a meeting this morning anyway. I've had word that Elena is homeward bound and will be arriving soon, but Raphael and the rest of the Cadre have left for Lijuan's territory."

Illium helpfully pointed out the correct directions.

Holly turned, concentrated, but shook her head. "Nothing," she said. "But the second I go back along this line"— she angled herself toward the heart of Michaela's territory again . . . and the glow pulsed—"there."

She turned away to rub at her chest. "It's as if I'm tied to something with an invisible thread and it's pulling me closer. It's getting increasingly difficult to fight the urge to head that way."

Venom ran her tail of rainbow-colored hair through his fist. "Do we need to reloca—"

"No." A scowl up at him, her voice firm. "No more running. I need to know what this is, and I need to face it." She looked across to Dmitri. "I want permission to leave the territory and follow the pull, wherever it leads."

Dmitri held her gaze for a long time before shifting his attention to Venom and Illium. "Security assessment?"

"New York will be fine without me," Venom said, because they all knew Dmitri wouldn't authorize Holly to head into another archangel's territory on her own. "The squadrons are strong, and you have access to both Janvier and Trace." Neither vampire was as powerful as Venom, but together, they came close.

"And," Illium said, "if we are going to send our small kitten into Michaela's territory, what better time than when Her Beauteousness is absent?"

"It's possible that Michaela parted ways with the Cadre," Dmitri pointed out.

Illium shook his head. "No, I can't see it. Michaela would never permit such a large gathering of power to occur without her."

Looking back over her shoulder, Honor met Dmitri's eyes. No words passed between them, but the leader of the Seven put his hand on his wife's shoulder. "If you leave now"—his gaze catching both Holly and Venom—"you can probably beat Michaela back to her territory."

Adrenaline punched through Venom's blood, but the leader of the Seven wasn't finished. "You've both got reckless streaks," he said bluntly. "But this is an archangel we're talking about—you could be the two most powerful vampires in the universe and you couldn't take her down. Don't be stupid." An order. "And don't try to deal with something that you simply can't."

"Reckless doesn't mean suicidal," Venom said to the other man. "As you'd know."

Dmitri's smile was that of the man who'd raced them through the streets of Manhattan. "Stay under the radar.

We don't want to incite a political incident." A pause before he added, "If she comes to harm, Venom, I'll take it out on you."

Beside Venom, Holly scowled, but Venom nodded.

Holly couldn't believe it. She hadn't imagined the entire conversation with Dmitri. She was actually on a high-speed jet that was about to land in Michaela's territory. The pilots had gone in the direction she pointed, and not eased up on their speed until Holly told them they were nearly at the point to which she felt drawn.

Not Budapest after all, but the mountain range prior to it. Where Michaela had a hidden and far more private stronghold than her stately showpiece of a palace on the Danube.

The knowledge was an eager, dark whisper in her head.

Glancing at Venom while trying not to listen to the words spoken by that mad voice, she said, "How did you find a landing strip so close to Michaela's stronghold?"

"We didn't." Venom rose from his seat. "The plane is going to keep going on a path that leads to an international airport. Officially, they're here to pick up an artist from Raphael's territory, a woman who was permitted to come to Michaela's territory to study under a master."

"Then how are we—" Holly stared at the backpacklike thing he held up with a wicked grin. "Is that a parachute?"

"I hope so, kitty. Or we'll have a long fall."

"Not funny." She went and stared some more at the thing. "No, seriously?"

"Naasir gave me the idea." Another grin, his eyes brilliant and unshielded. He was dressed in camouflage green cargo pants and a black T-shirt, along with combat boots; it was the most casual she'd ever seen him outside the training ring.

It was ridiculous how good he looked. Wild.

Then he put on the parachute backpack and did up the straps across his chest.

"Where's mine?" Holly put her hands on her hips and began to tap her boot-clad foot. "If you're planning to leave me here, I'll deck you."

"Do you know how to jump out of a plane?"

"Well . . . no." She scowled at him when he pulled out another harness.

"Come on, then, Hollyberry." That grin just kept digging its way further and further under her skin. "Let's get you ready."

Ten minutes after that dangerous invitation, Holly found herself jumping out into the ink-black skies above the light-less dark of the uninhabited land below, while harnessed to an insane vampire who laughed when they tumbled out into the cold air. "Oh my God!" She'd always wondered what it would be like to fly.

They raced through the air, Venom having told her how to hold her body during each phase of the jump. He gave the countdown in her ear. "Brace for the tug," he said just before he opened the chute and they swung up a little be-fore gliding back down through the silken darkness. When Holly looked up, she couldn't see the parachute canopy ex-cept as a patch of darker blackness against black.

It made sense now that Venom had asked her to dress in black, and to wear long sleeves. His skin tone blended bet-ter than hers.

They hit the ground with a smoothness she hadn't ex-pected. She was unclasped seconds later, Venom pulling in the chute with a speed that told her this was far from his first jump. She watched the deathly quiet of the landscape around them while he finished. It looked like they'd landed on top of a small and flat mountaintop.

The landing area wasn't that large, so she had no idea how Venom had pinpointed it in the dark.

Those beautiful eyes.

The plateau proved to drop off into a steep gorge about thirty feet to the south. When Holly looked down in the hope of spotting their supply packs, which had been dropped behind them, she had the sense of dense foliage, the same as grew in every other direction surrounding their landing spot.

No visible sign of the packs.

When she turned to look back at Venom, she belatedly realized that this "plateau" was just a ledge that jutted out from a much larger mountain. And she had the feeling they were going up. "I can't see the packs down there." Taking out the little tracking device Venom had given her on the plane, she switched it on.

Two quiet, blinking dots appeared on the grid.

Holly blew out a relieved breath. "Both are higher up on the mountain."

"Good. We can get them on the way." Venom hid the chute under a bramble of some kind, ignoring the resulting bloody scrapes on his arms. "Do you feel anything?"

Holly shook her head, her braid sliding across her back. She'd taken off her black knit cap for now, stuffing it into a back pocket—even with the crescent moon, there wasn't enough light for the colors in her hair to shine and betray their presence. "I haven't felt a directional pull since I told you we were at the right spot to jump. Do you think we drifted too far?"

"No. I think *it's*"—the faint brush of his fingers over her breastbone—"satisfied now that you're headed where it wants you to go." He began to climb up the mountainside. "Only way to find out for sure is to infiltrate Michaela's stronghold." A dangerous smile over his shoulder. "Haven't you always wanted to risk death and torture at the hands of an archangel?"

Holly grinned. "Let's do it."

The moment of levity faded quickly, the two of them becoming more wary the higher they got in the darkness. It wasn't the darkness itself—Holly and Venom were both creatures who had no fear of the night. It was what that darkness might conceal. This was the heart territory of an archangel, after all. Michaela had many residences, but, according to Dmitri, this one was considered her most private retreat.

"Stop." Holly checked the device again. "We're almost on top of a backpack."

Venom looked around. "Got it." He grabbed the pack from on top of a bush. "It's yours."

They located his larger pack two minutes later.

Sliding away the device, she continued to walk with him through the massive old trees. Their large canopies meant there wasn't too much undergrowth. When Venom held up a hand, she froze. He looked up. Following his gaze, she saw nothing . . . but heard the distinctive sound of wings in the air.

They pasted themselves against the closest tree trunk.

The angel passed overhead seconds later. He was skimming the tops of the trees, clearly doing a patrol. A single pale feather drifted down to lie against the toe of Holly's boot right before he flew out of view.

Her heart thundered. "That was close."

"We have to be more careful. We must've hit the secure border." Venom began to walk nearer the trunks of the ancient trees, using their shadows to conceal himself.

Holly had no hesitation in copying him. He'd had a lot more training than her. They flowed through the forest like ghosts, dropping to the ground to make their profiles smaller the instant the sound of wings whispered on the air.

A half hour, and they had bare minutes between each drop. "They know we're here." She'd pulled on her knit cap twenty minutes earlier and stuffed her hair underneath, just in case.

"Something's certainly stirred up security." Lifting his finger to his lips a few minutes later, Venom slipped behind a tree after nodding at her to do the same.

Holly went motionless in a way most human beings couldn't do. Dmitri had been very clear that they weren't to get caught or to leave behind any evidence of their presence. Raphael did not need a war with Michaela. So neither one of them could take out the vampire prowling the woods unless they did it in a way that could never be linked back to Raphael.

As a result, Holly stayed immobile, even when the vampire guard passed within a foot of her tree. She closed her eyes, in case they were glowing, and she surrendered to the thing inside her, the otherness that knew instinctively how to evade detection. She'd fought that surrender for a long time, believing she might not come back from it, but tonight, her resistance could get them discovered.

So she gave in.

And could feel herself literally fucking *disappearing*, her awareness overlaid with a layer of acidic green that made her stomach roil because it was a silent indication that she wasn't in any way human. She knew that. Of course she knew that. But . . . she liked to pretend sometimes.

A movement she felt as a change in the air around her.

She opened her eyes a sliver and saw that Venom had stepped out from his tree. And, that quickly, she was visible again. Relief kissed her blood. He paused a second before waving her forward. She moved, flowing in the darkness behind him in a fashion that wasn't like him, but worked. He was sinuous, a cobra snaking its way through unfamiliar territory with silent ease. She was a creature of the night, a bat with silent wings.

Great, thought the part of her that was still Holly. Now she was imagining herself as a bat. When was the sonar going to kick in?

An alert pinged off her consciousness. *Oh, no fucking way.*

Reaching forward, she touched her fingers to Venom's shoulder. His muscles flexed as he came to a total halt. She shifted so that she was pressed against his front and he had his ear right next to her mouth. "There's a group up ahead. Maybe five."

27

Venom didn't ask her how she knew. That was good, because she wasn't ready to tell him she might be a human bat. Real sexy, that. He just pointed right. She looked that way and felt no sensation of danger, of a presence. "Safe."

They went right, moving away from their destination for at least ten minutes before angling back, hopefully to come up behind the guards prowling the woods. It left them crouching higher up on the mountain, hidden in the night shade of a thick-trunked tree whose branches rustled in the wind. Holly looked up, loving the feel of the wind on her skin, loving how the canopy moved in the night.

"There."

Glancing back behind them, she followed Venom's pointing finger. It took her several seconds to spot what he already had—the men and women creeping about lower down the slope, stealth in the way they held their bodies. Probably vampires.

Holly smiled. "Let's go before they realize we slipped the net."

A dangerous grin.

And they were moving again, two creatures designed for this environment. Not like a tiger was designed for a forest. No, they were the shadows that whispered *behind* the tiger, unseen, unnoticed. The climb was hard, and Holly felt it in her calves, in the backs of her thighs—especially when the acid green that had lingered in her vision since the eerie but awesome invisible trick faded from view.

Damn. Turned out she was human enough that she couldn't just slither her way up a mountain with boneless ease. "Do you have bones made of jelly?" she muttered to Venom when they paused to make sure there were no threats up ahead.

"No. Spaghetti."

Holly nearly snorted out a laugh.

Hitting him lightly on the shoulder with a fisted hand, she took the bottle of water he handed her. They drank from the same one rather than risk the faint sounds of opening a second bottle. Then, skin flushed with heat and her blood pumping, the two of them carried on across unfamiliar territory.

When her senses pinged once more, she just glanced at Venom and pointed in another direction, and they went that way. More climbing, more changes in direction, sweat beading on her brow despite the cold night air.

The stronghold appeared out of the darkness in a shock of light.

Holly had been so focused on avoiding vampires and hiding from angels that she hadn't put much mind to how close they were to their target . . . or that Michaela had been the muse of artists across the centuries, many of whom had worshipped her.

Her stronghold was as beautiful as its mistress.

It rose up out of the primeval forest like a castle built for a queen. Delicate spires and spiraling walkways, a white stone that glowed even in the scant light of the stars and the small crescent moon. The light within was a soft gold, the angels she could see landing on the high balconies graceful silhouettes that made her heart ache.

A flag flew from the highest point of the highest tower. Probably Michaela's emblem. Just barely visible from their position were the exquisitely maintained gardens that wove in and out through the stronghold. There were dark patches, too. Probably water, ponds or pools of some kind.

"I'd heard it was a wonder, Michaela's home of the heart," Venom murmured. "But this is unexpected."

Holly's own heart was too full of the beauty of what she was seeing to speak. An artist had spent years creating this, piece by piece, and their work had been cherished through time. The stronghold showed no signs of neglect or ill use. It made Holly furiously curious about what lay within, what wonders and beauties. She'd had such good times inside, and Michaela's laughter, it had ensnared him until he'd been—

Holly didn't hesitate. She shoved up her sleeve and deliberately bit down on her forearm, hard enough to draw blood.

Venom's head jerked toward her, his eyes narrowing. "Problem?"

She bit down even harder, until the pain had chased the last of the fog from her mind. When she looked at the stronghold again, it hadn't turned into a squat ugliness, was still graceful beyond compare—but she could admire it without being overwhelmed.

Releasing her abused forearm, she took several deep breaths. "Was Uram intimate with Michaela?" She hadn't lived in the immortal world then, but she could vaguely remember an article in a magazine dedicated to immortal gossip. A reporter had written a gushing piece about how Uram and Michaela made the ultimate "power couple."

"That's a very specific question, kitty," Venom murmured. "The answer is, yes. He was her lover before he became bloodborn."

Holly dug her fingers into the earth where they crouched. "He loved her," she whispered. "He saw her scheming mind and pitiless ambition, but he loved her anyway." A wet heat burned her eyes. "When she laughed, he thought eternity might not be so full of ennui after all."

Venom closed one of his hands over hers, lifting it from the earth. "You have his memories?"

"Flashes only. Mostly of her laughing or smiling." She stared out at the stronghold. "I've never felt anything like this before from the otherness." It didn't surprise her when her chest began to hurt.

She didn't have to look down to know the wings had reappeared.

Turning so that the glow was blocked by Venom's body, she quickly shrugged off her pack and retrieved the outdoor jacket she'd packed for exactly this possibility. Once on and zipped up, it followed the lines of her body without bulking her up—most importantly, it was thick enough to block the glow.

"Okay?" she asked Venom to be sure.

He nodded, his hair sliding forward a little. "You can still feel it?"

"Oh, yeah." Slipping her pack back on after stuffing her knit cap in it, as the jacket had a hood, she squeezed her eyes shut for two long seconds. "I may become a liability if these memories take me over. He was consumed with her."

"Maybe Uram should remember that Michaela was probably the one who stoked up his ego to the point that he—" Venom cut himself off. "It's fucking irritating that you don't have the Tower clearance to know certain things."

"Tell me about it," Holly muttered. "Who do I have to sleep with to make that happen?"

Her question had been facetious, but Venom smiled slowly. "Let me get back to you on that."

She gave him the finger.

His smile deepened, and suddenly, she was back to being herself, Uram's memories held at bay. "Ready?"

A nod.

They flowed down the slight slope, then back up toward the stronghold. When Venom veered left, she didn't disagree. He was attempting to get them behind the stronghold, which made a lot of sense. The area directly in front of the stunning structure was clear lawn interrupted only by a fountain that created a delicate fall of sound.

Hopefully, the back would be better in terms of hiding places.

Holly hugged the ground when two angels passed by within seconds of each other. The only reason the angels hadn't spotted her and Venom was that they were in the narrow band of shade thrown by a foliage fence. Her heart drumming inside her chest, Holly padded along behind Venom, and when the green overlay appeared on her vision, she didn't fight it.

She listened.

And stopped Venom as he was about to go around a corner. Instead, the two of them pressed their backs against the same foliage fence and blended into the night. The guard passed by within a few feet. There was no way he wasn't going to see them when he turned left to continue his sentry duties.

Shit, shit, shit.

The guard turned.

Holly didn't realize she'd thrown out her hand until it slammed quietly against Venom's chest, halting his nascent movement to take care of the threat. His muscles quivered under her touch, his body held at taut readiness.

The guard looked straight at them.

His mouth began to open, but it was too late. Holly had caught his eyes. Caught him. He was an old vampire, but she was something *other*. And she was far, far stronger than she'd been before Daisy's energy joined her own.

"We're not here," she whispered. "You thought you spotted something, but it was only an animal." The latter was a deliberate choice of word. She didn't know if Michaela kept cats or dogs or peacocks for that matter. The guard's mind would fill in the blanks with the most appropriate image. "You're on high alert, miss nothing, but there's nothing here to see."

The guard yawned before absently scratching his shoulder. She thought for a moment that she'd failed, but then he muttered, "Damn cats," and moved on.

Holly sagged.

Venom tugged her around the corner before the guard got too far away. He knew as well as she did that the mesmerism had limits. The guard would remember exactly what she'd told him to remember—but once he was far enough away, he might decide to turn, double check.

"That was clever, kitty."

"Why didn't you think of it?" He was stronger than her, could control people far longer. "You were going to get physical." She'd felt it in the violent tension of his body.

"I'm not used to not needing to leave a trace. It's usually Jason or Naasir or Janvier who do any necessary sneaking around."

They went silent again, crouch-walking for a distance that was long enough to make Holly's back ache like she'd been twisting herself into a pretzel. Michaela's stronghold might be an astonishingly beautiful edifice, but it was also fricking huge. They didn't hit the turn for the very back of the property until what felt like an hour later.

Thankfully, it was worth the pretzel torture.

Trees filled the backyard—though those trees were controlled and noticeably shorter than the ones on the mountainside. Peaches and apricots hung from the branches of the ones nearest Holly and Venom. "An orchard."

The night air was a crisp bite as they crept under the trees, sneaking their way to the back of the stronghold itself. The wings inside Holly's chest, they pulsed, the sharp edges shoving brutally hard against her skin.

Holly had touched angelic wings—Elena's mostly.

The Guild Hunter had offered the contact so that Holly could overcome her traumatic fear of wings. It was probably *only* Elena who could've helped her conquer her throat-choking fear—because it was Elena who'd found her, rescued her. Holly's brain was imprinted with that knowledge. As a result of her deliberate tactile experience, she knew that while angelic wings were powerful, they weren't sharp. Ellie's feathers had been silky soft under Holly's fingertips.

Whatever it was that lived in Holly, it wasn't natural.

Something brushed her leg.

She couldn't help her jump.

Yowling, the black cat ran off.

"Damn it." Hoping the sentries were accustomed to the feline sounds and wouldn't pay them much mind, she carried on, Venom a dark silhouette in front of her. He took them not to the center of the back of the house, but to the right side. She saw why once they got closer—the back door was heavily guarded, but there were high windows on the side.

Not all of those windows were closed.

The structure of the stronghold also meant the guards on the door couldn't see the windows from their position. It was only the angels doing security sweeps in the sky that could prove tricky.

She and Venom made it to the wall without problems. Holly crouched down beside him, their bodies brushing. Heat emanated from him, his flesh very much warm-blooded despite the mark of the viper that defined him. "How are we going to reach the window?" she whispered, as the first accessible one was at least two floors above ground level. "Unless . . . I heard you can slither up walls."

His grin told her he'd caught her own and knew she'd meant no insult. His snakelike tendencies were a part of him and Holly had no intention of ignoring them—that would be like accepting one aspect of his nature and not the rest. And Holly was fascinated and compelled by the whole.

"Depends on the wall." He ran his hand over it. "This one is extremely smooth from age. Even the seams in the stone have been worn away, leaving nothing in terms of a gripping surface. If we were at home, I'd try it, but as we're not . . ." Opening his pack, he took out a coil of rope with a four-pronged hook on one end. "Here's where we need some luck, kitty."

Acid green filmed her vision as Holly listened to the night. "Wait." His arm was rigid muscle under her touch, his skin warm. "Now," she said the instant the wings in the air were at an optimum distance.

He threw.

The hook caught on the ledge of the open window, and when he tugged, it held. "Go."

Grabbing the rope, Holly tried to remember the lessons she'd had. She was no expert, but one of the hunters who was friends with Ashwini liked climbing and Holly went with him sometimes. He didn't know what she was, of course, just thought she was a badly Made vampire, but that didn't matter. Demarco was fun and uncomplicated, their relationship centered on climbing.

The problem was, with this wall being so slippery, she had to rely on her upper-body strength and her thighs to get herself up. She could do it—thanks to her training schedule over the past four years—but she felt like she'd gone through the wars by the time she managed to crawl over the window ledge and into a well-lit passageway.

Pressing her back to the wall the instant she was inside, to avoid being silhouetted against the light, she made sure the hooks were holding tight. The rope went taut a second later. Venom made it up at ruthless speed and was rolling up the rope and putting it back into his pack before her heartbeat eased from its frantic tattoo.

Agony speared Holly's chest without warning.

She could see that this place was as beautiful as she'd imagined—a chandelier up ahead fractured light into rain-drops that cascaded over the deep blue carpet patterned in cream and jewel red. But the beauty was lost on her, her mind a clawing obsession painted in acid green.

She couldn't stop her head from snapping to the left. "That way."

28

Holly's body wanted to go through the wall that stood between her and her destiny.

Taking her hand, Venom squeezed. "Stealth, kitty." A murmur against her ear. "We have to go down the hall and find a way to get to that wing of the house. We can't afford to crash about and get caught—the angels and vampires on guard within will be dangerous powers."

She had the feeling he was talking as much to the thing inside her as explaining what they were about to do. But the otherness didn't want to listen. It shoved so hard at her skin that she thought it was going to explode out of her like the ball of deadly energy that had erupted out of Daisy.

No. This is for both of us. Daisy, who never had a chance. And Holly, who came back from the dead.

She was a *person*.

Not a suitcase taking this . . . *echo* of Uram from one place to another.

"Go," she said to Venom through gritted teeth, conscious that her control over the entity within wasn't absolute.

Viper green eyes connected with hers before he moved silently down the hall, his hand linked warm and strong with hers. He broke contact only when they reached a corner and had to hug the wall before it to check if the way forward was clear. Venom looked very carefully around before jerking back his head.

He held up two fingers, then formed the shape of wings with his hands.

Holly pointed to her eyes and made a questioning face. Her mesmerism didn't work on angels—Izak, the youngest angel in the Tower, if you didn't count Ellie, had allowed her to try to capture him, the experiment supervised by Ash and Dmitri. It had proved a total failure.

Venom, however, was older and stronger. Now, he made a motion with his hand that she read as there being a fifty-fifty chance of success. Given his strength, it meant the two angels up ahead were old, possibly even people he recognized.

The wings inside her *shoved*.

Deadly cold flowed over her, her hands tingling and flexing without her conscious volition. *I can kill those angels.* The thought was as clear as if someone had spoken in her ear—and the voice wasn't hers.

Fuck.

Holly wasn't about to become a goddamn zombie. She lifted Venom's wrist to her mouth and bit down without warning. Blood potent with power . . . blood that was deeply familiar hit her bloodstream, thrusting out the acid green mist crawling through her veins. Flicking her tongue over the wound to help close it, she released the strong weight of his wrist. *Thank you*, she said with her eyes when she met those of a far wilder green.

He ran his knuckles over her cheek, then took out a small mirror from his pocket. As she watched, curious, he held that mirror low by his leg and angled it—*Oh*. It allowed him to see around the corner without having to stick out his head.

Clever.

It was two minutes later that he said, "Now."

Holly moved, Venom at her back. The upper arches of the wings of the angels who'd stepped off the railingless mezzanine were still visible, the central core of this part of the stronghold a vast empty space that soared to the ceiling far above. If the angels looked up, Holly and Venom were screwed, but the two men appeared to be focused on landing on the polished wood of the floor below. Holly ran with all her inhuman speed, but the passage was long and the angels landed before she reached the other end.

Falling to the carpet as close to the wall as possible, she began to crawl.

Voices drifted up from the ground floor, but the words were difficult to understand. She didn't try, just focused on her destination and kept going. Now that she was going in the right direction, the serrated wings inside her chest had stopped trying to breach her flesh, but she could still feel them, lying just beneath her skin.

The distinctive susurration of wings, as if one of the angels was rising back up.

The end of this part of the mezzanine was too far for her to win a race against a being with wings. Holly rolled left and into an open doorway. Venom rolled in a heartbeat later and they moved behind the door to flatten themselves against the wall. Holly's heart thudded hard, but below that was another pull far more visceral. Whatever it was that drew her, it was now so close that it was a hand around her throat that attempted to override her free will and haul her closer.

Holly thought of Mia, of their mom and dad and brothers, of Ash and Janvier, even Arabella and Zeph.

All people who saw *her*. Knew *her*.

No one more so than the vampire who closed his hand over hers and gripped hard. She wove her fingers through his and she stayed determinedly Holly.

She and Venom were in a darkened bedroom. Not Michaela's, that much was clear now that her eyes had adjusted to the darkness. The furniture was lovely, the bed made with flowing white sheets, the bed itself edged by four exquisitely carved posts. A chair with curved legs as elegant sat by the antique white vanity, and it looked like the light in the center of the room might be a small chandelier.

It was very pretty, but without personality. The kind of room where no one lived on a permanent basis. A guest room then, a nice one. It looked like it might even have a private balcony beyond the lacy curtains that hung on the other side of the room. The view—

She elbowed Venom . . . only to glance over and see him staring at those same balcony curtains. He lifted a finger to his lips, then began to slide along the walls in that direction, motioning for her to stay and keep an ear on the external hallway. He was halfway to his destination when the angels' conversation became suddenly more audible. They'd moved to right outside the door.

Holly couldn't understand a word of what the two were saying. They weren't speaking English.

Of course they weren't. She was in freaking Hungary.

She had a smattering of high school French and German, but the language was neither of those. Hungarian made sense. And maybe she was pulling a language out of her ass because she had no idea. What she did have was an app on her phone that Illium had told her to download. As Venom whispered closer to the curtains, she slipped the phone carefully out of her pocket but didn't press the button to bring up the home screen.

First, she unzipped her jacket slightly—and silently—and tucked the phone up near her chin so the glow from the screen would be contained. It wasn't the best way to see the screen, but she could *just* do it if she tucked her chin into her chest.

Bringing up the home screen, she swiped into the translation app. She'd already put the phone on silent, so the app wouldn't speak. However, words began to crawl across the screen, with gaps where the app couldn't pick up the sound. According to the screen, the language being spoken *was* Hungarian . . . right before it became ancient Greek.

Two angels, two preferred languages, but it was obvious they understood one another.

A cheery note popped up over the text, stating that the app's ancient Greek module had been verified by a vampire professor who was an actual ancient Greek. It also helpfully noted that this was no longer a dominant dialect, but still popular among a "statistically significant percentage of immortals."

Holly quickly got rid of it, far more interested in the conversation outside.

". . . restless."

"What . . . sentries . . . ?"

"Nothing, but I'm . . . alert."

". . . a good position . . . make it into the house, but we should be vigilant."

"Agreed. No one can get past us."

Holly winced as the sound of wings opening then closing came from almost directly outside. Well, that made that decision clear. Sliding away her phone, she did what Venom had and made her way silently to the balcony doors he'd parted the curtains very slightly to expose. He shot her a speaking look.

Shaking her head, Holly risked taking out the phone to show him the transcript of the discussion.

His jaw firmed before he returned his attention to the locked door. When he gestured at her hair, she frowned, having no idea what he wanted. He made pointy motions. What? *Oh.* Holly had braided her hair tightly for this operation and had no hairpins to give him. Making a "wait" motion, she reached carefully into her pack to triumphantly reveal a penknife. It was pink, with golden stars on it.

Venom rolled his eyes at the petite thing.

Making a face at him, she pulled out the metal toothpick tucked into the top of one side of the casing. She'd never understood why the otherwise girly penknife, given to her as a gift by Rania—yeah, it still hurt to remember her friend was gone—and filled with things like nail files and a tiny, slender mirror, had a disgusting, meant to be reused, toothpick. Needless to say, Holly had never put it anywhere near her mouth. It had, however, come in handy when she wanted to dig out the last of her lipstick from a tube.

The other side of the casing featured a much more sensible pair of tweezers.

Venom's eyes widened when she produced the toothpick. Grinning, he surprised her with a quick hard kiss before he began to fiddle with the lock again using the spike of metal. Holly's lips felt swollen, sensitive, her mouth curved into a smile. They both froze when the shadow of angelic wings flowed into the room via the open wedge of the door, only relaxing when it became clear one of the angelic sentries in the hall had just moved to stand with his back to this room.

Venom's muscles quivered, his body held in an awkward position.

It took Holly a second to realize he'd picked the lock, but that the last move would make a noise. So they waited . . . and then the angel called out to his partner and Venom twisted. The final click floated under the sound of the conversation outside. But when he would've opened the door, she put her hand on his arm and nodded beyond the glass.

Wind rustled through the trees. Not a gale by any means, but enough to slam the main door to this room closed should they open the door to the balcony. Again, they had to wait. And wait. Holly's muscles threatened to cramp, the unnatural wings in her chest shoving and shoving, but she held it together.

The one good thing about being stuck here was that they could time the sweeps of the angel who was on security in the skies directly above and was most likely to spot them. It looked like they'd have approximately two minutes of clear air if they timed it right. Holly made sure her hood was secure, checked that Venom's knit cap showed no signs of slipping.

And waited.

Venom squeezed her calf.

The wind had paused. And the angel had just passed.

One hundred twenty seconds before he'd turn and see them.

Opening the door, Venom waited for Holly to slip out before coming out himself and pulling the door shut with utmost quietness. Then he crouched down and relocked it using her toothpick. After which, he handed her the toothpick and she put it neatly away into the penknife, that knife going into her pocket.

All the while, she fought the compulsion that sought to turn her into a zombie.

The view from the balcony was magnificent, looking out over an intricate garden maze, and beyond that, the other mountains that formed this range. Stars glittered in the night sky, the beauty of it turning the agony within into a piercing ache of memory. So many times, she'd flown through those night skies. So many times, she'd landed on the flat roof high above that was hidden within the spires. So many times, she'd twined wings with her beloved underneath those stars.

Holly felt her throat lock. "I only ever thought of him as a monster," she whispered to Venom. "I never even considered that he'd had a life before he became a monster. That he loved a woman and flew across a starlit sky with anticipation in his blood."

Venom's hand closed over hers. "He and Raphael were friends once."

Holly tried to see it and today, she could. Two angels, beautiful and strong, laughing together, their feathers glinting in the sunlight, and their eyes bright. "It must've hurt Raphael to have to kill him."

"There was no choice." Venom pointed forward to the next balcony. "Do you think you can cross the gap?"

Seventy seconds to go.

She had to force her eyes away from the sky, the wings deep inside her wanting to stretch out and sweep off this balcony. The urge was so strong that she had to remind herself that she wasn't an angel. She wouldn't soar; she'd crash to the earth, bloodied and broken. The internal battle ate up five precious seconds.

"Yes," she said after mentally measuring the gap.

Venom went first, landing on the opposite side in a silent crouch. Breath shallow, Holly crept up on top of the balustrade . . . and then she flew to land on the far side of the other balcony. Venom's eyes gleamed when he turned toward her. She lifted her shoulders and opened her hands in a silent *I don't know how I did that* answer.

Another balcony lay beyond.

Sixty seconds to go.

Jumping again, they found themselves at the corner; a turret rose up on the far side of the balcony. And Holly's chest glowed so hard that she could feel the rays attempting to pierce the black fabric of her jacket.

She gritted her teeth and, putting her hand on Venom's arm, pointed up with her other. Whatever it was that called to her, it was in that turret. Venom ran his hand down her back as he put his lips to her ear. "There were rumors Michaela might be pregnant. Any chance we're about to break into a nursery?"

Joy and anger unfurled within her. Along with a violent dose of jealousy.

"I don't know," she said through the dark pulse of it. "Unless archangels stay pregnant for years, any child won't be *his*."

"Michaela could've inadvertently transferred part of Uram into the child."

All the blood left Holly's face, to be replaced by chill horror. "What do we do? If it's a child?"

"We do the only thing we can," Venom answered. "We tell Raphael."

"Just like that?"

"We are talking about the child of an archangel."

Yes, said the powerful whisper inside her head, *the weak have no place here.*

Holly closed her hands into fists. "It's getting harder to stay me."

Venom's jaw grew tight. "Turret windows look like they're welded shut," he murmured as he crouched in the darkness, "and there's no way to climb that surface. We'll have to go through these balcony doors, then figure out the rest." He glanced over his shoulder. "Twenty seconds left by my count. If we don't make it in before he turns, go flat on the balcony."

Horror a twisting intruder in her gut at the idea an infant might be dealing with the same dark urges that howled inside her, Holly nonetheless took out her penknife and gave Venom the toothpick. It took him fifteen agonizing seconds to access the darkened room. Entering just as the sentry angel began his turn, they waited for their eyes to adjust.

A shirt thrown over a chair, boots lined up neatly near the doorway, a comb and what might've been cologne or aftershave on the small dresser. An opening to the right, darkness beyond.

The bed was empty.

Not relaxing, Holly padded quietly across the carpet to peek into what turned out to be a large dressing area with sanitary facilities on the right behind a glass door. All empty. She gave Venom the thumbs-up and he emerged from the pool of black where he'd concealed himself so he could provide stealthy backup should Holly be caught. Their next problem was the closed door to this room. It would open out into the same mezzanine passageway that held the two angelic sentries.

Turning the doorknob with jaw-clenched care and tortoise slowness, Venom nudged open the door a fraction of a fraction. Barely enough of a crack to slide out his mirror to examine the passageway. His grim expression told her what he'd seen.

Now what? she mouthed.

29

We wait, Venom mouthed back.

They both took a seat on the floor behind the door.

"What about . . ." She pointed at the bed and its missing owner.

"Vampire or mortal from the size of the bed," Venom murmured directly against her ear, his lips brushing a part of her body she'd never before realized was so sensitive. "I can mesmerize vampires far older than I am, so as long as it isn't someone of Dmitri's age, it won't be a problem."

"And how did that happen?" Holly whispered after tugging down his head with her hand pressed against his cheek. He was warm under her palm, his stubble having begun to emerge to give his skin an intriguingly rough texture. "I get that you're still developing, but from mesmerizing human prey to old immortals?" The surge in Holly's power made sense because of the creepy stuff that had forced its way into her body, but Venom had no such excuse.

"Dmitri says he grew stronger in sudden bursts, too. As

if the body builds up to a certain point, then pushes over in one go."

That made sense in an immortal way. "Well, hypnotizing powers or not, it's not a good bet to hope this guy is under your mesmerism age limit. We're in an archangelic stronghold."

Venom grinned and shrugged.

When she scowled at him, he mouthed, *Kitty.* She punched him lightly on the arm. He took her fisted hand, pretended to sink his fangs into her knuckles. Her lips twitched . . . and it was okay. Because they were in this together.

An hour passed, with Venom using his mirror to check the hallway every few minutes. The pain in Holly's chest slowly intensified to the point that she pressed her palm to her chest in a futile effort to ease it. Venom saw the movement, put his hand on her thigh. She gripped that hand, held on hard. And tried to breathe.

"The angels are walking in the opposite direction," he said three minutes later. "The turret entrance should be directly to our left."

"Let's do it." Trying to sneak past under the angels' noses was a massive risk, but so was sitting here when her chest was threatening to crack in half, leaving her a bloody, broken mess.

Opening the door, Venom slipped out to watch the angels while waving her out. Holly didn't argue or hesitate. She padded on silent feet to the only possible door that could lead to the turret—it was angled into the corner.

Her hand fell on the doorknob.

It was locked.

Shit.

She looked over her shoulder to see that Venom was backing up toward her. She knew he was keeping his gaze forward in the hope he could mesmerize the angels should it come to that. But those angels would turn onto the other part of the mezzanine within seconds. No way they could avoid being seen.

There was no time for Venom to pick the lock.

Holly stared at the lock . . . and a whisper of acid green rolled down her arm and into it. Oddly calm, the pain no longer agonizing, she turned the doorknob again. She was inside the next second. Venom moved with viper speed to join her, the two of them managing to shut the door without making a noise.

Tongue dry and heart a drum, Holly stared at him. It was dark in this part of the turret and her chest, it was glowing. So were Venom's eyes. She touched her fingers to his left cheekbone. He was strong and extraordinary and unique . . . and she'd always wanted to have him in her court. But he was ridiculously loyal to Raphael. She'd never understood why. Raphael was a strong pup but she was thousands of years older, had far more power. Yet Raphael was able to hold the loyalty of not just this vampire with the eyes of a viper, but that of Dmitri.

He'd never been able to do that. He'd had friendships once. A long time ago. Raphael had been his friend. They'd raced through the Refuge on wings of air and fire, or that was what it had felt like. It was after Raphael's ascension that things had changed. The pup had become too strong, and he'd had trouble accepting that.

Such a fool he'd been.

He should've killed Raphael before the young angel he'd known had ever ascended.

"Holly."

Holly stared into eyes slitted like a snake's, Venom's hands gripping her upper arms. "I'm here," she rasped, her throat gritty. "It's strong now. He keeps sliding into my thoughts, making me into him."

"Drink." Venom held his wrist up to her mouth.

Once again, the punch of his unique and brutally powerful blood helped her shove the echo to enough of a distance that she could function. "I won't be able to last long," she warned him. "He's very strong in this place." Stuck in Holly's weak body, but flush with a power that had lain dormant since the attack.

"Then let's finish our recon and get out of here."

Holly turned to the stairs that spiraled up to the top of the turret. They were narrow but well maintained and a metal railing ran along the right side. She went first. Venom didn't try to stop her.

He will never limit me. He will help me fly.

It was a gift, one she held on to tight.

The closer she got to the turret, the more difficult it became to ignore the violent pressure in her chest. Holly unzipped the jacket in a futile effort to ease that pressure. Acid green light blazed out of her, spearing through the darkness. It glimmered on the iron of the huge padlock that hung on the door to the turret room.

Break it.

Digging the nails of one hand into her palm, Holly retrieved her penknife with the other, then pushed out the toothpick using her thumbnail. "One more lock to pick," she said to Venom. There was no way to hide a broken padlock and they'd promised to leave behind no trace of their presence.

Venom crouched down to begin.

It took him long enough that sweat began to trickle down her temples, the pressure inside her a cauldron. Stripping off the jacket and her pack, she left them both by the door. Venom unclipped the padlock right then and put it down quietly beside her things, before quickly taking off his pack and placing it next to hers.

Rising to his feet, he placed his hand on the doorknob. "I'll go first."

Holly nodded because she *had* to get inside, and agreement was the fastest way to ensure it.

Venom took hold of her chin, made sure her eyes locked with his. "Take what blood you need to stay in control."

Only after she'd nodded did he open the door.

The room within was lit only by an acid green glow. Holly thought at first that it was her chest . . . but that light was coming from something in the center of the circular space. Gripping Venom's hand viciously tight, she stared at the frightening sight that met her: a crib. White and delicate.

Her stomach roiled. A baby?

No. Please no.

She felt Venom suck in a breath and then the two of them walked silently closer, close enough to look down into that horrifying crib. Only . . . they hit something before they got within touching distance of whatever lay in the crib. A barrier blazed up against them, repelling them with enough force that they both stumbled, barely keeping their feet. Its color was a shimmering bronze that reminded Holly of Michaela's wings. As they watched, it formed into a lattice that enclosed the entire crib in a ball of glittering power.

"What is that?" Holly raised her fingers to the bronze power but didn't touch it.

"It looks like Michaela can leave behind static pieces of her power." Venom scanned the glittering structure. "Probably a Cascade-born ability, or else there would've been rumors about it before now. My guess is she'd have to recharge the construct at some point."

Holly didn't care about the answer anymore, even though she'd asked the question. The green glow in the crib called to her. Heart pounding, chest pulsing, she stepped close enough to look through the lattice cage . . . and saw a misshapen and twisted . . . Not a child.

It had no head. No eyes. No nose. No limbs. No rib cage. No hips. No spinal cord.

It looked like *nothing* human or immortal or even animal. It was nothing but a lump of clay mashed together and turned into meat. But that distorted lump of flesh rose and fell in a pattern of breaths and its pale brown skin was as fragile as a baby's beneath the acid green glow.

There was a twisted and sickeningly soft-appearing bone sticking out of its center that vaguely resembled the shape of a wing. But, it *wasn't* a wing. And what was that? The tip of an *adult* finger, complete with a hard, square nail, jutting out below the wet shine of a patch of flesh that appeared to be rotting beneath the false life of the acidic glow. And oh, God, there were three adult teeth sticking out on the other side of it.

How could it breathe? It had no nose, no mouth. No brain. How could it be *alive*?

Her stomach roiled.

Bile rising, Holly began to back off . . . and the wings stretched and stretched and tore out of her before she could do anything to fight the migration.

Venom saw Holly's back stiffen, her spine arching in a dangerous curve. Her mouth opened on a soundless scream, spears of acidic green light pouring out of every cell of her body. Even as he moved toward her with inhuman speed, the light coalesced into a single tight beam and began to stream toward the lattice.

The lattice bounced it back into Holly with brutal force.

She shuddered, blood streaming out of her nose and her eyes, *her*, but her body bowed again nearly at once, the acid green energy punching once more at the lattice. Venom was ready when it was repelled this time. He grabbed Holly in the split second after the power returned but before it re-took control.

He connected with her eyes. But, as he'd feared, Holly was immune to his ability to mesmerize. Her eyes glowed as the power rose again. And where his hand pressed against her stomach from his attempt to capture her, he felt wetness. He didn't need to look to know what it was.

Every vampire knew the sharp metallic tang of blood.

The energy inside her was literally tearing her apart in its frantic efforts to get to the energy . . . receptacle in the bronze lattice cage. Venom made a split-second decision. He gripped Holly's throat in a single powerful hand and squeezed hard, cutting off her blood flow. Her body spasmed in his grip for nearly a minute before going limp.

A human would be dead.

He was counting on the fact that Holly wasn't human. Because if he'd killed . . . Pain such as he'd never again expected to feel tore through him as he scooped her up into his arms and carried her to the far side of the room. Placing her on a window seat, he checked her pulse.

Relief was a cold punch in his gut.

She was alive, and the glow had stopped. It made him believe that the thing inside her needed her to be conscious to do what it had been doing. Which meant its own consciousness wasn't whole, couldn't exist without being a parasite. As with the pulsing horror in the crib, it was twisted and created of pieces. It needed to use Holly as a host. However, like an insect that erupted out of its host's body after consuming that body from the inside out, it'd kill her in an effort to get out.

Leaving Holly on the seat, Venom went to look through the lattice again; he needed to give the sire every detail he could. His gut told him that thing shouldn't exist and wasn't alive in any known sense, the rise and fall under its skin having only a superficial resemblance to breathing. As he watched, that rise and fall pulsed and faded in random jaggedness, pulsed and faded. Flickered.

And he caught a hint of putrid green below the surface: *decay.*

All details stored in his mind, Venom moved to the next thing on his list and touched the bronze lattice directly. It threw him back against the wall, but he'd prepared for that outcome and rolled with viper fluidity. He'd been with Raphael long enough to identify the power that had repelled him as archangelic.

He wouldn't be getting through it.

Which left him with only one choice: he had to get Holly out of here before she regained consciousness and the malignant energy inside her began to once again attempt to reconnect with this other piece of itself. He also had to keep her away from it until he could talk to Raphael and figure out a solution that didn't end with Holly's death.

Because Venom wasn't okay with that.

Keeping an ear open for any sign that Holly was regaining consciousness, he went to the windows around the turret to see if he could open one. The answer wasn't good: as he'd thought earlier, the windows were welded shut. They were also designed so that smashing the glass would have no real impact—the panes were too small for anything bigger than a bird to get through, while the window frame itself was formed of thick metal.

Michaela clearly understood that this *un*being could not be permitted to escape. Why, then, did she allow it to exist? For power? Or had she loved Uram enough to hold out hope for his return?

None of that was important in this time and place.

Only Holly mattered.

Venom would have to take her out the same way they'd come in.

He'd always liked a challenge, he thought grimly.

Going back over the room, he made sure they'd left behind no trace of their presence. It was evident that Michaela wasn't mentally connected to the power lattice, else the room would've been swarming with guards a minute after their entry. After he'd confirmed that no drops of Holly's blood lay on the floor to betray her, he picked up her body and exited the room, then placed her on the ground and carefully relocked the padlock in the same position in which he'd found it.

Getting Holly back into her jacket and zipping it up proved easy enough; he made a note to needle her by calling her a doll. She'd glare daggers at him before replying with some equally needling riposte. Her pack was a problem. However, she didn't have much more than food and a change of clothes in it now that her jacket was out. So he emptied everything into his own larger pack, then managed to squash her empty pack in there as well. Slinging it on, he picked her up again and tried not to look at the purpling bruise around her neck.

He'd done that.

He, a man who'd been very careful through time to never become without conscience, to never treat women as disposable commodities. His sisters might have forsaken him, but that didn't change that he was a man who'd grown up knowing it was his duty to care for, not harm them. "I'm sorry, kitty," he murmured, rubbing his cheek against her hair before he started down the stairs.

Getting to the bottom wasn't a problem—Holly didn't weigh all that much. She was pretty small, even though she seemed such a huge presence when she was awake and snapping back at him. Placing her on the ground again once they'd navigated the stairs, her back to a wall, he risked cracking open the door the tiniest fraction.

Two angels stood not fifty feet in the distance.

Venom decided to wait. From what he'd seen so far, this turret was off-limits to any and all. The angels' job was to ensure that no one breached the house and got to the crib above. Michaela had also left a huge warning sign with that bronze lattice. Given her reputation for creative and cruel punishments, he didn't think her people would be disregarding her orders.

Not so long as Venom didn't give them a reason to check the turret.

The problem was keeping Holly unconscious long enough to distance her from the unbeing in the crib. Venom hadn't forgotten the wings that blazed in her chest in Central Park, but that had been fleeting. The power hadn't attempted a total takeover until it was within touching distance of the receptacle. And it was only inside the stronghold that the memories had begun to merge with Holly's own mind.

An hour of screaming patience later, her eyes began to flutter open.

"I'm sorry," he whispered again, and choked her out of consciousness.

Tears clogged his throat, threatened to roll down his cheeks for the first time in over three centuries.

30

A minute afterward, bile yet burning his throat, he looked out into the hallway. The two sentries had disappeared. He dared stick out his head to check that the entire mezzanine was clear. *Yes.* He realized the angels must've decided to stretch their wings by flying down.

But they'd be back soon.

He threw Holly over his shoulder, wincing at the damage he was doing to her already wounded abdomen, and pulled the door shut behind himself. He'd used the wait to fix it from the inside so that it would lock behind him, but he checked to make sure. Then he made his way in quick silence to where they'd entered the stronghold.

The area was still empty and the window was still open.

After placing Holly against a wall, he slid off his pack, removed his hook and rope, then anchored the hook as strongly as possible. They'd already left a few marks. Others were unavoidable, but hopefully, no one looked too carefully at this window ledge at the end of a distant hallway.

Climbing down with Holly wasn't going to be easy, but

he finally decided on moving his pack to the front and tying her to his back with an extra rope. It wouldn't be the most comfortable position for her and she'd probably wake with one hell of a backache, but she'd be alive. Pack and Holly in position, he waited for a time when there were no wings in the sky close enough to spot him.

Ten excruciating minutes passed before the sky was clear.

Venom swung out the window.

With the weight on him, the rope tore at his palms. He barely felt it. His Making had hardened him to many other types of pain. When you were tied down, then had angry vipers and cobras thrown onto your body, their fangs sinking poison into your unguarded flesh over and over again until agony and horror were all you knew . . . Well, there weren't many nightmares that could terrify Venom and little pain that even came close to destabilizing.

He moved with preternatural speed.

His feet landed on the grass without an alarm being shouted. Untying Holly and placing her on the grass, he swung his backpack into the correct position before flicking the rope in a hard ripple designed to dislodge the hook.

It held.

He tried again, the motion one he'd practiced and practiced and practiced again over the centuries. The stupid thing didn't budge.

Venom took a deep breath, reached for the ice coldness of the creatures who'd marked him, and flicked again.

The rope slithered down, the hook falling.

Catching it, he wound up the rope and hooked it onto his backpack, careful to do so in a way that wouldn't hurt Holly when he threw her over his shoulder. Which he did the next minute. She groaned partway through his run through the orchard but he didn't stop. And when he ran into a guard, he mesmerized the vampire without thought, giving the male much the same instruction Holly had the other guard: *You saw nothing but a cat. There were no intruders.*

He was gone a heartbeat later, lost in the darkness. He made it to the treeline using viper speed, timing his bursts of movement to avoid sweeps by the angels flying overhead. He didn't stop even once under the tree canopy. Though he usually only used his speed in sporadic bursts, tonight he ran full tilt for as long as his body could bear it.

It wasn't an endless period. He was only three hundred and fifty or so years old and yet growing into his power. When he finally came to a standstill and looked back, he could see the stronghold, but it was a toy castle now, the distance he'd put between the unbeing in the crib and Holly a significant one.

"Venom."

Releasing Holly from over his shoulder at that sluggish sound, he sat her down with her back to a tree and cupped her face in his hands. "Talk to me, kitty." It came out a plea.

She lifted her hand to weakly close over his wrist. "Where . . ." Her voice was a rasp.

"Wait." Shrugging off his pack, he took out a bottle of water, helped her wet her throat. "Is that better?"

A faint nod, her head turning in the direction of the stronghold. "I can still feel it." Her chest glowed.

"Can you fight?"

A taut moment before she nodded. "Yes. He's not in my head as much." Another breath that sounded too rough, not quite right, the damage to her throat obvious.

Cold deep inside in a way that had nothing to do with his Making, Venom stroked tendrils of hair off her face. "We need to check your chest and stomach." He'd known he was hurting her further by carrying her over his shoulder, but it had been the only way to get her to safety.

Holly didn't fight him when he unzipped her jacket and gently pulled up the black top she wore underneath. The only mercy was that the blood hadn't dried, so he wasn't ripping the fabric off her. He didn't need a flashlight to see the damage—her chest glowed acid green, illuminating her skin.

Cracks spread out across that skin.

Her heart was the epicenter of the bloody quake.

Venom's fangs shoved against his lower lip, not because of the scent of her blood—though Holly *did* smell very good—but because seeing her hurt, in pain, it did things to him he hadn't permitted anyone to do for centuries. She was fragile, Holly.

Venom didn't hang around fragile people.

He lifted his wrist to her mouth. "Drink."

Her eyes met his, the pain in them searing. "I've taken blood from you more than once already." A scowl that made her seem herself again. "You can't be weak if we're going to survive."

Venom chuckled, the knots of his muscles easing slightly. "It'd take more than a couple of bites from you to weaken me."

When she continued to hesitate, the stubborn line to her jaw one with which he was intimately familiar, he reached into his pack and pulled out a bottle of blood in an insulated carrier. "Courtesy of Ashwini. She said I might need it." Elena's hunter friend—and Janvier's wife—had what Venom's mother would've called "the third eye," so Venom hadn't fought the extra weight created by the two insulated bottles.

"Drink it first," Holly ordered, her breathing uneven. "I'd rather . . . I don't like drinking like that."

Not about to waste time arguing when she was hurting, Venom screwed the top off the bottle and began to gulp it down . . . only to rip it from his mouth with a curl of his lip. "It's *flavored.*"

Holly's lips curved, a spark in her eyes. "What flavor?"

He brought the hideous thing back to his lips, took a sip. "Spiced." And, he grudgingly accepted, the taste wasn't so bad. He drank more. And thought of home. Of the warmth of the inn's large kitchen as his mother threw cinnamon and cloves and cardamom into the pot during Diwali. The Festival of Lights, full of color and joy and the sweetest of scents, had always been his favorite time of the year.

Holly reached out to clasp her hand over his, her grip weak but steadfast. "What is it?"

Venom didn't talk about his past. It was long buried and turned to dust. But at that moment, with the spices lingering on his tongue and the memories uncurling with warm stealth inside him, he couldn't stay silent. "Home," he whispered. "This blood reminds me of home." His smile was a thing formed of equal parts sadness and happiness. "Long ago."

"Let me taste."

He didn't give her the bottle. Leaning forward, he pressed his lips to hers. Her free hand coming up to lie against his cheek, she accepted his gentle kiss and when they drew apart, her eyes were wet. "You miss it."

"Yes. Sometimes." New York was his home now. It was where his family lived—the Seven, Raphael, Janvier, even a few of the younger idiots, but part of him would always be that boy who'd come to adulthood in an inn on the Silk Road. The hot air, the sound of voices raised in conversation in a thousand distinct dialects and languages, the color and chaotic wildness of it, the piercing starlight so far out from the smoke and dust of a large city, the memories would live in him forever.

"Can you go back?"

Holly had no idea what she was asking. He shook his head. "Not home. I can't go home."

Her fingers tightened on his.

"But I can go to India," he said, brushing back her hair again. "Neha likes me. She calls me and Janvier her Charm and Guile. We have never figured out which one of us is which."

"I've always wanted to go to India," Holly said on another shaky breath. "And to China. My great-grandparents came from a place called Xi'an."

"We'll go." With that promise, Venom brushed his fingers down her bruised throat. "I'm sorry."

Catching his hand, she pressed a kiss of unexpected sweetness to his palm. "I'm not. Thank you for helping me stay Holly. Now drink."

Venom finished off the bottle of blood that held some magic that had made him speak of the past—and thought deliberately of the future he wanted, the future he'd fight to the death to win. "On our trip to India," he said, "we'll ride a motorcycle through the streets of Delhi, dodging bullocks pulling carts, and spindly rickshaws, and pretentious vampires in town cars, and we'll surprise Neha with you. We'll just have to be careful she doesn't try to keep you."

Holly's fangs sank into his wrist when he held it up. She cradled that wrist as if it was a precious thing that could be hurt. So strange, was Holly. She made his heart hurt in ways that he'd have thought were impossible. But as she drank, he saw the cracks in her body begin to heal inch by inch.

She drank more than she normally would, and when she flicked her tongue over the wound to help it heal, she did so with utmost gentleness. He smiled. "Careful, kitty. You start being nice to me and I'll begin to think you like me."

"I'll consider it, Viper Face."

Grinning, because she was back, he rose and held out a hand. "Can you move?"

She accepted his help and slowly got up, then flexed as slowly. "Yes," she said at last. "I feel bruised and the flesh on my chest and abdomen is new and fragile, but I'm not weak. I'll just have to be careful not to tear open the wounds."

He'd been going through the pack as she spoke. "Here," he said, having found the long-sleeved black T-shirt she'd brought along as a change. "We need to clean the blood off you, too."

Taking off her jacket, she stripped off her bloody top. Then she used water from a nearly empty bottle to sponge off the dried blood. "Am I clean?"

Venom looked at her small, sleek, perfect form. And wanted to bite her in ways that had nothing to do with survival. "Turn around."

When she did, he nodded. "Blood's gone." Droplets would've sunk into the waistband of her jeans, but that wasn't something they could deal with right now.

"How much got onto your jacket?" he asked after she'd pulled on the clean tee.

It turned out that the inner lining of her jacket was waterproof, and they were able to wipe it clean using the already damp top. Close as they were, the scent of her curled around him like the kitten he called her. He wanted to tumble her into his arms and explore her, find out if the passionate, fascinated, protective pull he felt toward her had become that most precious of things: *home*.

But first, he had to get her to safety.

Taking the bloody top they'd used as a rag, he said, "I'll be back in five. Anything dangerous appears, poison it with those baby fangs."

The sound of her snarl stayed with him as he faded into the trees, his destination the waterway he'd glimpsed not long before he'd stopped. *There*. A small stream tumbling over rocks. The large gray wolf standing on the other side was no surprise, not in this region. Its eyes gleamed at Venom as Venom washed out the top; it'd get rid of the concentrated smell of wet iron. Vampires had good noses, but they weren't bloodhounds. This should keep a vampire from using their scent trail to mount a pursuit.

It'd have been a different case if Michaela had one of the hunter-born in her employ, but the former Queen of Constantinople and current Archangel of Budapest had a strange blind spot when it came to hunters. She used the services of the Guild and, according to the hunters Venom knew, she treated the hunters in her territory with courtesy. However, she didn't have any deeper connection with the Guild.

Then again, neither had the Tower until Raphael fell in love with a mortal hunter and the world turned upside down. Most mortals, even the strongest, stayed away from immortals. It was good for their health.

"Good hunting, my friend," Venom said to the wolf across the way, the one who'd stayed in place but had made no aggressive moves—like recognized like, and the wolf knew Venom wasn't prey.

He was on his way back to Holly seconds later. He found her sitting with the backpack, her jacket on but open; the green glow continued to pulse. She hadn't taken out her pack from inside his, probably well aware she'd need all her strength just to move, but she appeared to be repacking. "I organized it so the stuff we might need first is at the top," she said without looking up.

Venom knew he was silent when he moved. "How did you know I was here?"

A shrug. "I could feel you."

Unconcerned about that when he'd normally be otherwise, he walked over and hunkered down to look into the pack. "Why did you put that bottle of blood near the top?" It was the unopened one. "I already drank one."

"I don't think it'll stay cold and good for longer than maybe till morning, so you should have it then." A wicked smile up at him. "Wonder what flavor it is?"

"I'm never accepting gifts from Ashwini again," Venom muttered, but of course it was a lie. He'd take anything the seer gave him. No one called her that, but they all knew it was what she was. Ash saw things that hadn't yet happened, and if she liked you enough to offer you a helping hand, you'd be an imbecile not to take it.

Of course, Ashwini's motives weren't always linear. "Has she ever told you anything?" he asked Holly as he put her damp—but clean of blood—top into a plastic bag that he then stuffed into a front pocket of the pack.

A long pause before Holly nodded. "You sure you want to know? It might make you question the nature of fate and destiny and free will."

Venom was immediately intrigued. "Tell me."

31

"One day," Holly began, "after we'd sparred on the lawn at her and Janvier's place, and I was sitting on the grass, looking down at the Hudson and feeling sad for the life I'd never have, Ashwini sat down next to me and said, 'Holly.'"

Wild green eyes met his. "I was still Sorrow then, but that day, she called me Holly very specifically. I didn't correct her because she had this tone in her voice that told me to be quiet and *listen*. And she said . . ."

"I've already strangled you twice," Venom murmured with lethal silkiness, though he still wasn't all right with what he'd done to save her from the entity inside her. "They say the third time is the charm."

Her laughter was reckless and fearless and he wanted to drink her in until that laughter was his own. "I was focused so hard on her," she said with a smile lingering on her lips. "My body was almost quivering to hear what she had to tell me—my future? My death? What? At last, Ash opened her mouth and said, 'Don't forget to learn Hindi.'"

Venom blinked. "What?"

"Uh-huh." Her shoulders shook. "I'd have thought her completely mad, except that I'd been around Ash long enough to realize that when she says one of her weird things, you should listen. So I joined an online class." The last sentence was spoken in the language of Venom's homeland.

Something huge spread out inside him, a wild joyful thing without a name. "Your accent could use a little work," he said in the same language.

"And you can't speak Mandarin, so shut up."

He replied in that language, saw her eyes widen. "I grew up on the Silk Road," he reminded her. "I also spent over a hundred years in Neha's court, and she has many courtiers who come from across the border." Not all spoke the same dialect as Holly; he'd had to learn multiple variations—as he'd had to learn the languages favored in other parts of India. "Naasir always says he doesn't like not knowing what secrets people are talking about. Neither do I."

Holly's smile was a wide-open thing of utmost delight. "My grandma made me attend Mandarin school all through my childhood. I used to get so mad because I had to spend my Saturday mornings there instead of watching cartoons." She spoke the words in a mélange of the three languages they shared. "But as I grew older, I was glad. I can speak to her in the language she used with her own mother. And it's something special, you know?"

Venom understood. "Janvier speaks Hindi, as does Ashwini," he told her. "Most of the Seven have an excellent grasp of it, too. Part of it is they're just old enough to have had the time to learn multiple languages . . ."

"But the rest is because they're your family," Holly said, raising her hand to brush her fingers over his cheek. "So, *jaanuu*, is it time to go? Also, did you know there's a wolf behind you?"

"He's just curious about the other predators in his territory. Don't challenge him with eye contact, but also don't appear weak." Venom looked back to let the wolf know they were aware of it. "He wants to make sure we're only passing through."

Venom pulled on the pack and got up.

Accepting the hand he held out, Holly used it to haul herself up. "Is our safe house within a distance we can travel on foot?"

"Yes. But we might not make it before dawn." Holly was weaker than she should be, even with his blood twining with her own. "We'll have to camp in the forest if there's any chance we might get caught out in the open."

"Yes, that would suck after we successfully pulled off the stealth infiltration of an archangelic home." Tugging the hood of her jacket on over her hair, Holly zipped up the jacket so that her face was neatly framed, her body a sleek black outline. "Let's do it."

They began to run, the wolf running alongside them for over an hour before it peeled off to return to its territory. Venom had kept the pace at one Holly could also maintain. She was doing better than he'd expected. Even at full strength, she wouldn't be as fast as him—but she'd be fast enough to make it fun.

Flying over a log in their path, she turned to grin at him over her shoulder.

He grinned back, and they ran.

Wings flew overhead now and then, and when they did, the two of them crouched low, became motionless. The farther they got from the stronghold, the less Holly's chest glowed— Venom knew because she'd unzip and check every so often, until, by the time they ran into a small mountain village, there was no wash of acid green pulsing off her body.

Dawn hovered a red line on the horizon, but it was just far enough off that the farmers who ran goats up in these mountains weren't yet awake. Venom and Holly moved like shadows through the village, not stopping when dogs barked.

They were long gone and back in the forests before anyone so much as twitched a curtain in response to the canine alarm. If anyone *had* seen them, all they would've spotted were two dark silhouettes. Venom had pulled the knit cap back over his hair and made sure to keep his eyes open only a sliver so no one could identify him.

Sunglasses pre-dawn would've been a dead giveaway.

Safe in the trees some distance from the village, they stopped so Venom could drink the second bottle of blood, after which Holly would feed from him to continue her recovery. Before that, he gave her the prepackaged food she'd brought along: he never forgot that Holly wasn't a vampire in the known sense, needed actual food, too. As she munched on a packet of cheese and crackers, he opened the bottle of blood and—forewarned by the last bottle—took a cautious sip.

Pretzels and coffee and roasting nuts.

He laughed. "Ashwini gave me New York this time." Another home of his heart. He drank it down without hesitation, then kissed Holly again so she could taste it. And so he could taste her.

She licked her tongue playfully against his. "Shall we indulge in wildly-inappropriate-on-the-run sex?"

He sank his fangs into her lower lip, just enough for it to be a sting.

"Ouch." She did the same back to him and when they drew apart, they were both panting.

"A bed," Venom said silkily. "I want a bed and time." The luxury to stroke her softly, slowly, drink her in.

Holly's breath caught. "Then let's move it."

"Feed first." But he didn't give her his wrist.

Instead, he did something he *never* did . . . except with her. He leaned in so she could feed from his throat. Slender fingers curving around the side of his neck, a soft breath kissing his skin, her scent slinking around him like an affectionate cat.

His already rigid cock went stone hard when she sank her small fangs into his vein. To feed her, to care for her, it gave him so much pleasure that he knew he was in trouble beyond anything he'd ever before handled. He cradled her head to him regardless, glorying in the pleasure of the intimate blood kiss.

She took her time, sipping slowly rather than gulping and getting it over with.

When she did end the kiss, it was with a press of her lips against his skin. "Okay," she said in a husky tone that stroked him just right, "maybe I could grow to enjoy drinking blood in some very limited circumstances." A nuzzle against his throat. "Will you feed from me?"

Venom shuddered. "When we're safe." He wouldn't take much, the act more about the offer and the acceptance than sustenance.

She nuzzled his throat again, small and fierce and strangely gentle with him. "I want to curl up and sleep."

"Soon." Forcing himself to break the skin-to-skin contact, he took a quick breath before rising, tugging her up at the same time. "We're nearly there."

They eased their way into a fast run, Holly moving more fluidly after the fresh injection of blood and food. Her distance from the abomination in the crib was also likely helping; the less strength she had to expend on fighting the alien energy from taking over, the more she had for herself.

The two of them made it to their destination just as true dawn cracked the world in spears of burning gold and brilliant red. That destination was a lodge deep within the trees. There were other lodges scattered through the forest, but all were far enough from one another that privacy was assured. Owned by the very wealthy, these lodges were winter homes meant for the skiing season.

The actual runs were a short distance away, which meant the forest around the cabins was thick, cocooning the homes in lush green solitude.

It so happened that the wealthy vampire who owned this lodge was part of Jason's network of spies. Venom had once

asked Raphael's spymaster—a fellow member of the
Seven—how he could be certain that a vampire who'd been
so long in Michaela's territory could now be loyal to Raphael. "Michaela has her moments," Venom had said, "but
she's not evil for the most part, and she protects the inno-
cents in her territory."

"She also flays vampires alive and uses their skin to make
purses," Jason had replied, his wings blending in with the
night as they stood on a Tower balcony on a moonless eve.

Shrugging, Venom had said, "Aside from that."

Jason's eyes had actually glinted with humor, the tribal
tattoo that covered one side of his face an astonishing work
of fine curves and dots. "Michaela ordered the death of a
vampire our ally loved deeply," he'd answered at last, the
humor fading into a cool darkness. "It was not a deserved
death—Michaela was capricious in giving the order and
though she was apologetic in the aftermath, her remorse
couldn't breathe life back into the dead. Our ally and his
lover were together for five centuries and devoted to one
another always. He will never forgive Michaela for the loss,
no matter how long he lives."

It made more sense than a non-immortal—or even a
young immortal—could ever understand. Love was a gift
that came along rarely in their world, especially love so
true that it lasted through centuries—that was beyond a
gift. It was a *treasure*.

"Michaela doesn't understand the depth of her crime,"
Jason had added with spymaster quietness as his eyes
tracked an angel with wings of peacock blue and emerald
green who flew with Elena around the Legion skyscraper.

"She's never loved that much, that desperately." The passion in Jason's voice was not a thing of fire, but of thunder,
deep and potent. "She thinks he has gotten past it in the
hundred years since the death. She has no idea that he sits
every night at a table set for two and drinks blood in com-

plete silence while looking at a painting of his love done three centuries earlier by Aodhan."

Venom's eyes went to Holly's profile as she pulled back her hood and shot him a wild grin. And he knew. She'd *never* bore him, not through centuries and centuries and centuries. And if he won her heart, the fierce wildness of her would be endlessly loyal. He'd never, ever have to worry that she'd reject him. She'd drive him insane on a regular basis, but he'd be *hers*.

"We made it," she said, but didn't pad her way to the wide steps that led onto the porch fronting the A-frame structure. "You sense any danger?"

Venom shook his head, though she was the most dangerous thing in his world. "It's safe to go in."

Holly moved forward, stopping when he didn't follow. "Come on, Viper Face." Laughter in her expression, her hair rainbow strands across her face where it had escaped her braid. "Your eyes are pretty in the dawnlight, light green fire mixed with gold."

No one but Holly had ever called his eyes pretty. Eerie. Striking. Unique. Yes. But never pretty. Not until her. "And you look like a unicorn kitty who wants to curl up and sleep."

Sticking out her tongue at him, she ran up the steps and, after locating the hidden key exactly where they'd been told it would be, walked into the house. He ran after her in deadly silence. Once inside, they locked the door and—though need pounded at him—he told Holly to duck into the shower while he prepared something for her to eat. She needed more fuel. Her body was burning up what she already had too fast. He was certain she'd lost weight over the night, her cheekbones were so sharp against her skin.

"This 'little winter cabin' has at least three showers," she told him after a short exploration, her eyes wide at the idea of such luxury. "You should use one, too. Jeez, some people are so freaking rich."

Venom wondered when she'd realize *he* was rich. It made him smile to think of the gift he'd ordered her—she'd either shoot him when she saw it or she'd laugh in amused delight.

Because Holly *would* make it.

Showering quickly, he dressed in a pair of jeans and a black shirt with long sleeves that he folded back; clothes in multiple sizes had been left in one of the guest suites for those who might come through. When he went into the kitchen, he found it stocked with food as promised. Had anyone from Michaela's court become suspicious about so much food in the home of a vampire, their absent host had a ready explanation: it was for the human mistresses he kept for blood and sex.

Nothing unusual about that. According to Jason, the women never knew that they were literally only conveniences as well as smoke screens. The vampire treated them with politeness and generosity for the time that they hung on his arm and, when it was time to part, he made sure they were in a good situation. "He uses them for cover," Jason had said, "but his heart is never going to belong to anyone else. I think he lives only so he can wreak vengeance on Michaela through such methods as are open to him."

Venom had witnessed that kind of love through time, but he'd believed himself incapable of it after his Making. He was too cold inside, the vipers and cobras that had been part of his Making marking him far more deeply than most people realized.

Bone-deep friendship? Loyalty? Fidelity? That he could do.

But the kind of love that softened a man and made him vulnerable? Love that was so intimate it dug its way into the soul and anchored in with millions of tiny hooks? Love that understood no boundaries, put up no walls, exposed its defenseless throat? How could a viper be capable of that?

Yet Venom was starting to believe he wasn't only capable of it, he'd been built for it. Built to love with the same relentless will that had powered his psychic survival after the unthinkable horror of his Making. All he'd needed to awaken his heart, to turn on that switch of unyielding devotion, was one specific smart, fierce, and deadly woman who took no shit and whose fire was so bright that it embraced his cold without a blink.

Holly Chang. Sorrow. Kitty. Hollyberry.

No matter what he called her, she was the most dangerous adversary he'd ever faced.

Because once that switch flipped on, he knew it would never, ever turn off.

32

Holly stepped out of the glorious heat of the shower to find that Venom had thrown clothes on the bed in the spare bedroom she'd claimed. A loose white sundress with spaghetti straps and little eyelet holes in the lined fabric. It wasn't what she'd have chosen, but, to be fair to Venom, there probably wasn't much of a selection. She pulled it on . . . and had to laugh. She hadn't seen the front, as it had been lying on the bed with the back showing before she tugged it on over her head.

That front had splatters of color across it.

"Okay," she whispered into the mirror, "you do get me."

Not bothering with underwear since her spare pair was shoved in their backpack, which was probably still in the lounge, she brushed her damp hair until her scalp tingled, then headed out . . . straight into a rich, savory scent. Underneath that lay a softer undertone of sugar and cardamom and spice. Her stomach rumbled.

She ran to the kitchen.

And came to a sudden halt.

Feet bare and a pair of well-worn jeans hugging his butt, the black shirt he wore a little worn at the seams and his dark hair falling forward across his face, Venom was . . . She took a deep breath and, bracing her back against the doorjamb, pressed her thighs together. Tight.

When he looked up, she found herself caught in the lethal beauty of his eyes, as if he'd mesmerized her. Holly gripped the doorjamb, her hands behind her back. If she got any closer she might jump his bones, and watching him cook was way, way too much fun for her to end it just yet. "What're you making?"

"Here." The gorgeous man who'd given her the most wonderful vampiric feeding experience of her life put a plate on the counter. "Sit. Eat."

When Holly padded over to scoot up onto one of the three breakfast stools that lined this side of the counter, she saw that he'd made her an omelet with all kinds of things in it. Onion, ham, green peppers, mushrooms. Her stomach rumbled. She'd eaten half of it before she looked up and saw him watching her, a smile playing with the edges of his lips. "Get back to your cooking," she ordered.

And he laughed.

God, he was beautiful.

Her heart went all askitter despite what she knew of his view of relationships. Because Holly wasn't thinking about just a fun time in bed. Not with him. Not with the one man who'd always pushed her buttons and who challenged her on a daily basis.

No matter what they'd convinced themselves, it would never be simple, not between them.

Eating the second half of her omelet with a little more grace, she watched as he picked up a covered bowl of what proved to be dough. After using his fingers to quickly bite off the dough and shape the bites into small, flat circles, he began to roll out each piece. The tendons in his forearms shifted with every move, the burnished brown of his skin taut over pure muscle. She suddenly understood the obsession with cooking shows on television. Because if the chefs all looked like this . . .

Her toes curled.

Dough rolled out, Venom cut each circle in half before turning on the power to the wok he had on the stove. It only took him a few seconds to pour in enough oil for deep frying. He'd already made something else in a little pot—the man was *fast*—and now shifted it next to the rolled-out dough. Then his hands were moving to create small triangular pockets so fast she could barely follow the movement; as she watched wide-eyed, in went the filling before he sealed up the final edge of the pocket.

"Are you making samosas?" she whispered, barely daring to interrupt the magic.

A quick nod before he dropped the prepared samosas into the hot oil. The sizzle of frying dough filled the air, making Holly's stomach rumble all over again. The omelet had barely touched the hole in her belly. "Why am I so hungry all the time?"

Venom gave her a considering look. "Elena's hungry a lot of the time, too."

"That at least makes sense. I mean, she turned into an angel and grew wings. There's probably all kinds of stuff going on inside her." Holly drew in the delicious smell of Venom's creation. "Can I *please* have one?"

"A little longer." Venom flipped the samosas. "Keir," he said, naming the senior-most angelic healer, "says Elena is still becoming, still growing into her new skin."

"You think that's happening to me." Holly's eyes widened as he lifted up another pot she hadn't noticed at the back of the range, and poured a milky light brown liquid into a small mug for her.

She almost cried when she lifted it to her nose and sniffed—to be hit by the smell of cardamom and tea and the bite of other spices she couldn't identify. "You made me masala chai?" It was stupid, how her throat got all thick. He couldn't know how much she loved the stuff. So much that she'd given it up during the dark time when she'd wanted to end herself—she'd thought herself a monster who didn't deserve anything nice, not even a simple cup of her beloved chai.

Venom said, "I saw the tea packets at your place in New Jersey before I was transferred out of New York." A disdainful curl of his lip. "Real chai is made from the ground up. This is the quick-and-dirty version, until I have time to grind the right spices for you."

Even though she knew it was too hot, Holly dared take a sip. The slight burn was worth it. The sweet, spicy taste swept through her like lightning. "If this is your quick-and-dirty version, I'll probably orgasm at the real thing."

A sharp look, Venom's eyes glinting. "Drink your chai and eat this." He put several samosas on a plate he'd already layered with paper towels, and then, as soon as the excess oil had been soaked away, he transferred the hot pockets to her plate.

Holly forced herself to put aside the delicious, delicious chai he'd made for her *because he knew she liked it*, and picked up a piping hot samosa using the tips of her thumbs and forefingers. "What's inside?" she asked in an effort to make herself wait so she didn't sear her tongue.

"Potato and peas," Venom said. "Fastest option."

Holly took a bite and flavors exploded on her tongue. Potatoes and peas? Hah! He'd mixed in all kinds of spices that took those prosaic items to a whole new level. She basically inhaled an entire one before coming up for air. "Where did you find the spices?"

"Our host must've told his housekeeper to fully stock the kitchen. There was an entire unopened spice set." He put the extra samosas to drain. "What do you want for dessert?"

Holly had her mouth full of most of a second samosa—

she was well past trying to look in any way elegant—and had to wait to reply. After swallowing the samosa down with chai, she dug up a smidgen of shame. "Are you sure? You already made so much." All things she loved.

And the aggravating viper expected her to keep her emotional distance?

"Seeing how much you can put away is currently my favorite entertainment show."

"Ha ha." Holly decided she'd kick him later. When he wasn't cooking for her. "Do you know how to make cinnamon pinwheels?"

"No. Describe them to me."

After she did—around bites of a third samosa—she met his eyes. "Are you—"

"The bottled blood I've already had should keep me going for a long period, but there are more bottles inside the fridge. None are flavored."

Holly laughed. "You liked the flavors, admit it."

"Do I look like a barbarian?" Seeing that she'd almost finished her chai, he refilled her mug with an easy motion.

Holly had never before felt so incredibly spoiled. It softened things inside her that she hadn't even realized were still hard. Hopping off the stool, she walked around the counter and wrapped her arms around Venom from behind, pressing her cheek against the muscled warmth of his back.

He went motionless in a way that wasn't human. "Holly."

She didn't let go despite the warning in his tone. "I'm stubborn," she whispered. "Especially when it comes to people who matter." And he *mattered*. "You don't get to do the lone viper thing anymore."

"How will you stop me?" A cold purr of sound.

"Do you really think I'd warn you?" A snort. "This is war." Pressing a kiss to his back on a raw wave of affection that scared her with its strength, she drew back . . . but only *after* running her palms down either side of his chest.

The gauntlet? It was thrown.

* * *

Venom had fought countless battles, had faced down enemies and dangerous allies alike, but even after his earlier thoughts about how lethal she could be to him, he hadn't been ready for this. For a Holly who hugged him and smiled at him and stood next to him asking him to teach her how to roll the pinwheels.

This woman was . . . soft. Vulnerable.

He knew that was only the here and the now, a time when she felt safe, that Holly was dangerous and tough and a fighter, but even this fragment of vulnerability, it terrified him. "We're not dating, kitty," he said harshly. "I'm not a boy who's going to go steady with you."

Holly's eyes flicked up, the hurt in them an iron-handed blow to the gut. And he knew. It had taken enormous courage for her to lower her defenses and retract the prickles she used in self-protection, and he'd just taught her that it had been a mistake. One more nudge—or just silence—and he'd break her precarious confidence that he was worth her vulnerability.

That was the correct move, the smart move, the move that would make sure the damn switch inside him never turned on. Holly's future was a dark unknown that could end in a single fucking day. If he allowed her in, what would be left after she was gone?

"Fuck." Gripping her face in hands covered with flour, he pressed his forehead to hers. "I'm broken inside," he said, his voice ragged. "I function so well that even my closest friends think I'm healthy and whole, but I'm not."

Her hands came up to close over his wrists. "And I'm the poster child for mental health," she said in a tone so dry, it was dust. "Stop trying to drive me away by snapping like a cobra." Tilting back her head, she kissed him and it wasn't hard, wasn't demanding. It was a lush, feminine type of kiss. The type of woman Holly was below the anger and the rage and all that had been done to her.

She liked color and pretty beads and painting her boots with daisies.

"Even if you survive that monstrous thing in Michaela's turret, you won't survive immortality," he ground out. "Not being so soft inside."

"Maybe not," Holly said with clear-eyed serenity, "but I'll be myself until the day I die. That's good enough for me." A squeeze of his wrists. "The question is, do you like who I am when I'm not sniping at you?"

He bit her. Out of frustration at all that she was asking of him. Out of arousal at the scent of her. Out of a viciously powerful emotion that had been building inside him for years and had burst to the fore only when he saw that she was healing, becoming herself again. He'd never been tempted to take her while she was so badly psychically wounded. But this Holly?

She didn't fight his fangs sinking into her throat, didn't fight that he had a death grip on her hair, pulling her head back to arch her neck taut, didn't fight the hand he shoved under her dress to grip at her hip. Her blood flowed into his mouth and went straight to his cock. He didn't drink. He wouldn't hurt her. He just needed to taste her.

Her blood pulsed with the rapid beat of her heart.

Venom moved without conscious volition. Shifting his hand around to the front of her body, he moved it down . . . to find she wasn't wearing panties. Spearing his fingers through her delicate folds, he discovered she was wet, so wet. *Wild, sensual creature.* He found the nerve-rich little nub hidden within, pressed hard at the same time that he penetrated her with a finger.

"Venom!"

He removed his fangs long enough to say, "Tushar. *Say it.*" He thrust in and out of her in a demanding coda.

"Tushar." Acid green eyes holding his, her pupils hugely dilated. *"Tushar."*

He sank his fangs into her again, and then he drove her over. Once. Twice. Until her body quivered and her flesh was liquid for him.

And still she held him, this stubborn and deadly and complicated and soft woman who'd decided to claim him.

Caressing her down from the edge, he removed his fangs, licked the wound closed. But not totally. He was strong enough to have done that, but he didn't. He left two bruises that made it obvious he'd bitten her. And though he'd just shown her he wasn't human, could strike without warning, she smiled at him, her hazy eyes dancing. "Do I have flour on my face . . . and other places?"

"Yes." Removing his hands from her naked flesh, he lifted her up and put her on an unused part of the counter. "You're playing a dangerous game."

Throwing her arms around his neck and her legs around his hips as if he hadn't just warned her in his coldest voice, she said, "My mom is going to adore you."

His heart kicked, memories from a lifetime ago crashing so hard into him that he wrenched away—or tried to. Because even with that old anger riding him, he couldn't hurt her and so he didn't pull as hard as he should have, and she held on.

"Who was she?" A deadly question.

The viper in his blood raised its head in interest at the reminder of the poisonous danger that lived beneath her feminine surface. "No one."

A narrow-eyed look. "Spill it." Poking at his abdomen with a finger, she added, "Don't make me mad."

He could take her at her worst, but he found himself opening a box of memory he'd sealed centuries ago. "I was pledged to be married before my Making."

"And you went ahead and got Made?" Eyebrows drawing together in a dark vee. "That seems like asshole behavior."

"It would've been—but she was to be Made, too. Our marriage was to take place five years after our Makings, on the condition that we were assessed as having achieved full control over our vampirism."

"So what happened?"

"I was accidentally bitten by one of Neha's pet vipers a month before my Making. My body's reaction was to shrug off the bite—the only indication I'd been bitten was a faint soreness at the site of the bite."

Holly's pupils dilated in a flare of understanding. "That attracted Neha's attention," she said.

"No one knew why I had such a strong tolerance for snake venom—others in my family had been bitten by far less venomous snakes over the years and they'd all had a severe reaction." Venom had been curious, too, not realizing he'd sentenced himself to a nightmare. "Neha told me she couldn't waste me, that I contained within me something that might make it possible for her to create a vampire unlike any other."

"That bitch," Holly spit out. "She hurt you to satisfy her own arrogance!"

"She is a queen and an archangel." Venom had never expected her to act human. "The end result is that my betrothed came out a normal vampire. I didn't." He and Aneera had deliberately been placed in different parts of the country, to ensure they didn't breach the rules. It wasn't until four years after being Made that they'd met again.

Venom's eyes had only partially changed by then, but one look and Aneera had run screaming, the same horror on her face that he'd seen in the faces of his family when they'd begun to glimpse the depth of the changes in him. Fear had been acrid in their sweat, their refusal to touch him a staggering hurt, the wards against evil they'd made behind his back brutal blows.

He'd been almost glad when one of his sisters had found

the courage to tell him he was no longer welcome—at least then, no one could question his honor in walking away. Because that was all he'd had left. "The marriage pledge was deemed invalid since I was no longer 'human.'"

"Well, duh, you were a vampire." Holly flashed her fangs. "Is she still alive, this woman who couldn't handle it when things didn't go exactly as planned?"

Venom shrugged. "I don't know. I left the past behind long ago."

"Then what's all this baggage you're carrying, huh?" Tightening her grip on his hips, Holly moved her hands to his hair. "Did you love her?"

"I barely met her. It was a different time." A time when his parents and hers had made the arrangements and he and Aneera had agreed to it. "With both of us from similar family backgrounds, and all other concerns in alignment, it was considered the perfect match."

It felt so strange to say that, to think about his parents and about a time in which he'd been the dutiful eldest son who'd seen nothing wrong with pledging to marry a woman who was a stranger to him. "If I'm being honest, I've never understood why her reaction hit me so hard." As if he'd been kicked.

"I know why," Holly said, her eyes seeing right through him. "You'd committed to her and you're not a man who breaks his commitments. It left you totally unprepared for her defection."

A quiet pause before she added, "Especially coming as it must've done on the heels of your family's rejection. That's what hurts, isn't it? Not the loss of a stranger who didn't know the incredible gift she was throwing away. That woman was just the foul icing on the really shitty cake."

Venom wanted to bite her again for stripping him bare, punish her for making him face wounds he'd thought long-scarred and only now realized were still oozing. Most of all, he wanted to sink his fangs into her and hold her down until even an archangel's fucking ghost couldn't steal her life.

Pulling away from her before he gave in to his inhuman nature once again, before he betrayed far too much, he went to wash his hands. "I'll finish making your dessert."

33

Holly looked at Venom's back as he began to work on the pinwheels again. She knew pushing him would gain her nothing. He wasn't stubborn like her—but he held his ground. And whatever he'd been carrying around for three-hundred-plus years, it wasn't something he was ready to share. Fair enough.

She hopped off the counter—and had to do it. "I have to go clean up. I'm all wet and sticky."

His entire body froze.

Lips curving, she sauntered out of the kitchen, feeling his gaze on her every step of the way. He might be fighting it with all he was worth, but Venom—

Tushar. Say it.

Her heart stopped.

He'd given her his real name. She wasn't sure anyone else knew or remembered that. And he'd *given* it to her.

Holly released a quiet breath . . . and her chest, it pulsed. *No. Just no.*

Striding into the bathroom, she cleaned herself up—

Venom really had done a stellar job of turning her flesh erotically wet—then lifted up her dress to look at her chest. The image of those menacing serrated wings was a faint outline that faded completely toward the edges. "Do what you will, you bastard. And so will I." The latter words were a vow. "I don't plan to be easy prey like poor Daisy."

When she returned to the kitchen, it was to discover the treats already baking and Venom missing. It wasn't hard to find him. He was standing on the back porch, staring out into the forest as sunshine brushed the treetops.

Padding past him down onto the grass, Holly spread her arms and did a little twirl that sent the skirt of her sundress flying around midthigh. "Okay, that's enough nature," she said afterward, the grass soft underneath her bare feet and the air so clean it nearly hurt. "When do we go back to New York?"

Venom's face was expressionless when he said, "We don't go back. We wait."

"For Raphael?"

A curt nod.

Holly's heart squeezed, the playfulness gone and her dreams of a future in which she seduced Venom into a relationship in ashes. It had all been a fantasy anyway, an illusion the two of them had created with their refusal to refer to the reckoning to come. Because Holly had known how this would end from the moment she'd seen that distorted, monstrous fleshy thing in the crib.

She was a carrier of part of Uram. And now the insane archangel was trying to what, come back to life? The only way for Raphael to make sure that didn't happen, to *absolutely* ensure a powerful and insanely murderous being didn't once more stalk the streets, was to end both her and the receptacle in the crib.

"I won't run," she whispered to Venom when he continued to watch her. "I saw what Uram did." Grief was a bruise deep inside her that had never quite healed. "I watched my friends die. I heard their screams. I'd do anything to make sure he never again hurts anyone."

Even die.

The unspoken words hung in the incongruously luminous morning air, her vow unbreakable for all that it was silent. "It won't come to that," Venom said, responding to the words she hadn't spoken.

"Don't be a liar, Viper Face." Gentle, chiding words as she walked back up the steps toward him, a small woman in a vivid sundress, bare feet, and a fall of hair as bright as her soul. "There's no other way."

This time, when she put her arms around him, he crushed her close. And he knew it was far too late to try to distance himself. She'd already reached that sliver of the man he'd once been. Not only that, but she'd charmed the cobra, twined the viper around her arm. And flipped the switch.

He was hers.

They stood there in silence for untold minutes, until Holly lifted her head from his chest. "I don't want my pinwheels to burn," she said with a smile that couldn't hide the sadness within.

He followed her inside, watched her take the sweets from the oven and put them on a cooling tray on the counter before picking up the small jug of glaze he'd prepared. Glaze drizzled on, she used a fingertip to touch one of the sweets, hissed out a breath. "It's so hot . . . but I still want to stuff my face."

Sucking on her burned finger, she shot him a look that asked him to laugh with her.

Venom had no laughter inside him.

Only anger and pain and *need*.

Tugging her finger from her mouth, he kissed the poison

and sugar sweetness of her with a greed that should've terrified her. But this was Holly. Who thought his eyes were
pretty and who wanted to introduce him to her mother.

Mouths fused and bodies in passionate sync, they ended
up in the room she'd claimed. Pulling her dress up over her
head and throwing it aside, he palmed her breasts. When he
bent his head to caress them with his mouth, she tugged at
his hair as if she wanted another kiss.

He resisted, squeezing her other breast to make his point.

A shiver ran through her. Satisfaction a curve on his lips,
her pleasure soothing and calming the raw edge of his need, he
got to work. She jumped at the scrape of his fangs, moaned
when he sank them in without taking blood. She was sensitive
there, not just to touch, but to the kiss of his fangs.

He took full advantage of that knowledge to tease and
torment her. First, he let the taste of her sink into him, before licking the wound closed. It was only a small one, a
wholly sexual thing that had nothing to do with drinking
blood to survive. Then he licked his tongue over her nipple
before closing his teeth deliberately over it and tugging.

Jerking, she ran her hands down his back, scraping at
him through his shirt. When she pulled impatiently at it, he
managed to unbutton the shirt without taking his attention
from his worship of her breasts. Shrugging it off, he gloried
in the feel of her nails sinking into his flesh as he bit and
licked and kissed.

Only when her heart was a rapid tattoo and she sounded
like she couldn't breathe did he move his lips to the centerline of her chest and kiss his way back up to her mouth,
holding the silken heat of her body close to him.

Small but strong, that was Holly.

Her kiss was a demand and it was a branding. Holly had
decided on him and he knew no matter what happened, she
was it for him. He'd be like Jason's vampire contact, that
man who still loved his lost mate so many years after her
murder.

Some things a man knew.

Breaking their kiss, he nuzzled his way down her throat, nipping at her carotid as he did so. She shivered but made no attempt to stop him. He was lethal, dangerous, could've torn out her throat . . . but that wasn't what they were to one another.

Lifting her up in his arms, he threw her onto the bed.

She laughed, her hair a glorious stain of color on the white bedding, and her eyes so full of pure happiness that it stopped his breath. "Tushar," she said, using a name no one had spoken in centuries, a name he'd told everyone was of a dead man.

Turned out he'd lied.

"God," she said suddenly, "imagine if past-Holly could see me now. Naked and about to be led astray by you. The poor girl would be shocked, *shocked*."

Laughing at her reference to their antagonistic beginnings, the memories ones he would guard fiercely against time and age, he got on the bed and began to kiss his way down her body, ignoring all her attempts and orders to him to speed it up. Venom had no intention of rushing this, his patience a sinuous, covetous thing focused on marking her as his.

She writhed on the bed, her musk making his nostrils flare.

Crouched over her, his head by her navel and his hands on her hips to keep her still, he flicked up his eyelashes . . . to see her looking down, her breath coming in short, desperate gasps. "You," she said on a sucked-in gulp of air, "are a menace."

He felt his lips curve. It had been an eon, forever, since he'd played this way with a lover. Perhaps he never had. Before his Making, he'd had only three lovers, all traders passing through who wanted nothing but a little physical ease. Since all three women were on settled routes, he'd had the pleasure of their bodies in his bed a number of times. They hadn't been strangers who met only for a single night and never again—but neither had they wanted one another for anything but bed sport.

After his Making . . . A man couldn't be free, couldn't love, when he knew his lovers saw only part of him. Vampires, angels, mortals, the women glimpsed his eyes, thought they understood, but no one did, not really. Not until Holly.

Venom didn't have to hide anything from her.

Not his needs.

Not his movements.

Not the inhuman coldness that was as integral a part of him as his eyes.

And not the human core with its scars and its memories and its devotion.

To Holly, he was all of that and more. He was Venom. He was Tushar.

Prowling up her body, he said, "If I am the menace, then you must be the trouble."

Delight sparked in her, the fangs she sank into his throat all about play.

"Kitty, I seriously don't know how you drink through those tiny, tiny things. Are you sure they're not just for show?"

She sank her fangs deeper in punishment.

Laughing, he tumbled them over so that she was on top. She kissed the wounds closed, detoured to devour his mouth, before slithering down his body to attack the top button on his jeans and undo his zipper. She'd stripped him bare in a matter of seconds, his impatient, fiery lover.

Holly would never treat him as anything but an equal. They both knew he was stronger, faster, but that was simply a consequence of time. All he had to do was be with her as she grew into her own strength. But . . . that was a gift that could yet be stolen, their future torn to bloody shreds.

Not here. Not in this bed.

This time was theirs; he'd allow nothing to destroy it.

Drawing her up over his body on that silent vow, he palmed her breasts again before sliding his hands to the curve of her waist to bring her over his erection. "Come on, then, my wild Holly," he murmured. "Ride me."

Teeth sinking into her lower lip, she rose up, then oh-so-slowly took the hard ridge of his erection inside herself. A shudder rocked him. He watched her move with erotic grace, a thin layer of muscle underlying her skin and her pleasure in him unhidden, and he stood no chance. None at all.

"Tushar."

That was all it took. His name. His long-ago true name on her lips and his back bowed as he lost control for the first time in hundreds of years.

34

Venom and Holly spent the next three days in a cocoon of privacy that shut out the world and all its horrors. They loved, they played, he cooked for her all the things she wanted to eat. When she needed to talk to her family, he sat with her, holding her close and lending her his strength so that she could laugh with them without betraying the battle on the horizon, the fight for her very survival.

"If I die," she'd said to him, "if the only way to contain Uram is to end me, then I want you to tell my family that I died in an accident. A simple crash that burned my body to ash, a crash I never saw coming." Her hand in his hair, her gaze telling him she knew exactly what it would cost him to keep that promise. "I want them to believe I went out smiling."

In pursuit of her goal, she told her family that she'd come to Europe with Venom on a little runaway trip. Romantic and fun. She left out the danger and the horror and the blood. And when it was done, she put away her phone and she curled into him and they didn't speak of what was to come.

Venom spent hours in bed with her, just holding her as she held him in turn. "I had six brothers and three sisters," he told her on the third night, the sheets tangled around their legs and their bodies aligned, breaths kissing.

"You were the oldest, weren't you?"

Venom nodded. "My youngest siblings, they were still children when I decided to become a vampire." It was hard even now to look back at what had once been, the noisy, laughing family that had once existed. "You see, my father, he was a good man, but he wasn't the best businessman and he could deny my mother nothing. Not silks bought directly from the best merchants, not jewels that caught her eye, not the most piquant spices."

Frown marring her brow, Holly asked the question he'd known she would—because, for Holly, love didn't seek to insulate to the point of blindness. Love was wide-open eyes and a raw honesty that permitted no barriers. "Didn't your mother wonder where it all came from?"

"She was convinced we were wealthy, but when my father died, we discovered our inn was heavily in debt." Venom felt the reverberation from that blow through time. "The creditors he'd managed to mollify to that point demanded an immediate sale."

"You loved that place."

"I'd worked in the kitchen since I was ten. It was my home." Closing his hand over hers where she'd placed it on his heart, he took a breath infused with aching memory. "Not that it mattered—by that point, the debts were so substantial that a sale would've left us homeless paupers."

Tears wet on his sisters' cheeks.

White-faced shock in the faces of those of his brothers who'd been old enough to comprehend the dire reality.

His mother's grief-stricken wails.

"As the eldest son, I had to make the choice, and the only choice I could make that would save them all was to become a vampire." He remembered sitting alone in the inn's kitchen, the accounts open in front of him and his heart cold with realization.

"How?" Holly frowned. "Vampires don't get a payout until after the century of service."

"Neha was a familiar face at the inn." An archangel who had a liking for Venom's cooking, and whose patronage gave the inn such cachet that, had the inn been managed well, they would've never ended up in such grim financial straits. "I spoke to her about our situation in the aftermath of my father's death—"

"Hold on." Holly's eyes were wide. "You just rocked up to speak to an archangel while you were still a mortal? Funny, you don't look demented."

His lips kicked up. "The first time she requested to speak to the chef after stopping at the inn because she'd heard good things about it from her squadrons, I'd just turned seventeen and I'm sure my bones clattered from knocking against each other." Never in his life had he been near anyone who burned with such violent power. "But when she kept dropping by . . . well, a chef has his own arrogance—and what seventeen-year-old boy wouldn't be puffed up with self-importance by an archangel's open pleasure in his creations?"

Laughing in an affectionate way that told him she saw the boy he'd once been, Holly said, "So by the time your father died, you were used to talking with her?"

Venom nodded. "She was, I think, sincerely sorry for my grief—I had become a person to her, not just another mortal who'd exist then die in an immortal heartbeat." He wasn't so certain she'd been truly aware of anyone else in his family. "When I told her our situation, she reiterated her invitation for me to become a vampire—and offered to advance me three quarters of my post-Contract payout. It was more than enough to cover the debts and keep the inn going."

The Queen of Poisons had also authorized the Making of the woman to whom he'd been betrothed, the match arranged by Venom's father just two weeks prior to his death.

And that choice, to become a vampire or not, had been solely Aneera's. No one would've held a broken betrothal against her, not in those circumstances, but she'd hungered for near-immortality, been ecstatic at the chance.

"Say what you will about Neha," Venom murmured, thinking of the horrific torture of his actual Making, "but she is not ungenerous. Not human in any sense, but not evil, either."

"And after you sold yourself into bondage for your family," Holly bit out, "they turned their backs on you?" It was a cutting denunciation.

Shaking his head, Venom ran his fingers through her hair. "They weren't sophisticated folk, Holly. They didn't know something like me could exist."

"Bullshit." Holly's tone took no prisoners. "My parents didn't know. My sister didn't. Neither did my brothers. And yet you've witnessed how they treat me. What your family did to you was a horrible, nasty thing and you're allowed to be angry."

Venom went motionless.

All this time, all these *centuries* and he hadn't admitted it wasn't only grief that he carried deep within, but a primal anger that the people he should've been able to trust without compunction had forsaken him in his darkest hour.

Releasing a shuddering breath, he gripped Holly's hip hard and said, "Yes, I'm angry. I've *always* been angry." It was a searing heat inside him. "The young ones, I don't blame. Mohan was only five. Later, when he was an old man, he made overtures. He wanted to see his *bhai*, introduce me to his descendants. But I couldn't go."

Venom fisted his hand in Holly's hair as the memories crashed through him. "I'd seen too many of them die by then. I stood in the shadows through the decades and I watched their pyres burn one by one, until my mother and all nine of my brothers and sisters were gone, and I was the only one left."

Tears burned his eyes, tears he'd never allowed to fall.

Holly tucked his head gently down to her shoulder, saying nothing, just holding him. And then, the man with the viper's heart, the man the world thought as cold as the snakes that marked his eyes, cried tears that were very much human.

Raphael got in touch two hours later.

It was in the gray hour before dawn of the next day that Venom spotted Raphael high in the sky above Michaela's stronghold, at precisely the time the sire had told Venom to expect him. Venom and Holly were hiding in the forest out of sight of the sentries, ready to move the instant Raphael gave the order.

Venom. The single word sang with a power so immense and dangerous that even most immortals wouldn't be able to bear it.

To Venom, it represented a loyalty he'd chosen and one that would never hold him in chains. *Sire,* he replied, *we're ready.*

Michaela appeared above her stronghold right then, flying up to meet Raphael on wings of finest bronze.

Raphael's voice in Venom's head again. *Get to the location.*

We're on our way. Turning to Holly, he nodded, and they both began to move. The two of them had already known they'd have to get in on their own; Raphael was dead certain Michaela would, under no circumstances, permit anyone in that turret.

Regardless, Venom had every confidence the sire would get in.

As for him and Holly . . . "You remember how we practiced, kitty?"

She winked at him, this wild and strong woman who was probably racing to her death. When they ran into the first guard, she caught the vampire's gaze like a champion, mesmerized him in a matter of heartbeats.

Venom took the next—much older—one. Then it got hard. They no longer had tree cover *or* darkness and the angelic squadrons had begun to buzz closer with Raphael in the air with their mistress. Those squadrons could do nothing if it came to a battle between archangels, but their loyalty to Michaela would allow nothing less than utmost vigilance.

For that, they had Venom's respect.

"Venom, *it* wants me to . . ." Breaking off her words, Holly slid her arm around his waist, bit down hard on her lower lip . . . and they ceased to exist.

He whistled soundlessly. "That's a good trick, Hollyberry."

"It's the proximity to what's up in that turret—he's stronger." A trickle of sweat dripped down her temple, her eyes glowing such a vibrant acidic green that it would've made her stand out like a cat deep in the night had anyone else been able to see them.

Holly felt a little sick at having listened to that mad whisper.

Not that there was any point doing otherwise. The echo of Uram had spread stealthily into every part of her during the run here, now felt fused into her cells. Holly might have cried at the loss of herself, but there was no time for tears, for sorrow. If this went as predicted, she'd be gone before she ever had the chance to mourn who she'd once been.

It was a good choice, she told her screaming heart; she'd go out destroying an evil that shouldn't exist. "This," she whispered through her focus, "what we're doing. It's important."

"Yes," said the fascinating, beautiful, aggravating man with whom she wanted to explore eternity. "It might be the most important thing either of us ever does."

Holly nodded. She'd needed to hear that, needed to know that the pain she'd cause would be for a reason.

Mia, Wes, Alvin . . .

Holly couldn't think about her brothers and sister without emotion overwhelming her in a crushing wave. And when it came to Venom, she simply couldn't think about it, full stop. She'd done a terrible thing. She'd brought him out of the self-protective cocoon in which he'd existed for three hundred and fifty years only to teach him that he should've stayed deep within it.

The woman who came after her would have one hell of a job getting through the carapace he'd grow around himself. Because Venom's dirty secret was that he loved too long, too hard, too much. "Promise me," she whispered.

"What?"

"That you'll love again."

A deadly stillness in his muscles. "Focus on the glamour, kitty."

Holly went to respond when a large angelic squadron flew right overhead. She froze despite herself, only continuing forward when they didn't so much as glance in her direction. The sleek Abyssinian cats did, however, prowling up and hissing from a distance, but those cats were too far below the squadrons for the angels to hear and become suspicious.

Her arm began to tremble around Venom as they walked into the stronghold through the open front entrance, her entire body taut enough to snap and the hard-faced guards on either side blind to their passage.

His own arm came around her waist, strong and warm and unwavering.

Hold, girl.

Gritting her teeth at the aristocratic command, Holly fought not to throw up. Whatever part of Uram lived in her, it was growing stronger inside her, becoming more and more a separate personality.

The walk up the stairs to the mezzanine floor was an exercise in brazen confidence. She and Venom passed within inches of a tall vampire so powerful she made the hairs rise on the back of Holly's neck. The well-built blonde woman frowned, stopped, and looked around, her hand on the hilt of her sword . . . before finally shaking her head and continuing on down the stairs.

Holly had been aware of Venom going dead silent beside her, even as he reached back a hand to close it over the hilt of one of the two blades he wore on his back.

Now, he relaxed his ready stance and they carried on without bloodshed.

Only to enter the mezzanine and find an angel standing directly in front of the turret door. The angel, his wings white streaked by gray, wasn't looking at them, couldn't see them. But Holly could feel the pulse of his power buffeting her even from halfway across the floor.

Venom spoke right against her ear. "He's mine."

Removing her arm with exquisite care once they were only a foot away from the suddenly tautly alert angel, Holly tapped Venom's back once to let him know she was about to drop the glamour . . . and then she did. The angel's hand moved with predator speed to the hilt of his sword, his body reacting even before his mind understood what it was he'd seen. Venom, however, had already mesmerized him.

It wasn't, Holly quickly realized, in any way an easy capture.

Venom's opponent was *strong*—and he was fighting the compulsion. It was there in the rigid line of his jaw, the locked fury of his muscles. A vein pulsed in Venom's temple. She could tell he was using every ounce of his power to force the angel to move away from the door step by single excruciating step.

There. Just enough of a gap to get to the door.

Breaking the lock with a pulse of power, Holly stepped inside. Venom slipped in viper fast behind her; shutting the door, he held the broken lock in position. "I managed to cloud the guard's mind," he murmured to her. "He shouldn't remember us, but he was too strong to fool totally. He'll feel—"

The doorknob was tested right then from the other side. Venom made sure it moved only as much as it would have had the lock been unbroken. The angel stopped, as if satisfied the lock was as it should be. But Venom didn't step away, despite the urgency of their task. Three painfully slow minutes later, the doorknob was tested again.

Only after that test was over did Venom release the doorknob and nod at her to go ahead. Holly had had to fight the compulsion to race up the entire time they'd stood waiting for the guard to be satisfied. No way had she been about to leave Venom alone to face an angel who had to be a couple of thousand years old at least and powerful with it.

But the defiance had taken everything she had.

The otherness in her an icy rush through her veins, she flowed up the steps as if she were made of living acid. Even Venom, fast as he was, couldn't keep up with her. She'd broken the foolish padlock and was in the turret room almost before she was aware of taking the first step.

The host inside the crib glowed in time with the beat of her heart and that was as it should be. It was part of him. And he was an archangel.

He was Uram.

35

Venom had never seen *anything* move like Holly had just moved. She'd been untrackable with the eye—and he had better tracking senses than most beings on the planet. He was out of breath when he reached her.

Horror slammed into him like a concrete fist.

She stood staring down at the crib; behind her glowed acid green wings spread wide. Those serrated wings made of illusion and power reached the floor, were angelic in size. And they were held with warrior control.

Her head jerked toward him at that instant. "You," she said, and her voice wasn't hers. It was deeper, masculine, the tone arrogant with age and power. "Open the roof."

Open the roof?

Venom looked up, and spotted what he hadn't during their first incursion. The entire ceiling came together like a jigsaw, with locks designed to fall in place. Now the narrow staircase made sense. Michaela had never come up those stairs. Looking around, he quickly found the control—it was easy to see once you knew it must be present in a position Michaela could easily access once inside. Before, he'd dismissed it as just another light switch.

Michaela must have a remote to open it from the outside.

He glanced at Holly as he reached the switch and, though it enraged him to see her swallowed up by a mad being who should be long dead, he played the game. For better or worse, this would finish here today. That was what Holly wanted, and Venom would do anything for Holly, this strange, wild, beautiful creature who'd come into his life and taught him that it was all right to be weird and different. That you could be loved not in spite of it all, but simply because you were you.

"Should I do it at once, Archangel?" He made his tone respectful, as it should be when addressing the man he served. Uram wasn't his sire, would *never* hold that position of respect and honor in his heart, but he was talking to a madness. And that madness gave him a pleased smile and an incline of the head.

Venom pushed the button, turning his face skyward.

He glimpsed Raphael and Michaela at the same time that they became aware of the roof splitting apart like a huge metal flower, the "petals" slowly rising up and away from the central point. The two archangels were almost directly above, though some distance up. Michaela dropped first, spreading out her stunning wings to control her rapid descent; her hair flew up in a tumble of mahogany and dawn-kissed gold behind her.

She was exquisitely beautiful and brilliantly powerful and she did nothing for Venom. This same archangel had once thrown him so violently against a wall that she'd broken his spine, fractured his skull, one of his ribs piercing his lung to collapse it. But that wasn't the reason he wasn't drawn to her. From the instant he first met her, he'd known there was something wrong with Michaela. A vital piece missing.

His eyes went to his sire. Raphael was descending directly behind Michaela, clearly having realized the roof wasn't big enough to allow the two of them to enter at the same time. His wings were white gold and powerful, the Legion mark on his right temple a violent blue lit with incandescent white fire against the midnight shade of his hair.

When Venom looked over to Holly, he saw that her eyes, too, had turned skyward.

The smile on her face was a mix of pride, love, and rage.

Overlaying it all was unadulterated arrogance.

Venom had never once witnessed that particular fault in Holly. If anything, she wasn't as conscious of her strength and skills as she should be. And that depth of arrogance? It took eons of unchallenged supremacy to develop.

A wash of wind buffeted his face as Michaela landed, snapping her wings shut behind her. She'd seen Venom but ignored him in favor of facing Holly over the lattice of power that protected the crib, a lattice that had flickered to bronze life before Venom ever entered the room. The archangel's eyes grew wide, her lips parting, but Raphael landed before she could speak.

The small room hummed with so much power that Venom's bones ached with it.

"My love." Holly's mouth but not her voice, the acid glow of her eyes locked with Michaela's. "You betrayed me."

Michaela's hair blew back in a wind that affected no one else in the room. "You are not him." It was a flat statement . . . but a hidden and oddly fragile note sang underneath.

Need? Want?

Was it possible the Archangel of Budapest had truly loved the archangel who had taken over Holly's body? The same man whose territory she'd claimed a large part of in the aftermath of his death?

Holly responded in a language Venom didn't recognize. Michaela clearly did, her cold expression crumbling into a shock so harrowingly naked that it could only be real.

Sire. Venom reached out to Raphael with his mind.

Do not intercede, Venom, Raphael ordered, the pristine blue of his gaze focused on the disturbing tableau being played out in front of them. *We must understand what this is to know how to end it.*

Venom couldn't see anything that a rational being would ever understand, but he'd trusted Raphael with his life for centuries. Now, he trusted the sire with Holly's. *She would rather die than live as Uram's puppet,* he said. *If that is the only choice, we must end her.* The words were like shards of glass in his throat.

I have promised your Holly this, Venom. I will not forget.

Because this was Raphael, an archangel forged in honor and tempered by a love that had shoved back the ice of immortality, Venom held his silence. And forced himself to listen to a dead and insane archangel's words coming from the mouth of the woman to whom Venom had handed his heart with full knowledge that she would soon break it.

Raphael had killed Uram above the ruined skyscrapers of Manhattan, building after building falling during their battle, the wreckage crashing to litter the streets below. He *knew* the archangel was dead. But the man Raphael had once called a friend had also been six thousand years old and had spent over half of those years as an archangel.

A member of the Cadre *could* come back to life even after being blown into a million small pieces . . . but only if he hadn't been killed by angelfire utilized by another archangel.

Raphael's angelfire had obliterated Uram. His heart. His mind. His body. Whatever inhabited Holly Chang's body, it wasn't Uram. But as he'd told Venom, they had to watch first. Even as he thought that, he knew what he was asking from this member of his Seven. In all the years that he'd known Venom, he'd never once seen the other man look at anyone as he looked at this small woman Raphael had first met as a brutalized victim.

It was the same way Raphael looked at Elena.

"Are you certain?" Uram's voice asked from Holly's mouth. "You feel me." She turned her gaze to the crib. "You kept a part of me safe until I could retrieve it."

Michaela shook her head, her wings spreading and beginning to glow. "You are dead."

"Then why do you keep this piece of me?" It was a sinuous whisper, Holly running her fingers along the power lattice without being affected by it. "Why do you protect it?"

Raphael's healing gift had confirmed that Michaela wasn't pregnant the time she'd tried to fool him that she was, but it appeared she'd . . . *birthed* the thing in the crib at some point afterward. So either his gift hadn't recognized what Venom called the "unbeing" as life, or Michaela *had* been playing games back then and the seed Uram had left hidden in her had begun to grow much later, fed by the rising power of the Cascade.

"You are dead!" With that shaken shout, Michaela raised a hand ringed with deadly energy. Before she could release it, however, Holly spoke again in a language Raphael didn't immediately recognize. It was old. *Very* old. And had been used only in a small area of Europe over a thousand years earlier. Raphael hadn't spent enough time there to have learned it well, but he'd picked up just enough during his friendship with Uram to translate the words.

"We danced above Szeged the first time."

Michaela's fire died.

Trembling, she stared at Holly. "Uram?" The whisper held so much hope it was a keen of sound.

Raphael was near certain it was Michaela's poisonous whispers that had either encouraged or pushed Uram to make the decision that had led to his madness. But at that moment, he was also sure that part of Michaela had loved the fallen archangel with whom she'd been for five decades.

Uram said a word Raphael couldn't translate, but the caressing tone of it was unmistakable. Michaela just stared, her chest heaving. "Uram?" she whispered again. "Have you returned to me in truth?"

Her eyes went to the crib and its monstrous inhabitant that still did not register as alive to Raphael's healer senses. "I thought this was all I'd ever have of you. I hoped you'd grow under the influence of the Cascade, become yourself in time."

"You were right to wait," said the being inhabiting Holly. "It is time for me to be whole." Slender fingers running over the power lattice once again. "Undo this, my sweet."

Swallowing, Michaela raised her hand.

Holly felt as if she was struggling through molasses. Her mind was heavy and slow. Her limbs heavier and impossible to move. But she fought. If she died, it wouldn't be because she'd goddamn given up. This was *her* body, *her* mind. And her fucking heart!

That heart loved her siblings, her mother and father . . . Venom. As that heart had once loved five girls a monster had tortured and murdered.

Shelley.

Cara.

Maxie.

Rania.

Ping.

The bastard who'd butchered them didn't deserve a second life, a second *chance*, even if he had somehow found a way to return from the grave. He didn't get to live happily ever after with his lover while her friends rotted in their graves, their last moments on this planet full of horror and pain.

Her rage and grief gave her strength enough to grab hold of a little more of her mind.

"You were right to wait," the ghost of Uram was saying through Holly's mouth. "It is time for me to be whole." Her fingers caressing the power lattice, neutralizing its power but unable to breach the obstacle. "Undo this, my sweet."

The words came to Holly's ears through a thick barrier that dulled the words to a flat monotone, but she understood their meaning. She had to keep listening, had to keep learning. Because she was inside him. Or he was inside her. She didn't know. She *had* to know.

Holly fought desperately for a foothold that would keep her from sinking into the darkness again, but she was battling the echo of an archangel. Even far less than whole, he was powerful. And—

Oh, that was the answer. She'd had it all along. Uram wasn't coming back to life. He couldn't. Raphael had destroyed all the essential parts of him. She'd watched the footage of that destruction—caught by countless amateur videographers—over and over. She'd talked to people who'd been there that day, who'd seen Raphael wipe Uram out of existence.

Nothing had remained of the Angel of Blood.

This otherness that was trying to steal her body and mind was exactly what she'd thought—an echo, a lost fragment. Glimmers of memory, flashes of thought, bursts of impulse . . . but, now that she was paying attention and looking carefully, she got no sense of an actual whole person. If he had been whole, Holly would be erased by now. An archangelic mind was simply too powerful for anyone but another archangel to resist.

Which all meant this echo could never exist as a whole being outside of Holly and that terrible thing in the crib, no matter what it thought in its ghostly madness. But it looked like Michaela was ready to believe in the same madness.

Holly could forgive her that, even understand it.

Love had a way of making you a little insane.

Viper green eyes in her vision, Venom staring at her from near Michaela. He hadn't been standing there earlier. He must've moved while Uram totally controlled her vision, to put himself in her direct line of sight, exactly as she'd asked him to do.

No one had eyes like Venom.

No one *was* Venom.

And Venom was hers.

The reminder she'd spoken over and over through the night, the mental foothold she'd created using her emotional response to him—always, she'd responded to Venom—gave her a touch more strength.

Light flashed, a glittering bronze shower that was astonishing in its beauty. Wonder tried to catch Holly in its shimmering grasp. Michaela really had struck the jackpot when it came to the beauty stakes. Horror soon curdled the wonder. Because the lattice was down and she could feel acid-green energy gathering inside her, as the echo of Uram prepared to leave Holly to merge with the part inside the fleshy receptacle in the crib.

Should that happen, Holly would die just like Daisy had died. Uram would steal all her energy, all her life force to make himself stronger. Holly thought furiously as Michaela turned to Raphael, slamming out a palm laced with power. "Do not interfere here, Raphael. If he's powerful enough to have survived angelfire, then he's powerful enough to fully regenerate from a stump of flesh."

You're wrong, Holly wanted to say. This echo would never be anything but a madness stuck in a moment of time. It didn't even know why it wasn't whole. It didn't remember dying. Because that death had taken place *after* Uram transferred—whether purposefully or by accident—fragments of his energy into Holly and Michaela and Daisy. It did remember loving Michaela because Uram had loved her as he went into his insanity, the emotion imprinted into every fragment of him. And it slyly remembered the craving for blood, for violence, for torture.

Whatever grew out of that thing in the crib would be nothing but a horror.

She was conscious of Raphael replying to Michaela, but she wasn't listening to the archangelic conversation any longer. She had to have a critical discussion of her own.

Is that what you want to be? she whispered from deep inside herself, as Uram's echo had whispered to her. *That twisted piece of flesh that has no life to it?* Inside Uram, she understood that it was literally just *meat*. Created of Michaela's cells and Uram's tainted energy, it was an external host meant to act as the core for Uram's resurrection. It hadn't rotted away only because . . .

My sweet dripped her blood over that which will become my flesh.

Which Michaela hadn't been able to do while at the Cadre meeting, explaining the putrefaction Holly had glimpsed during her first visit. A few more days and there'd have been maggots crawling in that crib.

Holly's stomach lurched, but she didn't lose the precious control she'd regained. *You will be totally dependent on Michaela.*

Her body moved closer to the crib, looked down. "I will soon grow strong," the Uram echo said aloud, capturing the attention of everyone in the room.

Are you sure? Holly whispered. *Do you have enough power? Or will you be trapped in that hunk of toxic meat forever?*

Rage in her muscles, a burning pain her body wasn't designed to handle for long. "I am an archangel."

Tell me when you and Michaela first met, Holly said through the agony.

"Silence!" The voice that wasn't her voice boomed into the air.

36

Raphael, Michaela, Venom, they all watched without interrupting, as if aware something was taking place that they couldn't perceive. Luckily for Holly, *she* didn't have to be silent. The echo of Uram could do nothing more to her.

You don't remember, do you? she murmured. *Do you remember coming to New York?*

A deadly silence.

You are not an archangel. You are an echo, a mad ghost created of fragments of energy left behind before your death. Holly felt an unexpected sadness spear her heart. *You must've been an incredible power to do that, to leave behind energy that survived for so long.*

"I am an archangel!" It was a roar that shuddered against the walls of the turret that Michaela had turned into a nursery and a prison both. "I am Uram!"

"My love." Michaela reached out a hand across the crib, her face a thing of power softened by grief. "Become whole."

The power inside Holly coalesced into a tense knot, ready for the transfer.

If you go into that flesh, Holly said in a voice she forced to be calm, *you will be sightless and without hearing, without voice, the entire time it'll take you to recover. You'll be helpless in Michaela's hands, a child she has to raise.* She stopped herself from saying anything more, from pointing out that Michaela could use any such opportunity to shape Uram as she saw fit.

The truth, of course, was that Uram would never be a child. Would never grow. There wasn't enough of him left. Even now, his few memories were less sharp than they'd been before, as if having degraded once brought out into the light. If he went into that lump of flesh, however, then Michaela would fight for him to be allowed to exist. And, given Michaela's love for Uram and for the meat host in the crib, sooner, or later . . . *Oh, that wasn't it at all.*

The knowledge was a faint whisper at the back of her mind, but it came from the echo that was part of her. And it told her the echo would try to take over Michaela the instant it had bathed in enough of her blood.

Would it succeed?

Holly didn't think so, but the risk was too horrific to chance. For if the echo did succeed in maddening Michaela, Uram's blood reign would begin all over again.

Take this body, she whispered. *At least until you are strong enough to create a full adult body in which to transfer yourself.*

This time, the answer was internal . . . and thoughtful. *I will have to leave a splinter of energy in the other to make sure it grows.*

You know you need all of you to return to greatness.

A long pause before Holly's hand reached into the crib and spread over the lump of flesh below. A single touch and she knew it was *wrong*. There was no warmth to that flesh.

It was cold. Dead. Animated only because Uram's energy, fed by Michaela's blood, ran in its veins.

Venom watched Holly's hand spread on the lump that was the unbeing, acid green wings continuing to glow behind her. He wanted to tear that acid green from her, set her free. But to do that would be to kill her.

He refused to believe she was already gone, that this was now a matter between archangels. When the Holly/Uram hybrid looked up without warning and said, "I will keep this body," Venom knew he was right. Holly had done something, changed the script.

Sire. Venom didn't look at Raphael as he spoke. *I think we should let this, too, run its course.*

There's little choice. Raphael's voice was a storm of power in Venom's head, so much of it that Venom sometimes wondered how the sire could bear it. *If there is even the slightest chance that Uram can come back, I cannot strike without it being an act of war. To attack an archangel rising from a long Sleep is to breach all the rules that keep the Cadre from destroying one another and the world. We have already had one such incident; I will not be responsible for a second.*

Venom stared directly at Holly, willing her to look at him. Just one second, that was all he needed. A heartbeat.

Holly's eyes scanned the room. "Do not interfere," her mouth said before she frowned and shook her head. "I do not remember how I came to this place, but this is my resurrection."

Even as Holly's mouth moved, her eyes were processing what she'd seen in the echo's scan. Venom's hand had moved so quickly that most people wouldn't have caught it. She did, because she was a little like him. And— *Why am I like Venom?* she asked the echo inside her. *Did you have an affinity for snakes? Except . . . I'm not all like him.*

A buildup of pressure. *Quiet, mortal!*

Holly forced herself to sound subservient. *Please. I'll be gone once you come to power. Answer this one question before you take my flesh for your own. Did you have an affinity to snakes? Like Neha.*

Holly's head fell back, laughter pouring out of her mouth. When the echo stopped laughing, it said, *I am not Neha with her poisons. I am Uram.*

And she realized the echo didn't know. The echo didn't remember what powers it'd had that had fed into Holly. It couldn't tell her the "why" of her, couldn't explain if she was the way she was because the toxin that had fueled his madness, had twisted the abilities he'd had as an archangel. She'd have to do her own research . . . if she survived this. *Yes, you are an archangel,* she said, setting her endgame in motion. Because she'd recognized that move of Venom's hand.

It was part of a silent language he'd taught her during their sessions while he'd been away from New York. He'd made her practice the rapid hand movements until she could use them without thought. Similar to sign language, but much faster, it could, Holly had originally thought, be utilized only by people who had their reflexes. Which would've made it pretty useless.

But it had turned out it could also be used in combat situations with other angels and vampires in the Tower. She just had to slow things down so they could see the movements. The speed he'd taught her was so, should the two of *them* be in a hostile situation, they could talk without anyone being the wiser.

The move he'd just made, it meant: *Ball's in your court.* Holly shuddered deep within. He was telling her that

Raphael and Michaela wouldn't interfere. If the horror was to end here, *she* had to be the one to end it. Only she knew what was at stake. Only she understood that this echo of energy was created of the most horrific part of Uram, the part that had existed right before his death. When the archangel had been a being driven by madness and blood-hungry for the pain of others.

Shelley. Maxie. Cara. Rania. Ping. Kimiya. Nataja. Daisy.

Her friends' names, and those of three other women who'd never stood a chance, they were a silent mantra in a hidden part of her consciousness as she spoke again to the echo. *Thank you*, she said, as if he'd answered her question when he'd done no such thing. *I hope my body serves you well.*

A pause. *You have served me well.* Swirled in the madness was a regal graciousness. *Now it is time for you to cease to exist.*

He pulled energy from the lump of flesh in the crib. It ran up Holly's arm in an acid-green electrical storm that threatened to melt her brain and explode her heart. She gritted her teeth . . . or tried to. The echo had control of her body and it wouldn't let her take that instinctive action. When the energy threatened to erase her brain, her memories, she hunkered down and fought back using the very power he'd given her.

Because she still had access to part of that power. It had become fused into her cells and this body was yet hers, each and every part of it imprinted with the force of her life. If he truly *had* been an archangel, she couldn't have regained any access to the strength forged of his energy and her determination. But he was only a faded echo. Powerful, but not a *power*. Not like Raphael or Michaela or the Uram he'd once been.

Steeling her mind, Holly refused to be crushed, but she made no move to betray herself . . . not until the echo ripped her hand off the now-lifeless lump in the crib. As she watched, the fleshy host quickly turned a putrid green at the

edges, the rot snaking so swiftly through the rest of it that
it was clear it had been rotting for a long time, the putrefaction held back only by Michaela's blood. A foul smell began to emanate from it.

Flicking out a hand, Michaela incinerated the thing
she'd birthed.

Ashes lay in the crib.

And Holly's skin glowed with an acid green power this
body wasn't built to contain. With the extra power came a
stronger echo. More knowledge. A vague, *vague* hint of
sanity. Holly had been winging this, and the best plan she'd
come up with, given her limited control, had been to force
one of the archangels to kill her—kill them both—by incit-
ing the echo into an act of total insanity.

Such as attempting to tear off Michaela's wings.

But now, she paused, thought. *Do you see what you've
become?* She made her voice non-confrontational, never
forgetting that she was talking to an immortal who was
used to having people bow and scrape to him. That wasn't
always the way—from what she'd seen of Raphael's rule, he
preferred strength around him. Venom didn't bow and
scrape to anyone, and Raphael's hunter consort was a warrior through and through, one who held her ground.

Uram had been different. From an older time. She knew
because she'd researched him obsessively. *You were considered an archangel among archangels. Neha admired you,
called you the most handsome man she had ever met aside
from Eris—and you forgave her bias there, I think. Even Lijuan respected you and she respects very few people.*

The echo rumbled inside her. *I will have all their respect
once more.*

Will you? Holly fought his hold on her mind to bring up
the images she'd tried to bury for four long years. Of nightmare and horror and Uram sitting on a thronelike chair, his
mouth rimmed with blood while a severed arm lay in his lap.

A roar erupted from her mouth. "Lies!"

She glimpsed confusion in Michaela's eyes, battle-ready tension in Raphael. Only Venom watched in motionless, expressionless silence. He understood what was going on. He knew Holly wasn't dead.

Ask your fellow archangels, she whispered. *Ask them what you became. That nightmare is the only part of you that remains. Not the archangel who was considered the fastest among the archangels. Not the archangel who ruled with an iron fist but had the respect of his generals. Not the archangel who had the most beautiful woman in the world as his lover. Just that ravenous monster who thirsts endlessly for blood.*

Her pulse leaped at the thought, her mouth watering.

Nauseated, she forced herself to continue. *You feel it. You feel the urge to drink. You're looking at Michaela's throat. You want to rip it out.*

Another roar of sound, her hands fisting without her conscious volition.

"Uram." Michaela circling the crib to come cautiously closer. "It's all right, my love. This body will frustrate you until you can reshape and regrow it to your requirements, but that will not take you long."

A memory flash that wasn't her own: Michaela flat on the ground with her wings outspread and her chest ripped open, a glowing red fireball in place of her heart. The female archangel's body jerked, blood streaking the smooth brown of her skin.

The terror in her expression shocked Holly into silence.

Archangels didn't get terrified. Archangels *were* the terror.

Holly's hand rose, her fingers brushing the taller woman's cheek. "My sweet."

No terror today. Michaela's eyes shimmered, the bright green dazzling beyond the wash of water. "You are the only one who ever understood me."

Holly's fingers played along the swanlike length of Michaela's throat, stopping for a heartbeat at her pulse, before running down between the archangel's breasts to eventually spread over her heart. It beat rapidly under her palm. "I tore this open," came from her mouth. "I put myself inside you."

Michaela's hand closed over hers and the punch of archangelic power rocked Holly's entire body. Michaela was glowing and when an archangel glowed, people usually died. However, this archangel wasn't in a murderous mood—and didn't believe she was dealing with a mortal. "It is no matter," she said with a soft smile. "I didn't understand then. I didn't know you were asking me to keep you safe until you could return."

Why am I so weak?

It took Holly a second to realize the question was for her. *Because you are only a faded echo of a great archangel. You are a ghost.*

I will grow strong again.

Do you truly believe so? Holly asked seriously. *Can you draw power from the world around you?*

Her eyes went unerringly to Michaela's neck, and to the pulse that beat there. Her fingers curved slightly over Michaela's heart. *Blood will feed me. Blood will make me grow.*

The madness is returning, Holly said before the shred of sanity slipped away forever. *You will once more become enslaved to blood. A monster who will be feared but never respected. Even then, you will never be what you once were.*

Rage in her veins. "I need your blood, my love," her mouth said to Michaela. "Just enough to give me a little more strength."

Michaela angled her neck in a trust that shook Holly. She'd always thought of the Archangel of Budapest as arrogant and beautiful and manipulative. That was how Michaela came across in the media that so loved her. And, blinded by the differences in their power and age, Holly had never once thought about how Michaela was a woman, too, one who'd loved a man who had died.

Holly ran her fingers over the line of Michaela's throat before rising on tiptoe to bend her mouth to that pulsing spot. Blood spurted onto her tongue, hot and fresh and so powerful that it made her physically stagger. But still she drank and drank, until she could literally drink no more.

When she did finally tear away, it was to see Michaela's throat wound close up in front of her eyes.

The archangel didn't look weakened or as if she'd been hurt.

And Holly's body swirled with power that threatened to burst her cells, burn out of her skin. Dear God. How did anyone survive feeding from an archangel?

"Was that enough?" Michaela's question was gentle, her own hand rising to lie against Holly's cheek. "I have waited for you."

Holly's skin cracked across her back, her chest, her soul in danger of drowning as pain ripped at her insides. *Are you more yourself?* she asked through the haze of it. *Are you more Uram?*

I need more blood. Her head turned toward Raphael. *Stronger blood.*

You are glutted on the blood of an archangel, and yet you seek more blood. Agony twisted at her guts as things began to crack inside her, too, her body full of too much archangelic power. *You will always seek more and more and more.* The craving clawed at her even as her body began to fail. *You are starting to want blood with violence, aren't you? You want to tear at Michaela's throat like a wolf gnawing on his kill.*

"No!" Holly's body staggered back to press against the cold stone wall.

Sweat dripped down her temples.

Are you any stronger? Holly kept on pushing through the unbearable pain of a body bursting from the inside out. *Even a little?* The surge of archangelic blood, archangelic *power*, should've had a violent effect . . . and it had. *Or are you unable to transmute that energy into a form you can use? Because you are only an echo.*

Blood. A red haze. *I need blood.* A sudden, cunning thought. *This body is weak. I need hers.* The power wrenched out of her before Holly could do anything, bending her spine so far backward that she knew it was about to snap.

37

"No!" The shout left Venom's throat as Holly's back bowed violently, acid green light pouring out of her in a brutal surge.

Uncaring of the two—perhaps three—archangels in the room, he ran across to catch her body as it collapsed to the floor. He was too fast to allow that to happen. He caught her bloody, broken body in his arms, stopped her head from cracking onto the hard polished wood.

She weighed too little, his Holly.

And the power was still screaming out of her in a burn of acidic green.

When it did finally cut off, her head lolled to the side, blood trickling out of the corner of her mouth . . . and her face riddled with hundreds of tiny cracks. Blood filled those cracks, iron-rich wet against every part of her that he was touching. As if her entire body had fractured.

Venom's heart was pounding too hard for him to sense her pulse.

He kept on trying.

Nothing.
No, kitty, no.

Raphael watched the energy erupt out of Holly, saw Venom catch her as she fell. And he saw unvarnished terror on Venom's face for the first time in all the years he'd known the vampire.

But Raphael could do nothing for Venom's love at that moment. "Michaela," he said in warning.

She wasn't listening, her eyes wide with hope. "My love," she whispered . . . just as the ball of power smashed into her, covering her body in a slick of acid green fire.

Raphael could've stopped it. He didn't. The instant he stepped in, he ignited a catastrophic war. The choice had to be Michaela's.

Her eyes glowed the same distinctive acid green for a single piercing instant before she shoved the power out with a roar. "Get out!"

The green glow coalesced in the air again, crackling with veins of red. Blood red. Raphael wasn't Michaela. He'd accepted long ago that the man he'd once called a friend no longer existed. When the malignant energy went to smash into him, he held up a hand ringed with angelfire. The energy drew back . . . and headed toward Venom. The other man moved with viper speed to evade it, Holly in his arms.

Raphael moved at the same time to put himself in front of Venom and the fallen girl he loved. This was a war between archangels. Venom and Holly had done their part. They'd done *far* more than could be expected of a vampire of only a few centuries and a mortal who'd been Made too young.

It was time for Raphael and Michaela to end this. "Michaela."

Tears ran down her cheeks as she raised her own hand,

her power glittering bronze around her fingertips. She couldn't form angelfire, but the bronze lightning she could create felt stronger than it had the last time he'd been close enough to witness it.

The Cascade in effect.

Her lack of angelfire mattered little. She had other ways to kill a fellow archangel. That was one of the markers of ascension: the ability to kill your peers. "I loved him," she whispered, the sick energy held frozen between his power and hers. "He truly saw me. The darkness, the light, the glory, the rot."

It was the most honest appraisal he'd ever heard Michaela make about herself. "Is he who he was?" Raphael asked, because they *had* to be sure. "You felt him just now. Can he come back?"

"He is . . . a ghost. A fragment. Of the worst part of him." The tears continued to fall. "We must end him, Raphael. He is worth so much more than this mad existence driven by blood."

Raphael thought one last time of the friend who'd raced with him through the canyons of the Refuge, of the man who'd laughed as they sat around a bonfire, his wings spread out on the grass. That Uram had been lost to time and to his own arrogance well before the insanity, but he had existed. And their long relationship demanded this act, for a sane Uram would've never wanted to exist as this mad phantom.

"Good-bye, old friend," he whispered. "This time, it will be forever."

Sobbing openly, Michaela released a crackling bolt of her power. It encircled the energy, began to crush it to death. Raphael added his angelfire. The echo stood no chance. It wasn't Uram. It wasn't even a part of Uram. It was only a faint shadow left behind by a powerful man lost to blood.

And then it ceased to be, burned out of existence.

Michaela collapsed to her knees, her wings spread out

behind her in a splendor of delicate bronze. "I wanted *more*, more power, more everything. And I lost him to that greed."

Turning, Raphael focused on his own people without discounting Michaela. As she'd just admitted, even her love had a price—and she might yet blame him for Uram's death. "Venom."

This member of his Seven who had always been so self-contained and coolly sophisticated, his humor often so dry it was cutting, raised eyes wet with tears. "She's dying, sire." It was a broken statement, Holly clutched tight to his chest.

The girl's face was a smear of blood and broken skin, her pulse near impossible to detect. Blood trickled out of her nose and pasted her black top to her body. Wiping away the blood from her nose with a gentle touch, Venom pressed a kiss to her wrecked face. "She refused to let evil win. She *fought*."

Raphael held out his arms. "Entrust her to me, Venom." He didn't want to be here, in this place with an archangel he'd never fully trusted.

Venom's responding glance was shattered, but he nodded; he was one of the Seven and even nearly broken, he understood the reason behind Raphael's request. "I will meet you there."

As soon as he had Holly in his arms, Raphael rose into the sky without saying good-bye to Michaela. Lost in her guilt and horror, she wouldn't have noticed if he had. He'd wrapped glamour around himself and Holly while still inside the turret, ensuring no one could follow him to the cabin of Jason's informant.

He wasn't worried about Venom. The youngest of the Seven was resourceful; he'd make it out of Michaela's stronghold and if he needed assistance, he'd call out to Raphael.

As it was, Venom outdid himself, arriving at the cabin only minutes after Raphael.

Sweat drenched his body.

Going to his knees beside the sofa where Raphael had placed Holly, Venom stroked back her hair, then looked at Raphael. "Can you do anything?"

Raphael already had his hand on the girl's bloody chest, his palm glowing blue as he called on his Cascade-born ability to heal. He could feel the energy penetrating her skin, but it had no discernible effect. She was unique, this girl who had found the will power to defy the ghost of an archangel. "She has courage, your Holly."

"Yes. Too much." He hissed at Holly, the sound dangerous. "You made me fall in love with you. You don't get to go now!"

Raphael had never seen Venom like this. He poured more power into Holly's motionless body, but her faint heartbeat didn't strengthen, her breath didn't become less shallow. And his Cascade-born power was young yet. It flickered and died without warning, while Holly lay bloody and motionless.

"Would a mortal hospital be able to help her?" Venom asked.

Raphael shook his head. "Her wounds are immortal in nature." Created by the remnants of archangelic force. "Do you wish to stay here?"

"No. I want Holly safe. Will you fly her home?" Torment lived in the distinctive eyes that were all many people saw of Venom. "If she dies on the journey . . . hold her safe for me."

Raphael shook his head, for he would not steal this time from the other man. "Carry her. I'll fly you both to the plane." It was parked in a part of Michaela's territory that hosted a large international airport. As of this morning, secrecy was no longer necessary—the former Queen of Constantinople knew they were here and she knew why they'd come.

Though Venom had never before accepted being carried

by any angel, he scooped Holly's small body carefully into his arms and nodded. For love, Raphael thought, a man would do anything, bear anything. Raphael would've made the same choice had their positions been reversed.

Holly survived the journey to the plane.

Venom placed her on the bed. "She's still fighting."

Raphael was far more impressed by this slip of a girl than he'd expected to be. Elena and Dmitri had updated him about her on and off through the years since Uram's attack, but he hadn't expected a woman with this kind of grit. "She's survived Uram twice." Raphael looked at the girl with new eyes. "I wouldn't bet against her."

An hour after Raphael had left the plane to fly home on the wing, Holly still breathed as the jet soared above the clouds, but her pulse was no stronger, her breath as shallow. Venom hissed at her again. "Wake up!" He knew he was being unreasonable and erratic, but his heart was in a vise, being crushed to nothing.

Holly remained motionless under the clean, crisp sheet he'd just pulled over her, a sheet that was already spotted with blood. She was naked beneath; he'd stripped off her bloody clothes and wiped the blood from her ravaged flesh, then left it in the hope she would heal. Maybe he should've left her body open to the air, but he couldn't bear to see her so vulnerable.

Three hours later, the North Atlantic Ocean glittered below and Holly's fractured skin was no longer bleeding. Venom tried to see that as a sign that her body was mending itself, rather than a sign that her overstretched heart was growing sluggish. Her ravaged skin was cool to his touch, her pulse still so faint that he had to press his ear to her chest to be sure she remained alive. Her breath was nearly impossible to detect. But it *was* present.

Venom had long ago tucked her into his chest, holding

her warm against his body as they lay in the private cabin of the plane.

The pilots hadn't interrupted after their initial greeting.

Cocooned in the silence, Venom began to talk in the language in which he'd spoken his first words. He told Holly of his childhood in that bustling inn on the Silk Road, of how he'd learned to cook at his father's knee, and of how he'd been considered an adult at eight years or so of age. He wasn't sure. Records hadn't been kept so well at that time.

"I didn't consider that strange," he told her. "I had five brothers and sisters by then. It was normal for the eldest son to take on the mantle of protecting and providing for the family, together with his father."

Venom's mind drifted back to those long-ago times. "My father had a good heart. He just lost his way a little because he couldn't say no to my mother." His lips curved. "That is a fault that runs in my line. My brothers were the same with their wives."

He didn't know about their descendants. "It was hardest to put Mohan to rest. I remembered him as a baby, all swaddled up in my arms." Eyes red hot, he swallowed. "I can't bury someone I love again. Not ever." He pressed his lips to hers. "Please don't make me, Holly."

A whisper of breath against him, fingers uncurling on his chest.

His heart thumping hard, he looked down, but Holly's lashes still shadowed her cheeks, dark fans against the cream of her skin. She'd lost weight during the silent battle in the turret. Her cheekbones were prominent, her fingers impossibly thin. But . . . he could hear her heartbeat without having to press his ear to her chest.

And, as he watched, a fine crack across her cheekbone began to seal itself.

Venom shuddered.

He wanted to give her his blood, but Raphael had warned him that Holly was showing signs of blood toxicity. "Uram caused her to ingest too much archangelic blood. Feed her *only* when she is hungry. Her body needs to get rid of it. If she bleeds, let her."

She'd sweated blood for the first two hours, her body desperately rejecting the power it had no way to handle. He'd wiped her clean, kept her warm.

Fighting his need to do more, he kept on talking.

He told her about his first days in Neha's court, and of the time he'd spent in the tunnels below, and of how he'd come to a slow consciousness. He'd been clothed in rags and filthy with dirt the day he woke and realized he was a man, and not a viper like the ones with whom he'd bedded.

"They were draped over me, twined around my neck, my arms." He should've been horrified, but he'd changed in the months after his Making, his threshold of horror a high one. "Even when I moved, they didn't bite, just slid off."

It had taken him another week to make his way out of the labyrinth under Archangel Fort. "Ncha hadn't given up on me," he told Holly. "But she *had* lost me. It turned out I was faster than any of her trackers—and though I was a viper, I didn't react to her connection to snakes. I never have."

For that, he could only be grateful. "It would've been a leash she could tug on anytime I was in the vicinity. I like to think I made that happen with my defiance." He released a breath. "I've never hated Neha, though. She was just being an archangel. It was my family who made the choice to turn their face from me." To see only a monster and not the brother and son who'd done everything he could—given up his entire human existence—so that they'd have lives free of deprivation and shame.

"Venom."

It was less than a whisper, but he heard.

Heart thundering, he rose to look down into Holly's face. Her lips were slightly parted, her eyes closed. "Kitty." His voice shook.

"Umm." It was a lazy, sleepy sound . . . right before she curled into him in a way that said she had no plans to wake.

He pressed a kiss to the rainbow shine of her hair, his entire body trembling. "Sleep. We'll talk later." All of what he'd said while she was asleep, he'd tell her when she was awake. She had every right to his secrets and stories. Naasir was right about having someone to share secrets with—it was a gift beyond price.

38

Holly stretched awake with the sense that she'd had the most luxuriant sleep of her li— "Fuck," she whimpered, "that hurts." Every muscle in her body felt as if it had been pounded with a hammer until it was pulp, then flung into a freezer to become locked into its misshapen form. "Oh, *God*."

"No need to go that far, kitty. Venom or Tushar will do."

Slitting open her eyes, Holly found herself looking into eyes of viper green that were dancing with light.

Happiness.

She'd never seen Venom this innocently happy in . . . ever. Her own lips curved. "Stop being snarky and do something."

His smile deepened. "I've drawn you a hot bath with mineral salts. Will that do?"

"For starters." She frowned as the sprawl of the room penetrated. "Where are we?"

"The Tower. View's behind you."

Groaning, Holly managed to turn just enough to look at the glittering lights of Manhattan. "Last thing I remember,

I was in Michaela's stronghold, trying to convince Uram's ghost it wasn't a good idea for him—it—to exist."

"He's gone for good." Venom scooped her up in his arms and held her against the bare skin of his chest.

"Mmm." She snuggled in, running her palm up that toned muscle all warm and tensile. "You're so pretty."

He chuckled. "You're still half asleep."

Yawning, Holly continued to stroke him until he set her in the bath . . . and only then realized she'd been naked on the stone floor in his living area. "What happened to my clothes?"

"I took them off—they were drenched in blood."

Memory flashed of her skin cracking, her *insides* fracturing. But her hands found only smooth, unbroken skin anywhere she touched—and while she ached, it didn't feel like she was dying. "How long since the turret?"

Venom moved to another side of the large bathroom, his buttocks flexing under the loose black pajama pants that were all he wore. "You've been asleep for forty-seven hours."

"Are you wearing satin pants?"

"No. I have better taste than that." The fabric moved like air and liquid both as he strode back to her, a bottle in hand. Opening it, he poured a shimmering and creamy something into the bath.

The scent of frangipani filled the air.

Holly's toes curled. "You're so pretty and so nice, too." Her muscles began to loosen up. Slowly.

Lips curving, Venom went behind her. "I'm going to wash your hair."

Holly had absolutely no desire to protest. She just lay back and stayed half asleep while he washed her hair with a care and a gentleness that surprised her. "How do you know how to wash long hair? Did you have a ponytail phase?"

"I used to wash my sisters' hair sometimes." His words were a surprise. "When they were very young and it wouldn't be considered scandalous. Just to help out my mother." A smile in his voice, he said, "My father never did it for my sisters, always acted so stern, but I saw him washing my mother's hair once. He loved her from the roots of his own hair to the tips of his toes."

He began to massage her scalp.

"Venom?"

"Hmm?"

"Are my eyes still acid green?" She was awake now, wide awake, and she was starting to remember that she should be stone dead.

"I think you need to see for yourself." Getting up, he wiped his wet hands on a towel, then rooted about in a drawer until he found a small handheld mirror. It was ornate, the back mother-of-pearl painted with vipers. "Gift," he said at her questioning look. "From a friend in Neha's court who enjoys poking fun at what she deems my vanity."

Laughing at his scowl, Holly accepted the mirror, but then couldn't make herself turn it to the reflecting side. "Just tell me."

He'd gone behind her again, was once more massaging her scalp with clever fingers. "You won't be sorry, Hollyberry," he murmured. "Look."

She released a long breath before slowly beginning to turn the mirror. If her eyes remained acid green, then part of Uram might yet be hidden inside her. That color was his energy. If her eyes were brown again . . .

She sat up before she'd finished moving the mirror enough to see, water sploshing as she felt for her fangs.

Venom came to face her. "They're still just as small," he said with an amused look to him.

Shoving at his chest without effort, Holly did nothing to hide her relief. "I thought I might not be a vampire any longer."

His gaze turned solemn. "You never wanted to be a vampire."

"Yes, but that was before you." Holly could imagine a different eternity now, one filled with happiness and love and a shared recklessness that led to wild adventure. "I don't mind sucking your blood for millennia."

Smile returning, he tapped the mirror. "Are you going to look?"

"I'm too scared."

"This from a woman who derailed the plans of a psychotic archangelic ghost?" Slipping one arm around her back and placing his other hand around hers on the handle of the mirror, he said, "Ready?"

Exhaling shakily, Holly nodded at last. And they turned the mirror.

At first, she felt a punch of visceral joy . . . only to wrench the mirror closer and stare. "What *is* that?" Her eyeballs stared back at her from the mirror. "What the hell. What am I supposed to put on my driver's license now?"

Venom's laughter filled the bathroom. "I think they call the color hazel," he said solemnly when he stopped laughing.

"Be quiet, Viper Face." Because her eyes *weren't* hazel. They were a strange mix of darkest brown and acidic green.

"Anything you say, kitty." Tipping up her chin, Venom kissed her hot and deep and a little desperate.

Holly let the mirror fall to the water. "Hey, hey," she said when he broke the kiss, both of them breathless. "I'm here. I'm okay."

Shuddering, he wrapped both arms around her and dropped his head to the crook of her neck. Holly stroked his hair, kissed his temple, held him. Held this man born in torturous pain and horror who let no one see his vulnerability. "I love you," she said simply, honestly, forever. "You make the idea of forever a journey into adventure rather than a thing to be endured."

He didn't raise his head for a long time. When he did, his eyes held joy and pain and echoes of terror. "As long as you live, so will I."

Holly's heart smashed against her ribs. "Venom, no," she whispered. "My life span is unknown."

"And I've lived long enough alone." No give in his expression. "How can you ask me to go back to it after I've known you? Loved you?" A shake of his head. "We take this leap into eternity together."

Tears rolled down her face. "I'll badger you every day to change your mind."

"Nag, nag, that's what kitties do."

She scooped up a palmful of water and threw it at his face. He laughed. And he was so incredibly beautiful that she wanted to kiss him and kiss him and kiss him. "Come here."

He came, sploshing water all over the place, his pants still on. None of that mattered. Because he was kissing her and kissing her and kissing her, and she was home. Always in his arms, she'd be home.

As he would be in hers.

Sitting astride him when she came up for air, Holly said, "What do my eyes mean?" That strange amalgam of who she'd once been and who she'd become with Uram's energy inside her. "Is he still alive in some way?"

"Keir was at the Tower when we arrived," Venom told her. "The healer says yes, Uram is alive, but only in the way any father is alive in his child. You are a being all your own now."

Holly made a face. "I have a father. And it's not that psycho."

"Perhaps 'blood sire' is the better term to use," Venom said. "Uram is alive inside you the same way Neha is alive inside me."

Holly ran her hands over his shoulders. "That doesn't make me feel better," she admitted. "I wanted him erased from my body." She pressed her finger to his lips when he would've spoken. "But if he was . . . then I wouldn't be a vampire, and I wouldn't be like you just enough that we fit." And so he no longer felt alone. "I figure the trade is worth it."

Venom leaned forward to kiss her.

Frowning at a sudden thought, Holly pulled back. "Wait. What powers do I have left?" Scrunching her eyes shut, she tried to go invisible. "Can you see me?"

"Your breasts are lovely."

She flicked her eyes open to see that he did indeed have his admiring gaze on her tiny chest. But he seemed to like that chest. Who was she to argue? "I've lost the ability to create glamour."

"Unsurprising." He rubbed a thumb over the wet point of her nipple. "That is an archangelic trait that has never manifested in any other immortal."

"Can I still move the way I did?" Hating that she might've lost that which tied them together, she went to get out, check, but Venom held her in place.

"I love you," he said, his eyes locked with hers. "From the roots of my hair to the tips of my toes. From yesterday to tomorrow and every tomorrow we will ever see. From this moment to the mystery beyond death. Every part of you, slow or fast, small or big, strong or weak. I love you, Holly."

Her lower lip quivered.

Throwing her arms around his neck, she held on tight. When he rose, it was with both of them together, water dripping off their bodies. He somehow managed to get his pants off, and then their wet bodies fell onto the bed. There was no foreplay. She didn't want it. She drew him inside her, held him, and they rocked, their eyes locked to each other's.

Slow and gentle and forever.

It was some time later, while she sat on the kitchen counter wearing one of Venom's shirts and watching him quickly put together a pizza for her, that Holly snapped something out of the air. She stared at the plum in her hand. "Why are you throwing me plums? Though, it does look nice." She took a bite, hungry for food if not yet for blood.

"I threw it at my speed," said the vampire who'd be aggravating her forever.

And she'd caught it.

Holly began to smile. She still had the speed, could still dance with him in their unique and inhuman way. Even if she'd lost everything else, that was enough.

"Want to hear my theory?" he asked as he grated cheese over the base he'd hand-made.

"Uh-huh." She nodded around her succulent bites of plum.

"I think you'll have retained all the abilities that integrated fully with you. The speed, the ability to become boneless in a fall, the mesmerism. The things that felt yours."

"The glamour was never easy," Holly admitted. "It was like I was wearing someone else's coat." She kicked her feet. "I'll test the other stuff tomorrow." She was far calmer now that she knew she had the speed. "Tushar?"

"Kitty?"

"Why am I alive?" Holly had felt Uram pull *everything* out of her body. "The ghost or echo or whatever it was, it tried to suck me dry."

Her lover looked up from chopping green peppers. "You're not going to like this."

Holly frowned . . . then groaned. "I swear to God, if you tell me I have some of Michaela in me now . . ."

Not having mercy on her, Venom nodded. "Uram fed deeply on her. Too much for your body to digest or process. Keir believes a significant amount of her blood was still pooled in your stomach when the echo left you."

"Ugh, ew!" Hopping off the counter, Holly threw away her plum pit and found a big glass; filling it with water, she drank it down in desperate gulps. "I know my reaction isn't rational," she said afterward. "But ew!"

Venom's lips were curved as he watched her little freak-out. "Michaela's blood nearly caused your own to go toxic, but its power also saved your life. The echo inadvertently helped by draining so much energy out of you that it left a void—into which Michaela's power flowed, giving your cells what they needed to survive."

Holly made throwing-up motions before putting down the glass and moving sulkily to his side. "How come I have to be the weird one who has archangelic blood messing with me?" Other people probably prayed for archangelic attention, but Holly had had enough of it. "Raphael didn't feed me, too, did he?"

"No, the sire gave you his energy, but only in an attempt to heal."

"Good, but seriously—the idea of Michaela's blood sitting around in my stomach?" Shuddering at the thought, she dropped her head against his side. "Oh well, at least it wasn't Charisemnon's blood." Any bastard who could orchestrate an act as heinous as the Falling was not someone she wanted in her bloodstream.

"Speaking of whom," Venom said, "our friend Walter came through."

It took Holly a few seconds to remember who Walter was and why she should care. *Walter Battersby*, her brain supplied, *fixer to the immortals.* "Oh, right, the bounty on me." The entire situation felt like a lifetime ago now. "I suppose we should follow that up."

"I'm happy you're taking this seriously."

"Possession by a mad archangel, and gross blood pool in my stomach," she pointed out, stealing a piece of cheese to wipe out the latter image.

Hopping up onto the counter to retake her seat as she nibbled on the cheese, she said, "So what did Walter say?"

"First, Vivek managed to link the bank account Walter was paid from to a company that functions under Charisemnon's banner." Picking up the pizza stone on which he'd created his delicious-looking masterpiece, Venom put it in the oven.

The wave of heat felt good against Holly's body.

"Walter, in turn, was able to trace his client as being a flunky in Charisemnon's court. It apparently used up every favor he had." Venom's smile was cold. "He should've thought of that before he decided you were an acceptable target."

Holly shrugged. "He's a hustler. He'll hustle up some more favors." Stomach rumbling, she looked around.

"Give me a second and I'll make you a sandwich."

Holly could've made the sandwich herself, but watching Venom moving in the kitchen was so sexy that she just waited. "So we have to go find this flunky?"

Venom's hands moved quickly as he sliced a tomato for her sandwich. "Dmitri already did. He thought we had enough on our plate."

Holly froze with a slice of tomato at her mouth. "Uh-oh."

"He sent the flunky home in pieces." Venom's eyes glinted. "Small, very precise pieces. All packed in a black gift box lined with red velvet."

Mouth falling open, Holly put down the piece of tomato. "Really? Isn't that an act of war?"

"The sire had a conversation with Charisemnon—our favorite disease-causing archangel denies all knowledge of his flunky's actions, and we have nothing that says otherwise." He fed her the piece of tomato she'd abandoned.

The tangy juice burst to life on her tongue. "Small pieces?" she said afterward.

A raised eyebrow. "You do realize Dmitri can be bloodthirsty when it comes to protecting the people he loves? And you are his little weirdling."

Holly glared at him, but her lips insisted on tugging up. "How do you know he calls me that?"

"He came by while you were napping. I may have eavesdropped on what he said to you."

"That is bad behavior," Holly said with mock-sternness.

Venom's response was an unrepentant kiss.

Happy, she said, "Did the flunky confess why he was

after me?" She knew Dmitri wouldn't have executed him without first squeezing the man dry.

"All the archangels spy on one another—apparently, one of the reports that came in from New York included pictures of you and a note that you'd been attacked by Uram and altered." Venom's expression turned lethal. "Jason will soon find that leak and it will never again spill Tower secrets."

Holly gripped the edge of the counter. "The flunky wanted me for my blood," she guessed.

"For whatever Uram had left in you—it was your eyes that convinced him Uram *had* left something behind."

Sandwich made, Venom put it on a saucer. "The idiot stupid enough to put a price on your head told Dmitri he wanted to gift you to Charisemnon, but it's possible he wanted to use you to feed his own power, much as Kenasha did with Daisy." A liquid shrug. "Dmitri's cut off his head now, so it doesn't matter."

"That is so weird."

"What?"

"How you talk so casually about cutting off people's heads."

"My weapons of choice are razor-sharp blades, Holly-berry," he reminded her with a dangerous smile. "Eat your sandwich."

Holly bit into it with a groan of pleasure. She didn't speak again until it was all gone. "Why am I so hungry?" Even more so than before the craziness. "I swear I can feel that sandwich digesting at lightning speed."

"According to Keir, your cells have entered a state of flux similar to a newborn vampire's," Venom told her. "Those vampires are fed blood steadily until their need flattens out, but your body was permanently altered by Uram's energy. You carry angelic markers as well as vampiric."

Holly looked over her shoulders. "Nope, no wings. Damn it."

Laughing, Venom shifted to stand between her thighs,

his hands on her hips. "You're not a vampire, not an angel. You're like Naasir, like me. One of a kind."

"I like that." At some point in that cold room with a crib that held a twisted flesh host, she'd come to terms with the strong, strange fusion that was her body. "My species should have a name." She put her arms around the neck of the man who was to be her partner in crime for eternity.

Laughing, he said, "A Hollyberry."

She kissed his laughing mouth, drank in his happiness. And it was all right. The past was done. Gone. Dead. The future awaited. And for her, that future glinted viper green and searingly bright.

Two days later, she went to the garage to get into her car and discovered a number plate that had her glaring at a certain vampire.

He winked. "I told you I'd get you one that said *KITTY*."

NEW YORK TIMES BESTSELLING AUTHOR

NALINI SINGH

"The alpha author of paranormal romance."
—*Booklist*

For a complete list of titles,
please visit prh.com/nalinisingh